22/12/15

is

D0508810

'If
is

BRISTOL LIBRARIES
WITHDRAWN
SOLD AS SEEN

er
ce.
to

is

Please return/renew this item by the last date shown
on this label, or on your self-service receipt.
To renew this item, visit www.librarieswest.org.uk
or contact your library.
Your Borrower number and PIN are required.

up.
e."

os.
'

He was asking if she wanted him to kiss her. She
wanted it. Desperately.

* * *

Be sure to check out the next books in this series.
Conspira... ...n: Ally or foe?
No one... ...nd love.

"I don't play games," Serena replied.

"Asking me to meet you here?" Casimir said. "If I weren't more trusting of you, I would think this was a trap."

"How could this possibly be a trap?"

"I think you know how the king and his mother would respond to finding us alone in the palace. It would call your pending engagement into question."

"We haven't done anything wrong."

"Katarina seems to believe my very presence is wrong," Casimir said.

"She knows her son and I don't have a relationship. Any male is a threat to the little that we do have."

Casimir's eyes traced from her eyes to her lips. "Do you want to make me a real threat to him?"

He was asking if she wanted him to kiss her. She wanted a distraction.

Be sure to check out the next books in this series...
Conspiracy Against the Crown: Ally or...
No one can tell in this fight for power...and...

THE SECRET KING

BY
C.J. MILLER

Published in Great Britain 2015
by Mills & Boon, an imprint of Harlequin (UK) Limited,
Eton House, 18-24 Paradise Road, Richmond, Surrey, TW9 1SR

© 2015 C.J. Miller

ISBN: 978-0-263-25316-0

46-0915

Harlequin (UK) Limited's policy is to use papers that are natural, renewable and recyclable products and made from wood grown in sustainable forests. The logging and manufacturing processes conform to the legal environmental regulations of the country of origin.

Printed and bound in Spain
by CPI, Barcelona

To my brother, Dr. Andy.
Your sense of humor cheers me on my darkest days,
your love of adventure inspires me and your unending
support means the world. Love you, buddy.

C.J. Miller loves to hear from her readers and can be contacted through her website, cj-miller.com. She lives in Maryland with her husband, son and daughter. C.J. believes in first loves, second chances and happily-ever-after.

Chapter 1

Casimir felt the pulse of power in the ballroom of the Acacian castle. Three influential leaders, each with their axes to grind, were setting problems aside tonight in a public display of unity that hadn't been witnessed in the past twenty years. The king of Acacia was turning sixty and the night was meant for frivolity.

Too bad one of the kings would die tonight by Casimir's hand. He hated to ruin the party for the king of Acacia, but attacking the king of Rizari away from his palace made the logistics much simpler.

With the president of Icarus's help, Casimir had smuggled his weapons into the room. He was ready. He had mentally run the plan dozens of times. He had trained. He would do what needed to be done, shed his fake identity for good and he would disappear, taking asylum in Icarus.

Casimir was careful not to touch the gun at his side, a habit he'd formed in the military to ensure it was in place. The knife in its sheath at his hip brushed against his pants. He did nothing to call attention to himself. In addition to the three leaders, the room was filled with security—each of the king's guards and the president's servicemen, all armed to the teeth.

Danae, the eldest princess of Acacia had her guards close as well. She was the heir to the throne, and watching her, Casimir understood why she was being courted by the king of Rizari. Princess Danae looked like a woman who liked to have fun, but who couldn't organize her closet, much less a country. Her brunette curls bounced as she laughed and threw her head back in delight.

The younger princess of Acacia, Serena, was standing alone on the perimeter of the party. Unlike her sister's vibrant, fanciful energy, Serena had a quiet, serious beauty about her. Her blond hair hung around her shoulders and she looked almost ethereal in a light blue gown. She sipped her glass of wine and watched the party with little change in her expression. No one spoke to her. She had to be bored. Casimir had been studying King Warrington's social circles, and he found her behavior curious, very different from what he had experienced in Rizari. To blend in to the royal social circle, extraversion was critical.

Why was the princess so removed? He knew little about the king and princesses of Acacia. They didn't factor into his plan, except that he was using their castle to exact his revenge. He would send an anonymous note of apology once he'd returned to Icarus and was safe in his new life, revenge complete. Perhaps then his soul would be quiet and peaceful.

"She is beautiful, no?" Demetrius DeSante said. The president of Icarus, and his good friend, spoke softly. Though DeSante and Casimir were careful not to give away how close they were, especially in regard to this conspiracy, DeSante had been making the rounds through the ballroom, talking to everyone with a title or a fortune. Casimir was pretending to have the latter.

Though DeSante had been accused of many bad things, he was a good leader and one of his best qualities was his charisma. He could talk anyone into doing what he wanted. It was another way he was dangerous.

The lights flickered and then went out.

"Is this your plan? You're doing this now?" DeSante's voice in his ear.

The blackout was not part of his plan. Casimir was nowhere near King Warrington of Rizari. Casimir could only see by candlelight in the darkened room. Acacia was plagued by energy distribution problems. "Not my plan. Rolling blackouts—"

The sentence died in his mouth. At the sound of gunfire, Casimir dove for the floor, instinctively dragging President DeSante with him. The ceramic tile was cold against his hands, but his body broke out into a sweat and adrenaline charged through him. Gunfire had that effect on him. He had already been keyed up, waiting for his chance to kill Warrington and now, he was all systems go and on full alert.

The music died. More gunfire and the room was filled with screaming and shouting. Glass was breaking and objects hit the floor. A woman's heel pierced his hand. Damn stiletto shoes. Shaking off the pain,

Casimir belly crawled toward the darkness, away from the windows. If an active gunman was peppering the area with shots, he was safer in the darkest corner of the room. Once there, he would take stock of his position and kill whomever had decided to ruin his revenge.

Casimir assessed the area. Though his eyesight was compromised, his hearing was sharp and his nose searching. As if his senses had been attuned to violence, he peered through the candlelit glow of the room. The king of Acacia was slumped on the floor, the older princess next to him. In the dimness, it was impossible to know if the king was dead or injured. The sound of gunfire was elsewhere in the castle. Seeing no one guarding the king, Casimir filled in the blanks. Security had fled in the direction of the shooting, leaving the bodies of the king and princess alone. Were they already dead?

Dread consumed him when Princess Serena's face came into view. She was moving toward her father and sister. Was she trying to get herself killed? Wasn't she aware she should run away from bullets, not toward them?

Forgetting his own safety, Casimir rose to his feet and sprinted toward her. Princess Serena was pulling her father behind a table. For protection? Her face was grief-stricken and her eyes met his. They screamed for help, pleaded with someone to come to her aid.

Women in need were a soft spot for him. He could have used the darkness to search for King Warrington and kill him. But the probability of finding him unguarded was slim. More pressing was the beautiful woman who needed his help.

Serena shouldn't have come to the capital tonight. She had decided at the last minute to forgo her usual excuses and instead had driven to the castle for her father's birthday.

Serena's face felt sticky and her feet slid on the floor. She had to drag her father and sister to safety. Someone was shooting into the ballroom. No answers came to mind as to why.

She couldn't find her father's security. She had commanded her cousin and personal secretary Iliana to hide in the coat closet. But Serena couldn't leave her father and sister exposed. She had no medical training, but she could be with them until help arrived.

Pulling her father's weight was nearly impossible. Why was the floor so slippery? Her shoes slid out from under her again. Her dress tangled around her ankles as she fought to stand. A shadow blotted out the little light shining in her direction. Help had arrived! She lifted her head to welcome whomever had come to assist her.

Instead, she came face to face with the muzzle of a gun.

Before she could scream, not that screaming would have made a difference in the current environment, a hot and wet liquid hit her face. She closed her eyes and when she opened them, the lights were on again. She blinked as her eyes adjusted to the scene.

The man who'd been holding a gun at her was slumped in the arms of a stranger. A very dashing stranger, with reddish-brown hair, hazel eyes, a mustache and goatee, pronounced cheekbones and a perfectly straight nose. Serena was sure she had never met this man before and yet he seemed so familiar.

He threw the body to the side. She winced at the sound it made hitting the porcelain tile. The man slid his knife into a sheath beneath his black suit coat. A knife-wielding stranger had saved her life.

He extended his arms to her. On the heels of a violent attack, she should be more wary of him, but her instincts told her he wouldn't harm her. He had saved her life. If he wanted her dead, he could have allowed the gunman to kill her.

She took his hand. Her feet slid beneath her. Blood. It was blood she'd been slipping in. In stark contrast to the gruesome scene, the stranger was watching her with the kindest eyes she had ever known. She turned her head to look at her father and sister, to see what help they needed.

The man put his hand on her cheek. "Do not look, Princess. This is not what you should remember." He took a white handkerchief from his pants pocket and wiped her face. Blood smeared the material.

He began to escort her away. Suddenly, her father's guards flew in her direction, ripping her from the man's arms and slamming him against the wall.

"Release the princess!" More shouting and commands.

Serena held out her hands toward the stranger this time. "Please stop. Stop! I command you to stop! This man saved my life." Now the guards appeared again? In the chaos, they had left her and her family unprotected. Hysteria threatened to consume her. She stared at the stranger. If she looked away from him, she would look back at her father and her sister.

"Come, Princess, you need to be taken to the safe room."

The stranger looked over his shoulder at her. Her guards released him and he turned toward her, bowing slightly. "You will call on me again if I am needed."

He fled the ballroom, toward the sound of sirens. He was gone before she realized she didn't know his name.

President DeSante pulled Casimir away from the crowd. Everyone was being questioned by the police. In the circle of DeSante's guards, they could speak freely.

"Was this your plan?" DeSante asked.

"I already told you it was not." Casimir threw off his fury and focused. Someone had beaten him to the punch, but the assassins had killed the wrong king, at least in his thinking. "I had nothing to do with this." His plan had been to kill King Warrington of Rizari only. His revenge did not include a massacre.

"This was chaos. This was reckless." DeSante's fingers bit into Casimir's arm and his eyes were blazing with intensity. "This was not the revenge you had planned, but this is an opportunity. Don't squander it."

An opportunity?

DeSante spoke quietly. "Think like a king. Who is next to inherit the throne in Acacia?"

"The princess. Princess Serena." It had been difficult to walk away from her. But he couldn't stay. He had no reason to remain with her and if he did, too many questions would be asked.

"That's right. The princess, the woman whose life you saved."

Casimir mustered control of his anger over his lost chance. He focused on what his old friend was saying. They were not blood relatives, but they were brothers on the battlefield and DeSante owed Casimir a debt. A debt that would not be paid until Casimir'd had his revenge.

"I killed one of the assassins." Casimir had slit the throat of the man who had planned to kill the princess at point-blank range. The assassin had gotten what was coming to him and Casimir felt no regret for his actions.

"That you did. I promised you revenge and asylum from the fallout of that revenge, but this is more than I could have given you. Use her."

Use her for what? DeSante was a chess master, seeing many moves ahead in the game and in life. For Casimir, his anger often drove him harder than reason. He shook off his anger and took a cleansing breath. "You said she is to inherit the throne. Are the king and Princess Danae dead?" From what he had seen, it didn't look as if they had much chance of survival, but doctors could sometimes perform miracles.

DeSante inclined his head toward the ambulances. "An official announcement has not been made, but I would assume that yes, they are dead."

The ground had been covered in blood. The assassins had worked quickly.

True peace in the Mediterranean between Icarus, Acacia and Rizari had never been achieved. After tonight, Casimir guessed it would be impossible. Accusations would be made and blame would be spread around enough for everyone to be hit with some.

But perhaps DeSante was right and this was an opportunity for Casimir to achieve a goal he had never believed possible. As a royal, Princess Serena would be part of King Warrington's social circle. After all, he had been planning to marry Serena's sister. Casimir could use contact with Serena to keep the king close while Casimir planned his next move. If he was lucky and played his cards right, instead of killing King Warrington outright as he had intended tonight, perhaps he could clear his mother's name. Casimir could make a play for the crown and the throne of Rizari. The crown that rightfully belonged to him.

King Warrington would pay for what he had done to Casimir and his mother, but not with his life. Instead he would lose everything that mattered to him.

"Do you think that President DeSante is responsible for the bloodshed?" Iliana asked. She set a cup of coffee next to Serena's easel.

Serena didn't look away from her canvas. She had been painting since midday. Painting and thinking. Her long-term therapist, Dr. Shaw, had helped, but she'd had only a couple weeks to process what had happened the night her father, sister and fifteen others had been killed in a massacre the media had dubbed the Birthday Bloodbath.

Serena found the name distasteful, but she found everything about the situation distasteful and almost too painful to bear. "He denies it. The investigation hasn't uncovered who hired the assassins to murder my father."

According to the one killer who had been apprehended by the police, the deaths of her sister and the others had been collateral damage. As if they hadn't considered that firing bullets into a crowd in the dark would result in deaths. Serena wasn't surprised to learn the ME had found amphetamines in the assassins' bloodstreams. Their behavior had been aggressive and erratic.

Serena had never planned to be queen, and yet she would be Acacia's queen in a few weeks' time. She hadn't had a boyfriend, and yet negotiations were in progress for her to marry the king of Rizari. Samuel

Warrington had been courting Danae, and now, as if the two sisters were interchangeable, he planned to pursue Serena.

Serena had asked for a fortnight to grieve away from the public eye in the seclusion of her beach house, knowing that being granted that amount of time was a boon. Her personal feelings didn't matter. Her country needed a strong alliance with King Warrington and Rizari, the closest country to the east, to keep the dictator of Icarus on their western shores from attacking during a time of weakness. Acacia's Assembly would keep the country running while she grieved, but the country needed their princess.

King Warrington would provide military protection in exchange for uniting their countries and placing his own advisers in positions of influence in Acacia's Assembly. He had agreed to respect her country's culture and traditions and give Serena a certain amount of independence. It was the best and only offer she'd had. Her advisers were discreetly inquiring about other arrangements, but Icarus, through that detestable Demetrius DeSante, was rattling its saber, letting it be known that the death of the king of Acacia had presented them with an opportunity to strike. Rizari and Icarus had long been enemies and Acacia, being geographically in between them, was subjected to the fallout of that long-standing feud.

Serena's solitary time was up and she would need to paste on a brave face and pretend as if she could be a competent and strong queen. Danae had been the perfect princess and would have been the perfect queen, the perfect bride and the perfect wife. Serena would be none of those things. Her formal training was untried and she hadn't been blessed with the grace and elegance her sister had had.

Serena had much to do, much to plan, yet she was spending an inordinate amount of time thinking about the stranger who had saved her life. No one could give her his name. Witnesses who had seen him save her life provided varying accounts of the incident. He had been described as brown-haired and blond, tall and short, overweight and slender.

Someone recalled seeing him speaking to President DeSante, but when questioned, that loathsome man had claimed to know nothing about Serena's protector. Serena knew how to tell when DeSante was lying: his mouth was moving.

Serena wouldn't give up looking for the man with the kind eyes. Though her country didn't have the resources to launch a national manhunt, especially for a man who was a hero, Serena had a few private investigators searching for him. The birthday guest list was being reviewed to see if someone could discover his identity. Whoever brought her information would be handsomely rewarded.

Serena wondered about the man with the gentle, compassionate eyes. Could he have been from Icarus? From Rizari? That would explain why no one seemed to know him. He had been granted entrance to her father's birthday, meaning he was either invited or had attended as someone's guest.

Her emotions were volatile, grief amplifying every feeling, and Serena tried not to become frustrated with her inability to find him.

Serena heard tires spinning on gravel. Looking out her second-story window, she saw her uncle Santino driving to her beach house, his off-road vehicle kicking up dirt. Her guards stopped him for a moment and then waved him through. After parking in front of her house, he climbed out of his car, limping as he walked. Though he had a cane, he hated using it, believing it made him appear weak. Uncle Santino had a scar that intersected his right eye and as a child, Serena had called him a pirate. The scar was a result of a tragic boating accident that had killed his wife soon after they were married.

Serena set down her paintbrush. She met her uncle on the wraparound porch, holding up her hands. "I would hug you, but I need to wash up first."

"Painting again?" he asked.

"Yes." Art calmed her and the past two weeks had given her many reasons to need serenity.

Iliana poked her head out on to the porch, her long red hair swinging around her shoulder. "Why don't I prepare tea for everyone?" Iliana was her cousin on her mother's side and officially Serena's personal secretary. But their relationship went far deeper than boss and subordinate.

Serena and her uncle had met several times since the massacre. Sometimes they spoke about her father and sister, sometimes about the kingdom and sometimes about nothing of importance.

Santino sat at the kitchen table. With the curtain open, Serena counted four guards at the back of her house. With her being a potential target for yet unknown reasons, her security team wasn't taking chances.

"When are you meeting with King Samuel?" her uncle asked.

King Samuel had been her sister's boyfriend and according to Danae, he had been smitten with her. How could Serena put her heart into a relationship that should have been her sister's? It felt twisted. "He wants to meet tomorrow evening for a dinner party."

It was her understanding that others would be in attendance, which should make it less awkward in some ways, more stressful in others. Serena would need to behave and speak in a certain manner. Her every action would be scrutinized and criticized. The media would pick apart her clothing, hairstyle and how she accessorized. Serena dreaded it and promised herself she wouldn't read their articles, which would undoubtedly accent her every inadequacy and include a snarky review of her love life or lack thereof.

"You look tired. Are you getting enough sleep?" her uncle asked.

"Not really." Thoughts of her sister and father kept her awake and on particularly bad nights, she lay in her bed and waited for morning to come.

Nightmares about the night her family had died, nightmares about the mother she hadn't had in years and nightmares about her future haunted the little sleep she did have.

"Still thinking about the man who saved your life?" her uncle asked.

Sometimes. Often. "Now and then." Why was she so obsessed with someone she had met once, for no more than a few minutes? If he wanted to be found, he would be.

What if there was a compelling reason he wanted to remain anonymous to her? He might fear the media response. He might not enjoy the idea of his rescue story being printed in the papers. It was another reason she had to keep her search quiet.

"Let it go, Serena. You don't know what you saw. You'll go crazy if you let this consume you," her uncle said.

He had urged her to forget everything she could about that night. Serena wasn't in any hurry to relive it, although occasionally brief flashes from that night interrupted her thoughts. "I know someone saved me."

"And then disappeared. He could have been working with the assassins."

"Yet he chose to kill one of them to save me?" It didn't make sense. Unless her instincts were totally skewed, her protector wasn't involved in the plot to kill her father.

"Please let this go, Serena. You will only be hurt again. I can't stand to see you in more pain. You have enough grief to manage without adding to it. This fixation with him is unhealthy."

Maybe she was thinking about her protector because it was easier and far more pleasant to think about him than to think about her father's and sister's deaths or how much she missed them. Though she had not lived in the castle and had been happy to have some independence, knowing she could reach out at any time was a comfort. Now, she felt alone.

Serena's uncle wished to protect her. But he didn't need to protect her from the man who'd saved her. Iliana returned to serve the tea and Serena changed the subject. No point in upsetting her uncle who was wrestling with his own grief over losing his older brother and his niece.

Her uncle left around nine that evening.

"You're not giving up on finding the mystery man, are you?" Iliana asked.

"Not a chance," Serena said.

"Why don't you let me fly to Icarus and speak to DeSante? He knows something about everything and his spies are everywhere. Give me a few minutes alone with him and I can force the information out of him." She lifted her knee mimicking hitting the dictator in the crotch.

Serena cracked a smile, rare for her these days. "I don't think that's advisable. He has big, scary guards and you're topping out at five foot two."

Iliana set her hands on her hips. "For you, I'd kick his butt. You know I could. I'm pretty mean when I'm angry."

Serena loved that about her cousin. She was loyal and spunky and feared nothing. Her business phone rang and Iliana frowned and answered it, her tone professional and cool. "Princess Serena's office. Iliana speaking. How may I help you?"

Iliana swore under her breath. "He's a real piece of work. Hold on." She pressed a button on her phone.

Dread coiled inside Serena. "What now? What's happened?" Was her uncle okay? He had only left a few moments earlier.

"The coast guard is on the phone. The Icarus navy is preventing ships from entering our waters."

Icarus's navy, one of the fastest, biggest military operations in the region, boasted hi-tech equipment and sailors who came from generations of sailors. They were experts on the water. "What did you say?" Serena asked.

Iliana repeated her statement, this time slower. Serena had heard her the first time, but she hadn't fully processed the information. Was DeSante planning to attack? Serena had no military experience. How should she maneuver in this situation? Who should she call? Though she had the ear of the head of the Assembly and she was supposed to wield influence, she was green and DeSante knew it.

It was dark, but that wouldn't matter to the experienced Icarus navy. Was DeSante hoping to catch her off guard, ill equipped and scared? The idea incensed her. She might be weak now, but she wouldn't be for long.

"Has the coast guard made contact with DeSante? What does he want?" Serena asked.

"I don't know, hold on." After a few moments, she said, "They say they want your confirmation that it's okay to let boats through."

Her confirmation? That made no sense. Icarus wasn't in charge of screening what boats entered and exited through their waters. Acacia and Icarus had no such arrangement. "What do they really want?"

Iliana repeated the question into the phone. "He wants to speak to you. He being DeSante, the warlord."

DeSante wasn't exactly a warlord, but he wasn't a peaceable man either. He had come to be president of his country during a violent coup.

This was a warning, then, from Icarus. If she refused to speak to him, DeSante would place an embargo on Acacia.

The dictator of Icarus was playing a dangerous game, mostly dangerous to Acacia with its weaker navy and dependency on imports. If DeSante refused to allow boats into their ports, Acacians would starve. "Put Demetrius DeSante on the line." She sounded stronger than she felt. She had been avoiding the dictator's requests for an audience and instead had allowed Iliana to put him off and explain that she'd needed time to grieve. Apparently, that time was over.

Iliana handed Serena the phone.

"Good evening," Serena said, keeping her voice cool and polite.

"Finally, I have the pleasure of speaking with you," DeSante said.

She wasn't in the mood for a conversation with DeSante. "Let the boats through."

"I would be glad to. I am an ally who can secure your western waters from enemies."

What a load of crap. Her enemies consisted of him and whomever had killed her family, although Serena still suspected they were one in the same. "Let them through."

"As you command. I expect a meeting with you shortly or my navy may again feel the need to question boats coming close to your shores."

"You'll have your meeting," she said. She hung up the phone with a quaking hand.

Iliana grabbed her arm. "You did good, Serena. It's okay. You sounded strong and the right amount of pissed off and polite."

It wasn't okay. The sharks were circling because they smelled blood in the water.

"She's looking for you," DeSante said.

Casimir knew it. He needed to play it cool. If he came on too strong, Serena would be suspicious. Casimir needed to approach her in the right manner with his plan in place.

When he was ready, he would allow himself to be found. Or perhaps he would show up at her castle and catch her off guard. The biggest downside to his plan was living with his fake persona a little longer. Being a wealthy heir who liked to party didn't suit him, but it had been his cover to infiltrate King Warrington's social circles. Though he had never breached the inner circle, he'd gotten to know enough royals and hangers-on that he couldn't change his identity now.

"Someone may recognize me and tell her who I am," Casimir said.

"As long as they give her the cover story and do not reveal who you actually are, you can handle it," DeSante said.

Casimir could handle anything. He would leak the story that he had been the man who'd saved the princess's life. It might keep him interesting to the royalty of Acacia and Rizari. Staying close gave him leverage to manipulate the situation to his benefit. "I'm not worried." Yet. Living a lie every day was almost as hard as harboring the rage he felt toward Samuel Warrington.

"Call me after you make your move," DeSante said.

"Will do."

Casimir hung up the phone and slid it into his pocket. Few people trusted the president of Icarus, but Casimir did without question. Not only did DeSante owe him, DeSante had a vested interest in Casimir taking control of Rizari. Having allies in the region and preventing Rizari from interfering with Icarus had long been DeSante's goal. With Casimir assuming the throne, DeSante would have the freedom to do as he wished.

Casimir entered his mother's house. His weekly meetings with her were difficult to press through, and grew worse with each visit. Casimir hated the stink of booze and cigarettes. "Hey, Mom."

His mother, Anna, rarely greeted him. She was sitting in the dark in her living room, like she often did. She had the television on, but seemed to be staring blankly at it. Casimir muted it. His mother hadn't always been this way. Every year, she grew noticeably more withdrawn, tired and depressed. Now, he couldn't convince her to sit outside on a nice day. She was a recluse and if he didn't do something, she would die in this dark, dank house.

"He's still alive," his mother said. She was looking haggard, having lost weight, and her skin appeared sallow.

Samuel Warrington was still alive. Casimir hadn't killed him. He had told his mother he would take care of it, but he had failed. The knowledge burned him. But he wouldn't give up on his new plan. "There were other assassins in the room. They killed the Acacian king and his daughter Danae."

His mother lit another cigarette. "What's that have to do with anything?"

Casimir hid his frustration. His mother's sole focus was revenge. "I couldn't get to Warrington in the confusion."

His mother said nothing and her silence reeked of censure. Her history with the king and his family was a bitter one.

One year into her marriage to King Constantine Warrington, he had falsely accused her of having an affair with his brother, Charles, and had exiled her. Anna had blamed Charles's jealous wife, Katarina, for manufacturing stories about her. She had fled to Icarus with a new identity. Fearing for her life and the life of her unborn child, she hadn't told the king that she had been pregnant with his baby. She had lived in Icarus and raised her son with her eyes on one goal: for Casimir to return to Rizari in glory and take his crown when he was of age.

But when Constantine and his brother were killed ten years ago, Casimir knew presenting himself as the rightful heir would earn him a knife in his back as well. He needed to be more careful, more crafty. Martyrdom wasn't the goal. Making things right for his family and Rizari was.

Casimir's existence and true parentage was a secret from everyone in the world, except his mother and De-Sante, whom Casimir had allowed into his confidence when he was fifteen.

When his father had died, so had his mother's chance of revealing to her ex-husband his true heir. With false accusations about her participation in his and his brother's murders and her conviction without a trial, her life had spiraled further into darkness. Anna had sworn to Casimir all his life that she still loved his father. His death had robbed her of the family reunion she had not-so-secretly wished for. Anna had believed that Constantine would see that she had been loyal and that Katarina would be revealed as a liar.

That hadn't happened.

When Anna had heard rumors that Constantine and Charles had been killed by Charles's son, Samuel, in an effort to usurp the throne, she had made Casimir swear he would avenge his father's death by killing the king who had stolen his life.

Chapter 2

Iliana recognized the country calling code for Icarus and felt a jolt of adrenaline. She had arrived at the castle early that morning to start work and she was eager for a tussle with DeSante's goons.

They thought they could push Serena around because she was young and had been distant from her father for some years. There had been no bad blood between Serena and her father, but Serena preferred the quiet of her beach house and the private pursuit of her interests. She hadn't been idle. She had painted a number of amazing landscapes and was making a name for herself—at least, under her alias—in the international art community. Iliana had brokered deals for her in the United States, Canada, Italy and France as well as throughout the Mediterranean. Iliana's law degree had some use after all, which was a mild salve on her ego, considering she'd failed the bar exam three times.

"Princess Serena's office. How may I help you?"

"Iliana."

One word and Iliana knew instantly she was speaking with Demetrius DeSante, Serena's enemy and the biggest bully in the Mediterranean. He thought he could push around smaller countries like Acacia. Maybe he had the stronger navy and maybe his economy was larger, but he wouldn't push Serena around and he wouldn't push Iliana around either.

"This is she. Who is calling, please?" Pretending she was unaware would knock his ego down a peg.

He had the gall to laugh. Pompous jerk. "This is President DeSante. Iliana, I enjoy our talks so much. But please, call me Demetrius."

They had spoken twice before. Iliana had been openly hostile both times and she didn't regret it. "President? Is that your official title? I mostly hear you referred to as a dictator."

He was quiet for a beat and she wondered if she'd gone too far. Her mouth had gotten her in trouble before.

"I will take great delight in winning you over and hearing you call me by my given name."

A little shiver of relief mixed with pleasure danced over her. "I wouldn't hold your breath on that."

"Such hostility from someone I barely know. Of course, I would like to know you better. You've proven to be quite spirited. I like that in a companion."

Companion? What did that mean? Like a friend or a prostitute? She would be neither to him. Her heart raced and it was not because she found his confidence appealing. He was appalling. She would be wise to remember that. "What is it that you want? The princess is not available right now."

"Such a shame. I was hoping to speak with her this morning about several pressing matters."

"If you tell me what they are, I will relate them to the princess." She wondered if he would tell her anything. In the past, he had refused to give her details of why he was anxious to meet in person and speak with Serena.

"Her father kept the peace between Icarus and Rizari. I need to know the princess's stance on that."

Was DeSante interested in peace in the region or did he want to stir up trouble? "I can assure you the princess wants no bloodshed." Iliana shuddered, remembering the night of the king and Princess Danae's murder. Serena had commanded her to hide in a closet and then had run off to aid her father and sister. Risky and bold, it was the side of Serena that came roaring to life in defense of the people she loved. When Iliana had left the closet where she'd hidden with several other women, the ballroom had looked like a slaughterhouse. Even now, the ballroom had not been reopened. Iliana wondered if it ever would be.

"What do you want, Iliana? Because you sound like you want to wrap your hands around my throat and throttle me, which wouldn't be keeping with the princess's desire for peace."

She scoffed. "I don't want to wrap my hands around your anything." Why did that image elicit a strange stirring in her stomach?

"Perhaps you're attracted to me and you hate that, so you're lashing out."

"I am not attracted to you." Except it was a lie. The first time she had met him in person, she had had no defense against the rush of sensations. Her body had tingled and though he had been professional with her, she'd harbored some decidedly nonprofessional thoughts about him, his mouth, his body. She chalked it up to hormones. Her attraction to the dictator meant nothing. Handsome on the outside, he was a troll on the inside. Handsome could trick her hormones. Mean would prevent her from doing anything about it.

"What is it that bothers you most about me?" DeSante asked.

Listing his deficiencies could get her killed. At least, if rumors were true. "I do not feel safe enough to honestly answer that question."

"You are afraid of me?" He sounded surprised. Wasn't he accustomed to fear from his countrymen?

"I am afraid of nothing. I just don't want to disappear." Or be murdered in her bed.

"You have nothing to fear from me. I will not hurt you. Not today and not ever. If I found out that you had been harmed, I would seek vengeance for that atrocity. A lady should never be on the receiving end of violence."

Why did he seem sincere? Why should she believe that? Even more, why did he sound as if he were earnestly trying to convince her? "How many people have died at your hands, believing that same thing?"

"What I have done for my country is not something I am ashamed of. I have spilled soldiers' blood, but I have done so for the greater good."

The greater good, which had fortuitously brought him into power.

"What is most difficult is accepting that you believe I am a monster."

He was a monster. "Do you deny subjugating your people?"

DeSante made a sound of disgust. "I deny it emphatically. If you are asking if my methods of leadership are harsh, then yes, they are. But I am not ashamed that every Icarus family has food on their table and important work that contributes to our economy."

Iliana had heard that conditions had improved in Icarus since DeSante had come into power. She couldn't quite accept how he had come to power, but she felt a chink in her armor.

"I want you to come to Icarus as my guest. I will show you. I will let you see with your own eyes."

His guest? Nothing in those words was sexual and yet her heart was doing somersaults. He had been secretive with the media and yet he wanted her to visit? "No." Her reasons for saying no were complex. She couldn't leave Serena now. She would feel like a traitor traveling to Icarus to spend time with DeSante. Spending time with DeSante under certain conditions could bring up some emotions she didn't want to confront.

Iliana did not have a good track record with men. She was easily seduced. DeSante could break down her defenses. Iliana knew it. She was loyal to Serena and she would remain that way.

"Perhaps you will be persuaded in the future."

To sleep with him? She smothered her outrage, realizing he'd meant changing her mind about traveling to Icarus. Iliana pulled her emotions under control. What about this man riled her so deeply? "We will see."

"I believed you to be an open-minded woman. Did I misjudge you?"

"Of course I'm open-minded. But I cannot travel to Icarus unless Princess Serena decides she wishes it.

Did you have anything else you wanted to talk to the princess about?"

"Tell her she is contemplating marrying a cad."

She hadn't heard that term in years. "A cad?"

"King Warrington will not make her happy."

"And you would?" Iliana asked, feeling a stab of jealousy at the idea of Serena dating President DeSante.

"Not at all. I am not interested in marrying the princess. My interests in her are political and professional."

Right. Though Serena hadn't had many boyfriends, mostly as a result of her avoiding crowds and staying away from being the center of attention, she was a beautiful, voluptuous woman. "I'm writing this down. You're not interested in war, you don't want Serena to marry the king and you're interested in her. Professionally."

"Don't forget that last word. My personal interests lie elsewhere. Until we speak again, and I do hope that is soon, be well. Good day, Iliana."

She hung up the phone being more turned on from one phone conversation than she had by her last boyfriend in the year they'd been together. President DeSante was the trifecta of attraction: bad boy, bad ass and far too handsome for his own good.

Serena took her guard's hand and stepped out of the town car to catch her balance and not trip over her gown. A plane flight and a long car ride had brought her to the palace of Rizari, King Warrington's home.

She smoothed her green dress, hoping it was appropriate for the evening's events. Iliana had helped her select it and yet Serena was a bundle of nerves about the entire visit, including what she was wearing. This was not where she shone. She was not great at small talk and mingling, and preferred to stay on the outskirts of a crowd and watch. Or better yet, to sketch or paint from a safe distance. Even hiding behind a camera had a certain appeal.

Before her father's birthday party, Serena had not been to a formal occasion in years, avoiding them with carefully constructed excuses. Grief knotted in her stomach and she blinked away tears. How she wished her father and her sister were still alive!

"Your Grace?" her guard asked.

Serena realized she had been standing rooted in the same place, looking up at the palace. It was a breathtaking display of architecture and design. When Samuel had inherited the throne after the untimely death of his uncle, he had put energy and resources into renovating the two-hundred-year-old structure. The effort showed.

"I'm fine." Her guards flanked her and she took the stairs to the front door. It opened and she was escorted inside.

She had always believed her castle to be ornate, but the palace of Rizari made Acacia's royal home look like a straw hut.

This was her first date with King Warrington, although she wasn't sure if he would consider it a date. Officially, it was a dinner party with members of the royal social circle, some whom she knew by name and others not at all.

Her heels clicked against the floor as she was escorted by King Warrington's butler and her guards into the dining room. She was almost used to having her guards so close, but in her home, they didn't hover over her as they did in public.

Serena scanned the room for an inconspicuous place

to sit or stand, as was her usual technique when being in an unfamiliar place. Her eyes landed on a man across the room and her breath caught in her throat.

"Your Grace, may I offer you a drink?"

She held up her hand to decline, vaguely aware that she may have been rude, but she was impossibly fixated on one person. The man who had saved her life. As she crossed the room, she realized she could be mistaken. She could be imagining him. Thinking of him so often had a strange effect on her. She found herself almost subconsciously looking for him everywhere she traveled.

When she was a few feet from him, he took a sip of his drink and then turned his head toward her. Their eyes connected. She remembered those kind eyes, eyes of strength and compassion.

"Is it you?" she asked.

"Your Grace." He bowed to her.

"What is your name?" She had to know before he disappeared again. A swell of emotion and questions rose up inside her.

"Casimir Cullen."

Casimir. A regal name. His voice set off a sensation in her stomach, and excitement spiraled throughout her body. "Do you remember…" She didn't know how to finish her thought. He had to remember that night. Anyone who had lived through it would have it seared into their memory.

She had thought, upon their reunion, her protector would grab her, hug her to him, and now she realized, she had pictured him kissing her, banding his arms around her and making her feel safe for the first time in weeks.

"I remember."

She would have to settle for being the target of his warm, intense gaze. But the effect was much the same. "I've been trying to find you."

He inclined his head and Serena glanced at the person he had been speaking to. More specifically, the woman he had been speaking to. This was the king's dinner party. Was Casimir here with his wife? Why did that thought devastate her? Her entire being should be focused on grieving for her father and sister, and trying to wrap her arms around the tremendous tasks ahead of her. Yet part of her clung to Casimir as being something bright and good in her future. It was presumptuous of her to think they had a future.

"That night was difficult. I have been traveling, trying to clear my head," he said.

"With your wife?" she asked, gesturing to the woman standing across from him.

The woman smiled. "Cas and I aren't married." The look she gave him implied she would like to change that at some point.

Cas. The nickname suggested familiarity and Serena was confused. Was this his girlfriend? Suddenly, her mind was reeling from a barrage of thoughts. What was he doing here? How did he know King Warrington?

The king of Rizari. Serena's heart dropped and she felt sickened. She was at the palace to spend time with King Warrington and she was fixating on Casimir. She glanced around the room. As if reading her thoughts, Casimir spoke.

"The king has not yet arrived."

The woman giggled. "He tends to be late. You know the type."

Serena didn't know the type or understand the reason for the laughter, and while his tardiness might have been rude, she was grateful he had not yet arrived. It had given her this moment with Casimir. "Casimir, could I speak with you alone for a minute?"

The woman frowned but stepped away. Serena walked toward the double-wide glass patio doors. Casimir followed her, as did her guards. Casimir opened the doors and led her outside.

"I have so many questions," Serena said.

"Please ask them. I told you I was yours to call upon."

He had said those words and yet he had disappeared without giving his name. "Do you live in Rizari?" she asked.

"I do not. I live in Icarus, but I travel frequently throughout the Mediterranean."

Many follow-up questions came to mind. "What were you doing in Acacia?" Serena asked. She wanted to know everything about this man. Everything.

"Acacia is known for their world-class boat making and I am having one built. My friend Fiona," he gestured inside to the woman he'd been speaking with, "knew I was in town and invited me to your father's birthday party as her guest."

His story made sense. Acacia's boat-building history dated back a thousand years. Most of the royal naval fleet had been assembled in Acacia. To hear him refer to his companion as a friend soothed some of her worry. "I am pleased you recognize quality."

He glanced at her lips and then his gaze skimmed down her body. "I recognize it." His meaning was decidedly sensual.

"I have wanted to thank you for what you did that night. I don't recall if I did at the time."

She didn't want the conversation to circle around the worst night of her life. Serena struggled with her grief and anger over what had happened. Yet, she felt it was important to acknowledge what he had done and express her gratitude.

"I did what any man would have."

Except that he had done what no one else had. "My guards had left me." Before becoming the heir apparent to the throne she had only traveled with one guard. That night she'd had two, but they had been trying to stop the gunfire and in the chaos, they lacked the training to execute the proper response.

"Their mistake," Casimir said.

A mistake that could have cost her her life. Her uncle was reviewing and changing security measures to ensure nothing like it happened again. "You owe me nothing. But I want to know more about you."

"Your Grace, you may ask me anything you wish," Casimir said.

It was a cool evening and Serena noticed she could not see or smell the sea from the palace. "What do you do? I mean, besides saving the lives of princesses?"

He grinned. "My father owns a financial services company. He and I recently parted ways. A life of numbers and spreadsheets bored me. Until I figure out what I want to do next, I've been traveling, studying and having fun."

She didn't want to ask, but she needed to know about his relationship with King Warrington. She was aware, of course, that nothing could come of her attraction to Casimir. The king was courting her. This could be the only night she had with Casimir. The idea was beyond depressing. "How do you know King Warrington?"

"He and I have been traveling in the same social circles for years. Fiona invited me here tonight. I didn't realize you'd be in attendance."

Serena felt a mix of emotions about Casimir's connection to King Warrington. She almost wished no one in Rizari had known Casimir, that he could exist in some space with her where they would be free to have a friendship without the interference of others. A strange notion, since she was not a possessive woman. Casimir had saved her life. She owed him, not the other way around.

"Are you pleased to see me?" she asked, trying to understand if he reciprocated any of her feelings.

Casimir looked over her shoulder and then returned his gaze to meet hers. "Yes. I should not say things like that to the princess, and to King Warrington's future bride, but yes, I am pleased to see you."

Though two of her guards were standing inside the door and another two were on the patio with them, Serena felt the space surrounding her and Casimir closing in on them. "I've thought of you often." An honest admission that could cost her.

"I have wondered how you were coping. I read that your father and sister's send-offs were touching. Many people have had nice memories to share about your father."

A water burial, as was tradition in her country, had taken place for both the king and the princess. "I am glad to hear it. I've distanced myself from politics and the day-to-day duties of the royal family in recent years.

But I'll be forced into the center of the arena now and I have big shoes to fill."

"Why haven't you been involved in politics recently? I thought that was mandatory for a princess," he said. He took a seat on a concrete bench with birds carved across the back of it.

Serena sat next to him, thinking how to frame her answer and not give away what she had been doing while at her beach house. No one except Iliana knew she had been selling her artwork and building her career as a painter. "My sister was to be the queen. I didn't think my future entailed a throne, so I found other interests to pursue."

"Tell me about them."

Casimir hadn't asked about her art directly, but she wanted to tell him. They had shared an experience that had changed her life and now she wanted to share this piece of her life with him. "I like to paint. And do yoga." She spoke quickly, feeling strangely vulnerable.

"What do you like to paint?" He sounded both calm and interested without censure in his voice.

"The sea." The beautiful sea, a source of calm and joy for her.

"I've never had much success with art. Or yoga. But I'd like to try it."

"I could teach you to paint." She offered quickly, without checking the words before she spoke them. It wasn't like her to talk without thinking. She wanted a connection with Casimir, something to keep him in her life.

"Then it's date. I'll be in Acacia tomorrow to meet with my boat builder. Do you have time tomorrow?"

Tomorrow was Boat Day, a national holiday celebrating the water, and her schedule was full, but she would make time. She agreed, both nervous and excited about seeing Casimir again. Though this couldn't end in a friendship—or something deeper—perhaps another day with her rescuer would satisfy her curiosity and she would stop thinking about him.

But looking at his handsome face in the soft lights of the patio, she had the impression it would be hard to forget a man like Casimir.

Casimir was glad he'd arranged an excuse to be in Acacia before tonight's dinner party. His plan was unfolding as he had wanted, without as much manipulation as he'd expected. Tonight was about keeping the door open to his connection with Serena.

Convincing Fiona, the Countess of Provence in Rizari, to attend this party and bring him along had been easy. Making it clear that their relationship was platonic was trickier. He had been careful to keep their association on neutral ground. It worked out better for his plans for Serena. The princess had to see him as available.

Going through a traumatic experience, Serena's heart would be guarded. Casimir would have to be diligent to breech those shields.

He had learned through a friend that King Warrington had been with his mistress that afternoon. Based on the king's tardiness at tonight's dinner party, he may still be with her. The idea disgusted him. Had Warrington considered Serena's feelings before inviting her tonight and booking time with his lover earlier in the day?

The silver lining was that, for once, the situation was progressing to Casimir's benefit. The king was missing in action and Serena had been drawn to Casimir immediately.

Casimir had to help her see that she would be miserable married to King Warrington. Though Warrington could give her some freedom, mostly because he cared only for her position and not for her, she would be bound by her marriage vows. Casimir sensed she was a woman who would keep those vows sacred. She would be loyal and true and consequently, she would be lonely and disappointed. The king would see no reason to stop seeing his mistresses on the side.

He wouldn't treat Serena as an equal; he would devour her. He would exploit her, sleep with her, marry her and then keep her in his life in some superficial manner, maybe use her to give him legitimate heirs. He wouldn't give her the respect and love she deserved. It incensed Casimir to think about it.

Granted, almost everything King Warrington did or said fueled Casimir's anger. He wanted the man to suffer for what he had done. Killing his father, and dooming his mother to a life of misery, came at a heavy price and Samuel would pay it. That Samuel had killed, or arranged to have killed, his own father as well, spoke to the depths that Warrington would descend for power.

The doors to the patio opened and Samuel's mother exited the dining room. Katarina strode toward Serena, looking regal in a red dress. Her dark hair bounced as she walked. Casimir recognized the glint in her eyes. She, like her son, was hungry for power and she would do anything necessary to secure an alliance with Acacia.

Underestimating Katarina's ruthlessness would be a mistake. She held sway over her son and according to Casimir's mother and rumors, she was vicious. Casimir wasn't sure what role she played in the king's and her husband's deaths, but he guessed she was at least aware that her son had been responsible for it.

"Princess Serena, what are you doing out here?"

Serena blinked in the dark and rose from the bench. "Hello."

"I was concerned when I saw you exit the dining room." She glanced at Casimir and narrowed her eyes. "Do I know you?"

Casimir had been introduced to her twice before. Nice of her to remember. "I'm a friend of your son's. My name is Casimir Cullen." The word *friend* burned his tongue.

Katarina narrowed her eyes. Did she see the resemblance to his father? That resemblance had been difficult for his mother and she had made no secret of it. "Please excuse us. I would like to speak to the princess alone."

Serena held out her hand. "If you think something improper was occurring, I must correct you. My guards are with me," she gestured over her shoulders, "and Casimir saved my life."

"Did he now? And how is that?" Katarina looked irritated.

Serena swallowed heavily and Casimir detected a tremor in her lips. She blinked and Casimir saw the tears shining in her eyes. Speaking about the night her father and sister had died was difficult for her.

"I was close to the princess during the massacre at her castle. I prevented one of the assassins from attacking her." Short and to the point. No use drudging up the gruesome details of that night or saying "killing her." Hearing him mention the tragedy had to be hard enough for Serena.

Serena looked at the ground and Casimir knew she was trying to compose herself. Grief was a brutal, unrelenting animal. He would have done anything in that moment to take away some of Serena's pain.

Katarina folded her hands in front of her. "I see. Then allow me to thank you on behalf of my son for saving his bride's life."

Serena's chest lifted and lowered as she took a deep breath. She seemed to be pulling herself together and when she lifted her head, her expression was calm. "Has His Highness arrived?"

"Not yet. Please, Serena, let's have a little girl talk. What do you say?"

Before she could answer, Katarina turned to Serena's guards. "You may wait inside."

Serena straightened. "My guards stay with me."

"The king has guards to protect his palace. You are not in danger while you are on the premises."

"As you can imagine, after what I have been through over the past several weeks, I would feel better if my guards remained close." Serena's voice was saccharine sweet but there was no mistaking the edge in it.

"Very well."

Casimir bowed to the women and strolled inside. Serena was timid in some ways, but when pushed, she wouldn't hold back defending herself. He had thought Serena would be easy to manipulate, but seeing her strength in action was impressive. Made his plan harder, but notched up his respect for her.

Serena would not be shoved around by her future mother-in-law. Starting the relationship on that note would doom her marriage and Serena already had doubts about its future happiness.

"I know you are adjusting to your new position, but I should warn you, being alone with a man who is not my son is asking for trouble."

It annoyed Serena to be spoken to condescendingly as if she were a teenager and the implication, that she had been doing something wrong by talking to Casimir, pissed her off. Her emotions were on a hair trigger, admittedly, but she thought Katarina had crossed a line. "Casimir is a man of honor. I am not ashamed to be seen with him in any context." Maybe not naked with him in bed, which would certainly be inappropriate, but she was dressed and in view of her guards and the guests at the dinner party. But now that she was thinking about being naked with Casimir, she had trouble putting it out of her mind. Despite the coolness of the night air, heat flamed up her back and a new tide of arousal washed over her. Utterly distracting.

"I don't say these things to chastise you, but if you read up on the history of the royal family of Rizari, you will find the implication of any disloyalty is not taken lightly."

How would King Warrington react if she spoke to or flirted with another man? Behead her? "I will look into that."

Katarina lowered her head, but Serena did not mistake the gesture for subservience. She would need to watch her back when it came to Katarina. Serena hadn't planned to make an enemy of the king's mother, but if she felt attacked, she would defend herself. She wished her sister was around to ask about the queen. The thought brought another wave of loss crashing over her.

"I will have my son send over some literature."

"Speaking of your son, do you know where the king is?" Serena asked. Why invite her to a dinner party and then stand her up? He had to know she'd traveled a distance to be in attendance.

Katarina looked into the dining room. Stalling for time to manufacture a lie? "I know he had an important meeting this afternoon. Perhaps he lost track of time."

"I see. That does not bode well for our relationship."

"You cannot expect the king to be someone he is not."

What did that mean? Expecting him to show up for plans he'd made wasn't expecting too much. She was the princess and she had cleared her schedule. Serena had been second all her life. Everyone whom she'd loved had put her behind something or someone else more important. She could not live with being her husband's second, at least not in his heart.

"I will keep that in mind in the future." Serena walked away from Katarina, feeling daggers being shot at her back.

When Serena reentered the dining room, the same sense of dread and anxiety volleyed through her. Relying on her coping mechanisms, she found a chair in the corner of the room and sat, watching. Her gaze was drawn to Casimir. He was the most handsome man in the room. Apparently, the other women thought so as well. They fawned over him, touching the sleeve of his suit coat, practically stroking him to win his attention.

After several moments, he glanced toward the patio. Her heart thumped hard. Was he looking for her? Checking on her? He looked around the room and when he saw her, he said something to the woman he was speaking to and strode to Serena.

"Pleasant conversation with the king's mother?" he asked.

"I've been warned that you could sully my reputation."

"She said that?" He sounded incredulous.

"Not in those words. But apparently, I should have eyes and words only for women friends and the king. The king who is not yet here."

Casimir's eyes darted left and right. "Is this your first time in the palace?"

She must have made him nervous with her negative observation about the king. She had been thinking about Casimir so much, building him up in her head, she'd forgotten that she didn't really know him. He had no reason to trust that she would not relate anything negative he said back to the king. She felt embarrassed for putting him in that position. "It is my first time in the palace. It is beautiful. My one complaint is that I can't hear the sea."

"The sea is a distance from the palace."

"I won't live here," she said, thinking of the future.

"The king might be surprised when his bride moves to the beach," Casimir said.

She hurried to explain, trying not to make him think less of her. "I used to fish and swim laps in the Mediterranean Sea and walk along the shore where the waves met the sand, letting the water cool my feet. I can't give that up." Not forever. She wished she were in her beach house now, listening to the water with Casimir.

"Marriage in any context is a negotiation."

Except that in her case, she had none of the power

and it entailed a lot of personal sacrifice with little personal gain in return. Acacia needed Rizari far more than the other way around.

On their first meeting as intended fiancés, the king was late. Was this an indication of how she would be treated during their marriage? Serena had a sense of foreboding. On the heels of that emotion was anger that the king thought so little of her. Would he have been late if he were meeting with Danae? Or perhaps the king was dreading this marriage as much as Serena was and looking for a way out. But if he offered an alliance without marriage, she would be turning Acacia over to King Warrington without any legal protection. That didn't sit right with her.

Her father had always told Serena that she should not accept subpar treatment from anyone. She had tried to be pleasant and accommodating, despite the challenges she was facing. But the well of pleasantness was about to run dry. The last several weeks had depleted it.

A woman stumbled over to them and slid her arm around Casimir. She kissed the underside of his jaw. "I am so glad to see you. You make these dull parties fun."

The woman took a big swallow from her glass of wine and glared at Serena. "Who are you?" The question sounded borderline hostile.

Casimir took a step away from the woman. "This is Princess Serena Alagona of Acacia."

"Nice to meet you. Are you the one who'll marry Samuel?"

Casimir shifted on his feet, clearly uncomfortable, but Serena was intrigued by this intoxicated woman and what she had to say. "Nothing has been decided, but our countries are negotiating."

The woman leaned forward and giggled. "I could tell you some hot stuff about Samuel. Most of the women in this room can. We've all slept with him."

Serena hid her disgust and pretended she wasn't repulsed by the idea of a slutty king who had invited his conquests to a dinner party with his future fiancée. "That's a lot of women."

Another giggle. "Not all at once. I mean, not usually more than one at a time. But sometimes."

Serena's hopes for a monogamous and meaningful relationship drifted further out of reach. King Warrington had been engaged to her sister. Was this woman speaking of the distant past? Could the king have been wild in his youth? Serena desperately wanted something to explain his behavior so she wouldn't be doomed to a life of unhappiness. "The king enjoys spending time with a lot of women?"

"Sure. Of course. You'll see. I'm sure you'll receive the royal treatment, you know, one-on-one with him. But maybe not every night. He is easily bored."

Was this a palace or a house of ill repute? "I see."

She had been thinking that perhaps she could make this arrangement work, and maybe it was this woman's intention to run her off, but after an altercation with the king's mother and now this, Serena wanted more than ever to be home.

"That's enough sharing. We can swap stories some other time," Casimir said, leading the other woman away.

Everyone in this room must think Serena was an ignorant moron. If the women had slept with the king, were they laughing at her? The king might be tied to her in marriage, but would that mean anything to him?

She turned to her guards. "I'd like to leave now."

They would not question her. As she moved toward the door, she tried not to think about what a spectacular failure this evening had been for her and her future with King Warrington. She had not made a connection with him. If anything, the experience had driven spikes between them.

She was on the front steps of the palace when she heard Casimir's voice. "Your Grace, please wait!"

Her guards stepped between her and Casimir. "It's okay." She wasn't mad at Casimir. Embarrassed by the king's behavior and feeling like a fool, yes.

"Serena, those are wild tales about the king. He likes to have a good time. Don't let a little provocation from his friends upset you. They are probably just having some fun at your expense."

"He didn't show up tonight." Even if the stories the woman had related about Warrington's bedroom behavior weren't true, his absence couldn't be disputed.

"He is being a fool," Casimir said quietly.

"Seeing you again was the only thing that salvaged the night."

She shivered and Casimir removed his jacket and draped it over her shoulders.

"I hate seeing you upset," Casimir said. "And yet every time I am near you, you seem to be in that state. Let me do something that will make you happy."

Serena felt the air sucked from her lungs. Was he planning to kiss her in front of the palace of Rizari? With her bodyguards standing around her?

"I will meet you in Acacia tomorrow," Casimir said. "And I will bring a surprise."

Not a kiss, but a promise of tomorrow. "Okay, tomorrow, then."

* * *

Serena was too warm. She had her windows opened and the overhead fan running, but heat seemed to pour from her. Anger for one man and desire for another made her blood run hot.

King Warrington had humiliated her. She hadn't been looking forward to the evening, but it had turned out worse than expected. With as much anxiety as she had about her social awkwardness and lack of finesse, her usually low expectations of social gatherings hadn't been met.

Serena would rather focus on Casimir. When she thought of him, she felt white-hot desire. The emotion could be completely inappropriate given the recent deaths in her family, but it persisted. Having located Casimir, she'd thought thanking him for what he'd done for her would give her some closure about that night. But instead, she found herself longing for him more intensely. He had slipped his suit jacket over her shoulders and she had forgotten to return it to him. It was hanging on her bed post, which felt wild and forbidden. The pockets were empty, but the jacket smelled of him, like sandalwood and spices.

She rolled to her side, adjusting her sheets. Closing her eyes, images of her father and her sister's bodies on the floor of the ballroom struck her. Nausea rolled over her. She opened her eyes. Maybe television would lull her into a mindless state.

She heard music as if caught on the wind, the light strumming of a guitar and the melodic sound of a man's voice. Casimir's strong, yet soft voice. Where was that coming from? Was she hallucinating at this hour? It was 1:15 a.m.

Looking out her bedroom window, she saw one of her guards patrolling her front yard. She knew at least two others were on the premises. Tugging a short robe around herself, she took the stairs to the main floor. On her wraparound porch stood Casimir, playing an acoustic guitar and singing quietly. She watched him for a moment, taking in how gorgeous he was. His dark silhouette was framed against the moon and the sea.

She memorized the image, thinking she could sketch it later.

Her heart was thumping as she walked outside. He continued playing, but had stopped singing.

"What are you doing here?" she asked. The wind blew and she shivered.

"We made plans to see each other today. Since it's past midnight, this counts," Casimir said. "I couldn't wait longer. I needed to see you now. I was serenading you."

Her knees felt weak. She had never had a man anxious to see her. She held on to the back of one of her porch chairs.

She glanced at her guard, surprised he had allowed Casimir onto her porch.

Her guard's shoulders tightened. "Do you wish to be alone, Your Grace? I overheard you agree to see him at the palace."

She had agreed to meeting Casimir and she was happy he was here, at her beach house. Though they were not lovers, this had the makings of a secret rendezvous. She shivered at the thought. "Let me get dressed." It wasn't as if she had been sleeping anyway.

"You don't need to change. You look good to me," Casimir said.

Her legs were bare and her nipples were pebbled against the cotton of her tank top and robe. It was hard to believe he was actually here. "Want to come inside? I can show you where I paint."

He shook his head and set his guitar on the porch, leaning it against her wooden chair. "No, we'll save my first painting lesson for another day. Being in the princess's house without a chaperone could be trouble."

"My guards can be trusted," she said.

"Perhaps I do not trust myself," Casimir said. "Let's go for a walk. You said you loved the sea."

They started down the stairs and her bare feet sank into the cool sand. Her guard followed at a distance. As they walked along the water's edge, Casimir didn't touch her, didn't hold her hand. His hands were tucked into his pockets in a boyishly charming manner. He had changed out of his suit and was wearing a pair of khaki shorts and a navy T-shirt. She could make out the muscles of his shoulders, arms and chest. She suppressed the urge to run her fingers down the hard planes of his body.

"I'm glad you came to see me tonight," she said.

"I'm sorry if I woke you."

"I wasn't sleeping."

Concern dotted his face. "I imagine you've had a hard time sleeping since that night."

He bent to pick something up.

"I miss them. I go over the sequence of events and try to think if there was more I could have done. I try to remember the last thing I said to each of them. I don't even understand why it happened." Who had wanted her family dead? Why that night? The questions yielded no answers, only more frustrating questions.

Grief made her throat tight and she went still, closing her eyes and gathering her strength.

"You don't have to be strong in front of me. Cry if you need to. I'll be strong enough for the both of us. For you."

A great heaving sob shuddered over her.

"I want to hold you. Let me hold you. Is that okay?"

She answered by stepping into his arms.

Casimir gathered her against him, his powerful arms clutching her to his muscular frame.

He held her while she cried. The water lapped over her feet at uneven intervals, the cool sensation soothing the burn of grief. The wind blew and the quiet of the night made her feel as if she and Casimir were hidden from the rest of the world.

When the tears stopped, only deep unrelenting sadness remained, heavy in her heart. Taking a deep breath, she rested her head on his chest. "A queen shouldn't cry."

"Where did you hear that? That's nonsense."

"My country needs me to be strong."

"Crying and showing emotion doesn't make you weak. It takes real strength to open up about how you're feeling," he said.

She broke away and sat on the sand. He sat next to her. He had his elbows propped on his bent knees. "You can say anything to me, Serena. I won't sell you out."

"I hardly know you," she said. Yet she trusted him more than a princess should.

"When two people have been through something like we have, there's a bond. It's hard to ignore that connection. You can trust it. If you listen to your instincts, you'll know I'm right."

Then he had felt it, too. She would be careful what she said to him, knowing a woman in her position should be, but she had someone to talk to and that was what she needed most. "I was humiliated tonight. The king never showed and he never called."

"It was a jerk move," Casimir said.

Then she wasn't the only one who thought so. "Why plan a party and invite me if he had no intention of coming?"

"I am not sure that he had no intention."

"He could have called. Texted. Had someone else call or text."

"That's true."

"I didn't want to see him tonight."

"Then why were you at the palace?" Casimir asked.

A complicated situation made more complicated by the day. "I don't know how much you follow politics, but my country needs me to marry the king."

"Why?"

"We're in a difficult location being between two life-long enemies. If Icarus decides to take a shot at Rizari, we're in the way. Therefore, Icarus may want to use us or invade to have easier access to Rizari."

"The president of Icarus told you this?"

She had yet to have a reasonable conversation with the president on the matter. "No, but Danae was planning to marry King Warrington to form a strong alliance with Rizari. Rizari's military presence can prevent Icarus from seeing us as an easy mark and attacking. The Assembly believes it's inevitable for Icarus to make a play for more power and more land."

"I see," Casimir said. He didn't seem eager to share his thoughts on the matter.

"What would you do?" Serena asked.

"That's not for me to say."

She wanted to know. "I asked your opinion."

Casimir glanced at her, amusement on his face. "Is that a royal request?"

"It is," she said with a smile.

"I would hate to belong to someone in marriage who I could not tolerate as a person and who did not respect me."

"I belong to no one," she said. Yet even the denial was a lie and she knew it. From the weaker position, she would be forced to agree to Warrington's terms. He would own her.

Serena watched the endless waves and thought about running away, just getting in a boat and sailing off. "I was never meant to be queen."

"Life has its own sense of humor. Perhaps you never believed you would be, but you have what it takes."

She scoffed. "If you knew me better, you would not say that." He didn't know about her social anxiety, the complete lack of experience and the fact that she had zero desire to be the figurehead of a nation.

"What I know tells me you are strong, faithful and loyal. What better qualities to have in a queen?" He handed her a piece of green sea glass.

She held it up in the moonlight.

"A broken shard of glass, someone's trash. It's been tumbled by the water and smashed by the rocks and the sand until it's beautiful and shiny."

"What it's gone through is what makes it beautiful," Serena said. She held the sea glass in her palm.

Casimir had the soul of a poet, the strength of a fighter and the bravery of an explorer. Everything she had been looking for in one man and had never found. Her heart clamored at her to crawl into his lap. But she couldn't.

She belonged to another man.

Chapter 3

Serena picked up the small globe from her therapist's desk. Dr. Albert Shaw had been her therapist for five years and she had seen him more frequently in the past several weeks. He had been helping her with her social anxiety and more recently, with her grief. He asked her prying questions, he was perceptive and she wanted to convince him she was fine and healed, as if that would actually prove she was better.

She had to fight through this period of her life and be strong, not break down into tears and sob about her father and sister—which had happened twice in this office—and remain calm. Immediately after the morning's session, she would be heading to the Spear's Point Marina to give a speech for the start of the boat-racing season, locally and affectionately known as Boat Day.

Water and related sports and hobbies were integral to Acacia's culture. Almost every child she knew—herself included—learned to swim at a young age, learned to captain a water vessel as a teenager and learned to fish somewhere in between.

Serena thrived when she was on the water. She hoped to hang on to those feelings while giving her speech and not let the stage fright that plagued her consume her. Stage fright was not a good quality in a queen. She knew it and her father had known it. To a large degree, he had tried to help her through it. Speech tutors and public-speaking lessons hadn't worked. When she'd turned twenty, he'd given up and switched to helping her avoid the limelight. It was one of the reasons it had been easy for her to stay out of politics.

Serena had instead focused her time and energy on her artwork, a fine hobby for a princess. Serena had crossed a line when she'd asked Iliana to help her sell her work. Yet those sales had meant something to her. She had felt as if she had worth beyond her title and breeding.

Dr. Shaw entered his office, his gait implying he was in no hurry. He had a full beard, a warm smile and rosy cheeks, making him look a little like Santa Claus. But his leisurely movements, advanced age and jovial appearance were misleading. His mind was sharp. He missed nothing and he saw through lies. Serena didn't bother lying to him. Lying to herself, however, could still be a problem in tough situations.

Serena sat on the same chair she always did during her sessions.

"Have you had an easier time sleeping?" Dr. Shaw asked, taking his seat.

Serena had declined a prescription for sleeping pills, but had agreed to try lavender oil and some calming breathing exercises before bed. She'd tried to cover the dark circles under her eyes with makeup, but Dr. Shaw had a way of seeing through smoke and mirrors.

"A little."

"What's helped? What hasn't helped?"

Though she hadn't slept long, after Casimir had left her on the porch of her beach house, she had found the deep sleep she'd craved but that had been out of reach. "I found the man who saved my life." Saying the words made her feel breathless and excited.

Dr. Shaw shifted in his chair, dragging his hand over his beard. "Tell me about that."

Serena related the situation. She left out how attracted she was to Casimir, how much she wished she could have a relationship with him.

"What did you feel when you had to part ways?" Dr. Shaw asked.

A combination of emotions, sadness and loss, but also hope and excitement. "The same grief I've been carrying around, but I felt better."

"Sounds like he's a good man to have around."

That was putting it mildly. He had been helpful to her in every situation they'd been in together. But she had to be realistic about her boundaries and accept her new life and responsibilities and that meant she had to let him go. "He and I can't have a relationship and we both know that. It wouldn't be appropriate."

"Inappropriate to have a friend?"

The way Dr. Shaw posed the question, he had picked up on the fact that Serena was attracted to Casimir. They weren't simply friends and to pretend so was to lie to herself, to Casimir and to Dr. Shaw. "I'm attracted to him."

"Grateful for what he has done or attracted to him?"

"Both."

"What does he feel about you?"

Serena didn't know. He had been courageous for her, attentive to her and had made her feel desired and wanted. But he hadn't made any advances toward her. Could he want to be friends? What reason did he have to pursue a friendship with her? "I don't know. I assume he likes me. He acts like he does. But maybe he's just using me." Being a royal hanger-on was a full-time occupation for some.

"Nothing you've told me would suggest he is using you, but I would be cautious about requests in the future. When there's an emotional debt, it can be exploited."

Serena heard a commotion outside the office. Dr. Shaw rose to his feet. The door banged open and a man in a ski mask entered. He fired his gun at the window and it shattered.

Fear torqued through her. Immediately, the night her father and sister had been killed snapped to mind. Not again. This couldn't be happening again.

Casimir wasn't here to save her and she would have to save herself. She leapt to her feet, diving behind the couch.

One of her guards burst into the room, weapon drawn, and fired at the masked man. Two. Three. Four shots.

The man fell to the ground.

Serena climbed to her feet. Her guard rushed to her. She was fine. Rattled, but physically okay.

But Dr. Shaw was not moving. He was lying on the ground, blood pouring from his shoulder. A scream died in Serena's throat. She peeled off her sweater and hurried to him, pressing it to his wound.

"Help me!" Serena shouted to her guard.

He rushed to her side, taking over trying to stop the doctor's blood loss, and Serena fumbled for the phone on the doctor's desk to call for an ambulance.

Two of her guards had been killed by the masked men who had stormed the therapist's office. Her security had killed one of the men outside the private office and the other had been gunned down in front of her.

With those images pulsing in her brain, Serena changed her clothes. Iliana was helping her and for that Serena was deeply grateful. She couldn't think of anything except Dr. Shaw. He was in the ICU at Thorntree General and his fate was in his doctors' hands. When he was more stable, he would be helicoptered to a larger hospital in Rizari with better equipment.

The media was reporting on the incident as another failed attempt on the princess's life.

"Serena, are you sure you want to do this?" Iliana asked, sitting next to her and putting her arm around her shoulders. "Because if it's too much, we can come up with an excuse and you can go home."

Serena would have critics no matter what she planned today. In the past, she had been blasted for being too shy and too quiet. She had been called slow, although testing proved what she had tried to tell her father and her doctors. Her mind was fine. It was her mouth that didn't want to work. Even when she tried to say the words that came to mind, they sounded garbled when they left her lips. And worse still, she hated the look on people's faces after she spoke. They'd look confused or bored. She had a unique talent of making awkward silences fall over a conversation. It was her superpower.

Her sister had known what to say, even in tense situations. Her sister had charmed men into doing what she wanted. But Serena was not her sister.

Serena wouldn't go down this dark road, especially not now when she was rattled, her emotions in tatters. Her public failings were in the past. She had a new life path and she had to get on board and give it everything she had. Serena took a deep breath. "I want to do this. I want to show whoever is targeting me and my family that I won't be intimidated by threats and violence."

Iliana's eyes were deep pools of worry. "If you're sure…"

"I am sure."

The Spear's Point Marina had been decorated in Acacian colors: red and gold. Flags were posted at the ends of the docks and boats were likewise decorated. Citizens wore red and yellow T-shirts. Bands played patriotic songs. Over five thousand people were expected to attend this year's Boat Day celebration.

Iliana left Serena alone for a few minutes inside the marina's private suite. Serena looked out at the water and tried to center herself and her thoughts. She needed to appear strong and in control. While she did not want to look hard and distant, she had to keep her emotions on a short leash.

Iliana returned, looking excited. "The king is here!"

For a brief moment, Serena thought she could mean her father, but Serena then remembered it couldn't be so. Iliana meant King Warrington.

King Warrington had been scheduled to be part of the day, but had not committed to specifics. Serena's feelings about him were mixed, at best. They hadn't spoken since he had stood her up the night before. No calls or text messages with an explanation.

"Are you excited?" Iliana asked.

Serena hadn't told Iliana about what had happened with King Warrington or about Casimir's late night visit. She didn't have time to discuss the details now.

"Of course," she said.

Iliana narrowed her eyes. "You sound just the opposite. Did something happen with him last night?"

"Nothing happened and that's why I'm anxious. He didn't show up."

Iliana winced. "That bad? You should have called me. We could have commiserated over glasses of wine."

"It was late when I arrived home. I didn't want to bother you."

"You are never bothering me. You can call me anytime you need to. I'm not saying that as an employee. I'm saying that as a friend."

Iliana was loyal and steadfast. Serena would be lost without her. "Was the king headed in this direction?" Serena asked.

"I don't know. I didn't see him myself. Your uncle told me he was here. Speaking of…"

Her uncle entered the tent. Worry etched his face. He hugged Serena. "Are you okay? I heard about what happened this morning."

Serena blew out her breath. "I survived."

"And I am grateful. Do you need anything?"

She considered asking him to give the speech, but she wanted to honor her father and sister's memories. She wanted her father's legacy as a good and strong leader to continue with her. "I have the speech written.

I'll be okay." Her uncle didn't know the full scope of her public-speaking anxiety. Her family had concealed it even from him.

"That's my girl," her uncle said and kissed her cheek.

"Ready?" Iliana asked.

Serena stood on shaky legs, but at least she was standing. Heat flamed up her back. Her chest felt tight and she couldn't pull enough air into her lungs. This couldn't happen now. She had four minutes until she was scheduled to speak. A panic attack was unacceptable.

She had practiced her speech a number of times, but she couldn't recall how it started. Then, somehow, she was standing on the platform overlooking the crowd. Balloons blew in the wind, streamers whipped in the air and every eye was on her.

The head of the Assembly was making his opening comments and introducing her. She stepped forward, scanning the crowd for King Warrington. When she reached the podium, she opened her mouth to speak. Her tongue was impossibly dry. She took the water cup from the hidden ledge inside the podium and drank.

"Hot day," the head of the Assembly commented.

Uneasy laughter rolled over the crowd. Serena started again.

Her tongue felt heavy. Her hands felt sweaty and she was clammy and hot. She glanced at Iliana. She appeared concerned, but smiled encouragingly. How much time had passed? Seconds? One minute?

Serena tried again to read the words of her speech, but they were blurry on her notecards. She hadn't had time to memorize it. That could have helped.

Then King Warrington was at her side, moving her

away from the podium. "Good thing I'm here to save the day. Please allow me to welcome you to this Boat Day celebration."

Serena felt dismissed and overshadowed. She had flailed, but she would have pulled it together. She hid her frustration and pretended to gaze on King Warrington with affection.

She had to give him credit. The man had presence. In seconds, he had the crowd laughing and hanging on his every word. Serena couldn't track what he was saying. She could hardly define how she felt, a combination of annoyed and embarrassed.

It was the second time in two days that the king had made her feel that way.

"As for Princess Serena, I will be taking her to my palace in Rizari for a few days. She can relax under the constant vigilance of my guards and then I'll return her to you."

Serena felt a jolt of outrage. He hadn't consulted her about taking her away from Acacia. He was likely trying to imply they were closer than they were or to start planting the idea of a union between their countries. Either way, she was furious.

With that, Warrington led her away from the podium. He more than led. He practically carried her. Her legs were weak and her stomach roiled.

When they were back inside the marina suite, King Warrington poured himself a scotch from the bar in the room.

"What happened out there?" he asked. His dark brown hair was perfectly styled and his brown eyes were cold. Why had she never noticed how much he looked like a boy bander before?

Serena felt as if she were slipping into misery, deep and dark and all-consuming. This was her first private conversation with her future husband? What a nightmare. "I've had some anxiety since my father and sister were killed." Add to it what had happened that morning and she thought flubbing the speech was understandable.

"You'll need to pull it together. I can't have that kind of crap happening on a regular basis."

Serena had been this way since childhood. When she and Danae had played with their friends, Serena had been teased and mocked. Her sister would stand up for her, but it had still hurt. Now her sister was gone. She didn't have anyone to protect her in that same way and Serena felt resolute in protecting herself and making Danae proud.

Iliana entered the room and rushed to Serena, taking her hands. "Are you okay?" She glared at King Warrington. "What happened?"

"I just felt hot. And overwhelmed."

Iliana gave her a sympathetic smile. "It's been a very bad month."

"I am not leaving Acacia. I am fine here," Serena said.

"Your recent history proves otherwise," King Warrington said. He took a swig of his drink and stared at her, looking bored.

As if she didn't have enough to deal with, her uncle entered the room.

How could she explain it? She had taken on more than she could handle. She had screwed up. She had pretended she could make it through a short statement and keep her cool, but under the circumstances, the task was beyond her.

"Serena, I have tried to be patient with you. I have tried to give you space. But a stunt like that will make everyone in the country think you're on the verge of a nervous breakdown. Do you know how this will look for the royal family? Do you realize how weak we seem? President DeSante could attack and take over our country. Is that what you want?" her uncle asked. He seemed at his wit's end.

Serena didn't feel on the edge of losing her mind. She had a lot to learn and an overwhelming number of tasks ahead of her, but she was prepared to tackle them and work until she had the country's problems under control and they were united with Rizari. "I am not having a breakdown. I do not wish to turn our country over to a dictator. I've had a bad day."

Her uncle threw his hands in the air. "This is too much for you, Serena. I hate seeing you struggle this way."

Serena glanced over her shoulder at Iliana and Warrington. "Could you give us a few minutes?"

Iliana and Warrington left the room.

"I need time," Serena said.

"To do what? Leaders of countries do not have the luxury of time. You don't get to recover in your remote beach house and ponder the meaning of life and death. When your mother died, do you think your father took a vacation from his responsibilities?"

Her father had not taken vacations. It was a harsh truth she was well aware of. No family trips out of the country for pleasure, only the mandatory appearances at social functions. "He didn't. I remember."

"The media will be asking for a statement. What should I tell them?"

"Don't tell them anything. Give me a few minutes and I'll walk through the crowd, just as I planned. I will say I've had a tough day, but I'm fine. We don't need to overreact." Her words sounded stronger than she felt.

Her uncle sniffed. "Now you're decisive. Do what you must." He turned on his heels and stopped once to look over his shoulder. "Just remember that your weakness reflects on the entire country. Your unwillingness to be the princess you were raised to be leaves us vulnerable to attack by our enemies. Unless you want a hostile takeover by a dictator, you had better marry King Warrington and do it soon."

Serena was pinned between four bodyguards. Her security team was controlling the scene the best they could, under the circumstances. Boat Day was a huge holiday for Acacia. Docks were full, the marinas were crowded and banks and schools were closed.

Serena couldn't enclose herself in her beach house and sulk about her embarrassment or worry about Dr. Shaw. Especially after what had happened during her speech, she needed to save face and inject some confidence into her countrymen. She focused on the task at hand: shaking hands, posing for pictures and smiling. The crowd was stifling and after an hour, Serena needed a break. She was dizzy and tired and her brain felt foggy. She was wearing a bulletproof vest under her dress and it felt hot and heavy.

"Could we grab some lunch?" she asked the guard closest to her.

She was scheduled to have lunch at one of her favorite restaurants in the area and now was a good time for it.

Her guard nodded, said something into his wrist-watch communication device and she was led in a different direction.

Then, she saw him. As if a shot of adrenaline had hit her system, the fog lifted and her senses were completely focused. Casimir was speaking to a boat vendor, perhaps the vendor who was selling him the boat he'd mentioned.

"I see a friend. I'd like to say hello." Before her guards could stop her or warn her about the security risks of deviating from the planned path, she moved through the crowd toward Casimir.

She knew the moment Casimir had spotted her.

He had stopped talking and was staring in her direction, his lips slightly parted. Her guards held the crowd at some distance. The boat vendor bowed to her and moved away, giving her and Casimir a few feet of privacy.

"Casimir, hello." She wished she had said something more clever to him. She wanted to hug him in greeting, but knew the crowd was watching her and cameras were snapping pictures.

"Your Grace," he said, bowing to her. His body language was formal and he did not touch her, but his eyes conveyed heat and desire. Would the crowd pick up on that? Did she care?

"I didn't realize you would be here today," she said.

"I mentioned I was planning to buy a boat. And so I am. Best day of the year to get one. Fire sales, I tell you."

It was a big week for the boat trade. Serena had

bought her first boat around Boat Day when she was sixteen. "I am happy to see you."

"I am happy to see you as well. I heard you had trouble this morning." Lines formed around his eyes as his expression shifted to concern.

"I'm surprised you heard," she said. "I thought the police wanted to keep it under wraps."

"Most of the island heard about what happened through unofficial channels. I tried to call you." The second sentence was spoken so softly, it was almost impossible for her to hear.

She was pleased he had been concerned about her. That might be the only good thing that came from the attack that morning. Nothing like finding the bright side. "I haven't been near my phone."

"That wasn't an accusation. Just expressing concern."

"Could you meet me somewhere for lunch?" she asked quietly. They couldn't leave together or rumors would run rampant, but she could meet him.

Casimir straightened. "I could. Where?"

"The Steel Anchor Lounge? Now?" she asked. Her guards had reserved the top deck for her to have a lunch in a safe place away from the crowds. The restaurant also happened to serve the best lobster bisque.

"Sure. I am almost finished here. Are you sure I'll be allowed past security?"

She could have stayed with Casimir all afternoon. She wanted to know more about his boat, to see it, to find out if he had enjoyed their time together on the beach as much as she had. "I will make it so," she said.

Every moment with Casimir felt like borrowed time, but Serena would take what she could until she belonged to King Warrington.

* * *

Casimir had known that Serena would walk near this location. DeSante had a source on Serena's staff. Casimir didn't know the details. Either DeSante was paying for information or he had positioned one of his spies close to her. DeSante played his cards close to the vest, even with Casimir.

The situation with Serena had played out how Casimir had hoped, except for one small problem. He had expected to look at her and see a potential ally, one he could easily negotiate with once he inevitably won his throne in Rizari. But those thoughts were far from his mind.

He looked at her and he saw a woman whom he wanted to sleep with. He struggled to control his emotions when she was near. The relief that had consumed him at seeing that she was safe after this morning's attack was a clear sign that she wasn't another political tool to use. Then he had been concerned watching her on the podium giving—or rather not giving—her speech. It had taken speaking to her personally for him to feel that she really was okay. Physically at least, and that she wasn't so far down that she wouldn't rebound. She was stronger than she gave herself credit for. Some people who had experienced what she had wouldn't yet be out of bed.

Among his emotions was jealousy, jealousy that Serena belonged to another man. A competitive spirit urged him to pursue her regardless of her ties to the false king of Rizari. A bone-deep desire commanded him to throw her over his shoulder and carry her to bed. King Warrington had announced Serena would be coming to Rizari with him and it had angered him. Though it had been brief, her reaction told Casimir she hadn't known of the plan before Warrington had publicly announced it. That had shifted Casimir's anger into fury.

He didn't want Serena pushed around because she was inexperienced and in the weaker political position.

But overthinking her relationship with Warrington and being consumed with thoughts of her meant his goals were becoming muddled. Serena wasn't supposed to be his concern. Her well-being was her and her administration's problem. She had her uses and those should not extend into any real concern for her. Revenge against Warrington was his primary objective. When Samuel was no longer king, Casimir's mother could stop harboring anger and hurt. And he could take his rightful place on the throne.

But Casimir was troubled by how much he felt for Princess Serena. He was preoccupied with her and was spending more time than he needed to in order to accomplish his goal. Time he didn't have to waste. His plans with DeSante were complex and involved many moving pieces.

At the close of his negotiations for the boat, the boat vendor sized him up. "You and the princess seem close."

It was best to deny it. "Not really. I'm friends with King Warrington," Casimir said. The words tasted dirty in his mouth. He would never consider that liar, thief and murderer a friend.

"I see. I thought I caught something else between you two. Must have been my imagination."

The man walked off and Casimir didn't pursue the comment. To go out of his way to explain things would only make him seem as if he was covering up the truth.

He wasn't sure where the truth lay and he didn't want to look too deeply into how he felt about that.

On his way to the Steel Anchor, he resolved to stay the course. This meant winning Serena over, making her an ally and keeping her out of King Warrington's despicable, lying hands.

At the restaurant, Casimir was hustled through security and then he took the wooden stairs to the upper deck.

Serena was alone, save for three of her guards. She smiled at him and gestured to the seat across from her. To his left was a gorgeous view of the sea.

Casimir sat at a red linen–topped table. "I didn't realize this would be a private lunch." He assumed she only took audiences with groups during this highly anticipated and well-publicized event.

"The only way I can recover from a huge crowd is to have some time to myself."

"But I am here."

She smiled. "That's true. But you don't exhaust me."

He was glad to hear it. "If I may speak freely, I need to tell you that I was troubled to hear rumors about what happened to you this morning. I didn't want to ask you about it earlier when others could overhear."

She took a sip of her water. "I don't know what you've heard, but let me clarify. I was at a regularly scheduled meeting with my therapist, and two masked assailants broke into his office and attacked us. Dr. Shaw was gravely injured."

"I am sorry to hear that," he said. A second failed assassination attempt. Either these assassins were completely inept or they had another motive. Was it to scare her? Force her into some agreement?

Her hands trembled. "I care a great deal about Dr. Shaw. I heard from his doctors a few minutes ago. He is stable, but time will tell if he'll fully recover."

"Any news about the men who attacked you?"

DeSante had hired a few investigators, some of a violent persuasion, to obtain answers about who was targeting the Acacian royal family. Whatever information Casimir could feed him from Serena would help narrow the search.

"Nothing yet. Or if the police have discovered anything, I haven't been kept abreast of that part of the investigation," Serena said.

She had removed her sweater and it was draped over the back of her chair. The dress she was wearing fit tightly at the top and when she leaned forward in her chair to set her hands on the table, he had the most enticing view of her cleavage.

He tried not to focus his attention there, but rather on her.

He had to get his attraction to her under control, or better yet, stamp it out completely. He had allowed emotion to rule his thinking in the past and that never turned out well.

"I plan to sail my boat to Rizari later today," he said.

Serena lifted her brow. "Did you hear the announcement King Warrington made? Apparently, I am headed there myself."

"I would be happy to escort you," Casimir said. Not a smart offer. Being with her in the small confines of a boat wasn't a way to put distance between them.

Serena drummed her fingers on the table. "I was planning to tell Warrington that I wouldn't go, but being in Rizari will give Samuel and me a chance to talk and see if we can come to an understanding. Our relationship is off to a strange start and I don't want it to become hostile. To make matters more awkward, I know he's dealing with his own grief over Danae's death."

The idea of Serena alone with Warrington, a perpetual philanderer, was enough to drive Casimir insane. He needed to find a reason to be around the palace. Warrington regularly invited his social circle to the palace for a large number of events. Casimir would need to contact the Countess of Provence again and use her to get inside the palace. It was a tricky proposition. Fiona had seemed annoyed at him for leaving in a hurry the night before. No good-night kiss and no plans made for the future. Casimir hadn't even promised to call.

His hurry had been spurred by his anxiety to see Serena again. As much as Fiona claimed she understood that they were friends, Casimir sensed she had hopes of being something else in the future.

He would work his contacts, make excuses or lie. He couldn't leave Serena alone with Warrington. The man had proven he was capable of anything.

"If you had something to do with the attack on Serena this morning, I will gut you," Iliana said. She was gripping her phone so hard, she was afraid she would crack it. But the more she thought about Serena and how close she had come to being hurt again, the more intense her anger had become. She was almost blackout angry. All she could see and taste was her fury.

"Are you aware that threats against the president of Icarus are grounds for an investigation and jail time?" DeSante asked.

He sounded entertained, as if he was toying with

her, which set her temper on edge. "Don't make light of this. Serena was almost killed."

"*Almost* being the operative word. If I had set out to kill her, she would be dead."

"Are you threatening her?"

"Not at all. Just pointing out a simple fact. When I choose to do something, I do it. I don't bungle it repeatedly." He had the nerve to sound calm and unconcerned.

"You are deplorable!" Iliana said.

"You are the one who called me and made an unfair accusation based on emotion. Tell me, do you always make decisions based on how you feel in the heat of the moment?"

Iliana felt an emotion akin to desire ripple over her, dimming some of her rage. But she did not feel desire for the dictator. She hated him. *Hated.* He was pushy and rude and thought his title and position meant he could do whatever he wanted. In his country, maybe he could. But she was an Acacian citizen. He had no hold over her.

"I was hoping you were calling to tell me you had reconsidered my offer to visit," he said.

That wouldn't happen in her lifetime. "I am calling to make sure you know that if Serena is hurt, I'm looking in your direction."

"As much as I would enjoy you looking at me, I must tell you that you are looking in the wrong direction. I have no reason to harm the princess."

Iliana despised how smooth his voice was and how composed his tone. "I can think of a few reasons. It would clear your path to taking over Acacia."

"That is factually untrue. Someone else would be crowned king or queen and then I would be forced to negotiate with that person. As it stands, I don't have enough information about the princess to say whether or not I will find her to be a hindrance or an asset. All I really know about her is that she keeps a pit bull for an assistant and a rather fearless one at that. If she prefers strong people around her, then I imagine she is a smart woman and will be reasonable to deal with. As was her father."

Iliana was disarmed by his words. Serena's father had been key to keeping the peace in the region. He had often served in an unofficial capacity as mediator of disputes between Rizari and Icarus. Without him, Iliana was concerned how long peace would remain in place.

Iliana kept her tone sharp. She'd show no weakness. "I am worried about Serena and I wanted to make sure you were clear that you are not to harm her."

"It's rare to have a friend so loyal that she is willing to directly threaten the leader of a nation."

Iliana would do more than threaten DeSante if he attacked Serena. "Serena is my boss, but she's also my friend. We're family." Their mothers had been sisters, close until Serena's mother died when Serena was a child. Then both of Iliana's parents died in a car accident while Iliana was at university. She was no stranger to grief and that experience made her ache that much more for Serena.

"You're doing what any blood relative would do. Setting the expectations and making sure I don't cross them. Tell me though, what would you do to me if I did cross them, by say, showing up at the castle in Thorntree?"

His voice had taken on a dangerous tone, but she didn't feel afraid. She felt turned on. Iliana wasn't certain how to respond to him. Flirting was unacceptable, wasn't it? And what if she was wrong? What if he wasn't flirting, but rather using her to dig for information about Serena? Her temper flared anew. "You are not welcome here. Good luck getting past our security." Although the words were bluster. The Acacian military was weak. It was the main reason that Serena had to marry King Warrington and form a strong alliance with Rizari.

"Loyal and patriotic. I like that."

She felt as if she was a mouse and DeSante was a cat, watching her, deciding when to strike with his enormous claws. "I've made my position clear. Don't hurt the princess and don't send any of your goons after her. If you do, I promise, I will make you regret it."

"I suppose it's too late to tell you that you have nothing to fear from me. If you do not get in my way, I will not hurt you or the princess. I will only do what is necessary to protect Icarus."

Chapter 4

Spending time on the water had put Serena in a better mood. She was smiling and laughing, sitting close to Casimir as he steered his new boat toward Rizari. Casimir was pleased with *The Buccaneer*'s inaugural trip on the Mediterranean Sea. The water surrounding Acacia was blue and tranquil. The sun was high in the sky and the clouds blocked some of the light, providing relief from the heat.

Serena was wearing a pair of red pants that fell midcalf, showing off her shapely legs, and a sleeveless red-and-white-striped shirt. The pants emphasized her hips and rear, and Casimir had a thing for women with curves.

"Have you been boating long?" Serena asked.

"Since I was a boy." He had liked being on the water, whether it was kayaking or canoeing or taking out the fishing boat he had found and refurbished to be sea-worthy.

"Me, too."

Casimir glanced at his GPS. Two boats were moving in his direction. His instincts put him on guard and he reduced his speed. From what Serena had related, Samuel Warrington had not been thrilled about her arranging her own transportation to Rizari. Though he doubted Warrington would aggressively intercept his boat, other dangers lurked. These waters were not controlled or policed by anyone and pirates took advantage of that.

Casimir had a sidearm within reach. Was it enough to protect her?

"What's the matter? Why did you slow down?" Serena asked. She was too experienced of a boater not to recognize the change in their speed.

"Two boats are moving in my direction."

Serena stood behind him and set her hand on his shoulder. She looked at the GPS. Her guards were on board and she called to them. They arrived on deck, guns drawn, Iliana behind them.

"We may have a problem," Serena said.

It was too early to call the situation a full-fledged emergency. He could be overreacting, though his instincts had served him well and he did best when he followed them.

When the boats turned in their direction, Casimir knew his concern wasn't an overreaction.

As the boats came into view, Casimir felt simultaneously relieved and worried.

Both boats belonged to DeSante. The Icarus flag was stamped on the side, identifying the boats as vessels of the navy of Icarus. Demetrius wasn't in stealth mode, meaning he intended the boats to be seen.

The vessels pulled closer and slowed almost to a stop. Casimir's radio beeped and he answered.

"Good afternoon crew of *The Buccaneer*. This is the president of Icarus. Who do I have the pleasure of speaking with today?"

Serena's eyes were wide. Casimir didn't like Demetrius strong-arming Serena into speaking with him, but it was his style to get in Serena's face and force her to deal with him. Demetrius had been keeping tabs on Casimir while he was in Acacia, but had said nothing about forcing a confrontation today.

"This is Casimir Cullen, the boat's captain. This is my vessel."

"Your guest is the princess of Acacia. Don't deny it. I can see her."

"She is my guest and I will protect her as such."

DeSante laughed. "I mean her no harm. May I come aboard? Or perhaps I can send a dinghy and we can speak aboard one of my boats?"

Casimir released the radio so DeSante couldn't hear them.

"He is very insistent, isn't he?" Serena asked. She swallowed hard.

"I would suggest allowing him onboard. We can't outrun the boats and we're outnumbered."

Serena extended her hand for the radio. Impressed with her nerve, Casimir set the radio in her palm. "President DeSante, how interesting that we should meet on the open water. Tell me how I had this good fortune today."

"Your beloved alerted me to your travel plans hours

ago, as he did the entire country. So much for security protocols," DeSante said.

"Then you were lying in wait," she said. She released the radio button and added, "Like a snake."

Iliana had pushed to stand next to Serena and set her hand on her cousin's back protectively.

"I'd hoped to meet you. Decide, princess. We will have a conversation today."

She glanced at her guards. "You may come aboard. Just you. No one else."

"I agree to your terms and I will warn you that I will come armed."

Casimir wouldn't let this situation escalate to the point of using guns. He needed to maintain everyone's emotional calm. Usually he was on the other side of that arrangement, with DeSante asking him to stay in control. Though DeSante wasn't the type to shoot at Serena, her guards seemed twitchy. That could escalate the situation and DeSante would return fire. He always did.

DeSante sped to their vessel in a small powerboat. He threw Casimir his line and Casimir drew him close and then helped him aboard.

"You could have warned me," Casimir said under his breath.

DeSante ignored him. "Good afternoon, Princess. And Iliana, it is a pleasure to see you."

Iliana's expression could have iced over the sun. "President DeSante, I thought I made myself clear."

Serena glanced at Iliana. Casimir was equally confused. Was Iliana in private communication with DeSante? He had not said anything. DeSante did nothing without intent and Casimir wondered what his intention was with Iliana.

"I am a man of my word. I have no plans to harm the princess."

Was it Casimir's imagination or did DeSante look at Iliana with interest? His gaze seemed to linger longer than it should.

DeSante turned his attention to Serena. "You have been a difficult woman to reach."

"I have a country to run," Serena said.

"As do I. But I find time to speak to my neighbors and make sure we don't have any misunderstandings," DeSante said.

"What misunderstanding are you concerned we've had?" Her voice was arctic. She was holding her own and DeSante would respect that.

"Your father had been keeping the peace in our corner of the Mediterranean. With his untimely passing, you can understand that I have misgivings."

Casimir caught the first crack in Serena's composure at the mention of her father. Casimir moved closer to her. He would step in if needed. He didn't know what DeSante had planned here and he wouldn't allow the other man to bully Serena.

"This is a wonderful opportunity. You've refused my other requests for a meeting and now we are together."

"You have my attention. Please speak plainly," Serena said.

"I wish for our countries to unite. I won't be so crass as to require you marry me."

A dig at King Warrington and Serena's arrangement. Casimir hid his amusement.

"You may pass me control of your islands and I will make sure you live comfortably for the rest of your days," DeSante said.

Serena looked at him as if he was insane. "Give you Acacia in exchange for a comfortable retirement? Surely, you don't think so low of me that you expect I would sell out my entire nation for myself."

"Not for yourself. An alliance with Icarus is the better option. Our military strength and our protection are incomparable and unbeatable."

"Who is it that you would be protecting us from?"

The implication being that Serena wanted to be protected from Icarus. DeSante caught her meaning. "With the shift in power, Acacia is weak. Others may choose to strike."

"A threat?"

"An assessment," DeSante said. "And if protection does not appeal to you, we are a profitable trading partner and I can help build the infrastructure to boost tourism in your country."

Serena shook her head. "I must decline your offer. You are aware of my plans to marry King Warrington."

Casimir felt a jolt of surprise. She spoke as if it were a done deal. He had hoped he had sowed enough seeds of doubt on that matter.

DeSante didn't like being refused and he wouldn't view this as a final negotiation. Casimir recognized the glint in his eyes. He was just getting started. "King Warrington is a fool. He will run your treasuries into debt, probably planning parties. You will be totally dependent on foreign aid to feed your children."

Serena's eyes flashed with indignation. "As yet, I require no such aid to feed my countrymen and women."

DeSante looked at Casimir. "Who are you exactly to the princess? Her lover? I find it strange that she tells me her plans to marry one man while sailing on a private boat with another."

Though Serena seemed shocked, Casimir didn't let his old friend rattle him. "I am a friend."

"That's all? She looks at you as if you are more."

"I have earned the princess's trust," Casimir said.

"Then maybe I should be speaking to you, learning what it is that I need to win her over."

"I am not a person to be won," she said, sounding angry.

"You control access to something I want. That means I will not stop pursuing you. Say it however you wish. Winning you over or buying you out, but I will have my way."

"Bullying me won't get you far," she said.

DeSante came closer, but Casimir put up a hand to stop him. "Don't touch the princess or I will be forced to restrain you."

"Even knowing my reputation and that I am armed, you make a threat against me?" DeSante asked.

It was his opportunity to show Serena he would stand with her. "I would sacrifice my life for the princess's safety and well-being."

The president smiled between them and then looked at Serena. "If you negotiate with me, you could run away with your friend and live the life you want."

"That is a ridiculous statement. Casimir and I are not planning to run away from anything. Not bullies. Not assassins. Not responsibilities."

DeSante was planting ideas. He wanted Serena to think about having a relationship with Casimir. Casimir had considered it from a purely lust-fuelled perspective. He wanted to get Serena in bed, but he thought it better to keep those desires buried. Why did DeSante want to force this line of thinking? To keep Warrington further out of Serena's thoughts?

"Tell me what it will take and I will give it you," DeSante said.

"There is nothing you have that I want."

DeSante looked away. "I ask that you reconsider. Think carefully about the future you want. This is not the end of our negotiation." He looked at Iliana. "I hope to see you again soon."

Iliana shot daggers at him. "I hope that you slink back to Icarus and stay there, quietly."

Casimir gave both women points for boldness. Not many people had the courage to stand up to Demetrius DeSante.

As they docked *The Buccaneer* in Rizari, Serena composed herself. The altercation with DeSante had left her shaking and concerned. The Assembly and her uncle had warned her that President DeSante was a threat and he had made that clear today. He wanted Acacia and he would stop at nothing to have it.

Casimir drew her into a hug. "It's okay. I promise that you're safe with me. I will not let him harm you."

"He trapped me like a rat," she said.

"His tactics lack finesse," Casimir said.

Iliana approached, typing on her phone with her thumbs. "Serena, I need to talk to you about something."

From her tone, it was more bad news or more problems. "Is it Dr. Shaw? Is he okay?" Serena asked.

"Nothing about Dr. Shaw, but I will call the hospital again and request an update. This is about King Warrington. I heard something that might be a rumor and could hurt you for no reason, but I need you to know. I've always been honest with you."

Her cousin was reluctant to cause her pain unnecessarily and she understood. "Just tell me, Iliana." Even if it stung, how bad could it be?

"The night that Warrington stood you up, the night of the dinner party, he was with his mistress." Iliana's breath left in a rush.

Serena felt as if the air had been sucked from her lungs. She was so angry and frustrated, she wanted to demand that Casimir return her to Acacia. Or if he wouldn't, she would take the next flight home.

Iliana touched her forearm. "Did you hear me? Serena, are you okay?"

"I'm fine."

Warrington's mother, Katarina, was strolling down the dock toward her and on the heels of this news, Serena was spoiling for a fight. She felt embarrassed and angry at both DeSante and Warrington, and while it was juvenile, they weren't around and she wanted to unload on someone. "Say nothing of this to anyone. We will discuss it later."

Casimir glanced down the dock. "That looks like an *un*welcoming party. I'll see you around the palace?"

"I hope so," she said.

Serena didn't know Warrington's plans for her stay. She hoped her time in Rizari included face time with him so they could talk, but given their history, she didn't expect it. King Warrington seemed keen on presenting a certain front to the people of their countries, but behind closed doors, he was dismissive to her at best.

Serena climbed onto the dock. Katarina had reached *The Buccaneer* and was frowning at her. "I see that you

didn't take my advice regarding the company you keep."
She pointed to Casimir's retreating back.

She had been holding her tongue and that comment
sent her over the edge. "Casimir is my friend. I don't
think you need to be worried about where I spend my
time. Perhaps you should speak to your son about where
he spends his."

To Katarina's credit, she appeared unfazed. "I do not
tell my son what to do."

Serena wasn't ready to back down. "Someone needs
to. Because I won't be second to someone's mistress."

"The king will do as he pleases."

"So will the queen." With that, Serena brushed past
her. Her guards and Iliana stayed close. Serena might
have burst into tears if not for their support.

It wasn't in her character to mouth off to someone.
She was accustomed to being polite and quiet. But polite
and quiet wasn't cutting it in these situations. These circumstances called for boldness she didn't know she had.

"Was that Warrington's mother?" Iliana asked when
they were out of earshot.

"Sure was."

"She's a real biddy, isn't she?"

"Every time I have spoken to her, which is twice,
she's been like that to me."

Iliana made a noise of disgust. "What is in the water
today? Everyone is acting crazy."

"Let's hope the day turns around," Serena said, but
had no reason to believe that it would.

Serena's guards escorted her and Iliana to the palace.
Serena was ushered to a room that was beautiful and
the view, while not of the sea, was spectacular. Iliana
was given a room nearby.

When she was alone in her room, feeling audacious, Serena sent a message to Warrington, asking when she could see him. She waited a full five minutes. No reply.

She sent a message to Casimir. He responded in less than five seconds with a phone call.

"Is your stay everything you hoped it would be?" Casimir asked.

Since she'd had low expectations, she supposed it was. "I haven't seen King Warrington. His butler mentioned he may join me for dinner."

"That's kind of him," he said dryly.

She snorted inelegantly. "Instead of waiting around for him, can you meet me here?"

"In the palace?"

"If you suggest somewhere else, I'd be happy to meet you. But that will mean my guards will have to join us." She wanted to be alone with Casimir so they could talk. Though her guards had sworn their allegiance to her, she was still unsure if they could keep secrets.

"I'll meet you in the king's library," Casimir said.

Serena agreed. It took her a few tries to find the library. It was on the main floor in the east wing. The mahogany double doors leading into the room were beautifully carved into an ornate design. She entered. Casimir was waiting.

How he managed to arrive before her, she didn't question. He was making her feel what she needed in that moment: wanted and worth his time.

They walked down the aisles of books and turned out of view of anyone who might enter the library.

"Does it shock you that the king could have been meeting with his mistress the night of the dinner party?" It hurt her more than she would ever admit.

"You can't ask me to speak ill of him here. That's treason."

She rolled her eyes. "The king's bedroom proclivities are hardly a matter for the court system."

"You may be surprised what's prohibited in Rizari," Casimir said.

Casimir socialized with King Warrington. Did he know more? "Tell me what you've heard about the king and his affairs."

"It's a story for another day."

"Then tell me what's the story for today," Serena said.

Casimir stopped so abruptly and spun, trapping her between his arms against one of the tall stacks of books. "I think the story for today is that the princess of Acacia is acting more like a royal and playing a dangerous game." His tone was downright flirtatious.

"I don't play games."

"Asking me to meet you here? If I weren't more trusting of you, I would think this was a trap."

"How could this possibly be a trap?"

"I think you know how the king and his mother would respond to finding us alone in the palace. It would call your pending engagement into question."

"We haven't done anything wrong."

"Katarina seems to believe my very presence is wrong," Casimir said.

"She knows her son and I don't have a relationship. Any male is a threat to the little that we do have."

Casimir's eyes traced from her eyes to her lips. "Do you want to make me a real threat to him?"

His meaning was clear. Did she have the courage to nod her head or say the word yes? She wanted him to kiss her. Desperately. Everything that had happened lately had been emotionally brutal and physically draining. Was it wrong to want something purely for herself even if it was for a brief period of time? Just to feel good for a few seconds?

She lifted her mouth. "Casimir."

His name communicated what she wanted. He reached for her, aligning their bodies, and his mouth came down on hers in a gentle kiss. She parted her lips and nipped at his, and a growl sounded in his throat. He deepened the kiss and she returned it with shameless abandon.

Putting her hand around the back of his neck to anchor herself, she gave herself over to him. His tongue left a tantalizing imprint and she felt simultaneously restless and excited. She lifted her leg and ran her foot over the back of his calf.

She knocked into books on the shelves, sending them to the floor in loud thumps. She would clean up the mess later.

The sound of an opening door had them both going still.

She moved her arm and another book landed with the others on the hardwood floor.

"Is someone here?"

Serena's eyes went wide. It was Warrington's butler. She gestured to Casimir to move deeper into the stacks. She snatched a book off the shelves and held it up as she exited the row of books. "Just me. Looking for a book."

Warrington's butler frowned. "You are certainly welcome to borrow any book you'd like. I didn't realize you were interested in weapons of the fifteen hundreds."

Serena glanced at the book in her hand. She wasn't

interested in weapons of any time period, but she smiled. "I enjoy reading about history when I have the time."

"Very well." The butler bowed to her. "Unless you need anything, I am here to retrieve a book as well."

Serena hoped that Casimir was finding his way out of the library. "I'll be returning to my room to read and work."

As she hurried out, relief tore over her. To invite Casimir into the king's library and then kiss him was dangerous. If anyone had seen them, the repercussions would be disastrous.

In her room, Serena checked her phone messages and, having none from Warrington, she attacked her email queue. The task was boring and her thoughts wandered. She steered them away from her father and sister and they landed in a curious place, or rather, on a curious person.

Curiosity got the better of her and Serena typed Casimir's name into an internet search engine.

His name popped up in connection with a financial-services firm, as he had told her. She found no social media accounts or personal websites. Was he an intensely private person? She didn't post information about herself online either. The media took care of that for her.

Though it was a mistake, she typed her name into an internet search. The first results were about her father's death and her sister's funeral. The further she scrolled, the more upset she became. Though she didn't click through to the articles, the headings were disparaging enough.

Speculation about her screw-up during her speech,

stating she could have a drug problem or that she was not mentally fit to handle the position, were the most popular posts. The accusations incensed her. She did not have a drug problem. She hadn't taken an illicit drug in her life. She was barely even a social drinker.

The drug accusations were blatant lies and easier to dismiss as ludicrous, but attacks on her character cut to the core. Was she strong enough to lead a country? She wasn't certain. Her sister had been fierce and brave. Her father had been driven and focused. But Serena wasn't bent on wielding power. She didn't have a strong vision for the country. She didn't have items on her political agenda. She wasn't even sure she had a personal agenda that she planned to use her position to achieve.

Should she address the media about the incident? She had thought it would blow over, but it seemed that hope was naive.

She typed a response, all the things she wished she could say, and saved it to her drafts. She would not send it. She wouldn't even know where to send it. But the more she stewed on it, the angrier she became. Her birthright was to be queen of Acacia and she would prove she could handle the task. After rereading her response several more times, she grabbed her phone and sent a message to Casimir. She could trust him. He wouldn't go to the press about anything they discussed.

What was it about Casimir that made him easy to talk to? He was a strange combination of genteel and strong, like a wealthy heir who had been raised to street fight.

A light tap on the door. Serena expected Warrington's butler. It was Casimir.

"You got here fast," she said.

"I never left. I ran into a few friends in the garden and I was chatting with them when I received your message."

She nodded toward her guards standing post on either side of the door. "Could we talk privately?" She stepped back and allowed him inside the room.

Casimir's hair was askew, poking up on one side, but he was otherwise perfect. Handsome and charming. Why couldn't she feel this way about King Warrington? Because the king was no Casimir. When she thought of Casimir, lust and desire radiated through her.

Was he flexing his muscles or was she turned on and looking for ways to satisfy her lust? Just like that, her worries about the media's vicious speculation about her took a backseat to her far more powerful feelings for Casimir.

"I've never been allowed to have a relationship that I've chosen," Serena said.

"That can't be true."

"It's very true. The only boyfriend I've ever had was paid off by my father to stay away from me."

Casimir winced. "That's pretty rough. What made your father hate him so much?"

"My father didn't hate him. He just wasn't the right man, at least, in my father's eyes. He wasn't rich and he didn't bring anything to the table that our family needed. No political connections, no military experience and no favorable trade arrangements. After it was over, I didn't have an interest in getting close to another man because I figured it wasn't worth it. I planned to wait for my father to pick someone and then I would marry that person."

"Then marrying King Warrington is exactly what you expected."

Not precisely. She found it hard to imagine her father forcing a relationship that was obviously a poor match. "I don't want to spend my life being unhappy." Marrying King Warrington would make it difficult to find happiness. He may allow her some freedom, like returning to her beach house and spending her life painting. But she would be alone, without a real partner in the truest sense of the word.

Casimir circled her room, looking at the artwork on the walls. "You have another option."

She inclined her head. "What option?"

"You could marry the president of Icarus."

The dictator? She laughed. "Demetrius DeSante is a tyrant and he would ruin our country. He stole power from the last ruler of Icarus and forced changes on his people. Besides that, he explicitly stated that he wanted Acacia, but without the marriage. He would take over and shut me out. I'd have no recourse to protect my people." In short, Demetrius DeSante was not to be trusted. Acacia was a monarchy, but they had the Assembly, a legislative group that was representative of the people and their wishes. The president of Icarus didn't believe in representation by the people or input from the public. He ran his country on his terms. He made unilateral decisions and showed no mercy.

"His coup was backed by a number of constituents and many in the country are faring better since he has been in power," Casimir said.

Sounded like political spin. "It's a firm no. I want happiness, remember? Not another relationship wreck."

"Then you are left with one remaining option. Stand alone and make it work. Your father did. You can, too."

She blinked at him. Her father had known keeping the peace was a tenuous balance. Icarus and Rizari were old enemies with a bitter past and a long list of reasons to attack each other. If they went to war, Acacia would be torn apart in the crossfire. "My father knew the time for peace was ending. He wanted my sister to marry the king of Rizari." And now tensions were escalating beyond the point of discussion.

"You have choices, Serena."

Did she? Why did everything feel decided for her? Every choice put her in a scenario where she was unhappy. "It doesn't seem that way."

"Then you don't see what I do. I've seen you be quiet and passive, but I've also seen you be bold. Tell me what's brought out the passive side of you. Tell me why you doubt your abilities."

"The media is questioning me as a leader." Questioning her in the same way she questioned herself at the darkest times.

He looked at her computer screen. "Do not read that gossip. Don't put any stock in a story in a tabloid. You will lose your mind. One minute, they will call you weak and useless, and the next, a power-hungry despot." He closed her laptop. "Forget about this trash. What do you want, Serena? Go after that."

She hadn't realized that she'd been walking toward him until the scent of him hit her and she extended her hand to touch him. He smelled great. The heat of his body beckoned and the power of the moment wasn't lost on her. He didn't move and she wasn't sure what to do next.

There were rules about what was and was not proper and what had happened in the library was decidedly not appropriate. That didn't stop her from wanting more or wanting him.

"I know what I want," she said.

"Then take it," he said.

Touching him was living a fantasy. His maleness was almost overpowering. His eyes were bright, greenish in some light, and other times, more brown. His hair was dark with flecks of copper. She wasn't usually a fan of facial hair, but his goatee was neat and well kept, framing his mouth.

She touched his chin and he remained still, but concern appeared in the corners of his eyes.

She drew away. "Is this too much?"

He laughed. An outright bark of laughter. "With you, it is never enough. I want this to happen. I'm letting you show me what you want. I know what's at stake. I will let you decide how this plays out."

Serena pushed on his shoulders to get him into her desk chair. The bed was far too…intimate. She wasn't ready to go there with him.

His eyes blazed with sex. She climbed into his lap, facing him, letting her legs dangle over the sides of the chair. What they were doing took on epic possibilities. Serena kissed him, soft, gentle and slow. She wanted him to take control. If she kissed him long enough, he would take over. It was in his nature.

She ran her hands over his shoulders and down his arms, relishing the feeling of his muscled arms. His goatee tickled her face and she smiled when he deepened the kiss.

In one smooth motion, he stood and she wrapped

her legs around his waist. He hit the light switch on the wall, plunging the room into darkness. Was he taking her to the bed? She made the decision in that moment to let this happen, to experience real passion and heat with a man who desired her.

Casimir carried her to the balcony, holding her with one arm and opening the door with his free hand. Outside, he laid her on the lounge chair and lay on his side next to her. It was almost completely dark, the last of the pink and purple of the sky disappearing into the deep blue of night.

"Why outside?" she asked. Not what she had expected and not what her hormones wanted.

"If you are quiet, you may hear the sea."

He had remembered that the water was a source of joy for her.

He half covered her body with his and returned to kissing her. He moved his mouth from her lips to her cheek and she angled her head to give him access to the spot on her neck where she loved to be kissed.

As her eyes adjusted to the dark, she could make out the features of his handsome face.

The man was masterful with his mouth. The right pressure and speed and she was melting in his hands. He moved his body down hers, stopping at her clavicle. "Tell me when to stop."

The words *no* and *stop* were light-years from her brain. "You don't have to do anything you don't want to," she said.

His eyes danced with merriment. "I never do."

He didn't continue down her body, a disappointment to her aching breasts and trembling thighs. Instead, he gathered her against him, shifting her to be close and held her in the nook of his arms. "Tell me why you're worried about what the mudslingers are writing about you."

Her stomach knotted. "It's not easy to read criticism, but it reminds me of my dad's disapproval. He didn't think I was smart enough or quick enough."

"Why's that?"

She'd given her father plenty of reasons to be disappointed. She wasn't an athlete or an academic. She didn't have many friends or a suitable boyfriend. People didn't like her. Her social awkwardness made them uncomfortable. "I am more introverted than my sister. After my mother died and my sister was of age, she took over as hostess for events. It was seamless for her to slip into the tasks that my mother used to handle." Their father had relied on Danae to deal with parties and the staff and the thousand other details that were involved in running and maintaining the castle.

"Your sister was organized and good at planning events. You have your own strengths."

Their father hadn't seen it that way and after Serena had moved to the beach house, she'd stopped caring. The tranquility of her home had provided more contentment than attempting to win her father's approval ever would. "I prefer the company of my art to people and I would rather have an intimate sit-down dinner than throw a splashy party."

"Nothing wrong with that."

"Everything is wrong with that when you're royalty and you need to cater to a country of people who want to see you and talk to you."

He kissed the tip of her nose. "You'll come into your

own. You'll let people see your strengths and they'll love you for it."

"A public figure who hates being in public?" It was a disaster.

"You don't need to be a political monster with a big mouth to get ahead."

It felt as if she needed a toolbox of skills she didn't have. "I guess we'll see. The next few weeks will provide plenty of tests."

"Don't worry about that now. Just think about you and me and this beautiful night."

Serena snuggled close to him and closed her eyes. Her problems would be waiting for her in the morning.

Serena's eyes popped open to the sound of knocking. It took her a moment to place where she was and what she was doing. Casimir was sleeping beside her on the lounge chair. She shook him. "Cas, you have to hide. Someone's at the door."

Another knock. This time sharper. "Princess Serena? You have not answered your phone and the king is concerned."

Serena had left her phone in the bedroom. She hadn't heard it ringing from the balcony. Serena gestured to Casimir, who ducked into the closet.

Adjusting the comforter and sheets on the bed to make it appear as if she had been sleeping, she cracked the door open. "My apologies. I turned off my phone. I was sleeping."

King Warrington's butler straightened. "The king requests an audience with you for breakfast."

Her stomach growled at the mention of food. She

had skipped dinner. "I'll need a few minutes. I'll meet the king at the top of the hour."

She closed the door and locked it. Casimir stepped out of the closet looking as handsome as ever. His hair was mussed, but it was a look that worked on him.

"That was close. I must apologize to you, Your Grace. I didn't mean to spend the night here."

Time with Casimir rejuvenated her spirit. She looked forward to spending time with him and every hour they spent together made her long for more. More days, more kisses, more Casimir. "I slept well for the first time in a long time. Thank you for staying with me."

"Sounds like you have plans with the king."

The king's expectation she appear at a meal with no warning annoyed her. She was a guest in his home, but he hadn't made much of an effort with her and that bothered her. Why should she center her schedule around King Warrington if he would not do the same for her? "I need to make myself presentable."

"You could meet with him looking like you do just now. You have no idea how beautiful you are."

Wrecked hair and everything? "You make me feel beautiful."

"Your beauty has nothing to do with me. I'm just a man who gets to enjoy it."

She looked down at her rumpled clothes. "I think the king expects something different."

"The king expects a lot from you, it seems."

It was true. "You'll need to be careful. If someone sees you leaving my room, it won't look good for either of us. I'm not sure how easily we could explain what happened last night." The circumstances were compromising. She had enough problems with King Warrington's philandering. If she opened the door to the concept of spending the night with anyone, things could only go downhill.

"I know how to go unnoticed," Casimir said.

Should she hug him goodbye? Kiss his cheek? Shake his hand? Spending the night with someone felt intimate. She decided to let it be his call. She waited and he leaned forward. He set his hands lightly on her waist and kissed her cheek.

His eyes indicated he would have liked for it to be more. But she didn't have time to dally. She couldn't risk Casimir being discovered in her room.

She stretched on her tiptoes to hug him, lingered and then drew away. "I hope I will see you soon."

"Same goes," he said.

Knowing she could have talked with him for hours more, she fled to the bathroom to get ready.

Forty minutes later, she was running at least ten minutes late for her breakfast with King Warrington. Perhaps he had invited a large group of people and wouldn't notice her tardiness. Perhaps he wouldn't show up at all.

She smelled fresh coffee, bacon and bread. As she entered the dining room, her heart dropped.

King Warrington was seated at the head of the table. He was alone.

Serena pasted a smile on her face and entered. "Good morning, Your Highness."

"Good morning, Serena. I trust you slept well."

Did he know she had spent the night with Casimir? "I did. Very well. Thank you for your hospitality."

"I have invited your guest to eat with us."

Casimir? A flare of panic hit her, but then Iliana

entered the dining room. She was all perky smiles and excitement. "Good morning."

Iliana sat next to Serena. "Sorry I'm running late. I've been awake for less than two hours and already half the country is demanding a statement about your relationship with the king." Iliana seemed comfortable with King Warrington, and Serena wished she had that same ease with him.

"What did you tell them?" Serena asked.

"That a statement was forthcoming. I wanted to talk with you first."

Serena didn't want to make a statement about her relationship with Warrington. Things were rocky between them at best. But being part of the Acacian royal family meant personal lives were not private and everyone wanted updates and explanations, even though Serena didn't have any.

The king's waiter brought her coffee with a small pitcher of creamer and a sugar bowl. As Serena made her coffee, she struggled to find words to break the silence.

Conversation with Casimir flowed without effort. She said what came to mind, but sitting across from King Warrington, Serena felt awkward and unsure.

A man hurried into the room. "Excuse me for interrupting, but the king is needed."

King Warrington appeared relieved. "Please pardon the interruption." With that, he fled the room.

"Thank God I can talk to you now," Iliana said.

"Tell me," Serena said, taking her phone from her handbag and looking at the emails Iliana had sent to her.

"A road washed out on the north side of the island.

Traffic is being diverted, but the highway administration is holding an emergency meeting to discuss repairs and how they'll acquire the money to fix it," Iliana said.

Serena typed notes into her phone as Iliana spoke.

"Cyrus Angelo is in the hospital. Heart attack."

Cyrus Angelo was one of the more outspoken members of the Assembly. His father and grandfather had been elected members and Cyrus wanted to make his own mark by being one of the biggest mouths in politics. Cyrus had been supportive of Serena's father. Serena didn't know where she stood with him. "Please arrange for flowers to be sent to him. How is Dr. Shaw?" Serena asked.

"I called the hospital this morning. No change in his condition."

"Please send flowers to his wife as well as a meal from the kitchen," Serena said.

Iliana nodded. As she continued to review the issues that had cropped up overnight, Serena grew increasingly frustrated. She didn't belong in Rizari. She belonged in Acacia. Why was she here? She had allowed herself to be persuaded. She needed to show more strength.

Serena had come to Rizari in good faith, hoping that she and King Warrington would have time together to talk. Publicly declining his invitation would have been seen as rude and hostile. But she needed to return to Acacia. She had made no progress here. "Please arrange for transport to the airport. I'm flying home immediately," Serena said.

Serena sent the king a text, brief and to the point. She was needed at home. She couldn't live this sham, not when her country needed her.

She sent a message to Casimir as well. He agreed to meet her in her bedroom before she left.

When she entered, he was pacing. "That was a quick meal."

Serena wished she could have had breakfast with Casimir, or that he had been in attendance. "The king had other priorities that required he leave after a few minutes. I have pressing matters to address as well. I am flying home in an hour."

Casimir drew her close to him. "Staying close to you is becoming a full-time job."

When he was near, she felt safer, more confident and more relaxed. "Is that what you've been doing? Staying close to me?"

He nodded. "I suppose it is. I find myself pursuing you back and forth across the Mediterranean Sea."

A thrill raced over her that he was making time for her. "When will I see you again?"

"I plan to sail my boat to Icarus. I have matters to attend to at home. I promise it won't be long."

She wished he had made firm plans with her, but Casimir seemed to show up when she didn't expect it. When she needed him. And she had a feeling that would be soon.

"Is something on your mind?" Iliana asked, as she entered Serena's office later in the day.

"Lots. Why do you ask?"

Iliana sat across from Serena. She set her tablet on Serena's desk. "You're brooding."

"Thinking," Serena said.

"About Casimir?"

How had she known? "Sometimes." Could she tell

Iliana she had spent the night with him? "He came to see me in Rizari yesterday."

"You mean after the boat ride?"

Serena nodded. "We fell asleep on the balcony of my room."

"You slept with him?"

Serena felt her face growing hot. The door to her office was closed, but she couldn't risk someone overhearing and misinterpreting. "Just slept. Nothing happened."

"Wow. Then he's more than a friend."

"I didn't say that."

Iliana rolled her eyes. "Were you touching when you slept with him?"

They had been curled on the same lounge chair, sharing their body heat. Her mouth went dry at the memory. "Yes."

"QED. Thus it is proved. You are more than friends."

Serena rubbed her face. She felt more for Casimir than just friendship. But she couldn't act on those feelings. It was a complication neither of them needed. "I don't know what to do."

"What do you want to do?"

See Casimir again. Spend time with him. Walk on the beach with him. Talk to him. "I miss him."

Iliana frowned. "What about King Warrington?"

What about him? Every time they were together, it was uncomfortable and obvious that neither of them wanted to be there. "Among other things, he's a big reason I should keep my distance from Casimir."

Iliana's phone rang and she answered it. "I am with the princess. I will be right out." She ended the call. "Flower delivery. Wonder who they're from?"

She left Serena's office door open, retrieved the flowers and brought them to her. Serena hoped they were from Casimir.

They were from King Warrington, and the attached card stated he apologized again for his abrupt departure at breakfast.

"Please send a thank-you note to the king for the beautiful flowers." She would feign that she was pleased by his empty gesture.

Serena carried the flowers to Iliana's desk and set them down. Iliana looked at her in surprise. "You want the king's flowers on my desk?"

She would prefer to shove them in the trash, but that could start a rumor. Besides, the flowers were lovely. "More people will see them on your desk. Their beauty should be enjoyed."

Iliana's phone rang again and this time, she sat at her computer while she spoke. From the sound of it, it could be a lengthy conversation.

Serena returned to her office and shut the door. She had tried to organize the dozens of tasks she had to complete and yet she felt out of control. Countless staff members, politicians and business leaders were waiting to talk to her and she needed time to process their requests.

At two in the afternoon, Iliana buzzed her to let her know that the police chief had arrived. They had a scheduled meeting to discuss the investigation into her father's and sister's deaths. She was simultaneously dreading this meeting and anxious for a culprit to be named.

Serena opened her office door and gestured for the police chief to enter. Perseus Valente was soft-spoken but commanding. He was young to be the head of the local police, but he had made a name for himself early in his career. From what Serena knew, he was above reproach. "Please, Chief, sit down. May I offer you a drink?"

He shook his head. "No, thank you, Your Grace."

She sat behind her desk and, based on his expression, braced herself for what would be an unpleasant conversation. "I hope you have good news to share with me."

"I am sorry to report that we've encountered a setback. The man we had in custody from the shooting at your father's birthday party was stabbed to death last night during a prison fight."

That man was the best lead they had and now he was gone. "Did you learn anything from him?"

Perseus shook his head. "He said nothing to his cellmates about who hired him or how much he was paid or even how he was paid. What we've uncovered about his life revealed a very isolated man who had no ties to the community. He had no personal effects in the hotel where he was staying week to week. He spoke to almost no one. I should warn you that we're looking at the possibility of someone on the inside being involved in the assassination."

A ball of dread formed in the pit of her stomach. "In what way?" Someone who worked for the royal family was working with the assassins?

"The assassins had a detailed list of who was scheduled to attend your father's party and an outline of the security protocols the royal guards followed. They exploited the vulnerabilities to smuggle their weapons inside the castle. I'm sharing our suspicions on that matter with few people. We don't know who we can trust. Until we find a mole, if there is one, we need to be on guard."

Serena felt sick. Feeling safe was nearly impossible, but she hadn't considered someone close to her being involved with the murderers. "I will be careful. Is there anything else?"

"I will keep you apprised of the investigation as it unfolds."

Serena stood. If the chief had no further information to share, their meeting was over. She didn't want to discuss her family's deaths any longer than was needed. Marshalling her emotions during those conversations was grueling and her objective was to appear in control. "Thank you for making the trip to the castle."

Perseus stood. "We haven't given up. We won't give up."

Neither would Serena. After the chief left, Iliana entered and handed Serena a dark brown folder. "One of the PIs you hired dropped this off. He has been following Casimir."

Serena had hired a few PIs to find Casimir and she had forgotten to call them immediately and inform them that their services were no longer needed. An oversight on her part and now curiosity got the better of her. She took the folder and opened it. Inside were photographs of Casimir, at least a dozen of them. The PI had tailed Casimir for the past several days, taking candid shots of him and noting what he did, where he went and whom he spoke with. Many of the photos had her in them. One picture in particular gave her pause. In the snapshot, she was looking at Casimir. The expression on her face was a mix of lust, admiration and intimacy.

Perhaps that expression was what Demetrius De-Sante had seen when he'd commented on their relationship. She searched the pictures for an expression revealing Casimir's feelings for her, but she saw only his stoic, unreadable look. Except when they were alone in private, his expression revealed nothing.

One photo had him looking serious, his hair wind-blown, and his eyes alive and taking in every detail. She hadn't missed that he was a handsome man. Turn-her-head-around handsome.

The office line rang and Iliana rushed to answer it. When Serena's phone beeped a few moments later, she remembered she had a scheduled conference call with the country's technology adviser. She lifted the receiver.

Forty minutes later, she was hanging up, her head aching with confusion. Too much jargon and new technology and catchphrases she didn't understand.

The door opened again and Iliana entered her office, her expression troubled. Serena's guard went up immediately. "What's happened?"

"I have some bad news. We—you—received a death threat."

Serena's heart raced. "Tell me what it said."

"It said, 'Fear not, darling princess, you will join your father and sister soon.' I contacted Perseus Valente immediately. He's called in his best detectives to investigate."

"I want to see it," Serena said.

"The card? Why? It's really creepy," Iliana said.

It was creepy and sick and twisted. The killer who had targeted her father was now targeting her. Why? Serena wouldn't cower in fear. "Maybe the handwriting is familiar. Maybe something about the card is familiar. I want to see it."

Iliana blew out her breath. "I think you're asking

for more nightmares, but I'll tell the chief you'd like to take a look."

Minutes later, after Iliana had placed a quick call to Chief Valente, the card was brought to her in a plastic evidence bag. It was a black card with silver writing. The envelope it had arrived in was plain. Nothing about it was especially notable. The handwriting was a large scrawl, the words properly spelled. The card was made of black stock paper, thick and textured, the kind available at any craft store.

Serena wanted to appear in control. But this card made her want to retreat to her beach house. The outer envelope had been addressed to her with only her name, meaning someone had been close enough to the castle mail room to hand deliver it. Security was supposed to be tight around the castle. Had the assassins uncovered another vulnerability?

What if the police chief was correct and the threat came from someone inside the castle? She had to consider the possibility that the person who had arranged to have her father killed could be someone close to the family. It could be someone whom she passed in the hallways, someone who worked in her kitchen.

The castle had never felt more unsafe. There were a hundred different ways for someone to get at her and now that the overt threat had been made, it was hard to call her worries paranoia.

"Iliana, do I have any social engagements coming up out of the country?" Getting away, putting some distance between her and what was happening in Acacia, in Rizari and in Icarus would give her perspective and a sense of security, however false.

Iliana retrieved her tablet and tapped on it. "Your

father and sister were planning to attend the wedding of the duke to his fiancée in Elion. I did not contact the wedding coordinator about the event yet. Do you want to go in their place?"

Serena liked the idea of honoring her father's obligations by attending as well as giving herself a breather from the stress. Though being in a crowd was a source of anxiety for her, she'd grow accustomed to it and, unlike events held in her country, she wouldn't be the center of attention in Elion. She would blend in with the many other royals in attendance. She would force herself to smile and appear happy to be there. A few photo ops could sway public opinion of her for the better. Maybe some of the media who were questioning her abilities as a leader would see her smiling and calm, and write about her in a more flattering light.

Serena could just as easily talk herself out of attending. Public, well-attended events were rife with possibilities for failure. She despised small talk, she didn't want to address issues surrounding her father's and sister's deaths, and she didn't have a firm enough grasp on the most pressing political issues to discuss them in detail.

Deciding she could handle this undertaking with a little guidance, she dialed her minister of foreign affairs to consult with him on the matter. If she needed to follow certain protocols, she wanted to know in advance.

Mitchell Wagner entered her office carrying a thick folder of papers. He was thirty years older than she was, a contemporary of her father's. He treated her with what Serena interpreted as disdain, or maybe he was uptight and surly by nature. Serena let most of his bad attitude slide because he was good at his job and she didn't know anyone with nearly as much experience to replace him.

"Thank you for meeting with me," she said.

"The pleasure is mine, Princess."

Now that they were meeting, more questions came to mind, those beyond the social and political implications of her attending a wedding in Elion. What did Wagner know about DeSante? Serena gestured for Wagner to sit. "I've had a run-in with President DeSante. There are rumors he wants to annex Acacia to have better access to attack Rizari. What can you tell me about him?"

Wagner appeared bored by the question and that annoyed her. "The president of Icarus won't back down until he accomplishes what he wants. He desires control of shipping lanes in this part of the Mediterranean."

"What is preventing him from attacking us?" The more powerful navy in Icarus could easily dominate the Acacian Navy. DeSante had flexed that muscle several times, perhaps to prove it.

"You're an unknown. No one knows what to expect from you. Perhaps he believes he can manipulate you or he's waiting to see how strong your bond with Rizari will become. DeSante is a vicious tyrant, but he isn't a stupid man."

Serena watched every dart of his eyes, twitch of his mouth and breath for a sign he was holding back. "What would you advise me to do?"

"I would suggest you keep DeSante at a distance, but close enough that we'll know if an attack is coming," Wagner said.

Serena considered that. She could make an effort to speak with DeSante more often, to keep her finger on the pulse of political movements. "I can do that."

Wagner wouldn't want his time wasted. She moved

the conversation along. "Tell me what I need to know about attending the Duke of Elion's wedding."

Wagner raised his eyebrows. "This is something you are considering?"

The doubt in his eyes made her question the choice. Did everyone believe her to be socially incompetent or was he concerned about her safety? Serena held her ground. "Yes."

Wagner settled in his chair. "I can provide the profiles of those in attendance and point out any political minefields that you'd need to avoid." He paused and rubbed his chin. "I think it would be good for you to attend. It may give you some ideas for your own wedding to King Warrington."

Again with the pressure to marry King Warrington. Why was everyone bent on it? Anyone who knew them had to see they weren't a good couple. A good political union perhaps, but nothing more.

"Your attendance would be noted and appreciated. The duke flew in for your father's funeral."

Serena didn't recall who had attended the service. Those days were a haze of decisions about psalms to read and songs to sing. "Is King Warrington attending the wedding?" She wasn't sure if his presence was a motivation to attend or a reason not to. She and Warrington had to appear a certain way in public, to look as if they were strong and reliable. Their countries wouldn't want to see a bickering, deeply divided couple running the countries.

"I believe he is planning to." Serena could do without the small smile that crept across Wagner's face. He, like so many of her countrymen, was eager to see her married, presumably because he had no confidence in her abilities to lead the country. She stifled the doubts that crept in at the slightest opening.

"I will attend." The words left her mouth feeling dry and her palms sweaty. She could have made an excuse, sent a lovely gift and a personal note, but she wanted Acacia—and herself—to be viewed as strong. She would prove that she was capable of running her country. She stood to lose too much otherwise.

Mitchell clasped his hands together. "I will communicate your intentions to the Duke of Elion and ask Iliana to make travel arrangements."

He left her office and Serena unfastened the top button of her blouse. It was too hot and the starched shirt was suffocating her. She reached for the phone and called Casimir.

The moment she heard his voice on the line, she felt better. "What are you up to?"

"What's the matter? You sound ill," Casimir said.

"I am ill. I agreed to attend a wedding. I can't go to a wedding. It's the Duke of Elion's. Lots of royalty will be in attendance looking elegant and refined, which will only highlight how ridiculously wrong it is for me to be there." She would make a fool of herself. She wouldn't say the right things. She would commit faux pas that would be printed in the tabloids, highlighting her ineptitude. Maybe she should call Wagner and tell him she had changed her mind.

"Cut yourself some slack. You can do this. I've seen you in social situations. I will be there, too, and you'll be fine," Casimir said.

Surely, he was exaggerating. She didn't feel fine in public. She felt unruly and loud and inappropriate.

A horn blared in the background and Casimir swore. "Sorry, someone just cut me off in traffic."

"Where are you?" she asked.

"Running errands."

"In Acacia?" she asked.

"In Icarus."

Why did that seem oceans away? She wished she could see him now. Her fascination with him had morphed into a crush, and it was becoming something deeper, stronger, the more time they spent together.

She had never felt this way about a man before. Their connection was intimate and she lived to see him again. She found him exciting and desirable. She had none of the same feelings for her future betrothed, the King of Rizari.

But even if the "right man" for her felt wrong, nothing could make what she had with Casimir right.

Casimir was enjoying the afternoon on *The Buccaneer*. Buying a boat had been on his mind for a long time. When he'd needed an excuse to be in Acacia, the purchase had filled in nicely. "You need to work on your charm," Casimir said to his old friend and handed him a beer.

"The princess was put off by my approach," DeSante said and twisted off the top.

Not a question. "Of course she was. You're treating her like a hostile and she isn't."

DeSante took a sip of his beer. "I am making it easier for you. The less she trusts me, the more she'll let you in. Are you making progress?"

He hoped he was. She was making time for him and confiding in him. "I'm getting to know her better every day. She trusts me." Knowing he had her trust and was misusing it bothered him. But this was for the greater good. It was all part of seeing his plan through.

"Learning anything I can use to persuade her to support our cause?" DeSante asked.

Serena was vulnerable. Her personal life was in shambles and her royal world was crumbling. He could give DeSante some information on how to get to Serena, which buttons to push, but he knew that DeSante would go for the throat and Casimir wanted to protect Serena. "Not yet. I'll keep working on it."

"I need you to work faster. She'll be in bed with the King of Rizari soon. Once that happens, I'm done. For that matter, so are you."

The image of her in bed with Samuel Warrington incensed him. Casimir was careful to keep his emotions concealed. President DeSante was not above using every weakness to his advantage and having feelings for Princess Serena was Casimir's flaw to be exploited. "I will not let her get into bed with that man. He's doing a grand job being a world-class ass to her. That helps."

"Make yourself a wedge. Do not allow their relationship to progress."

He wouldn't, though he couldn't take credit for how easy it had been. "What other methods would you suggest I employ to advance our cause?"

"Extortion. Play on her fears. Get inside her head."

DeSante's ambition knew no bounds. It was those extreme tactics that had garnered him the reputation for being cold, dictatorial and fierce. "I will get you what you want, but I will not hurt her or jerk her around."

DeSante sighed. "I should have sent Rolland."

The threat was clear and Casimir didn't appreciate it.

"Don't use him to pressure me. Rolland is a demon and I suggest you keep him in his cage." If Rolland showed up at the castle to convince the princess to bargain with the president of Icarus, he would take their goal to an extreme. Rolland didn't accept no for an answer.

"Consider him tamed. But if I don't see results soon, I'm sending in someone else to close the deal."

Casimir needed the afternoon to catch up on some tasks. From the time he'd left his place in Icarus, someone had been following him, so he made a good show of visiting a men's clothing store, a big box store, staying in character every moment and letting himself be photographed. Who was tailing him? It wasn't DeSante's style and DeSante had no reason to question Casimir's loyalty. Their conversation the day before told Casimir where he stood. He was still focused on his goals, but if he lost focus, DeSante would use someone else to get the job done.

Casimir didn't like the idea of someone digging into his life. DeSante had done a good job of establishing Casimir's fake identity, but nothing was bulletproof except the truth.

When Casimir was finished with his errands, he entered a busy part of the shopping district and disappeared. After he had doubled back twice to ensure he wasn't followed, he found an unoccupied bench in a crowded park and pulled out his smartphone.

He needed to check in with his spies in Rizari without anyone intercepting the messages and a public Wi-Fi network served the purpose.

Casimir was concerned about Serena and how she was affected by his schemes. He didn't want her destroyed when her plan to marry King Warrington fell apart, but he wouldn't allow her to make such a terrible mistake and marry a murderer.

He read his emails with a great deal of pleasure. Warrington had no idea what was coming. He thought he had stolen the throne and no one could challenge him. Casimir had every intention of making Samuel pay for killing his father.

Chapter 5

Elion was a beautiful green country. The fog hovered for most of the day and it seemed to rain often, as if precipitation was a constant. But Serena was glad to be here. Iliana was beside her, searching her schedule, ensuring none of her commitments were overbooked, while also setting aside time for Serena to be alone.

"The Countess of Provence is attending the wedding with a guest. Is Fiona's guest Casimir?" Iliana asked.

Casimir and Fiona seemed close, and though he'd said they were friends, Serena imagined Casimir being the perfect date. Good manners, textbook handsome and a total gentleman. Weddings could bring out a woman's romantic fantasies and having a man like Casimir close could fulfill them.

"Perhaps. It wouldn't surprise me. Casimir mentioned he was attending the wedding, but he didn't say if he was invited or if he was attending as someone's guest."

"Will it bother you if he's here with Fiona?" Iliana asked.

Serena didn't think that Casimir was interested in Fiona sexually. She was beautiful and charming, but Serena was more certain of her own connection to Casimir. "No more so than it might bother you if someone you liked was here with another woman." Serena had picked up on something between Iliana and DeSante. She was waiting for Iliana to admit to it.

"What are you getting at?"

"Just wondering if you have a crush on a certain president who will also be attending this wedding."

Iliana went ramrod straight. "A crush? On Demetrius?"

The use of his first name was telling. Serena reached across the car seat and took her friend's hands. "Iliana, you are my cousin and I love you. I've noticed things. Like how excited you become when you talk to him or about him. That you seem strangely giddy when his name comes up in conversation. The other day, I saw you lower your head to hide your smile when his name was spoken."

Iliana blew out her breath. "Is it that bad? Because I feel ridiculous when I'm around him. I can't help it. I know he is a jerk. Total jerk. But he's a cute jerk, you know?"

"I understand."

Iliana let her head fall back against the headrest. "I feel better that you know and it's out in the open. I've been worried but I can't talk myself out of it. This is the most absurd crush. Why would I like him?"

"I reserve the right to change my mind at any point, but I think he has some desirable qualities. He's strong and determined and resolute."

Iliana looked at Serena skeptically. "He forced you to speak to him. Again, that's a jerk move."

Serena shrugged. "He didn't harm me. I don't think his intention was even to scare me. I think he wanted his way. So, he's a little like a two-year-old having a temper tantrum, but definitely not evil-villain material. He hasn't moved on Acacia when we both know he could have and easily won."

"You were bent on hating him, but now you're cheering him on. What's changed?" Iliana asked.

Serena had never hated DeSante. Feared him, yes. But the more she learned about Icarus, Rizari and Acacia, the more she understood why the king and the president made the maneuvers they did. Her relationship with Casimir had also shed light on Iliana's relationship with DeSante. "We can't help who we're attracted to. Even when it's inconvenient and makes no sense, it's beyond us."

Iliana looked out the window. "I don't plan to act on my feelings."

"Nor do I," Serena said, thinking of Casimir.

As they drove up the driveway leading to their hotel, Serena was shocked by the crowd gathered outside the metal gate. "Why so many people?"

"The hotel has been fully booked for the wedding. The crowd is there to take pictures of the rich and famous guests that will be arriving," Iliana said.

Iliana was well informed on matters pertaining to this wedding and on social issues in general. When their car pulled through the gates close to the hotel, uniformed guards held back the crowd that tried to surge through.

Cameras flashed as photographers pressed them against the window of her vehicle.

"When we arrive at the front of the hotel, if you can, climb out of the car, turn around, smile and wave. Try to look relaxed," Iliana said.

Serena could do that. She wouldn't have to say anything, and appearing happy and in control for ten seconds shouldn't be hard. As long as she didn't trip or otherwise appear like a fool.

When the vehicle stopped to allow them out, she stepped out of the car, smiled, relaxed her shoulders and turned. She lifted her hand and waved to the crowd gathered.

Out of the corner of her eye, she caught a glimpse of King Warrington. Of all the terrible timing! Serena wanted to dive back in the car. Instead, remembering she was being watched, she smiled in his direction.

Samuel was a man with presence. As he strolled toward her, he wasn't smiling, but he seemed pleased to see her. The crowd grew louder and cameras flashed more incessantly. "Serena, what a happy coincidence."

The king bowed to her and she returned the greeting with a curtsy and the lowering of her head. "Your Highness."

"This will be our first weekend away together," he said.

He phrased it as if this was a romantic rendezvous between them and that made her terribly uncomfortable. They had not discussed this wedding or made plans to see each other while in Elion. "I am sure we will see more of each other."

King Warrington waved to the crowd and then set his hand on Serena's lower back, leading her into the hotel. As the doors shut behind them, he removed his hand as if he had been burned. "I'll have my secretary get in touch with Iliana to see when our schedules align."

With that, he strutted away from her. Serena gave him credit for knowing how to work a crowd. Serena would learn to do the same. So much was riding on her. It wasn't an option to appear a clumsy dope in public.

In her beautiful hotel suite, Serena pulled a bottle of water from the small refrigerator. She offered one to Iliana who refused with a shake of her hand. Serena twisted off the metal top and took a long swallow. Facing the crowd and running into King Warrington had been nerve-racking. She needed to keep her cool and not let a couple unplanned incidents derail her confidence.

The theme of the weekend was relaxed and happy. At least, *appear* to be relaxed and happy.

The bellhop arrived with her suitcases. Serena handed him a generous tip and he thanked her before leaving the room.

"I'll unpack your bags," Iliana said.

Serena shook her head. "We'll unpack together."

"Serena, you need to be more…"

"Mean? Rude?"

Iliana laughed. "No, not mean or rude. But you should let me do my job. You don't need to help me. Be a little more demanding to the staff."

Serena thought again of the possible mole in her midst. "Are you saying this for a reason?" Had Iliana heard something about the mole? Did she have suspicions about someone they worked with?

"I've been watching others and thinking about how they appear to their country," Iliana said.

"By others do you mean DeSante?"

Iliana rolled her eyes. "Not everything I think is about him. I believe the most successful leaders position themselves above the people around them and demand their respect. You want to rub elbows with everyone as peers. You are the queen. Try asking me to do something."

Serena liked doing things for herself. But she trusted Iliana's advice. "I'll start by asking you, firmly, to please show me what I'll be wearing tonight."

Iliana flipped through the dresses in the wardrobe case and frowned. She checked the other luggage. "Don't panic, but I don't see the dress I brought for you for the party tonight."

"I'm not panicking. Can I wear one of these other dresses? They're all so beautiful."

Iliana shook her head. "I have everything planned, the jewelry and the shoes. If you have to repeat clothes, it will reflect badly on Acacia. Don't worry. I'll check my suitcase and I'll be back. Maybe I have a few items mixed up with yours."

Iliana appeared rattled, but Serena was unconcerned. Iliana rushed to her room down the hall.

Serena returned to the living room and sat on the couch. She kicked off her heels and wiggled her toes. She couldn't let small bumps in the road turn this weekend into a nightmare. Staying focused on her goal, which was to make her father proud, represent her country and forge a few associations with others, was key. The rest of it, what she wore and what she ate, wasn't important.

A knock on the door brought Serena to her feet. Iliana had moved quickly.

Serena opened the door and came face-to-face with Casimir. He was wearing a black pair of pants and a crisply ironed, dark blue button-down shirt and tie. She had half a mind to grab the tie and pull him close.

He took her breath away. "Hey, you," she said.

"Hey, you." She stepped back and he came inside her room. If he lingered in the hallway, someone might see him and rumors would fly. Her guards were at their post and she hoped they would maintain their silence on the matter.

"Nice place. Much nicer than mine."

"Iliana booked it." Serena smiled.

"She's with you?" Casimir asked, glancing around.

"In her room." She was due back any second, but Serena didn't want to trample the moment by telling him.

He slid his hands into his pockets. "I'd heard you'd arrived and saw the bellhop bringing up your suitcases."

"How did you know they were mine?" Serena asked.

"Country emblem," he said.

Right. Not exactly traveling discreetly, but discreet hadn't been her goal.

"I saw you with King Warrington."

"Are you here with Fiona?"

The questions were asked at the same time. They were circling each other, not sure where they stood.

"I've missed you. It's been a few days, but I feel like weeks have past," he said.

Her heart surged in her chest. "I feel the same."

"You didn't call. But I know you are busy."

Was that hurt in his voice? Disappointment? "I have been busy." But also unsure if she should call, when she should call. When they were together, it felt right, but with distance came questions.

"I took a chance and came to your room, talked my way past your security guards, hoping to see you, wondering if everything we had was in my head."

So he felt it, too. "Not in your head."

"Can I see you tonight, after the party?"

Her heart thumped hard and loud, onboard with whatever he was offering. "Yes, of course."

Serena had so many questions, but she wanted answers to the one that roared the most: What did she mean to him?

Casimir's past kiss burned on her lips and she wanted to be in his arms so desperately. Would he reach for her? How could she tell him what she needed?

Casimir removed his hands from his pockets and extended them to her. She rushed into them and he folded them around her. "Did you get shorter?"

She rose up on her tiptoes. It was now or never. "No heels. Now kiss me."

He lowered his mouth to hers and she felt as if she was coming apart at the seams. Everything in her wanted this man in her bed. He made her feel so unspeakably precious. There was no comparison between Casimir and King Warrington.

Whenever she was with Warrington, she felt as though he was using her, as if he barely tolerated her. With Casimir, she felt part of something bigger and better.

Casimir's soft lips moved across her cheek to kiss her below her ear. She tilted her head, giving him more, wanting everything from him.

"Oh, my God."

He froze at the sound of Iliana's voice. He brought Serena upright and she straightened.

Iliana was looking between them and the door, a dress in one hand and her other hand plowing through her hair. She shoved the door closed. "Serena, are you okay? Do you want me to leave? What is happening? What is this?"

Serena held out her hands. "I'm fine. We're fine. Casimir stopped by to say hi."

"Serena, you can't do this. What if someone sees?" Iliana was hissing the words as if someone could overhear.

"No one will see. We're not doing anything wrong."

Iliana set the dress over the back of the settee. "I get it. I know where you're coming from. Things with Warrington have been—" she made a so-so gesture with her hand. "But this would be a huge scandal if it leaked."

"No one will find out. Especially not if you help us."

Iliana folded her arms across her chest. "I'll help you, but you know you are playing with fire. What about your guards? They know he's in here. What will stop them from telling someone?"

She made a good point. "They work for me. My guards can be trusted. You know I would help you if you needed it." Like if Iliana wanted to meet with a certain dictator and spend time alone with him.

Iliana heard her loud and clear. "Then let me return to my room so you two can finish…whatever this is." Iliana looked at the clock on the wall. "But you have four minutes, tops, because someone is coming to fix your hair." Iliana sighed. "Tell you what, I'll turn my back." She did and covered her ears, humming softly.

Casimir laughed. "Is she always like this?"

"Most of the time. She's the best."

Casimir wrapped his arms around her waist. "I want much more time with you than two hundred and forty seconds. I'll be thinking of you all night and counting down until our next rendezvous."

"Me, too."

He pressed another lingering kiss to her lips. Then he fled her room.

Iliana's eyes were wide. "I am not judging, but I had no idea that was happening."

"It's not something that's happening. It just happened."

Iliana removed the dress from the garment bag. "I need to steam this. But please be careful, Serena. This could be very bad. And we don't need anything else very bad to happen."

Serena's hands were shaking so hard, she couldn't button her dress. She had only glanced at the dress when Iliana had hung it in her closet, assuring her it was the appropriate dress for a royal cocktail party. Serena couldn't imagine how Iliana knew what was or wasn't appropriate for a specific event. Maybe there was a book on the matter that Serena was unaware of. But she wished she had chosen a dress more carefully, say, a dress with a zipper.

She hadn't slept well on the flight to Elion and now she had to attend the wedding festivities cranky, tired and nervous. Serena opened the door to the bedroom leading to the rest of the suite.

"Oh, Serena, you look a mess," Iliana said.

Since she had spent the past two hours being primped by makeup artists and hair stylists, Serena didn't want to hear it. "I'm fine. Just nervous." Thinking about being with so many people was enough to bring on a full panic attack. Serena fought against it. She would keep her calm.

"I wish I could go with you, but the invitation did not include me," Iliana said. "What's making you more nervous, seeing Casimir or seeing King Warrington or having to deal with the crowd?"

All of it. She wished she could fast-forward to 11:00 p.m., a good time to leave the party, especially with the wedding being held tomorrow morning. "I wish I was more like Danae." She turned around so Iliana could button her dress.

"Stop that. You are not Danae and she couldn't have been you. You each have your strengths. You're far more sensitive to others. That's a great skill. Use that."

"How will my sensitivity help me?" Most people were keen to tell her to toughen up and be more firm.

"If you sense someone needs a friend, be that friend. Listen. Don't worry about being entertaining. Half that room probably pays a therapist five hundred an hour to listen to their problems. You can do that for free."

At the mention of therapists, her thoughts flew to Dr. Shaw. Her shoulders tightened and she felt ill. "Do you think assassins will come after me tonight?"

Iliana hugged her. "No. You will be safe tonight. You have your guards in addition to the security for the wedding, and King Warrington and Casimir. And me. I'm a text away if you need anything."

Serena had come this far, she would go the distance. She would represent Acacia proudly.

As Serena entered the Great Hall where the party was being held, she was struck by its grandeur. She wished Casimir was beside her. She circulated through the crowd, clutching her handbag. It made her feel better to have something to do with her hands. In a room of famous faces and celebrities, she didn't stand out and it was the way she preferred it.

As if they had an invisible draw between them, Serena found Casimir. He was standing across the room, wearing a tuxedo as if it was made for him. She couldn't take her eyes off him. One of her guards was with her, walking close beside her. In a room of dashing, talented men, she only had eyes for Casimir.

Making it doubly a shame that King Warrington was in the room. He was speaking to a group and hadn't acknowledged or noticed her. Making a beeline for Casimir would be terribly obvious.

But she caught his eye and she felt as though he was looking into her soul. She would have given almost anything to be alone with him, to follow her heart and her instincts and run directly to him.

She considered her options. As the heiress to the throne, she should feel free to do what she wanted. Except the opposite was true. In matters related to her personal life and her political decisions, she was utterly caged.

Iliana had never been to Elion before. She might never have another opportunity to be in the country again. Instead of lying in bed, watching television and worrying about Serena, she pulled on her favorite jeans and a sweater, grabbed her handbag and planned to take a walking tour of the area, or at least the parts of it that she could reach on foot.

She opened her hotel room door and came face-to-face with Demetrius DeSante. "Oh." Her heart raced and her stomach dropped. Her handbag hit the floor and she bent to pick it up at the same time he did.

Their hands met as they were crouching on the floor. The air around them crackled and singed. They rose together, their eyes locked. Iliana struggled to compose herself.

Though he was flanked by two of his guards, she didn't feel threatened.

"Were you waiting outside my door?" Iliana asked.

"A happy coincidence that I caught you on your way out," he said. He had a lilting accent and her heart swelled a bit.

"Serena isn't with me."

"I am not here to see the princess. I am here to see you."

Iliana felt sure her heart would explode out of her chest. He cut an impressive figure, tall and darkly good looking. His face was that of a warrior, stern and strong. "How may I help you?" This did not feel like a professional visit. This felt personal. But Iliana wouldn't make the leap alone. He had to cross the line and then she would gladly cross it with him, if only for a night.

"Come with me to the party tonight."

Iliana looked down at her jeans. "I have nothing to wear."

"You look perfect in that."

Iliana laughed. "You are the only man to think that, I am sure."

"What can I say to change your mind? Of all the women I have ever known, you are the most difficult to persuade into doing what I want."

Everything the man said sounded sexual. "I can't go, tonight, Mr. President."

"Call me Demetrius. Please." He was looking at her with such intensity, she looked away for a moment and collected herself.

When her eyes returned to his, he was watching her. His tie was crooked and she reached for it.

His guards tensed, but he held up his hand. "I don't think she plans to strangle me."

Iliana shook her head. "Of course not. Your tie is uneven. But I like it. Very fashion forward. Where did you get it?"

"I have no idea."

"You don't do your own shopping, then?" she asked.

"No. For now, I have a personal shopper. One day, I will have a wife to perform that duty."

The word wife echoed in her brain. He wasn't speaking of her, but it did funny things to her heart. Iliana had never been a "take care of your man" woman. She was independent, lived alone and had never bought a man clothes. How could she imagine herself in that role, and for a dictator, no less? "Serena left for the party a while ago." Shouldn't he be there as well?

"Then I will be late."

"I was surprised to hear you were planning to attend," Iliana said.

"The duke is an old pal. He will understand if I am tardy."

It was strange to hear him speak of anyone as a friend. From what she had read and heard about De-Sante, he was cold and fierce. While she could see that side of him, he was showing her another side, too, one that was compassionate, warm and funny. "I should probably get going."

"Where are you going?" The question sounded casual, but she heard his concern.

"Touring the city."

"Would you allow me to accompany you?"

"I don't think it's a good idea." Except in some world where only they existed. But with the politics and the social issues between them, a relationship with Demetrius, especially a public one, would cause trouble for Serena. Serena didn't need more trouble.

"I will never force you to do anything you do not wish. But if you change your mind, here is my phone number." He took her phone from her sweater pocket and typed something into it.

She was startled by him offering the connection. She had called his office before and had thought that number was exclusive. This was beyond that. "Thanks. Thank you."

He bowed to her before leaving. When he'd disappeared down the hall, Iliana looked at her phone. He had typed *Yours*. And then his number.

Serena didn't like attending the party without a date. She should have considered this more carefully. It wouldn't have been appropriate to bring someone like Casimir, but she could have brought her uncle with her. King Warrington had technically attended alone as well, but he was not at a loss for company.

Serena circled the perimeter of the room and observed. Perhaps she would run into another wallflower and she could strike up a conversation. Her guard followed her, which made her feel a little less lonely, except like most of the other security present, he stayed silent.

Serena spotted Casimir speaking with Fiona. He was her date for the event. Her heart sank. Casimir could change his mind about Fiona, get swept away into an affair with the beautiful countess. Serena turned away, not needing to torture herself by watching them, and considered leaving. She had shown up. No one was tracking her. No one seemed to know she was there.

Her cell phone buzzed and she opened her purse. It was a call from the castle. Strange at this hour. She stepped out of the Great Hall into the hallway.

"Serena, I am so happy I caught you."

"Uncle Santino, what's wrong?"

"Are you safe, darling?"

She looked around. Her guard was hovering nearby. "I'm fine. You sound upset. What's wrong?"

"Terrible news. Someone tried to assault me!"

Serena's body tensed. "Are you okay? Were you hurt?"

Her uncle was breathing hard. "I'm fine now. I wanted to have a quiet, private dinner with an old college friend and asked my guards to wait in the car. I left the restaurant after my meal, walked to the car and someone jumped me from behind. I have a terrible headache and feel out of sorts."

Everything in her screamed in alarm. Another attack. "I'm coming home now," Serena said.

"No, no, there's nothing you can do. I only called to ensure that you were okay. I worried it may have been a conspiracy to strike out at the royal family again. After what happened to your father and your sister, I worry for you."

Serena shivered in the air-conditioned hallway. "I'll be okay. Are you sure you don't want me to return home?"

"No. Stay close to the king, though. He will keep you safe."

Serena frowned. Many, including her uncle, seemed to believe she had this amazing connection and relationship with King Warrington. Yet, a few hours ago, she had been kissing another man. "The king is quite busy."

"Never too busy for you. Remember, Serena, people will only treat you as badly as you let them."

"I'll do my best." That rarely seemed to be enough. "Please call if you change your mind and make sure your guards stay close," Serena said.

"It was a wise move to be out of the country. Give the dust some time to settle and give the police time to find who is behind these vicious attacks. You take time with the king and regroup. Your country is counting on you."

The city was so beautiful. Even with the heavy fog and light drizzle, the views were striking. Old buildings restored to maintain their character and charm lined the streets. No clutter littered the roads or sidewalks and every window had greenery to match the open fields and wide expanses of land surrounding the small town.

Iliana would like to live in a quiet place like this. She guessed everyone knew each other here and they were a close-knit and warm community.

"Give me your wallet," a man said into her ear. Something sharp pressed into her back.

Adrenaline kicked hard in Iliana's blood. She reached into her purse to hand him her wallet. The thief turned her around and grabbed a fistful of her hair. He held a knife to her stomach. She was afraid to breathe, for fear he would kill her.

"Let me go!" Iliana screamed.

"How lucky for me that a beautiful woman was stupid enough to walk alone."

"She isn't alone."

Demetrius DeSante came out of nowhere, fists flying. He had the thief on the ground and was pummeling him mercilessly.

The thief wasn't moving. Iliana grabbed his arm. "Stop, Demetrius. Stop. Please."

Demetrius landed another punch and then stood. His guards were ten paces away. They had not interfered and they seemed indifferent to the scene. Would they have allowed the dictator to kill the man?

Demetrius touched the side of her face with tenderness she wouldn't have thought he possessed after that display of violence. "Are you hurt?"

"I'm fine. Scared. Of him. Of you. What are you doing out here?"

"Following you."

Iliana blinked at him. Serena had messaged her to see if she was okay following an attack on Serena's uncle, so Iliana had been somewhat distracted. She had been walking the streets for close to two hours and hadn't noticed anyone following her. "But the party…"

"The party is just that. A party. But you are precious."

Her lips parted and she inhaled. He was looking at her intently and her heart fluttered for reasons that had nothing to do with fear. "Thank you. I didn't think…"

"This is not Acacia. You are a stranger in another land. You need to be careful."

He slipped his arm around her waist and led her to a black sedan parked at the end of the block. "Tell me what you'd like to see and I will take you."

Iliana felt she was in an alternate reality. "I was planning to walk the city and see the sites."

"Then may I suggest a place?"

"Sure."

"I know a small café on the edge of town that serves the most wonderful biscotti. Let's share some coffee, or tea if you'd prefer at this late hour, and enjoy the local specialties."

"You want to eat with me?"

"I want to do more than eat with you, but I am a gentleman."

She swallowed hard. Seeing this side of him was strange. What was his angle?

"You called me Demetrius."

Her mind was still reeling from the attack and fear was still trembling in her muscles. "Did I?"

"You did. When you were begging me to show your assailant mercy."

Iliana blinked at him. "You would have killed him."

"He should not have touched you. I wouldn't have beaten him for stealing from you, but touching you and threatening you is a grave offense."

"I was okay." Except she wasn't sure if she would have been.

"Iliana, I know you are afraid of me. But I want to undo those fears. I want to show you I am not a monster. I am a man, a driven man, and I will prove that you can trust me."

Iliana didn't know what to do with this information. Still rattled, she slid closer to Demetrius in the car.

Though he seemed surprised, he didn't move away. She laid her head on his firm shoulder and closed her eyes.

Inhaling deeply, she let herself relax. She had fantasized about Demetrius, dreamed of him, sparred with him verbally and now that she was in his arms, she didn't want any more drama. She just wanted him.

Despite being together for hours, Demetrius DeSante didn't touch her. He sat across from her in the café at the circular mosaic-topped metal table. He did not laugh easily and rarely smiled. But he made no attempt to end the evening. He asked interesting questions to further the conversation. He didn't look at his phone or the clock on the wall.

Demetrius was well read on a variety of subjects and strangely, they seemed to share several interests and were of like mind on many topics.

Best of all, his attention was completely on her.

Iliana wished she could text Serena about this, but she didn't know how to without appearing rude. And she already felt intimidated sitting across from the dictator. When the shop employees began wiping down tables, they reluctantly stood to leave.

Demetrius left a sizeable tip on the table. She wouldn't have thought he would tip so generously. Everything she had read about him seemed shaded and not representative of the real Demetrius DeSante.

When they returned to the hotel, Demetrius walked her to her room, oblivious to anyone who saw them together. Would he try to come inside her hotel room? Would he expect sex? She slipped her key card into the slot and the light turned green. She turned the door handle and cracked the door.

He did not advance forward.

"Iliana, I had a wonderful night. Thank you for the company."

She held the door open and debated inviting him inside. Reading him was difficult and it would be easy to make a misstep. "Thank you for rescuing me."

He seemed to blush and it was adorable. His hands were clasped behind him. He would leave without touching her or kissing her. Would it be wrong to kiss his cheek? To hug him?

She decided a kiss on the cheek was not out of bounds. She leaned up and pressed her lips to his cheek. He closed his eyes.

When she pulled away, she had left some lipstick on him. She wiped at it with her thumb. He caught her hand and kissed the inside of her wrist. "Leave it."

"It looks like I marked you."

"Perhaps I want to be a marked man. Good night, Iliana. You will call on me if you require anything."

He stepped back and she closed the door. After sliding the lock into place and taking several deep breaths to calm herself, Iliana peeked out into the hallway. Demetrius was gone.

She wouldn't know how to explain what had happened tonight. Was she being courted by the dictator of Icarus? Was he trying to use her for some ulterior motive?

If he was using her, what did she have that he needed?

As the party picked up the pace, wine and alcohol were flowing more freely and the volume of the room grew louder.

Casimir found Serena sitting at the bar. She looked bored. He seconded that emotion. He had spent time with Warrington, a task that taxed and angered him to no end.

"Having fun?" he asked.

Serena smiled halfheartedly. "I was planning to leave in a few minutes. I wanted to give you this." She pressed her room key into the palm of his hand.

The simple gesture meant volumes. Even after a night of socializing with the upper echelon of Elion, she still wanted Casimir in her room. The anticipation of being alone with her might kill him.

Casimir was pleased to know that if he was with Serena, she would not be with King Warrington. Demetrius DeSante would be pleased to know that information as well.

Serena slid off the bar stool and walked casually out of the room. Before he could follow her, DeSante approached.

"I almost killed a man tonight."

Casimir knew his old friend could mean that literally. "In what context?"

"I went out with Serena's assistant. A man touched her. I beat him senseless."

Casimir shook his head. DeSante rarely acted or reacted with pure emotion. There had to be more to the story. "You had a date with Iliana?"

"We were out together. It was not a date."

"What kind of man touched her? Like brushed by her on the street?"

DeSante gave him a droll look. "No, he tried to assault her."

The incident came more clearly into view. DeSante had no patience when it came to violence against women or children or anyone who could not defend themselves.

Zero threshold. It was a strange ethic. He would beat someone without guilt, but would defend to the death someone whom he believed deserved protection.

"Is Iliana hurt?"

DeSante shot him a look. "Do you think I would let someone hurt her?"

Casimir didn't know DeSante and Iliana had grown so close. DeSante's interest in Iliana was noteworthy because he rarely pursued a woman. "If you were out with her, I have no doubt she was safe."

DeSante stood taller. "I made it clear to her where we stand."

"And where is that?" Casimir asked.

DeSante touched his heart. Then he flicked his head upward to someone behind Casimir. "Excuse me."

Casimir didn't mind the abrupt end to their conversation. He and DeSante could be friendly. They made it their policy to be sociable with everyone. But they couldn't be linked together. It was too risky for their plan.

The last thread he needed to tie up was Fiona. She was having a good time, not drunk, but definitely feeling a buzz. He located her on the dance floor.

"I'm heading to bed," he said.

Fiona shook her head and winked at him. "Not unless it's my bed."

He wasn't sleeping in her room. They had booked separate rooms for a reason. "Not tonight, Fiona. I can't sully your reputation."

"Then make an honest woman out of me and put a ring on my finger." She threw her head back and laughed, but he heard the truth in the statement.

He had promised himself Fiona wouldn't get hurt

in his quest to destroy King Warrington. That might mean ending his relationship with her and giving her wide-open space to move on with her life. Not that he and Fiona had made any verbal commitments to each other, but Casimir knew that Fiona sometimes read into a situation and the more time they spent together, the more attached she became to him.

"Good night, Fiona." He kissed her cheek and she waved as he left the party.

He took the stairs to Serena's room. He needed to burn off some extra energy and give himself time to think about how to play this.

It had never been the plan to sleep with Serena. He didn't want to hurt her or put her in the middle of anything. He needed to be careful not to be seen entering her room at this hour by anyone other than her guards. They were, and should be, unavoidable.

Casimir stopped in his room, changed into sweatpants and a hooded sweatshirt. Then he went to Serena's room. He didn't see her guards. Were they posted inside?

Casmir entered the bedroom and he closed the door behind him.

Serena was in her closet, taking off her dress. His breath caught. She looked beautiful.

"Where are your guards?" he asked.

"In their rooms. Sleeping."

No one was watching her room? That seemed risky. All the better that he was with her.

She turned to show him the buttons. "I can't get my dress unfastened."

She was undressing in front of him? Score for his desire. He walked closer to her, trying not to appear too eager and trying to keep his lust in check. This might not mean what he thought it did.

"You picked a dress with the world's tiniest buttons. There's no way one person could get this off." His fingers brushed her bare skin as he worked with the tiny spheres, forcing them through the satin fabric loops.

"Maybe it's supposed to require two people. More exciting that way," Serena said.

Her tone was higher and she seemed anxious. "Everything okay?" he asked, still unfastening the buttons. They went down the back of the dress, well past the curve of her rear end. Should he unbutton every one, or leave some fastened? How far did she want this to go?

"I received some bad news from my uncle."

"About Dr. Shaw?"

Serena took a deep breath. "Thankfully, Dr. Shaw is stable and growing stronger every day. But my uncle was attacked leaving a restaurant."

Though he wondered if there was a connection, Casimir could not tell her about Iliana's near mugging without giving away his friendship with Demetrius. "He didn't have his guards with him?"

"He did, but they were waiting in the car," Serena said, emotion thickening her voice.

Casimir gently turned her by the shoulders. "I'm sorry." He drew her into a hug. She seemed as if she needed a friend and a support. He could be both. It wasn't exactly what he had in mind, coming to her room tonight, but he would be whomever she needed him to be.

"Do you want a glass of wine? Something to relax?" he asked.

"I've had enough to drink tonight," she said, turning again.

He had unfastened the last button. Her thong was exposed, giving him a peekaboo look at the rest of her.

"Have you looked in the mirror?" he asked.

She shook her head.

He led her to the mirror and she stared, mostly at him. They looked good together.

"You look like a princess," he said.

"I am a princess," she whispered.

Reading her signals and responding, he peeled the right shoulder of her dress away, letting it fall down her arm. She was wearing a black bra and now he could see the lace trim. Elegant and classy, exactly like her.

Then he slid the fabric down the other shoulder.

The dress fell to the floor in a heap. Still watching her face in the mirror, he kissed her neck, setting his hands on her hips.

She let out her breath on a sigh. He moved his hands to encircle her waist and she leaned into him. He had wanted her for so long, this could have gone lightning fast and been over in an instant. But he wanted to draw it out, to make his time with her last as long as possible.

Though he wasn't sure how this related to avenging his mother's honor or how it would impact his and De-Sante's plans, he knew exactly what he was doing with Serena. He knew how to please a woman, and tonight he would please Serena.

"Open your eyes and look at me," he said.

She did as he asked.

"Watch what I'm doing to you."

He reached into the front of her panties and found her hot and wet. His erection strained against his pants, but this was about her. He wanted her to come once, maybe twice. He massaged her and she swayed on her feet.

"Spread your legs."

She brought her legs apart and he plunged a finger inside her. She gasped.

Moving her panties aside, he knelt between her legs. Using only his fingers, he made love to her, his eyes never leaving her face. She reached for the full-length mirror stand to steady herself. She made the most astonished face when she came and pride tumbled over him.

He stood and kissed her and she melted against him.

"Let's go to bed," she said.

"My thoughts exactly."

Sweeping her off her feet, he carried her to the king-size bed. With a flick of his wrist, he pulled away the covers and blankets and laid her down.

She watched him from propped elbows, her back on the mattress.

He lifted her foot, removing her shoe and dropping it. Same for the other foot. He set her feet on the bed, her knees bent. He moved between them.

"What are you doing?" she asked.

"I want you to come again."

"I already…"

"That's why I said *again*."

She started to protest, but he ignored her and brought his head between her legs. After a few gentle laps of his tongue to gauge her reaction, he held nothing back, licking, sucking, tasting.

"I can't. I can't," she said, her hips thrashing.

But she could. He had seen it and now he wanted to taste it.

Adding his hand, he slid inside her. His free hand

reached to her breast and, pulling aside the delicate fabric, he stroked her. She climaxed in his arms.

He moved up the bed and lay next to her, feeling simultaneously tired and as if he could do this all night. The way she moved and the sounds in the back of her throat when she enjoyed him were awesome.

She rolled to the side and buried her head against his neck. "Casimir, please stay with me."

For tonight? Forever? His mind traveled to funny places and he considered what he had done. It complicated matters for sure. Was that bad?

Letting DeSante in on what he had done, not the details, just that his relationship with the princess had shifted, might give perspective, but Casimir wasn't ready to share this with anyone.

For tonight, Serena was his and his alone.

Chapter 6

Serena curled next to Casimir, basking in the heat of his body. The only light was from the closet. She was tempted to get up and turn it off, to pull on her pajamas and get more comfortable. But being next to Casimir was a comfort in itself.

She ran her fingers over his jawline, his beard tickling her fingers. Then she kissed him. Her skin prickled and the memory of the night they had shared simmered in her blood.

He looked so peaceful and handsome as he slept. "Casimir?"

"Yes, Your Highness?" He sounded groggy.

"Please don't call me that."

"What would you like me to call you?"

"My name. Call me Serena."

He brought his lips to her temple in a kiss that was as perfect as it was brief. "Serena, what's on your mind?"

"I was thinking about last night." Given the early-morning hour, it was an accurate description.

"About what happened with your uncle?" he asked.

"About what happened between us."

"It sounds like you're worried."

Of course she was worried. What did this mean? "I'm supposed to marry King Warrington."

He tensed. If she hadn't been touching him, she wouldn't have noticed the slight tightening of his muscles in response to the mention of the king. "I know that you do not and cannot belong to me. You belong to Acacia and the king." His voice was edged with ice.

The truth in his statement brought tears to her eyes. She blinked them back. "Can't I be yours for now? For a few days or weeks or however long we have?"

A dark expression passed over his face. She didn't know him well enough to say what it was, but he was holding something back. He had depths she hadn't fully explored and given the temporary status of their relationship, she couldn't demand he confide in her.

Secrets could bring trouble. "Will you tell me what you're not saying?" she asked.

He rolled to his side. "I'm worried about you. You don't seem cut out for this life. You aren't hardened and scheming. Everything you do is open."

"Is that wrong?"

"Not wrong, but not how most people play this game. You'll be hurt because someone will take advantage of your goodness and genuineness."

A warning traced up her spine. "Are you one of those people?"

He shook his head and closed his eyes briefly. "I have

no intention of harming you. But I see the path you are on, and it's not good."

He wanted to put distance between them before her path became tied to King Warrington's. Casimir seemed to be one of the few people in her life who saw that she and the king were wrong for each other. "Why are you pulling away from me?"

"You ask this as you sleep in my arms?"

She was overwhelmed with emotion. Though he didn't speak of love, he spoke of devotion and stead-fastness when she needed it most. "You have been the first person in a long time to become close to me. I can't define why it's so easy to let you in."

He let his forehead fall against hers. "I feel it as well."

"Stay close to me tonight," she said.

"I will. I promise. For tonight."

Inside the church and forced to make polite conversa-tion with strangers, Serena was grateful when the string quartet began to play music and she was escorted to her seat by an usher. The church was filled with pink and yellow flowers and a sweet floral scent hung heavy in the air. The church had been built a few hundred years earlier, its stained glass windows intricate and the fres-cos on the ceiling beautiful and ornate.

Surprised at how close she was to the altar, she looked around for Casimir, trying to appear noncha-lant. He had left her room early that morning before the sun rose.

No one could know they had spent the night together. It wouldn't be proper. One of her reasons for attending this wedding was to represent her country and to honor her father's memory by stepping in to his place. Starting rumors or problems ran contrary to her intentions.

When she visually located Casimir inside the church, seated a couple rows behind her and next to Fiona, he met her gaze. The eye contact closed the distance between them and her skin tingled as if she were standing in his arms. Afraid someone else would notice the look, she broke it.

Serena faced the altar and tried not to think about her own wedding. Many of the same people would be in attendance, her father's and sister's absence too painful to consider.

The groom walked to the altar with the minister and Serena was struck by the expression on his face. He was happy, excited even.

How would King Warrington look as he waited for her? Stern? Serious? Resigned? She hadn't seen him yet today. Would he think about their wedding today with the same sense of disappointment and dread?

When the doors in the back of the church opened and the bride entered, the groom's face switched from excited to elated.

Serena's heart broke for her misfortune. King Warrington wouldn't stare at her with affection and love. Their wedding would simply be a means for them to fulfill their obligation to their countries. Would he even want to share the same bed on their wedding night? Would she?

A mild headache formed at the edges of her brain. She had ibuprofen in her clutch, but taking it now would cause a distraction.

The rest of the ceremony was a blur, but Serena stood, sat and kneeled along with the people around her.

As the church emptied, she remained in her seat. She wished the day were over. This was supposed to be a small vacation from Acacia and her troubles there, but she didn't feel refreshed. She felt stressed and burdened thinking about her wedding. Arranging for her private plane to take her home was a simple matter, but she had to attend the reception. It was a private dinner for close family and friends. Although, given that Serena was invited, she wondered how close those family members and friends could be.

Casimir approached and sat next to her. "Enjoy the service?"

"The bride was lovely. The groom seemed happy."

The guests were outside throwing bird seed and blowing bubbles. The church was quiet. Could she stay here? She had made an appearance. Maybe she could skip the reception after all.

She reached for his arm, but she drew back when she realized her mistake. He wasn't her date and behaving otherwise was inappropriate. "You were gone when I woke."

"I had to leave before your guards returned."

Fiona approached, smiling, but something in her eyes worried Serena.

"I see you're talking to your princess again," Fiona said, glowering at Serena. Fiona slid her arms around Casimir's shoulder in an obviously possessive manner.

"Ready to go to the reception?" she asked Casimir.

Casimir smiled at her. "Sure. See you there, Serena?"

"Yes. See you both there."

Serena waited for them to leave. She was alone in the church, save for her bodyguard standing nearby.

She could hear the sounds of excitement drifting farther away.

Being in a church made her think of her father and her sister. Her sister would have loved to be married in a church like this. She would never have the opportunity.

Serena wiped at the tears that came to her eyes. She fished in her handbag for a tissue. She missed her father and sister so much, she wondered if the pressure on her chest would ever fully go away. Serena thought of them a thousand times a day and today was no exception.

She composed herself and then walked outside to her waiting car. Serena didn't want to socialize. She had too much on her mind. Was she accomplishing what she had set out to accomplish? Did anyone see her differently now, having spent time with her?

Needing to hear a friend's voice, she called Iliana who answered sleepily.

"How was your night?" Serena asked.

"I went sightseeing and instead of the sights, I saw Demetrius DeSante almost kill someone."

Alarm rattled her nerves. "What? Are you okay?"

"Thanks to him, yes, I'm fine. He was worried about me and he followed me. Sure enough, trouble found me and Demetrius kicked its ass."

"The dictator of Icarus kicked someone's butt for you?"

"Sure did. One of the most insanely disturbing and yet shockingly romantic things that has ever happened to me."

"Do you think your attack is related to the one on my uncle?" She had messaged Iliana the night before so she would be extra careful.

"The guy was a street thug. He didn't know who I was."

"Are you okay now?"

"Physically, yes. Emotionally, I feel totally confused."

"Same here."

"Oh, did something happen with Casimir?" Iliana sounded more awake now.

Serena filled her in, glossing over some details. "I know we can't be together, but I can't stay away from him."

"Give in and stay there for as long as reality allows. That's what I'm thinking about with DeSante. See where it leads. What's the worst that can happen?" Iliana asked.

"DeSante could kidnap you, take you to his country and add you to his harem."

Iliana laughed. "He would never. I don't share men. And can you see me as a harem woman? Please. I look terrible in jewel tones."

Serena had known Iliana long enough to read between the lines. Though she joked about her relationship with DeSante, they had something real. "Maybe you should give him a chance."

"You're okay with that?"

Serena wasn't sure she could pass judgment on anyone else's relationship. She was making a mess of her own. "I'll think on it. But as long as you don't spill state secrets, what's the harm?"

"Since I don't know any state secrets, I think we're safe there."

"We just pulled up to the reception. I'll call you later, okay?"

"Have fun!" Iliana said.

Not a chance.

Fifteen minutes later, Serena was struggling to follow a conversation with the duke of someplace. He was talking about his plans to take his yacht around the world. Normally, the conversation would have interested her, but since he was simply listing cities and dates, she found it tedious.

If she didn't get away, she would fall asleep. Not the impression she wanted to make.

She cut into the monologue. "You'll have to excuse me. I see someone I need to speak with." The duke didn't follow her and she was grateful.

Serena threaded through the crowd toward the bar. She asked for a glass of soda, hoping the caffeine would rouse her out of her funk.

Casimir was the only person in the room she could focus on totally. When their eyes met, he moved toward her. Given the number of people in attendance, hopefully Fiona wouldn't notice him speaking to her. Serena didn't want to make an enemy of the countess.

Casimir stood by her casually. They hadn't touched and Serena longed to close the distance between them.

Too many people to judge and too many cameras to capture the act to give in to that desire.

"Are you feeling okay?" he asked.

The crowds made her uncomfortable, but she was not the center of attention so it was tolerable. The bride and groom were drawing and holding most of the focus in the room, and deservedly so. "I almost didn't come. But I'm here."

A flurry of activity by the door caught Serena's attention. King Warrington had entered the Great Hall.

Serena's stomach knotted and she felt light-headed. The king of Rizari moved through the crowd, shaking hands. She wanted to disappear. She didn't want to talk to him, except decorum dictated she acknowledge him. She felt guilty for sleeping with Casimir and she resented Samuel Warrington for the hold he had over her life.

"Is it too late to leave?" she asked Casimir.

"He's blocking the main exit. I can take you out the side door."

Running away would look strange. Someone would notice and then Serena would have to provide a reason for her rude behavior. "I'm trapped." Today, tomorrow and in her future marriage.

King Warrington strode toward her and Serena took a slow, deep breath. Of all the times to feel dizzy and fuzzy, this was a bad one. She plastered a smile on her face and pretended she was happy to see him.

Extending her hands to him, she clasped his and leaned toward him, allowing him to kiss her cheek. He smelled of cologne, and she gagged a little.

"King Warrington, hello," she said.

"I've told you, call me Samuel. Even in public, we can be on familiar terms."

He had said no such thing, but it sounded good to anyone listening in on their conversation. "Did you enjoy the service?" Small talk. She hated it.

"It was well done. Hi, Casimir. I see you are keeping the princess company."

Casimir smiled in response.

People were moving closer to eavesdrop on their conversation. Serena hoped she was playing the role of his future betrothed convincingly.

Women, in particular, were jockeying for position to be near the king, openly staring at him and whispering to each other. His playboy reputation preceded him. She had to admit, he was handsome in a polished, preppy way.

But he was no Casimir.

"The bride is breathtaking," Serena said, trying not to become distracted by the thought of wearing a wedding dress herself.

With pleasantries exchanged, they were out of topics to discuss. They had little in common except her sister. It was inappropriate to talk about business or political issues at a wedding where others could overhear.

"My guards are signaling me, but I hope we'll share a dance tonight," Samuel said.

Serena nodded. "Looking forward to it." Not really. She would find some way to avoid it and him. Based on their interactions thus far, he would be thrilled to be relieved of the obligation. The women pouncing on him guaranteed he would have his share of women to keep him company.

One thing was clear: King Warrington wanted Acacia, but he did not want Serena as his wife.

Serena touched her hat to be sure it was in place. The room tilted and then Casimir's arm was around her waist and his hand on her forearm. "Your Highness, are you okay?"

In his voice, a worry. "I feel dizzy," she said.

Casimir was leading her somewhere, hopefully away from the crowd. She closed her eyes to dissipate the dizziness. When it grew darker, Serena opened her eyes. They were in the gardens outside the Great Hall.

Casimir led her to a marble bench and helped her

sit. He knelt in front of her. "Are you feeling okay?" Seeing him this way brought back poignant memories of the last time he had been in that position and desire stole the breath from her lungs.

Serena waved him off and tried to lasso her runaway libido. "I needed fresh air. It was hot in there."

Why had she come to this wedding? Why had she believed she could handle this? She had to prove something to everyone it seemed, including herself. "I don't want to marry King Warrington and when I think about it, I feel sick." She spoke the words in a whisper. She was sure this wouldn't come as a shock to Casimir. After all, he knew more about her relationship with the king than most. Serena set her hands in her lap. "Did you see how women frolic around him and throw themselves at him?"

"Frolic?"

"What word would you use?" Serena asked.

"Maybe another *F* word to describe what those women want, but why does that matter?"

Did he really not know or did he want her to explain it? "That's not a desirable trait in a husband."

"Some women would enjoy having a man who others desired."

"But that's the part we have wrong. Warrington doesn't desire me. I don't know that he ever will. What if he doesn't stop his dalliances after we're married?"

"That would be embarrassing for both of you."

Serena closed her eyes. She shouldn't have come to Elion. She should have sent a nice gift, a pleasant note and an excuse, like she had wanted to in the first place. "What should I do?"

"What do you want to do?"

She was almost never asked that by her uncle or her advisers. "I don't know." She considered her options. Could she demand more of King Warrington's time? Insist on fidelity being part of their arrangement?

Casimir shrugged. "You could offer him the country without the marriage."

She had considered that. "My people would revolt. They would fight a takeover and view it as hostile. They would feel they had no voice in the government."

"As his wife, will you have a voice?"

She had hoped they could come to terms and King Warrington would consult with her on matters involving Acacia. But who knew what would happen once the marriage papers were signed and their interests were merged? "I had hoped."

"You could live apart and lead your own life."

Her own life in her own house sounded good in some ways, but lonely. "You mean cheat on my husband?" Have a series of affairs that couldn't develop into anything real? She had that with Casimir now and it broke her heart.

She couldn't have a child with a lover. Did she want children? She hadn't stopped to make firm plans on the matter, although she had figured she would have children one day.

"Isn't that what he is likely to do to you?" Casimir asked.

Given the king's behavior during their first planned meeting, she guessed he wouldn't respect her feelings or honor their marriage vows. "I don't know him well enough to say."

Casimir slanted her a look.

"What do you want me to say? To admit I'm agreeing to a raw deal?"

His expression was unreadable. "I know you're getting a raw deal. But unless you force King Warrington to accept different terms, nothing will change."

"If someone sees us together and starts a rumor, something will change. I'll have let down my country. Warrington will marry someone else."

Casimir lifted his brow. "I doubt that. He still wants Acacia. He didn't agree to take it out of the kindness of his heart."

"He isn't taking it. It's a union." The words sounded flimsy, even to her own ears.

The music in the Great Hall stopped and Serena heard someone speaking on the microphone. Time to return to the party. Still feeling overwhelmed, Serena entered the hall, where the bride and groom were walking hand in hand through the crowd, speaking with their guests. Serena recognized the intimate body language between the bride and groom. They were in love. Actual love. Not trying to fool their countrymen and women or make a political alliance or please someone else. They had genuine warmth and affection for each other. Serena remembered reading that they had met at university and had been together since.

Watching them, loneliness descended on her. But that feeling was nothing new. Serena had been lonely since her last disastrous relationship.

To make matters worse, when Serena moved to her table, she saw she had been seated next to King Warrington. She should have expected it. Most members of their social circle knew about their pending arrangement. Few would stop and question how Samuel's history with Danae would impact their engagement, perhaps treating them as disparate relationships.

Serena sat and smiled at the king. Her worry increased when she noticed Fiona sitting across the ten-person table. If Fiona was at their table, then so was Casimir. Could she hide how she felt about him? She was accustomed to watching people and that had taught her that the smallest reaction, the lift of an eyebrow, a lingering look, a private smile, could give away so much. Too much.

"Where did you disappear to?" King Warrington asked.

Had he noticed her absence? Or was it that she hadn't followed him around the room as his other admirers seemed to do? "I'm jet-lagged and not feeling well. I went outside for some fresh air."

He leaned closer to her. Was she speaking loud enough?

"I'm sorry to hear that."

Nothing in his voice communicated real empathy. Serena worked to keep her voice low, but audible. "I know this is hard for you. I miss Danae, too."

Surprise registered on his face. Perhaps he had not expected her to mention her sister, but it was the big green-spotted pink elephant in the room and they might as well talk about it.

The king cleared his throat. "She was a good person." Now his voice held actual emotion. His eyes grew damp and she thought she detected some anger in his tone. At the situation? Toward her for bringing it up? "I know it puts us in an awkward position," she said. She felt better saying it.

"We'll make the best of it," Warrington said. He took

a sip of his scotch and looked straight ahead, avoiding eye contact with her.

Serena wondered why she had never considered the impact Danae's death would have on King Warrington. Perhaps some of his reluctance to spend time with her had to do with his lingering feelings for Danae.

The duke came to the microphone near the band. "Thank you for coming today. Many of you traveled a great distance to celebrate with my bride and me." He launched into a speech about how much he loved and cared about his new wife and how he looked forward to the days and years ahead. He was poised and collected. Serena wished she could behave that way in public, instead of floundering and stuttering her way through meetings and speaking engagements.

When he finished his speech, the duke pulled his wife onto the dance floor with him. He held her close as the music played. They seemed to move as one around the dance floor.

Casimir came to the table and sat. Fiona leaned into him, setting her head on his shoulder. He didn't push her away, nor did he slip his arm around her and hold her close.

Serena took a sip of her water and forced her attention on the bride and groom. Samuel Warrington didn't seem eager to talk about Danae, and Serena wasn't willing to give away anything about Casimir.

With her and the king harboring feelings for others, could they ever have an honest relationship built on trust?

Casimir could see the princess and King Warrington in his peripheral vision. Serena was leaning toward him, though she and the king weren't speaking.

The rage Casimir felt for Serena's future betrothed was potent, and knowing King Warrington was a liar and murderer didn't help matters. Yet rage had no place in revenge. It would skew his thinking, much as lust could.

Samuel Warrington tossed him several looks, but Casimir kept his expression neutral. He wouldn't tip his hand in Samuel's direction and give the king any reason to look deeper into Casimir's life.

King Warrington set his hand on the back of Serena's chair and Casimir forced himself not to look in that direction. He counted back slowly from ten. He had to stay calm. If he revealed himself now as the true heir to the throne, he would ruin the careful plans he had made.

When the bride and groom finished their dance, they motioned for their guests to join them. King Warrington extended his hand to Serena. She took it and he led her to the dance floor.

Casimir changed his position to keep Serena in his line of sight. He rationalized that he needed to keep her safe and therefore he had to keep her in view. But the room was filled with private security and few threats. He wanted to watch her for his benefit.

He needed to know that she wouldn't fall in love with King Warrington. A long line of lovers had fallen for Warrington's charms. Casimir couldn't stand the idea of Serena being in that line. Furthermore, he had promised Demetrius DeSante he wouldn't allow Serena's and the king's relationship to progress too far and once a promise was made to DeSante, it was a life-and-death matter to keep it.

When the song ended, a woman in a purple dress cut in between Warrington and Serena. Casimir saw the change in Warrington's posture. He pulled the woman to his body, he stared at her and rocked against her. She was one of his lovers. Did Serena realize it, too?

"Come on Casimir, dance with me," Fiona said.

Casimir escorted her to the dance floor and was lucky when the music changed and another man moved in to dance with Fiona.

Casimir let Fiona go, feigning disappointment. She winked at him. Fiona was a shameless flirt and loved men's attention.

Serena came to his side. "The king is awfully friendly with that woman. Do you know her?"

Casimir recognized her, but he couldn't place her. "She looks familiar, but no." The king and the woman in purple were practically grinding into each other. "Perhaps she is a friend."

"I don't touch my friends that way. They aren't strangers," Serena said.

"Perhaps she's an old girlfriend."

"Or a current one. I have been trying not to let the rumors bother me, but his reputation is making me wonder," Serena said.

He was glad she was more skeptical and questioning, but he hated the hurt in her voice. She was taking the king's behavior personally, when it had nothing to do with her and everything to do with the man's selfish motives. "She has nothing to do with you."

"Do you think he cheated on my sister?" Serena asked.

Casimir knew that Samuel had. One of DeSante's contacts in the government of Rizari had been following the king closely for years. It was easy enough to pinpoint when the king took a new lover. New lovers were sent flowers, gifts and given lots of the king's time for as long as the woman held his attention. "I don't know what arrangement your sister and King Warrington had."

Serena looked around the room. "There is so much I don't know. So much that is beneath the surface here. I can't really trust anyone. Except you. You've been there for me."

Casimir flinched. It was a knife to the gut. She trusted him? He would hurt her in the end. Casimir was lying to her, and while he was a grand liar, he hated that no part of her detected it. He wished she wasn't so trusting and naive. Anyone in power, especially someone new to politics, needed to question the people around them and keep some walls up. Serena's openness would get her killed. "You shouldn't trust anyone."

Her smile faltered but didn't fully fade. "What does that mean? Are you telling me I have misplaced my trust in you?"

Grossly misplaced. But Casimir needed to stay close to her. He searched for words that wouldn't hurt her, but that weren't an outright lie. Somehow, that seemed to cross a line. "I mean to keep you safe. I mean for you to understand that as the princess and soon the queen, people will want to hurt you and take advantage of you."

"I won't let that happen, but I was thinking it might be a good time for me to take advantage of you. Come to my room?" she asked.

A bold statement, coming from her. He went hard thinking of slipping into her room again. "Yes. You go first and I'll meet you at the hotel."

Casimir entered her room, his body keyed up and his arousal swollen to the point that it was painful against the fabric of his pants.

Serena rushed to him, throwing herself into his arms. He caught her and she wrapped her legs around his waist, her dress rising up around her hips. "I thought you wouldn't come."

"I'll come. We both will."

He carried her directly to the bed and laid her down, careful not to put his full weight on her. She rocked her body, simulating the act that his body wanted most.

"Casimir, please. Hurry."

He couldn't do anything except respond to her requests. Lust surged in his head, forcing out thoughts of caution. He was fully prepared for her to change her mind. Was this an emotional reaction to her sadness and hurt over King Warrington's behavior? There was no room for another man between them. "Are you sure?"

"I ache for you."

Simple, honest words. Casimir knew if he made love to her, he would never allow her to sleep with Warrington. They had spent the night together, they had fooled around, but they had never taken it this far. By sleeping with Serena, he was raising the stakes high. Everything was on the line.

She could not fall for King Warrington. She would belong to Casimir and Casimir alone.

If his revenge didn't unfold according to plan, he would lose the crown that was his birthright, his spirit would be crushed, his mother would sink further into darkness and he would fail Serena. She would marry King Warrington and if Casimir survived the inevitable backlash from the king, he would have to live with that knowledge.

Casimir would make her feel as good as he knew how, he would show her how a man should treat a woman and every other man she came in contact with would pale in comparison to him. He took great pleasure knowing that. If by some horrible twist of his plan, Serena married King Warrington, at least Casimir would know that he had been with her first and he had treated her like a princess, like a queen.

He ran his hand down her smooth hair. "I want you, too, Serena."

In one even motion, he flipped her onto her stomach and worked on unfastening her dress, kissing her skin as his fingers worked the dress open. "We need to have a conversation about picking dresses without so many buttons."

"Just rip it."

With a firm tug, he parted the fabric. Buttons bounced to the ground. "Much better."

He unsnapped her black bra. The black did something to him. She rolled over and he peeled away her dress and tossed aside her bra.

She was naked to the waist and he kissed her, brushing his lips over her cheeks, her chin and her throat. The longer he kissed her, the more he wanted her. She touched his hardness through his pants and let out a gasp of surprise.

He moved her hand away. "This is about you." If she touched him, he would embarrass himself. He was that turned on.

"What about—"

He silenced her with another kiss. He skimmed his hand between her legs. Serena lifted her hips into his hands, demanding more. More he was willing to give. Finding her ready, a charge of electricity burst through him, mind-numbing pleasure taking over. His finger easily slipped inside her and she cried out. They didn't need her guards coming to investigate, so he quickly returned his mouth to hers. Kissing was fast becoming his favorite way to spend his time.

He moved his hand, slowly at first, letting the tension between them build and grow. He watched her face, gauged her reaction to every movement. He slid her dress down her legs to give him more room to maneuver. Watching her was an utter turn-on. If he hadn't already been mad with lust, her gasps and sighs would have taken him there.

Nothing about this had been part of his plan. He had wanted to use her for information, but this act had nothing to do with his plan for revenge. He didn't want to consider his exact motives. She was beautiful and sweet and he was about to make love to her. That was enough.

The involuntary buck of her hips let him know she'd found completion. Gathering her close, he held her.

Her pulse was racing. When her hand moved to the tent in his pants, he shifted. "I'm fine." It would go away. Eventually. A cold shower. A bucket of ice. His hand when he was alone.

She didn't say anything else, just snuggled in tight. After a few minutes, her even, deep breathing indicated she had fallen asleep.

Serena rolled to her side and slung her leg over Casimir. "I'm cold." Based on the darkness that shrouded the room, sunrise was still hours away.

Casimir reached to the bottom of the bed and pulled the sheets and blankets over them. "When I was dancing with Samuel, I was thinking about you," she whispered.

Casimir watched her with soulful eyes.

"As the princess, you would think I would be allowed to make some of my own rules."

"When you are queen, perhaps you can."

She shook her head. "I'll be a queen in name only, a figurehead, but powerless."

"You have managed to have complete power over me."

He said the sweetest things that reached to her core. "Kiss me. Please."

He captured her mouth in a soul-stirring kiss. She felt the swell of his arousal against her belly. He deepened the kiss and she opened her mouth, letting his tongue stroke hers, lightly sucking on his lower lip.

"I have always planned to use great care with you, but you are making that impossible," he said.

His mouth found hers once again and their tongues collided and sparred. Her entire body was tuned to him. He had been attentive to her and she wanted to please him.

But Casimir seemed to have an agenda of his own. He palmed her breasts, sending molten heat surging through her. Instead of rising between her thighs and removing his pants, Casimir lowered his head between her legs. He took her into his mouth and she bit her lip to keep from screaming. His tongue moved up and down, swirling. He sucked her hard and she jerked against his mouth, desperate for release.

She had never felt this way about a man. The intensity, the intimacy, the incredible sensations were a whirl in her brain and in her heart. "Please, Casimir."

"Tell me what you need," he said, kissing the inside of her thighs.

"I need you." Every word was a pant. "You inside me."

He answered her plea by pressing two fingers inside her. He moved his tongue and fingers with expert precision. Serena knew she was close to finishing, but was unable to stop it. She looked at him and he lifted his head, making eye contact with her. She went off at that moment, tremors rocking her body, bringing every inch of her skin to attention and sending pulses of pleasure over her.

Casimir gathered her against him. He kissed her forehead. "Can I spend the night?" he asked.

"What about Fiona?"

"We have separate rooms. She won't know where I am," Casimir said.

"What if she comes looking for you?"

"Then I will tell her I was sleeping off an alcohol-induced buzz."

She rubbed her cheek against his shoulder. "I wish you would let me return the favor."

"I'm fine."

He didn't sound fine. Why didn't he want her to touch him? Casimir Cullen was a curious man. He had been a mystery from the very start, and Serena felt as if she was only beginning to scratch the surface of what lay beneath.

Chapter 7

The coronation of the queen was a grand affair in Acacia. It had been declared a national holiday. Banks, libraries and schools were closed. The formalities of the day were broadcast on television and streaming on news sites.

Serena tried to think about the day in pieces: the procession, the ceremony and the reception. She was hosting dozens of royals from around the world. The coordination of security, the staff and various events was a huge task.

Lucky for Serena, she had help. Iliana was handling her first major kingdom-wide event as Serena's personal assistant with poise. She'd provided Serena a detailed schedule, outlining where she had to be and with whom. Without her, Serena would be lost.

Her uncle Santino had overseen the details of her personal security and how to manage the crowds. Living through the day would be an accomplishment, as would her holding it together.

King Warrington was scheduled to meet with Serena before the procession. While he was not a part of the coronation, he had inserted himself into the day by making his travel plans known and arriving in Acacia by private airplane.

A physical reminder of her duties and future life, the Acacian crown, sat heavy on Serena's head. She had practiced wearing it, balancing it and walking with it. She would wear it today, but not many other occasions. It would return to the vault for safekeeping after the ceremony. Her biggest hurdle would be pressing through the coronation and the reception without stuttering and stumbling over her words. Her stomach was in knots. Someone might decide tonight was the day to take a shot at her. Or poison her food. Or slip into one of the private events and get close enough to hurt her.

A queen. The queen of Acacia. It was a position she hadn't thought she'd occupy. Immediately, her mind shot to Danae, sending grief to war with her worry. The crowning of the new leader of Acacia should have happened years from now, when her father was old and had decided to pass his crown to the next generation and live out his remaining days in the comfort of his seaside estate.

Her phone rang and seeing Samuel Warrington's private number, Serena almost didn't answer. But if she spoke to him now, perhaps she could avoid him later.

"Samuel, hello," Serena said, sitting on the chaise lounge in her bedroom.

"Good morning. I hate to drop in on you on such

short notice, but I'd like to congratulate you personally before the coronation. Stealing a moment alone with you later will be nearly impossible."

Why did he want to meet alone? She was immediately suspicious. Would he try to pressure her into agreeing to the engagement today? "My schedule is booked."

"It will only take a few minutes. I am sure you can squeeze me in. I'll see you shortly."

He ended the phone conversation. His tactics were strangely like Demetrius DeSante's. Why were the men in her life so quick to strong-arm her?

Iliana looked at Serena. "Everything okay?"

"King Warrington would like to see me before the procession."

Iliana squeezed her hands. "You need to bridge this gap with him at some point. I know it's hard and he hasn't exactly been Prince Charming, but you can make this work. I know you, Serena. You'll find a solution."

Like passing the crown to someone who wanted it and would happily marry King Warrington? "I've been trying."

Iliana pursed her lips. "Yes, but also no."

Serena knew what she meant. She was thinking about Casimir. Sleeping with Casimir wasn't helping her relationship with King Warrington.

Iliana consulted her tablet. "When he arrives, where would you like to meet?"

Serena considered her options. Not her bedroom—too personal. Her office seemed too formal. Many other parts of the castle were staged for various elements of the day's events. "The rose garden."

"Perfect. I'll message you when he arrives."

* * *

Serena was waiting in the rose garden's gazebo and stood as King Warrington approached.

He strolled as if he owned the castle and everything in it. She supposed it wasn't far from the truth. Soon, he would. She would struggle to keep control and fight hard to make her voice, and the voice of her countrymen, heard.

King Warrington sat on the bench across from her. "I won't keep you. But it dawns on me that we've been circling each other. We rarely talk. If we're to be married, this should be part of our routine, don't you think?"

What exactly did he mean? "I am not sure I follow."

"We'll share information. Figure out our best move."

Political strategizing was important if they would lead their countries jointly. "That seems reasonable. Did you wish to discuss something in particular?"

He sighed. "I received a call from the president of Icarus this morning. He wanted to discuss a meeting between the three of us."

DeSante wasn't showing his hand. What was his angle? "What did you tell him?"

"That I would think about it. Before we meet with him, I want us to present a united front."

Then King Warrington's reasons for being here weren't about their relationship or congratulating her. They were about ensuring she would side with him against DeSante. "On what matters?"

"All matters."

Unilaterally agreeing with King Warrington wasn't in her best interest. She didn't know what matters were most important to him and he didn't know those closest to her heart. "I think a meeting is a good idea. With my father unable to mitigate, we'll establish a new means of communicating."

Samuel ran a hand through his hair. "We need to move past this awkward formality between us. You look beautiful today and usually I am good with beautiful women."

There was a compliment in his statement somewhere, but she mostly felt uncomfortable.

"I can give you what you want if you'll just clue me in to what that is. Land. Money. Some heirloom jewelry. My advisers have been pressuring me to lock this down," he said.

How romantic. He was wrong, though. He wouldn't give her what she wanted because land and money didn't matter to her.

How could she be excited about this engagement? Samuel Warrington didn't love her. She wasn't attracted to him and he didn't seem interested in anything about her except her title. "We don't know each other."

"We can get to know each other if that's what it takes to make you comfortable," Samuel said.

He didn't want to spend time with her. He had made that clear. He treated her like an obligation he couldn't rid himself of fast enough. "How would you propose we do that?"

He leaned forward, snagged her around the waist.

"What are you doing?" she asked, pushing against his shoulders.

"Isn't this how husbands and wives get to know each other?" he asked.

Was he dense? Or maybe sex was how he became close to the women in his life. "This is not appropriate."

There was an awkward moment when he released her. "Figures you'd be frigid."

Her back went ramrod straight. "I am not frigid."

"Then let's sleep together, get it over with, and then work on the rest."

A man hadn't talked to her like this before and she was taken aback. "I am insulted you assume that sex is what I need to become close with you. What about finding common interests? Spending time on mutual hobbies?"

"Who has time for interests and hobbies?" He sounded angry.

According to what she knew of him, he spent much of his time throwing parties and vacationing. "I know this isn't easy because you cared for my sister. The pressure is making it worse for both of us. We can take things slow." How much slower, she didn't know. Perhaps they could start with a few conversations over email. Or text messaging. Become friends, which may lead to attraction.

Was it wrong to think attraction could be cultivated? She could find a trait in King Warrington that appealed to her and focus on that. She hadn't heard of anyone working that hard at a relationship, but she didn't know many women who had political marriages.

"We don't have months to waste. Demetrius DeSante is eager to attack you."

It wasn't far from her mind that the president was watching. But Serena hadn't been to war and her inexperience was a weakness. "I am aware of his intentions."

"Time is not your friend."

She didn't need threats and additional pressure from

King Warrington. "I know where my obligations to my country lie. I know what I need to do."

The king smiled as if he'd won. "I will call on you later this week. Perhaps you can articulate what other terms might make our arrangement acceptable to you."

He bowed to her. "Good day, Princess."

Serena watched him retreat down the landscaped paths of the garden.

Her skin crawled with revulsion and that was a terrible emotion to feel for her soon-to-be husband.

Casimir appeared and Serena gasped. "Casimir. How did you know I was here?"

"Iliana told me you were meeting with King Warrington in the rose garden."

Why did she feel she had been disloyal to Casimir? He knew about her impending arrangement with King Warrington. If he had seen them together a few minutes earlier, he would have seen that nothing happened except an almost kiss, which she had stopped. "He didn't leave me much of a choice about meeting."

Casimir said nothing with his words, but his look spoke volumes.

"Say what you want to say," Serena said.

"I have nothing to say that hasn't been said before. You said you didn't want to marry him, yet you're pursuing a relationship with him."

Was he hurt? She was unsure where they stood, but his presence renewed her feelings for him. Serena grasped the lapels of Casimir's suit jacket and pulled his lips to hers. He resisted for a moment, but then he returned the kiss, the heat of his mouth infusing her with a burning desire. She wished she had an extra hour to pull him away and do unspeakable things to him.

When she broke the kiss, she searched for the right words. "Some sad twist of fate has forced me into being queen. If I had my choice, you would be my future. I would be with you. But we know that's out of my control. I can't run this country alone. I can't protect us from Demetrius DeSante and his army without a better military. All I can do is make the best possible decisions for my country, given the circumstances."

Casimir ran his knuckles lightly down her cheek. "You underestimate yourself. But I am honored to know you would choose me. I know it's wrong to touch you and kiss you. I know I shouldn't but I can't stop myself."

Serena's phone chimed. A text from Iliana that she was needed in the solarium. "We will talk about this later. We will meet tonight?"

He didn't nod or indicate he would meet her, leaving her filled with uncertainty. "Good luck today. Be strong. Be the queen you were born to be."

His words infused her with confidence. "Thinking of you will get me through today."

Coronation Day was a blur of activities. Serena held it together through the procession and the ceremony, the pictures, the questions and endless small talk.

There had been a few incidences where her social awkwardness and lack of grace had been a problem. Serena had forgotten names, confused people and had been too nervous to eat, but she'd forged on, remembering Casimir's encouraging words.

She'd smiled until her cheeks hurt and waved to thousands of people. This day was about keeping Acacia on the path to a bright future. But Serena could not think of her own future. She could not think about Casimir leaving her, or about her marriage to King Warrington or her fears of what would happen when Acacia united with Rizari.

Prior to today, Iliana had warned the media not to ask questions about King Warrington, Rizari or her father's and sister's deaths. The press had complied.

During the ceremony those in attendance, dignitaries and commoners alike, held a moment of silence for their former leader. Serena had kept it together, but barely. At several different moments during the day, she'd felt the urge to burst into tears. The weight of her new title and the importance of this day was heavy on her shoulders.

One of the brightest moments of the coronation had been seeing Dr. Shaw in the front row when she was crowned queen. He had been seated beside his wife in his wheelchair. Though he needed rest and hadn't stayed long enough for her to greet him, she was pleased he had been in attendance. He was healing and that lifted Serena's spirits.

The final event of the day was an elegant party in the throne room with the doors opened to the lower level patio, which had been decorated with beautiful potted plants.

Serena needed to change her clothes before the evening's festivities. It was her seventh clothing change of the day. Iliana was waiting for her in her bedroom and she seemed distraught.

"What's wrong?" Serena asked. Iliana had planned the ceremony and related events to every last detail. Now that the coronation was almost finished, Iliana should be congratulating herself, having a glass of wine, and taking the next week away from work.

"Nothing."

Iliana had answered too abruptly. "Iliana…"

"It's nothing with the coronation. It's about Demetrius. A personal matter."

"You can tell me about it if you wish."

Iliana shook her head, fresh tears forming in her eyes. "I'm not ready to talk about it. Let's get you into your gown. It is my favorite. The most elegant by far. But it comes with a warning. I know that Casimir is here. Everyone is watching you tonight. Don't say or do anything that will start rumors."

Serena hugged her cousin. "Thank you for the reminder. I will be careful."

The morning after the coronation, Iliana had planned to sleep in late, maybe spend the day shopping in town or catching up on the errands she had neglected over the past weeks. When she'd received a message that Demetrius DeSante was planning to visit Serena, she rearranged her schedule, showered and beat feet to the castle.

She was upset with him because he had been so distant lately, but she wanted to see him. To confirm that their fling was over? To see if he still cared about her? She was a masochist, seeking out a situation that would inevitably hurt her. But like a moth to a flame…

Demetrius DeSante was waiting for Serena in the solarium on the first floor of the castle. He had finagled another meeting, perhaps by strong-arming any number of people. His official reason for the meeting was to congratulate Serena and formally acknowledge her as queen.

Iliana couldn't get over it. Serena as queen. Iliana was biased, but she thought Serena would rock the position. She was compassionate and warm and she cared about her country. Once she found her footing and some confidence, she would shine.

But her warm feelings for her cousin didn't negate her annoyance with DeSante. Demetrius hadn't informed her he was coming to the castle. She had seen the appointment on Serena's calendar that morning.

He had been so romantic and sweet in Elion and then Iliana hadn't heard from him. Being involved in a hot affair one minute, a freezing one in the next wasn't her jam.

Iliana entered the solarium. Demetrius's guards were in the room. Iliana nodded to them and they made no movement toward her.

"Good morning, Demetrius."

If the use of his first name when he was visiting in an official capacity offended him, he didn't indicate so. "Iliana."

"You didn't tell me you were coming by the castle this morning."

"I utilized the official channels to make this appointment."

What a load of crap. He hadn't wanted to see her and that stung. "I am the queen's personal secretary."

"Protocol and precedence dictate I book appointments with the queen through the minister of foreign affairs."

Iliana lifted her head proudly. "I must have misunderstood our relationship." He had alerted her to his official visits most times in the past.

"What did you understand our relationship to be?"

Iliana wasn't sure she could say it aloud without sounding like a perfect idiot. "In Elion you said... I mean, I thought we were…friends." What a weak word to describe what her imagination had led her to believe.

"We are friends. But you didn't call me," DeSante said.

"Was I supposed to call?"

"You are supposed to do whatever it is you want to do. You are strong enough to take what you want. I gave you my number to use at your leisure. You did not do the same for me. I would not use your professional contact information to pursue a personal matter."

He was putting the silence on her. "I coordinated the coronation. You didn't RSVP."

DeSante threw his head back and laughed. "You'll find a way to keep me in line. No infractions are acceptable. Even trivial social ones."

"That's right," Iliana said, unsure if he was making fun of her. "And the coronation was not trivial." She had spent long, hard and confusing hours planning that event, reading the details of past coronations and official protocols.

"My apologies. I know for you, it was a significant occasion. For me, it was an inevitable event that drew other matters to a head. I was dealing with those matters."

What did that mean? What was he getting at? "I see."

"Do you, Iliana? How would you feel if I told you I plan to speak to the queen about you?"

Her heart raced. "And tell her what?"

"That I wish for you to be our intermediary. I find Mitchell Wagner to be dull. I find you to be stimulating and infinitely more suited to negotiate affairs between the queen and me."

"What makes me more suited to that position?"

"It's my preference. I think you are glorious. Speaking to you excites me." He moved toward her like a panther stalking its prey. When he was close, he set his fingertips lightly on her hips. "I mean to have you, Iliana. I will court you and win you over."

Her legs felt boneless, but she remained standing. She wasn't a swoon-and-faint type. She was, however, a suspicious type. "Why?"

His eyes studied her face. "You never think of me?"

She'd be lying to deny it. "I think of you."

"In bed? When you are sleeping alone?"

"What makes you think I sleep alone?"

She expected her words to shock him, but he appeared unfazed. "You are a matter that concerns me and when matters concern me, I make sure I know everything about them."

She stepped back from him and shoved his hand away. "Are you spying on me?"

"Yes."

"That is so...rude!"

"For your protection."

"You know what, Demetrius? In Icarus, maybe women like that high-handed, man-is-king crap, but here, in Acacia, men and women are equals. I don't need a dictator peeping in my windows at night."

"I don't peep in your windows. I have hired parties watching out for you."

As if siccing strangers on her was any better. "Why? Why are you are so interested in me?"

DeSante inhaled and let out his breath slowly as if mustering patience. "You are of more importance than you know. One day, you will understand. Until then, I will keep you safe."

She should be creeped out, but he believed she required protection. "If pictures of me in the shower show up on the internet, I will blame you." Except somehow she knew he would demand lines and boundaries be kept to protect her privacy.

"If pictures of you in any compromising positions show up anywhere, you will see no end to how I will defend your honor and protect you."

Before Iliana could fully process or respond to that, Serena entered the solarium.

Seeing her cousin and the president of Icarus in intense conversation, Serena felt she had walked into a private exchange. Iliana seemed upset, but she could hold her own, regardless of her emotional state. Serena half expected, and would have found it highly amusing, to see her cousin let loose on DeSante.

DeSante and Iliana looked at her, and both went silent and still.

"Iliana, is everything okay?" Serena asked.

Iliana stepped away from DeSante. "Just confirming the president's plans."

Serena knew his unofficial reason for the visit was to pressure her again about merging Acacia and Icarus. Using the guise of offering his congratulations was flimsy.

Serena was firm in her resolve not to allow her country to become a dictatorship, least of all with Demetrius DeSante at the helm.

"I will take my leave," Iliana said. She glowered at DeSante and Serena hid her chuckle. Later, she would ask her cousin what their conversation had been about. She sensed a certain tension between the two. Perhaps it was the early stages of their relationship and they were smoothing out the kinks.

Serena and DeSante sat. Serena's steward rolled in a cart of tea and cookies.

"Thank you for meeting with me. I would like to extend my congratulations to you. Our previous meetings have not been productive. I am hoping that will change now that you have power of your own," DeSante said.

Their previous meetings had been forced by him and she had been unprepared for them. "I do not like to be manipulated."

"I have an offer for you that you might find more pleasing than others under consideration."

She doubted he had anything new to bring to the table. She gestured for him to continue.

"We will arrange an alliance without a marriage between us to muddy the water."

"I would like an alliance. Acacia is not spoiling for war."

"Neither is Icarus," DeSante said.

She didn't believe him. He wasn't looking for a war, but he would not turn away from any provocation. In her experience, provocation could be anything: a ship drifting too close to Icarus, an unintended flyover by a commercial plane slightly off its route or unfair trade arrangements. "Would our alliance leave me as queen of Acacia and the Assembly in place?"

"You would be queen in name and the Assembly would retain some limited powers."

Meaning she would be a figurehead with no power and no voice to speak for the people of Acacia. "I do not think that is an arrangement that will work for my country."

DeSante moved closer to her. Her guards were in the room, otherwise she might have felt threatened. "You will regret an alliance with the king of Rizari."

She would personally, but she believed it would be best for her country. "They have favorable trade arrangements with most of Europe and Asia. The king is offering us a part in those arrangements."

DeSante shook his head. "A part? Meaning you will sell what you have to him and he will take the lion's share of the profits."

Serena wouldn't listen to DeSante tear down every reason she was leaning toward a union with Rizari. "If you wish for me to consider your position, tell me why you are threatened by this arrangement."

DeSante leaned back in his chair. He regarded her carefully. Would he lay his cards on the table? Serena could guess why he didn't want her to marry King Warrington. The two countries being united would put Icarus in the weaker position. A man like DeSante did not like being in the weaker position. "The king of Rizari wants control of the Mediterranean. He will take Acacia and it will put him geographically closer to Icarus. When Acacia and your father provided a buffer, I had some degree of confidence that Warrington would keep his distance. My country does not want to waste resources defending ourselves from Rizari. We have more pressing goals and objectives."

His explanation was what she had expected. "I do not believe that the king of Rizari has plans to attack Icarus."

DeSante stared at her as if she were daft. "You have a lot to learn, Your Highness. Your naïveté is refreshing, but I won't like to see you taken advantage of, especially when it affects me."

"I am not alone in making decisions. I have my advisers and the Assembly."

"I will ask you to consider another offer that involves your secretary."

Serena was surprised he would bring up Iliana. Did this have to do with their blossoming relationship? She had no opposition to it as long as Iliana was happy. "What about Iliana?" She worked to keep her temper calm. She would protect her cousin at all costs.

"I believe her loyalty to you is preventing her from being loyal to me."

"Why would she be loyal to you?" Serena asked.

"I have power and am in a position to protect her."

"As am I. I would never allow someone to hurt Iliana. She is family."

"But you must realize that you do not know everything that happens in this region. I receive more intel. She is important and when critical information comes to light, she will need protection."

Serena didn't follow. Was he referring to the assassins who had killed her father and sister? "Tell me what danger Iliana is in and I will see to it that she is safe."

DeSante shook his head. "Only I can ensure her safety."

"You seem certain of that."

"I am."

Was he making a threat against her? It didn't sound as if he was implying he would harm Iliana, yet he was withholding important information. What game was he playing? "If information comes to my attention that makes me fear for Iliana's safety, I will see to it that I counter any attempts to harm her. But if you are simply maneuvering to have a personal relationship with her, I will tell you that I have no objection to her being friendly with you, as friendly as she would like. You have helped her on at least one occasion. For that, I thank you. But her life and her choices are in her hands. I will not stand between her and happiness, wherever she thinks she may find it."

"Would you consider brokering a marriage arrangement between myself and Iliana in exchange for an alliance between our countries?" he asked.

Serena blinked, feeling more than a little thrown. He could have knocked her over with a feather. "You want to marry Iliana?"

"Yes."

A dozen emotions played through her. She would not pressure Iliana into accepting any proposal or offer her to DeSante in exchange for the union. It let her off the hook, but Serena would not sacrifice Iliana's happiness for her own. Given her personal struggles, she wouldn't put another woman in that position. "My answer is the same. It is my cousin's choice to do what she wants with her life."

DeSante stood. "I will not take more of your time. Thank you for clarifying your position on Iliana. With regard to King Warrington, your future betrothed, I hope that you are correct and that he doesn't have war on his mind. When you realize I am your best option, I only hope it will not be too late to come to terms."

Chapter 8

Serena sat next to Iliana at the head of the table in the formal dining room. They were waiting for her lunch meeting to begin. Her uncle and her advisers wanted to speak with her. Given that she was newly crowned, it made sense to touch base on the most important issues the Acacian Assembly was working on.

Iliana handed Serena her tablet. "Bad news."

Serena took the device from her. Splashed across the local news website was a split photo depicting her with Casimir and King Warrington. The headline said, in bold capital letters, QUEEN'S NEW LOVERS.

Serena groaned and scanned the article. The picture of her and the king had been taken in the rose garden before her coronation. His arms were around her. The second image was a compromising shot of her and Casimir. Her face was visible, while his was shaded. It was hard to tell what exactly she and Casimir had been doing, but it didn't look innocent.

"Can I ignore it and hope it goes away?" Serena asked.

"Is it Casimir?" Iliana asked.

"Yes."

"Serena, you have to be more careful." Her rebuke was obviously out of concern.

"I made a mistake. I shouldn't have kissed him in the rose garden. But it may have been for the last time. He didn't come by last night after the coronation." And he hadn't returned her messages. Was it over? She couldn't imagine him abruptly ending the relationship, but she was unsure and saddened.

"Is there a way to spin the story, perhaps explain that he's a friend and the angle of the picture makes it look worse than it is?" Iliana asked.

Serena didn't like lying, but stating outright that she had been kissing another man on castle grounds would create massive problems for her administration and for her arrangement with King Warrington. "I should at least discuss it with the king."

Serena sent him a message, asking him to call when he had a free moment.

The door to the dining room opened and her uncle entered. "Serena, you are looking lovely this morning," her uncle said. He greeted her with a hug.

Two more of her advisers entered and sat to her left.

"Your Highness, I don't know if you've seen the paper this morning," one of her advisers started.

Now was the time to stop this story from spinning out of control. "I have. I think it is a flagrant attempt to discredit me."

Her uncle took Iliana's tablet from her and narrowed his eyes at the picture. "Have you spoken to King Warrington about this yet?"

"No, but I will," Serena said. She was tired of being questioned and prodded. She was capable of handling some matters on her terms.

Did anyone recognize Casimir? It would be ideal if she could keep his name out of this. Serena didn't know where they stood, but dragging him into a royal scandal would be the death of their relationship.

"I want to stay on topic today. I will not address rumors about my personal life," Serena said, channeling Iliana's advice to remember her position and stand her ground. Not that she had any idea where she stood. Her uncle cleared his throat as her remaining two advisers entered the room. "The purpose of this meeting is to discuss your personal life and how it will impact Acacia."

She was the queen of Acacia and that held power. Letting herself be steamrolled by her advisers or lowering her head and nodding in agreement to the king of Rizari's demands was unacceptable.

Her uncle slid a thick document in front of her. "Legal has reviewed the terms and conditions and marked the clauses that need our attention."

"Is this the king's marriage proposal?" she asked, glancing at the document. Not that she'd had high hopes from Samuel Warrington's proposal, as he had failed on the romance side of their courtship spectacularly, but this was dreadful, not even conducted in person.

"Not a marriage proposal exactly. The forms to become part of Rizari. Our laws must be followed and with your approval, the merger will be voted on by the

Assembly. We've polled the members of the Assembly and we believe we'll have majority agreement."

"I haven't seen this document before," Serena said, feeling caught unaware.

"We didn't want to worry you with anything before it was reviewed," her uncle said. His voice was gentle and in direct contrast to how she was feeling.

Worry her? She had been worried about this marriage since learning of its possibility. "I will need to read this." And have more time.

Her uncle frowned. "We don't want the king to think we are not interested. The picture in the news this morning will start rumors and he might decide to believe them."

The king couldn't think she would readily agree to anything he proposed. Unless he had deluded himself, he couldn't believe she was eager to become his wife—or hand over the reins of her country. "I will address this matter with the king."

"A few days won't make a difference," her uncle said.

A few days? She'd need a month. Or an entire quarter of a year. Her heartbeat quickened and she felt left out of an important conversation. Did everyone else in the room know about this contract? Was she the last to receive it? Why hadn't she been told the moment it had arrived so that she could read it and bring her concerns to the king?

She knew the answer and it saddened her. It was not brought to her because no one felt she was capable. They believed her only asset to her country was her gender because she could parlay it into a marriage to King Warrington.

"We'll start the marketing campaign immediately.

We'll need you to pose for pictures with King Warrington in our country and in his," her uncle said.

A marketing campaign? "Does the king know about this?"

The men and women around the table exchanged looks. Her uncle answered. "Yes. He thought it was a good idea for Acacians to see him and Rizari as an ally. Same for the people in Rizari. We want them to trust you."

Trust her? She wasn't the one drafting documents and negotiating with someone else's life! She took a sip of the water on the table in front of her. The room felt small and crowded. "I need time."

When half the room started speaking at once, her uncle held up his hand to silence them. "Please give me and my niece a few moments alone."

After waiting for Serena's nod, Iliana left reluctantly.

Her uncle might be upset about the picture in the news, but Serena was still the queen. She could hold her ground. If she couldn't with her uncle, how could she with King Warrington? Or Demetrius DeSante?

When they were alone, Serena looked between her uncle and the document. "You should have told me about this sooner. I feel blindsided."

"And I feel blindsided by the knowledge that you're rendezvousing with Casimir Cullen in the rose garden," her uncle said.

Her uncle had recognized Casimir in the picture. King Warrington may have as well. "Casimir and I are friends. He saved my life."

"That doesn't mean you should sleep with him."

Outrage surged hot and heavy in her blood. "That is not an appropriate way for you to speak to me."

"Yet I don't hear you denying it."

How had he known she had spent the night with Casimir? "What I do with my free time is none of your concern."

Her uncle appeared frustrated. "You are wrong, Serena. You are the queen now. Every moment of your time is the concern of the kingdom. Everyone wants to know what you're doing and who you're doing it with. If you're smart, you'll stay away from Casimir Cullen and any other man who decides to take advantage of your trusting nature."

"Does that mean I should stay away from Demetrius DeSante, too? Because he visited this morning. Do I have to worry that someone will accuse me of sleeping with him? Is that what I am? A woman who sleeps with every man she comes into contact with?"

"Calm down, Serena. The president of Icarus went through official channels to meet with you. From the looks of your meeting with Casimir Cullen, he did not."

Serena held up her hands. "I won't discuss Casimir with you. I need more time to think about the proposed arrangement with King Warrington."

"You don't have more time. Demetrius DeSante is not backing down. He's made his position clear."

"He thinks that Rizari will use Acacia to attack Icarus after my marriage to King Warrington," Serena said.

Her uncle quirked a brow. "That's ridiculous."

"How do you know?" she asked. Had her uncle spoken to Warrington about that issue directly?

"King Warrington isn't spoiling for war. He wants to merge our countries for the mutual benefit of both nations. Putting Acacia in the middle of a war wouldn't benefit us."

Serena didn't know what to think about Samuel Warrington's intentions. "I'll need to speak with the king directly."

And Casimir. She needed to call him and warn him that their relationship was no longer just a matter of speculation. If the media believed the picture held any truth or if a story was buried inside it, they would dig, looking for information about Casimir and their affair. What other damning evidence was out there waiting to be revealed?

Casimir swore aloud when he saw his picture on the front page of the newspaper. From the angle and graininess of the shot, it wasn't obvious who he was, nor was it obvious what he and Serena were doing, but it would raise questions.

His phone rang. It was Serena. He had missed several of her calls, having been working on some issues involving Icarus and Rizari. And since he didn't know where he stood with Serena, he had wanted to think about his next move.

He answered with a greeting, trying to sound casual.

"Have you seen the news this morning? There's a picture of us in the rose garden."

"I saw it," he said.

"Are you upset?" she asked.

It would drive a wedge between her and King Warrington, which helped his cause. But he didn't want to be exposed to scrutiny by reporters and King Warrington either. "I wanted to wait and talk to you about it."

"The picture is hard to see clearly. I hope it will blow

over without the media making it into an ordeal. Where are you now?" she asked.

"In Thorntree." He hadn't left Acacia yet. He hadn't been back to see his mother in a couple of weeks. He dreaded seeing what condition she was in and having to explain why it seemed no progress had been made. "Come by the castle?" she asked.

He wasn't sure how to answer.

"You didn't come over last night," she said.

"You're the queen. That changes things."

She sighed loudly. "It doesn't have to. Not yet."

The worry in her voice struck him. "It's not a good idea for us to be seen together. Why don't you meet me at the beach house?"

"Thirty minutes? Key is in the lockbox attached to the railing." She gave him the key code to open it and the code to disable the house alarm.

"I got it. See you then."

Casimir drove to the beach house, plotting his next move. He and DeSante were still working diligently to destroy King Warrington, looking for solid evidence of his involvement in the death of Casimir's father and uncle and proof of his launching a smear campaign against his mother. A scandal could bring their plans to a crashing halt. Problem was, he wasn't sure he could stay away from Serena if he tried.

Casimir entered the beach house and circled the front room, not touching anything, but taking in Serena's decor. She liked pale, soft colors and delicate things. He took the stairs to her bedroom. Her bed was covered by a white comforter with ruffles. Her curtains were a lightweight, shiny material. On the porch were fresh potted plants, some in bloom, and an empty easel.

She had another easel in her room, this one holding a painting of the sea. He could see the talent in her work.

"Casimir?"

He heard her voice from the main floor. Heard her drop her keys in the turquoise bowl on the entryway table.

"Upstairs," he called.

Serena ascended the stairs and appeared in the doorway. "I have terrible news I wanted to tell you in person."

"Worse than the picture?"

She nodded and looked on the verge of tears. "King Warrington sent over the agreement to unify our countries."

He didn't like that, and not just because he wanted to see King Warrington fail. "Unify your countries, meaning you marrying him."

Serena nodded. She seemed out of sorts, as if she had not fully considered the implications.

"What are you planning to do?" he asked. He had a response in mind. She would not sign the papers and she would stand strong and run her country alone.

She tossed a folder on the top of her dresser. "Read it if you want. I'll work something out that leaves me with power and ensures Acacia isn't swallowed into Rizari."

She was considering signing the agreement. She would marry him. Casimir hated that on so many levels.

The truth rose in his throat. Could he tell Serena the truth about who he was and what he'd planned? If he did, she might never trust him again. He didn't have the proof of Samuel Warrington's guilt and confessing his motives now could ruin what he and DeSante had planned and worked for. "Have you considered doing nothing?"

"Doing nothing? Like ignoring it?"

"You'd buy time." Time he would use to topple King Warrington. Though Serena would be angry that he had hidden his identity, she may be pleased to have control of her country without threats of war. She would rule Acacia without a marriage or interference from Warrington or DeSante and she would forgive him. Eventually.

"If I do nothing, Rizari and Icarus may make a play to take over Acacia. We'll be in the middle of a war. There will be casualties. I couldn't live with myself."

"You think the king of Rizari would attack Acacia unprovoked?" He hadn't considered that a possibility. Should he?

She ran her fingers through her hair. "I don't know what to think."

Casimir sat on the edge of the bed. "I think you should tell the president and the king you need time. You're still grieving for your father and your sister. I think that's enough of a reason."

"My uncle thinks postponing anything will show me and, by extension, Acacia as weak. Besides, I've spoken to King Warrington. After the picture went public I had no choice. He is coming for dinner tonight so we might discuss the matter privately and in detail."

No! Time alone with King Warrington was the last thing Casimir wanted for Serena. "Will he show up?" Perhaps if he reminded her of his past behavior he could keep them apart. Though he would have time before the actual marriage, he couldn't tolerate the idea of Serena promised to another man or in another man's arms. Especially a monster like Warrington.

"I don't know."

She moved toward him and he pulled her into his arms where she belonged. She laid her head against his chest. "You'll be okay. It will work out."

"I have to accept my duty." She looked up at him. "But I'm not married yet. I'm not engaged. For a few more days, I'll be a single woman."

She shifted, looped her hands around his neck and drew him down to her mouth. She pressed her lips to his and moaned. He was well aware of what she wanted.

DeSante wanted him to consider every angle before making a move that could be a game changer, but he couldn't do that with Serena now. Sleeping with her would have nothing to do with the plan and everything to do with desire and lust.

"The bed is right behind you," she said.

White candles in glass surrounded the space, helping to set the seductive mood. He hadn't planned for this to happen and while sometimes being caught in the moment could be great, she was worthy of so much, more than he could give her. "Let me light the candles." A small gesture.

She nodded and handed him a lighter from a drawer in the bedside table. She deserved romance and affection. When the last candle was burning, he laid the lighter on her dresser.

He looked at her in the dresser mirror, kneeling on the bed, watching him. He turned and they collided. In a frantic grabbing of clothes and unfastening of buttons, they tumbled onto the mattress.

"Do you need anything?" he asked. The desire to make this moment perfect and right for her was preeminent in his mind.

"Everything I need is here in this bed."

Casimir produced a condom from his wallet and slid it on. He kissed her, claiming her lips how he would claim her body.

"Why can't I have this? You and me, in this house. No crown, no title, no responsibilities?"

Because they both had crowns, titles and responsibilities. His were unclaimed. Could he confess to her his true identity? She was trusting him enough to sleep with him in her beach house. The impact wasn't lost on him. "Because that is not our fate."

She kissed him. "Then we'll pretend for now that we can have this together."

He bought into the idea because he knew that his confession would ruin her. Though it had not started this way, he had come to care for her. Deeply. He wanted her to be his. Some distant thought made him wonder if making love with her would prevent her from agreeing to marry Warrington. "Open your legs for me."

She slid her knees apart and he positioned his body over hers. His tip nudged at her entrance and he let out a low moan. "You're so wet," he said.

"I've wanted you for so long."

As he came into her, she spread her thighs wider. Her body beneath his was delicious and lithe. As he moved, it seemed to be in time with the waves as they lapped against the beach.

He rocked slowly and he loved the sensations of filling her. Their eyes met in an intensely intimate moment.

She lifted her hips, encouraging him to move faster. He responded to her silent plea, delving deep. Her fingernails dug into his shoulders and she closed her eyes, crying out her release.

Casimir groaned and finished moments later.

He collapsed on top of her and kissed her neck and collarbone. When he rolled away, he excused himself to dispose of the condom. When he returned, she was sitting on the bed, looking out her window at the water.

He came behind her and gathered her close, letting her settle against his naked body.

"I have to meet with Warrington in an hour."

He didn't want her to go. He didn't want this night to end. "Call and tell him you can't make it," Casimir said, hating the idea of Serena meeting Warrington tonight. He wanted this night to belong to them.

Serena groaned. "Don't tempt me. You know I can't. It would raise too many questions. I've been given enough passes."

He didn't think she'd been given anything. She had been expected to behave like a veteran leader of her country when she'd had less than a month in the position. She'd had to bury her emotions with her father and sister, and ignore the fear that multiple attempts had been made on her life and the fact that she was about to marry a stranger.

The marriage proposal had been delivered. It was up to her to sign and seal it.

Casimir hadn't intended to use sex to stop her. No room for regrets or second thoughts or the residual guilt he felt over his initial interest in her and his plans to use her. He had genuine feelings for her now and sleeping with her had been a natural progression of their relationship.

"I could stay here forever, but I have to return to the castle. I need to change before my dinner with King Warrington."

"Wear clothes you have here," he said.

"Like shorts and a tank top? I think that would be inappropriate."

"I think you should let him see the real you."

Serena pushed her hair away from her face and looked at him, bewildered. "You believe that."

He wouldn't have said it if he didn't. "Yes."

"Even though it would turn him off even more?"

"Even if that were true." If King Warrington shut Serena out of his life, then Casimir couldn't use her to gather more information about the king. The idea upset him less than the thought of losing her to Warrington.

Serena deserved a chance at real happiness with a man who could love and care about her.

Like him.

He threw the brakes on his thoughts. Like him? He didn't want to marry Serena. That hadn't been part of the plan. He cared about her, but he didn't see how he could have avoided that. She was so shockingly authentic and kind, he'd liked her immediately.

But he wouldn't fall for her. He didn't want a complicated love match. Love sharpened emotions like jealousy, anger and resentment.

Serena climbed out of bed and started dressing. He watched her with lazy fascination.

She circled the bed and kissed him. "You can stay as long as you'd like."

But not forever. Their romance was ending and he needed to turn his full attention to his revenge.

Serena smelled Casimir on her skin. Could King Warrington? She'd had enough time to change her clothes, but not to shower. King Warrington was waiting for her in the dining room and she needed to be prepared to discuss matters of grave importance: their marriage, their future, and the photo of her and Casimir.

Serena entered the dining room. A tense energy charged the air. She and Warrington's rocky relationship was about to be dragged through a storm.

Serena sat across from him. She had arranged for dinner to be served, but she guessed that neither of them had much of an appetite. "I assume you saw the picture in the media."

King Warrington's face was drawn into a hard line. "I saw it."

"He is a friend."

"Tell me his name."

Serena hedged. "I want to respect his privacy."

King Warrington seemed indifferent, as if he hadn't expected an answer to his question. "Maybe this isn't an ideal situation, but perhaps we understand each other better than I thought."

Serena didn't catch his meaning. "I don't follow."

"If you want to date other men, I don't have a problem with that."

Her heart sank. He wanted to use her indiscretion to justify his own philandering. "Even after we're married?" she confirmed.

"Right. I would ask that you be more discreet. I don't want my wife's picture splashed all over the media. It makes me look foolish. But carry on your affairs in private and I will turn a blind eye to them."

"You will expect that I turn a blind eye to your affairs as well?"

"Naturally."

Serena felt sick. She had slept with Casimir and

while she knew that was out of line, she had drawn a distinction between her relationship with Casimir and her arrangement with King Warrington. After she and Warrington were engaged, she would end her affair with Casimir. "Then you and I won't have a relationship?" Just a marriage on paper?

"We can play that however you wish. I will need an heir, of course, so perhaps you'd have to tolerate me for a few nights." He sounded repulsed by the idea.

Serena shook her head, trying to dash away her confusion. She had not expected this conversation. "I had a strange visit from President DeSante after my coronation."

"He did not attend the coronation in person."

"He sent a representative. But he was interested in speaking with me about our…merger." She wouldn't call it a marriage. Not after Warrington's declaration that they would openly cheat on each other.

"What did you tell him?"

"That we were working on it."

"Then he knows that if he wants to strike, it should be soon."

"If he were to strike before our merger, would you not protect Acacia? You have much to lose if Icarus occupies my country."

"You have more to lose," King Warrington said.

Then Samuel wouldn't help her country without the bonds of an official union. That didn't sit right with her. Wouldn't a man of honor protect Acacia no matter what, given what he stood to gain? "Demetrius DeSante seemed to believe that you would initiate a war against him once our countries were allied."

Warrington was quiet. Serena watched his mouth,

his eyes and his posture for any signs of truth to the statement. Several moments passed and Serena didn't fill them with idle prattle. She stared at Warrington, waiting for him to speak.

"It's a different world once we are merged."

Not answering the question. He was withholding something. "You believe Icarus will be a threat once we are united?" Serena asked.

"Don't you believe him to be a threat now?" Warrington asked.

Serena tilted her head. "He wants an alliance with us badly enough to make threats, but I don't think he would let those threats escalate into war. He has to know if he starts a war, neighbors will take sides and since he's made enemies with his hardline tactics, many will side with us. Perhaps not by sending troops or aid, but they may cut ties with Icarus completely, leaving them isolated."

"That's quite an analysis from someone new to the political arena."

Why did everything from his mouth sound like an insult? Warrington had an agenda and though Serena didn't know what it was, she was sure that whatever Warrington had planned, his needs would come first.

The king plowed his hands through his hair. "This is not how I envisioned our first date alone. I was hoping we could talk about more pleasant things. I suppose with you, that's impossible."

Serena wanted to throttle Warrington. It wasn't a good omen for their arrangement. Every time they were together, their relationship grew a little more hostile. She didn't know how to respond to Samuel's comment.

She stood. Listening to his insults was a waste of

time. "I suppose that gives you more time to spend with your girlfriends." Serena fled the room, regretting leaving Casimir at the beach house and regretting meeting with Warrington at all.

"A peace summit?" Serena asked.

Iliana set a leather folio in front of her. "The proposal arrived today. The summit is being organized by, get this, Demetrius DeSante." Iliana's excitement gave away how much she liked the president of Icarus.

His offer to marry Iliana replayed through her mind, but Serena wasn't sure what to think of it. Until she understood DeSante's angle, his actions were subject to suspicion.

"He sent this to you directly?" Serena asked.

Iliana nodded. "He's invited you and King Warrington to meet with him in Langun at a friend's ski resort."

Serena didn't understand DeSante's latest ploy. "Does DeSante want you on the premises as well?"

Iliana's eyes were bright. "Yes."

"I don't have a problem with you and DeSante seeing each other. My problem is that I won't go to this meeting in Langun and be blindsided. What does DeSante have planned? Has he said anything to you?"

"He seems like he genuinely wants to meet with you and King Warrington on neutral ground and no country is more neutral than Langun."

"Can you see what else you can find out?"

"Absolutely. Give me a list of questions and I'll call him."

Serena didn't like forcing Iliana to be the intermediary, but Iliana and DeSante had a good rapport and Serena would take advantage of it. That was as far as she would allow herself to request anything of Iliana in regard to DeSante.

After a busy day, Casimir met Serena in her beach house. Wrapped in Casimir's arms, Serena told him about the summit meeting in Langun.

"I hope you'll go," he said.

Serena groaned. "You sound like Iliana."

"It's a good opportunity. The three of you can speak on neutral ground."

"Warrington hasn't agreed to attend."

"If he finds out that you and DeSante are meeting, he won't miss it."

That was true. The three of them were circling each other, looking for allies and bonds. "I suppose it can't hurt. If DeSante tries to strong-arm me, I'll leave."

"That sounds reasonable," Casimir said, kissing the top of her head.

"Here's the follow-up question. Will you go with me?"

Casimir shifted her so he could look at her. "Of course. I'd love to."

Serena wished she had the same relaxed response to the summit that Iliana and Casimir seemed to. She couldn't shake the feeling that DeSante or Warrington would drop bombs on her.

"Are political and work conversations over for the day?" Casimir asked, shifting on top of her.

She slipped her hand around the back of his neck. "Conversations over. Time for some relaxation."

As their lips met, Serena turned her worries off and turned her body over to Casimir.

As Casimir had predicted, King Warrington had been quick to agree to the summit once Serena had informed him she was attending. Serena and the king's relationship remained tense.

Given the conversations and negotiations over the next twenty-four hours, she expected tense to shift into troubled.

Iliana was staying in the resort's main hotel and Serena was booked in a private château. Casimir had made his own travel arrangements, flying into Langun. He had texted Serena when his plane had landed. He was driving directly to the château. It was risky inviting him along and they would keep his presence a secret, but Serena needed his strength and his support. She needed him with her.

Her bedroom in the château overlooked the mountains. While the view wasn't as comforting as the sea, Langun was a beautiful country. DeSante had picked a calm, relaxing place for them to speak. Smart man. Then again, she had never questioned DeSante's intelligence. Only his morality.

Serena turned from the window and jolted when she came face-to-face with Casimir. She hadn't heard him come in or come up the stairs. He pressed a hand over her mouth to keep her from making a sound that would alert her guards.

"How did you get in here?" she asked.

"I used the front door." He was already pulling at her scarf and vest, tossing them to the floor.

"Did anyone see you?"

Casimir shook his head. "Did he try anything?" he asked, looking her over as if the evidence would be written on her clothes.

"I assume you mean Warrington, but no, I haven't seen him since I arrived."

She enjoyed the streak of possessiveness that whipped across Casimir's face. She removed her sweater and let it drop to the floor.

"Let's turn on the fire. I'm cold." The gas fireplace, located on the other end of the room, was operated by a remote.

"I'll keep you warm."

He folded her into his arms and she inhaled the scent of him. They stumbled to the bed, a tangle of arms and legs and kisses.

"I want you, Serena. I…"

She unfastened the buttons on his shirt. "You what?"

He stilled her hands, taking them in his. "I'm falling for you."

His words sucked the air from her lungs. She felt the same for him, but she didn't feel capable of returning the words. Too much was at risk. She couldn't back up the words with a commitment and it felt wrong to say them.

"I think of you when I wake up. I think of you when I'm sleeping alone. I miss you when we're not together."

The words sang to her, a bittersweet melody. She had found someone she trusted and cared for, who made her happy, and they couldn't be together.

She lifted her mouth kissed him. The kiss spoke the words she couldn't say and her body moved with his. "We're together now, let's make the most of it."

That night, while Serena lay in bed with her laptop open, Casimir sat on the edge of the mattress. "Could you see our arrangement as more than temporary?"

He hadn't planned to tell Serena he was falling for her, but the words, the truth, had sprung from his lips.

He had been disappointed that she hadn't returned the notion. She'd made love to him as if she cared for him, as if he was important to her, but that could be reading between the lines. Casimir didn't know what to think of her or of their relationship.

"So much of my life is not my own."

It could be hers. Why couldn't she see how far she had come in the past several weeks? How much further she would go in the next months? She had grown into a leader, and every day she was stronger, more dignified and confident. Casimir didn't believe she could be easily manipulated. She had held her own against a powerful dictator and a lying, murdering king.

Why couldn't she see that she could rule her country with grace and strength? That she didn't need someone at her side, telling her what to do, guiding Acacia forward? Casimir dispensed what advice he could. "When you meet with DeSante and Warrington, you need to remember that you are their equal in every way. You owe them nothing."

Serena closed her laptop. "Those are fighting words."

"I don't want you to fight with DeSante or Warrington. But I want you to stand your ground. Take what you want and give nothing, unless it is something you want to give."

"Is that so?" She set her laptop on the nightstand and stood from the bed. She positioned herself in front of him and pulled his shirt over his head. She ran her hands over his shoulders and down his arms. The past several times they'd had sex, he had done most of the work, seeing that she was taken care of, picking the positions she liked best. He'd wanted her relaxed and he wanted to win her over. The nagging thought that she would sleep with Warrington would not let go.

She gripped his biceps in her hands. "Let me take what I want now. I want you."

She wasn't quite smiling, but the corners of her mouth were turned up. Her eyes seemed to see deep into his soul. She had his head turned around. When he was alone, he could think clearly, but when they were together, his resolve and his intentions flew out the window and he only wanted her. In his bed and in his life.

Giving into the attraction, knowing he couldn't fight it, he let her push him back on the bed. She threw her leg astride him. With her knees on either side of his hips she lowered her mouth to his neck.

A sound of contentment escaped her lips and he went from intrigued and amused to rock hard.

He didn't reach for her. He didn't make advances to hasten it. He watched her, propped on his elbows, enjoying the show. "I had hoped this would happen. That you would see."

"See what?" she asked, and kissed his chest.

"That we are good together. That you have power over me. Power of your own."

She lifted her head and met his gaze. Taking the hem of her shirt in her hands, she pulled it over her head and tossed it on the ground. She removed her clothes, item by item, taking her time. When she was finished undressing, she unbuckled his belt.

She climbed into bed and threw some of the pillows to the ground. The bed had at least a dozen and they would be in the way. He and Serena needed room to maneuver. She slipped beneath the sheets. Casimir joined her, but he didn't remove his pants.

His eyes were fastened to hers. "There are some lines that once they are crossed, there is no returning."

"I don't want to return. I like where this is going," she said.

Serena grinned. She unzipped his pants and withdrew him. Her mouth came over him, hot and wet and slow. As she took him deep, he counted backward in his head, trying to control his release.

But Serena was persistent. Her hand and the suction of her mouth felt incredible. She moved faster, lifting and lowering her head. He touched the ends of her hair, threaded his fingers through the long strands, tangling them.

She moaned and the vibrations shot around his erection. Another few noises from her throat and she brought him to completion.

She moved onto the bed beside him. Casimir could have fallen asleep like that, with her tucked under his arm, her soft hair brushing the bare skin of his neck and her sweet scent surrounding him. But their time was limited and he had brought her a gift. "I have something for you."

He left the warmth of the bed and grabbed his duffel bag. He removed the navy velvet box. The necklace inside had been his mother's. It was a gift from his father to her on their wedding night. The king of Rizari's seal was engraved on the back of it.

If Serena recognized the seal as authentic, she would be curious where Casimir had acquired such a rare treasure. Perhaps he wanted to tip her off, to expose his lies, so they could muddle through those dark waters and face the future with truth between them.

Serena opened the box and gasped. She removed the

necklace from the satin liner inside, and held it up, letting it dangle between her fingers as she looked at it.

The necklace was platinum and diamonds. The setting was antique, but the style was becoming more popular. "What is this? It looks like there is a story here," Serena said. As the necklace spun on her fingers, she stopped and looked at the seal on the back.

"It's my family crest. The necklace belonged to my mother."

Serena's lips parted. "I don't know what to say. I am so touched by this beautiful gift."

It was the one item of value his mother had taken with her when she'd fled Rizari. She could have sold it, but she had been concerned someone would think it was stolen and she'd be arrested or her identity would be revealed because of it. "Take it. Wear it. It's yours."

Casimir was playing with fire. If Serena wore it and Warrington saw it, especially the back of it, he would question Serena about it. The necklace had to have been reported stolen due to the value of the diamond.

If Serena admitted the necklace was a gift from Casimir, this game would come to a head. Serena would know the truth and Casimir needed her to believe him and forgive him for keeping it from her.

"I can't accept this. It's so precious."

"Please wear it. For me."

He looped the delicate chain around her neck. She held her hair up while he fastened it.

Casimir reclined on the bed and Serena moved into his arms.

"What would you say if I told you I want to ride you?" Serena asked.

He tensed as jolts of anticipation shocked him. "I'd

be surprised to hear such frank words from your lips, but I would happily oblige."

She shifted on top of him. Casimir fumbled to find a condom quickly. He rolled it on and let Serena take charge. She rose above him, wiggling into position and sinking her body onto his. When he was deep inside her, she rocked her hips.

He held onto her, but let her set the pace. Like it was every time with her, emotions and feelings assailed him. Casimir placed his hand where their bodies were joined and moved them the way she liked, evoking as much pleasure from her as possible.

Release was just out of reach.

A tap on the door had her freezing. "Just a minute." Her eyes wide with panic, she rolled away from Casimir.

"Serena? It's Iliana."

Casimir had half a mind to let Iliana see them. She knew they were carrying on an affair. She would keep Serena's secret, wouldn't she? Though DeSante hadn't elaborated on the subject, he seemed to trust Iliana and DeSante trusted almost no one.

Serena gestured toward the bathroom. Though Casimir felt otherwise, he did as she asked. Still sporting a raging hard-on, Casimir darted into it and closed the door lightly.

Serena pulled on her robe and checked her appearance in the mirror. Her cheeks were flushed and her hair was a mess. She opened the door to her cousin.

Iliana was clutching a tablet in her hands. "I'm sorry to bother you, but I was surfing the web and I found something you should see."

Serena braced herself. Iliana turned the computer toward her and she gasped.

Posted on the main webpage of a local media site in Acacia was a picture of her and Casimir at the wedding in Elion. This time, the photo clearly showed him and he had been named in the accompanying article.

"How should we respond?" Iliana asked.

"To what?" What could she say that would explain away a picture?

"The press will want an explanation. This picture makes it look like you and Casimir Cullen are involved. King Warrington will ask. What should we say? The press knows he was the man in the rose garden." Iliana sounded distressed.

Serena didn't want a lurid story about her and Casimir spread over the internet. "This picture was taken out of context. We were photographed at the wedding of the Duke and Duchess of Elion. I spoke to many people that weekend."

That statement was loaded with lies, but she had no choice. To protect herself and Casimir, they had to deny their involvement with each other.

Iliana looked at the picture. "I will communicate that. But I have a hard time believing it and since the press connected the picture of the mystery man in the rose garden to Casimir, it will be a hard sell."

"We'll tell the press we're friends. Nothing more," Serena countered.

"You're protesting too much."

Serena wasn't great with lies on her feet, but when she caught the thread of one she hung on for dear life. "I know this could turn into a media circus and an outright scandal."

Iliana straightened. "I'll speak to your press secretary and see if we can't minimize the fallout. Would you like me to hire a local photographer to take pictures of you and King Warrington to counter what the news might print about you and Casimir?"

A good idea, even if the thought of acting as if she were in love with King Warrington made her sick. Could she fake that emotion? "That would be great. Please see if King Warrington is amenable."

When Iliana left and Serena closed the door, Casimir stepped out of the bathroom. He looked flushed.

"Hot in there?" she asked.

"Cold, actually."

He was still naked. It turned her on. "You know what game we're playing."

"I do," he said. "But sometimes, the lines between lies and the truth become blurred and it's hard to remember what's real."

"That's why we need to stay focused on the endgame," Serena said.

"The only endgame I can think about is the one tonight," he said, gesturing toward the bed. He scooped her into his arms and plopped her onto the soft sheets. Parting her robe, he buried himself in her and Serena lost herself in his intensity and passion.

Iliana muted the television when she heard the knock on her door. "Come in."

Her suite at the resort was top-notch. She was having a great time. Their host had mentioned that he'd have his butler check on her before bed to see if she needed anything.

Instead of the resort's butler, Demetrius DeSante

entered her room. He motioned to his guards to stay outside.

Iliana rose to her feet, grateful she was wearing fleece pajamas that, while not overly attractive, were decent. "Hi, Demetrius. Is everything okay?"

His dark eyes held her. "Everything is fine now that I can see that you are safe."

"Why wouldn't I be safe?" she asked.

Demetrius's eyes narrowed. "Many reasons. But I did not come here to upset you. I wanted to make sure you were pleased with your accommodations."

She shrugged. "Sure. I made the arrangements. This is a nice place." Television, internet, spa-like bathroom and room service. Everything she needed for a relaxing weekend.

Demetrius clasped his hands behind his back. "Would you be more comfortable in one of the châteaus?"

Iliana hesitated. She had been to Serena's château that night and it was gorgeous. The details and the luxury amenities were top of the line. "I am fine here."

"I don't want you to be fine. I want you to be happy. Pleased."

"What are you suggesting?" She could have stayed in Serena's château, but Serena liked her privacy and was insistent on having time alone. It was when Serena did her best thinking, so Iliana didn't press the issue.

"Come stay in my château, in your own bedroom, but close enough that my guards can watch over you and I can know you are safe."

Iliana wanted to say yes. She wanted to agree, toss her few items into her suitcase and follow him out the door. But how would that look to Serena and King Warrington? There could be no divided loyalties. "Your offer is very generous, but I need to remain here."

DeSante sighed. "Then you leave me no choice but to also stay here. I will be across the hall should you need anything."

DeSante turned and left the room leaving Iliana in stunned silence.

Chapter 9

Serena was filled with frustration when she returned to the château late in the afternoon. Warrington had abandoned the discussion with her and DeSante and was returning to Rizari, leaving many issues unresolved.

Casimir was sitting by the fireplace, a book open on his lap. "Rough day?"

Rough and unproductive. "No progress. I spent the morning dealing with two hotheads. Neither of them wanted to compromise or discuss anything. They shouted accusations. Waste of time."

"Why do you think that is?" Casimir asked.

Serena slumped into the plush couch next to Casimir. He set his book on the coffee table and reclined, putting his arm around her. "That's a matter of speculation. They don't want to say out loud what they want for fear the other will resist on principle."

"What do you speculate they want?"

"DeSante? I don't know. He's a blank slate. I try to read him and get nothing. Strangely, the only time I've seen him display any real emotion was in relation to Iliana. I've asked her if he's revealed his thoughts on the leaders' ability to reach an agreement, but she says their conversations aren't related to politics."

"What about King Warrington?"

Serena groaned. "My personal issues with him are coloring my judgment. DeSante suggested Warrington is planning to start a war between our three countries."

"Do you think that's true?"

"I can't be sure. Whenever I've tried to talk to Warrington, we argue. I don't see how our relationship will ever progress past that point."

"Samuel's mother's sixtieth birthday party is tomorrow night."

"I know." Serena's interactions with Katarina had been less than stellar. But Serena was planning to attend the party, especially since she wouldn't have the excuse of the summit to give her a valid reason to cancel. "I was planning on going. Do you think I should snoop around his office? See if I can't find something to hint at why he is resistant to talking and what exactly he wants out of our merger?"

"I don't like the idea of you undertaking that task alone. Can you ask someone you trust for help?"

"Like you?"

"Like me," he said.

She considered it. With her access to the party, she would be given more opportunities to move around the palace. Employees of the king, the king and his mother would be distracted by the party.

Her father's birthday party crossed her mind and she

shivered. She leaned into Casimir. "Do you think it will be safe to be in the palace?"

"I am sure Warrington is taking the necessary precautions. What happened at your father's birthday is fresh in everyone's memory."

It was never far from her mind, and Serena wondered if Katarina's birthday would be the stage for another assassination.

Serena was accustomed to being unseen in social situations, but as queen, her status—and visibility—had shifted. By the nature of her position, people were interested in her. Katarina's birthday party was no exception, making it difficult for her to operate in stealth mode.

If Samuel's guards spotted her where she was not supposed to be in the palace, she would give the excuse that she'd needed time alone. If she was caught in the king's bedroom, she would pretend she'd been planning a seduction. But Serena didn't want to wave the black-and-white-checkered flag for him. Despite their mutual dislike, she had no doubt Warrington would sleep with her for kicks.

Then there was the matter of slipping past her guards. If she was out of sight, they would be worried and actively search for her. An idea popped into her head, so crazy that it actually might work. She would need to use Iliana to help distract them. From a certain angle, she and Iliana looked alike. If her cousin could fool her guards long enough, she could accomplish her goal.

A quick call confirmed that—albeit hesitantly—Iliana would help.

When Serena arrived at Samuel's palace, she was immediately escorted to Samuel's side. She would have preferred a few minutes alone to collect her thoughts, but she'd been running late.

"After what happened at the summit, I was worried you weren't coming," he said, patting the hand she had slipped over his arm. When he kissed her cheek, he smelled of cologne and scotch. The scent made her dizzy and slightly nauseated.

"We ran into some traffic from the airport."

"My mother is anxious to see you."

Anxious to dole out more criticism? Based on how Katarina had spoken to her every other time they had met, she would have no problem commenting on the recent scandal involving Casimir in the rose garden and in Elion.

Serena kept her shoulders pinned back and her head high. She was queen of Acacia. She wouldn't be intimidated or cowed by anyone tonight.

She wished Casimir was beside her, but at least he was at the party, somewhere with Iliana, waiting for her to finish with her obligation. Samuel led her to where his mother stood, sipping from a glass of champagne and talking to the people around her.

As they approached, the guests speaking to Katarina moved away, bowing slightly. Katarina was not titled royalty, but at times, Serena wondered if she knew the difference.

"Katarina, it's a pleasure to see you again," Serena said, extending her hand. She took care to inject some warmth into her voice. "Happy birthday."

"Your Highness." Katarina Warrington accepted Serena's hand and clasped it.

"Everything looks wonderful. Your son did a nice job arranging the evening." Serena pulled her hand away.

Katarina laughed sharply. "My son didn't arrange this. The king doesn't have time to plan parties. We have event coordinators on staff to handle these affairs. When you're ready to start your wedding preparations—" Katarina said.

Samuel cut in. "Mother, not now."

Serena didn't want to think about wedding preparations. "It's customary to be engaged before planning a wedding." She tried to keep her tone light, but the look Katarina gave her indicated she'd failed.

His mother pursed her lips. "Engagements are merely a formality. Tell me, Serena, what is preventing you from agreeing to the engagement?"

Serena was taken aback by Katarina's willingness to put her on the spot in front of other guests. She hadn't anticipated this meeting would take a hostile turn so quickly. "Samuel and I are taking our time." And arguing and fighting and seeing absolutely everything differently.

"I see. I have some additional topics I'd like to speak with you about. Perhaps we can talk in private later?" Katarina's eyes were cold and hard.

Serena would rather chew glass. She gave a nod of acknowledgment, but she wasn't planning to follow through on a private whining session with Katarina. "If you'll excuse me, I need a drink." Releasing Samuel's arm, she strode in the direction of the bar. Being verbally accosted wasn't how she would spend the evening.

Samuel caught up to her. "You'll have to excuse my mother. She's protective. You know how mothers can be."

"No actually, I don't." Serena's mother had died when she was three and it stung that Samuel didn't know that. She strode away from him and didn't turn to see his expression. Maybe it was time for Samuel to put some genuine effort into their relationship. Or maybe it was time for Serena to think of other ways to secure Acacia's future.

Serena fled the drawing room, feigning that she was upset after the incident. Guests were flowing in and Serena pretended to be on her phone and distressed. When she was away from the crowd, she texted Iliana to meet her in the bathroom on the first floor. They would trade clothes and places. Iliana would have to take care not to show her face, but a walk in the darkened garden should accomplish that.

Serena waited a few minutes and following a quick tap on the door, Iliana slipped inside the bathroom. She locked up behind her. They traded dresses, Iliana wearing the formal purple gown and Serena slipping on Iliana's simple black frock.

"It's not too late to change your mind," Iliana said, adjusting her wig. "It's dangerous what you're doing."

"This is my opportunity. I can't let it pass," Serena said. She had to know for sure what Samuel wanted before she signed those papers, agreeing to marry him and turning over control of Acacia.

Checking her red wig and dress in the mirror, Serena slipped out of the bathroom. Samuel's office was on the second floor of the palace. She used the servant's stairwell, moving purposefully and quietly. Most everyone was working in or around the drawing room, so the hallways were clear. Serena took slow, deep breaths and tried to stay calm. Every footstep sounded loud, every creak of the stair echoing in the space. She rehearsed what she would say if caught. She wasn't a great liar, but she was prepared to sell it.

Once on the second floor, she strode toward Samuel's office. She set her hand on the door knob and turned it, hoping it was unlocked. It was! She entered the room and someone grabbed her hand, pulling her deeper into the office. She was composing her excuse, when she recognized his scent. "What are you doing here?"

Casimir pointed to the desk. "Searching."

"I told you I would look for evidence. You're supposed to be downstairs with Iliana."

"Iliana and I agreed. We couldn't let you do this alone."

"Great, now we'll both be arrested," she said drily.

"You're assuming we will get caught. We won't. Are you wearing a wig?" he asked.

"My guards won't be looking for a redhead. They are following Iliana in a blond wig." She patted the red hair.

"I thought you were pretending to be yourself on a mission of seduction. How will you explain the getup if you're caught?" Casimir asked.

"I'll tell Samuel I was shooting for a kinky role-playing evening."

"What role are you playing?"

"Red-haired, fiery seductress."

Casimir grinned. He kissed her then, pressing her up against the back of the closed door. Serena relaxed beneath his touch, letting his mouth plunder hers. His lips massaged hers, his tongue stroked against her tongue and his body rubbed with the right friction, the right movement to excite every nerve ending. A mewling sound filled the air. Did Samuel have a cat?

"Shhh," he whispered against her lips.

"I wasn't talking."

"You're moaning."

She straightened. "If you want me to be silent, you shouldn't kiss me."

"Shhh," he said again and went back to kissing her.

Her head was filled with Casimir. Kissing Casimir. Grinding against Casimir. Touching Casimir. When he broke away, she leaned against the door to keep from melting to the floor in a puddle of heat.

"I needed to get that out of my system," he said.

He strode to the desk and looked through papers using a flashlight.

It was out of his system, but now it was strongly in hers. She wanted to finish what he had started. They didn't have time now, but maybe tonight they could meet at the beach house. Being there with Casimir was one of her favorite ways to relax. But before they could relax, they had to finish this task and find something to clue her in to Warrington's agenda.

"I'll check his bedroom," Serena said.

Casimir glanced at her. "I need a few more minutes. I'll meet you there."

Serena wished they were rendezvousing in her bedroom. Instead, she was searching the bedroom of a man she hoped to never be in the position to share a bed with.

Samuel wouldn't leave incriminating information in the open for anyone to discover. Casimir had heard from one of DeSante's spies in the palace of Rizari that Samuel used this smaller office for the majority of his work, including personal matters. He had a larger office in the palace for official meetings.

Casimir had felt an instant connection to this space.

For good reason. It had once belonged to his father. His mother had some pictures of the palace, old, grainy photos, faded with age. The room was unfamiliar, yet being here was bringing to the surface emotions he'd thought long buried. He had never known his father, except in descriptions from his mother and stories in the news. He was torn between anger at his father and the crippling loss of never having met him.

Casimir heard a noise in the hallway and darted behind a plush couch, crouching to the floor. He should have been aware of approaching footsteps. His lapse in concentration might cost him dearly.

The door to the office opened, and Samuel and a black-haired woman entered. Casimir didn't recognize her, but she was tall and slender and wore a long black dress that was tied around her neck. Her breasts were spilling from the fabric and Samuel grabbed at her as they stumbled in the near darkness into the room.

She giggled and Samuel hushed her. After he closed the door behind him, he again advanced on her. She clawed at his clothes. Within seconds, she was bent over the desk, her dress around her waist, with Warrington behind her, moaning and groaning.

Casimir closed his eyes and tried to block out the noise. Even with his hands over his ears, the rhythmic thumps and high-pitched moans penetrated his hearing.

The episode was over in less than two minutes. Casimir gave his cousin no points for stamina or creativity. After a disgusting exchange of lurid compliments, Samuel and his fling left the office ten seconds apart. Casimir waited in case Samuel decided to return. When it remained quiet, Casimir resumed his search.

How was Serena doing? She hadn't messaged that

she'd found anything, but Casimir worried about her. He glanced at the time on his phone. It had been twenty-three minutes since Serena had left the office. Having found nothing himself, he sent her a message and then slipped out of the room to meet her in the king's bedroom.

Serena had a difficult time picturing Samuel sleeping and residing in his bedroom. It was almost hard to believe it was his. She had expected modern decor, possibly primarily neutral colors with a splash of bold tones, like red.

Instead, the room was decorated in soft fabrics, heavy drapes, and shades of green and blue. The decorations were simple and understated, though Serena had no doubt they were of high quality. The painting across from his bed was of a ship on the water, struggling against a fierce storm. What had compelled Samuel to choose that piece?

Serena opened his drawers, peeking inside. She found impeccably folded clothes that smelled of laundry detergent. Moving them aside, she looked underneath. She didn't know what she was searching for. He was unlikely to have saved documentation detailing his private thoughts on the future of Rizari. Samuel wasn't the type to keep a handwritten diary.

Pulling aside the curtain to the window, Serena took in the view. It was too dark to see anything except the dots of lights from the palace outbuildings. No view of the water. Serena released the curtain and returned to her search.

She opened the bedside table and found condoms, candles and lubricant. Feeling as if she had crossed a line, she closed it quickly. Serena knelt and looked under the bed. It was empty, save a condom wrapper.

"What are you doing here?"

A female voice. Serena rose to her feet. Samuel's mother was standing in the doorway, her silhouette outlined by the light from the hallway. Her hands were folded in front of her and she waited, watching Serena with narrowed eyes.

Serena had practiced her cover story so many times, it snapped to her tongue. "I was waiting for Samuel."

Katarina flicked on the light and stepped farther into the room. "Why are you dressed like that? What did you do to your hair?"

"Part of the surprise."

His mother lifted her brow.

Serena would let his mother think whatever she wanted. Let her believe it was a kinky fantasy, a lover secretly visiting in the night.

"I don't think you should be in my son's bedroom."

Serena lifted her head and tilted it to the side. She had seen her sister intimidate many foes with that same look. Would it work for her?

Samuel's mother set her hands on her hips. "We could call my son and speak to him about this."

Serena debated her next move. "That's a good idea." She could feed Samuel her story, that she was trying to smooth over the problems they'd been having by injecting a little fun into their relationship. Then she could pretend to be embarrassed or annoyed that she had been caught and return home.

His mother placed the call. Serena, astonished that she hadn't collapsed in a pile of nerves and sweat, sat on the chaise longue positioned under the window on the far side of the room.

Katarina spoke quietly into her phone, too low for Serena to hear. Serena tried not to let that add to her terror. She inspected her nails as if bored.

Katarina gripped her phone at her side. "You're not the good girl you pretend to be."

Serena glared at Samuel's mother. The woman knew nothing about her. "I am the queen of Acacia. I would appreciate if you'd show me respect. If you don't like me as your son's choice for a wife, that's your problem."

"His choice? My son doesn't have a choice. He has to marry you."

Serena saw another angle to explore. Katarina might know more about Samuel's motives than he had revealed to her directly. "We don't have an arrangement yet. He is free to marry whoever he chooses."

Katarina looked positively apoplectic. "That isn't true. My son sees the writing on the wall. War with Icarus is inevitable. He needs Acacia on his side."

Was Samuel expecting to defend himself against a war with Icarus or was he planning to be the aggressor? The information ricocheted around Serena's brain and made her feel dizzy. It wasn't the evidence she was looking for to implicate Samuel in wrongdoing, but it was more evidence that DeSante's suspicions were correct. Samuel had war on his mind. "I don't see it that way."

"Then you are a fool. Your sister would have made a better wife and a better queen. At least she had charisma and charm."

Serena tried not to visibly recoil. At the mention of her sister, Serena was assaulted by grief and curios-

ity. How much had Danae known about Samuel Warrington's plans for their countries? "I didn't realize you
and Danae were close."

Katarina sniffed. "We weren't. But my son tells me
everything. Everything."

The fact was unsettling, but Serena waited to see
what else his mother would reveal. Perhaps in her attempt to assert herself as the most important woman
in her son's life, she would step too far and divulge one
of the king's secrets.

"You aren't my son's type."

Serena knew that. Samuel wasn't hers. "I see."

"Do you? Because I am not buying this act you're
putting on tonight."

Samuel entered the room and appeared confused as
he looked between his mother and her. His hair was
mussed. "What are you doing in here?" He addressed
Serena.

Serena folded her hands and tried to appear exas-
perated. "Being thwarted by your mother. I took our
last conversation to heart and I had hoped to arrange
a surprise for you. Your mother didn't seem to think it
was a good idea."

He narrowed his eyes. "What surprise?"

Serena gestured to herself. "Me."

Samuel's lips quirked and his eyes lit up. It was the
first time she had seen genuine interest from him. Figured he'd be attentive when sex was implied. Serena
had opened a door she didn't want to walk through. She
rose to her feet. "But this is a mess. I'll be returning
home. It's your mother's birthday party. I didn't mean
to upset anyone. I wanted to have time alone with you,
but I can see that this is bad timing."

"Right. That sounds logical," Katarina said sarcastically.

Samuel looked at his mother. "Mother, you need to give Serena some latitude."

His mother straightened. "Aren't you planning to address the issue of her other lover?"

Samuel glanced at Serena. "I am aware of it and we've addressed it. That's all you need to know."

Surprised at the way the king had spoken to his mother, Serena stood and crossed the room to the door. "I'd rather not make another scene tonight and ruin your mother's evening. It is her birthday, after all." For once, Katarina had the grace to stay silent.

Serena fled the room and Samuel didn't stop her.

Serena ran into Casimir in the hallway. She shook her head and indicated he should turn and run.

She messaged Iliana to meet her in the same bathroom. This time, Iliana was waiting for her. They switched dresses again, and Iliana shoved both wigs into her oversized handbag. Serena exited the bathroom. Her guards were looking around for her and seemed relieved when they spotted her with her cousin.

Three hours later, at her beach house, Serena shared with Casimir and Iliana what she had learned. "King Warrington anticipates war with Icarus. I don't know if he plans to start it, but he expects it's inevitable."

Speaking freely in front of Iliana brought her cousin deeper into the circle of trust. She wanted both her and Casimir's opinions on the matter.

"He said that?" Iliana asked.

"His mother told me," Serena said.

Iliana made a noise of disgust. Casimir watched her with his deep intelligent eyes.

"I don't like his mother. She's strange," Iliana said.

"She's protective," Serena said, despite her feelings toward the woman.

"That's one way to describe it," Iliana said.

After discussing possibilities for an hour, Iliana rose to her feet. "I need to get going. I have an early morning tomorrow and the boss won't like it if I'm late."

Serena hugged her. "See you tomorrow. Drive safe, okay?"

After Iliana left, Serena was alone with Casimir, save for Serena's guards posted at the front and back of her house.

"I need to change out of this dress," Serena said, extending her hand to Casimir.

He took it, and followed her up the stairs to her bedroom. Her passion and her feelings for him were stronger than the confusing thoughts swirling inside her.

She unfastened her dress and let the satin pool on the floor. She was naked beneath the dress except for a thong and Casimir's eyes widened with lust.

She stroked his cheek and he closed his eyes, leaning into her touch.

He kissed the inside of her wrist. His lips trailed up her arm, moving their bodies closer together. "I want you, Serena."

She wanted him, too. He unbuttoned his shirt and let it fall over his broad shoulders. She kicked off her shoes, wiggled out of her underwear and pushed back on the bed, waiting for him. Watching him move, the sleekness of his muscles and the intensity in his eyes was throwing fuel on the fire burning hot and wild inside her. Casimir removed his pants and slid onto the bed with her, covering her with his body. He kissed her deeply, intensely, stroking his hand up and down her body.

Then he shifted, sitting with his back against the headboard and pulled her astride him. Her core touched his arousal, yet he made no motion to push inside her.

His kiss was ravenous, in direct contrast to the gentle caress of his hands on her bare back. She wanted his hands elsewhere on her body. Casimir palmed her cheeks. "I was worried you would have to protect your cover and stay the night with him."

She would have rather been arrested. "I wouldn't spend the night with Samuel. We haven't even shared a kiss. I think we'd have a few steps in between."

"Those steps can blur and blend," Casimir said.

"I'm with *you*. I don't want another man," Serena said, capturing his lips and kissing him.

Casimir rubbed his hips against hers and the friction hit her in the right places. She moved harder against him and she rapidly became frustrated. She wanted Casimir inside her. She'd come to associate him with mind-blowing orgasms and she was craving another.

Serena reached for a condom from her bedside table and fumbled to remove it from the packaging. After a few missed tries, Casimir took the foil from her hand and deftly handled the task. She lifted herself over him. He licked each of her nipples and reached between her legs, slipping a finger inside her and circling the tight bundle of nerves at her core with his thumb.

If he was checking if she was wet, the answer was obvious.

"Ride me," he said. The request came like a growl in his throat.

Serena lowered herself onto him in one clean motion.

Buried deep inside her, he held her close and kissed her. She swiveled her hips and broke the kiss, letting out a moan of pleasure. Passion and arousal were a hot blaze, urging her movements harder and faster.

Desire shuttered his eyes and she felt bolder with every response of his body. He was thick and hard inside her and she had the power to move how she wanted.

Timid at first, and then forgetting everything except how incredible it felt to be joined with him, she moved. His hands were at her hips, guiding her, sliding his body inside hers.

She felt the pressure between her hips and an orgasm built and exploded, ripping through her. Casimir swept her into his powerful arms. He flipped her onto her stomach and slid a pillow beneath her hips. He entered her from behind.

He thrust slowly. "Is this okay?"

Her overexcited body was tingling. She thought she would burst from his thickness. "It's good." She gripped the sheets to keep from sliding at the strength of his thrusts.

He increased his pace. He was taking her to new heights in his relentless pursuit of pleasure, bringing her with him. His thickness and length were almost too much, pushing her to the edge of another release. Casimir let out a growl and shoved hard into her, pausing for a beat before withdrawing and pressing inside her again.

Knowing he had finished, she let herself go, turning her body over to him.

How could she ever marry another man when her heart belonged to him?

Chapter 10

Santino burst into Serena's office at seven the next morning.

Serena stood to greet her uncle. "Good morning, what brings you by?" Serena had already skimmed the news that morning and saw no further mention of scandal related to her and Casimir, not even after he had attended Katarina's birthday celebration. Not that it was far from the minds of the press, but it didn't get top billing anymore.

Santino handed her a thick envelope.

"What's this?" Serena asked.

"The paperwork for the merger with Rizari, ready for your signature."

The merger, in other words, her marriage to King Warrington. "I haven't had time to review it." She had read it. But she wasn't on board with everything stated in it.

"You can't drag your feet on this. Enough time has passed. If we let too much time go…"

"Then what?" Would King Warrington change his mind? Would he attack Acacia and take it by force instead of by marriage?

"We are exposed. Icarus could attack while we dawdle and debate trivial details."

The summit meeting had not gone well. But Serena had hope that Icarus, Rizari and Acacia could still come to an agreement. Her marriage to King Warrington wasn't a done deal and she hadn't lost her bargaining power. She wasn't convinced that Demetrius DeSante and Icarus were the prime threats. She sensed more scheming and treachery from King Warrington.

Her uncle appeared worried. "If we renege on the arrangement with Rizari, that is an insult that King Warrington will not forgive."

"Do you think he will respond by attacking us?" Serena asked.

Her uncle seemed unsure how to answer. "I don't know what to think."

Serena tilted her chin proudly. "Maybe I'll run Acacia myself." She said it to test his response, to see if anyone would believe it was possible, aside from her and Casimir.

Her uncle shook his head. "How in the world do you intend to do that? You have no experience. You get nervous giving speeches. The press makes fun of you, constantly comparing you to Danae."

His lack of faith in her cut to the core. She had much to learn and she was open about that, but she was smart and capable. Her father had run the country for decades, just as her grandfather had before him. It was in her blood. She had watched her father all her life. She had learned from him and that counted for something. "I'll do everything I can. Our Assembly is strong and I have great hopes for the future."

"How can you possibly think you are capable of running a country?" Her uncle slammed his fist against her desk. "You've behaving like a spoiled child. You're wasting time pining for some commoner and imagining some fantasy where you're with him. You have a duty and an obligation to your country. This isn't an experiment for you to attempt. This isn't about making you feel good about yourself or boosting your self-esteem. The few times you've been in public, you've looked like a bumbling dolt."

His harsh words struck at her deepest insecurities. "I realize how important this country is and how important my position."

"If you realize it, then sign the papers. Stop exposing us to attack!"

Serena heard the shaking anger—or was it fear—in her uncle's voice and couldn't believe it was directed at her. "I will when I am ready." Then she thought about what finalizing the merger would mean for her and Casimir.

"You'll sign them now. The enemy is at the gate. The enemy has been in this space. In our home."

Serena felt tears come to her eyes. It wasn't solely her uncle upsetting her. The painful emotions that tightened her chest were rooted in her unresolved feelings for Casimir, her raw grief for her father and her sister, and the tremendous responsibilities that had been set upon her shoulders. "Give me time." Perhaps her uncle felt responsible for her and that stress was affecting him.

"Serena, I have always tried to protect you. This is a time where I need to protect you from yourself."

Serena stood and strode toward her office door. If her uncle wouldn't leave, she would. Santino grabbed her arm and his grip tightened. "Sign the papers, Serena. You won't be a good queen on your own."

She tried to shake him off, but his grip held. "You have no faith in me."

"Neither does anyone else in the country."

Serena felt as if she'd been slapped.

"You were practically estranged from your father and you've been dragged back to a position you don't want. Why are you resisting?"

"Because what I want has changed," Serena said.

"So help me, if you make this about some puppy love with that man, then I will have to take drastic action."

"Drastic action?"

Her uncle's expression was menacing. "I will do whatever is necessary to protect the people of Acacia, even if it's from their queen."

Casimir's judgment was clouded. He had set out on this path of vengeance years earlier and thought he knew what he wanted: to avenge his father's death and his mother's honor.

Serena had unexpectedly become part of that plan, a game changer. She was supposed to bring him closer to Warrington and the evidence he needed to take his rightful place as heir to the throne in Rizari. His father's killer would be brought to justice and his mother would have peace.

Serena wasn't supposed to be hurt in the process. She wasn't supposed to know anything about him. His goal had been to get in and out, with zero emotional ties and nothing to trace him to Rizari.

Casimir couldn't see Serena as a piece in a chess game. She was a woman, a strong and beautiful woman, who was coming into her own. She could handle so much more than the people around her gave her credit for. He had underestimated her and he had been wrong about her.

Casimir needed to tell Serena how he felt about her. Tell her the truth about who he was. Serena's beautiful face filled his thoughts. Could he find a way to come clean with her without hurting her? The truth was brutal.

He walked toward Serena's office, needing to speak with her. He didn't know what he would say, but he needed to clear his conscience.

"What are you doing here?" Iliana asked, standing from her desk.

"I need to speak to Serena," Casimir said.

Iliana glanced nervously at the door. "She's talking with her uncle."

That didn't matter. Casimir needed to see her. He burst inside the door. Santino was gripping Serena's arm.

"We're in the middle of something. Come back later," Santino said.

Not a chance. "Let her go. Now."

Her uncle released her. Lucky for him. Casmir had killed a man for less.

"What exactly is going on here?" Casimir asked, feeling his protective instincts rising.

"I'm handing this," Serena said.

"This is none of your concern, commoner. I'm trying to prevent my niece from ruining her life and running this country into the ground."

"By forcing me to sign the marriage agreement," Serena said.

"Instead, she is caught up in a fantasy about you and refusing to sign," her uncle said.

"I am not a girl caught in a fantasy. I am queen of this country and I am trying to do what is best for Acacia," Serena said.

Her voice was strong and clear. Casimir was proud of her for standing up for herself.

"Name your price," Santino said to him.

"Price for what? Walking out of here and leaving you alone with Serena? I have no price for that."

"Your price to walk out of her life completely," Santino said.

Even if Santino offered to kill Samuel Warrington in exchange for abandoning Serena, Casimir wouldn't do it. That truth felt like a bowling ball in his stomach. She meant too much to him. "You can't buy me off."

Serena smiled at him. Santino glared.

Iliana stepped inside the office. She was deathly pale. "Serena, it's happened. There's been an act of aggression between Rizari and Icarus. This will mean war."

The words *act of aggression* rang loud in Serena's head. What had happened? She couldn't reach either King Warrington or President DeSante.

Serena called for the heads of the Assembly and her advisers to gather at the castle. She wanted to be prepared to make decisions quickly. Though her uncle had not left, he was quiet.

After several more tries, she finally reached King Warrington.

"I need to know what is going on," Serena said. She was shocked by the hardness of her own voice.

"One of DeSante's submarines came too close to our shores and we fired at it."

"You opened fire on an Icarus sub?" Serena asked. She had anticipated Icarus being the aggressor. If they had traveled close to Rizari's shores, it was provocation, but a full-on attack was a declaration of war.

"We didn't open fire. Our navy is trained to respond to attacks and follow protocols, and they did." He didn't sound happy. He sounded angry and bewildered.

"Have you spoken to DeSante?" Serena asked.

"No."

Serena wanted to scream in frustration. It was absolutely critical that communication stay open between the two leaders. "Stay on the line. I'm calling him."

She put Warrington on hold and called for Iliana. "Get DeSante on the phone." Using her cousin's connection to him had never been more important.

Iliana nodded. When DeSante came on the line, he didn't sound upset.

"I warned you that Warrington wanted war."

She hadn't gotten the impression from Warrington that war was the goal. "I just spoke to him. I think we need to discuss this incident. It may have been an unfortunate training issue."

DeSante scoffed. "Training issue? No, Your Highness. If you believe that, you aren't the intelligent woman I believed you to be."

She was momentarily struck by the compliment, but she pressed on. This wasn't about her. "DeSante, no one wants war." Especially not her. Acacia would be the loser in this scenario.

"Aren't you supposed to back your boyfriend?"

Serena thought of Casimir first, then realized DeSante was referring to King Warrington. "I am behind peace."

"At any price?"

"I am willing to do whatever you need to keep this discussion going and not have the situation turn violent."

"It has already turned violent. My sub was manned. Four deaths."

"May I conference in Warrington so we might speak about this together?" Rationally and calmly as three leaders who didn't want additional casualties.

"The time for speaking was at the summit. Now it is time for action."

Serena tried again. "Please, President DeSante, if you would reconsider your position."

"Demetrius, please listen to Serena. You know that this is a difficult time for our administration. If you attack Rizari, you will force Serena into marrying Warrington." Iliana was on her extension and had jumped into the conversation. She sounded desperate and scared.

Though Serena thought it was inappropriate, given Iliana's relationship with the president and his soft side when it came to her, it might help. Peace at any price.

"Iliana, I did not realize you were on the call," DeSante said.

"I wasn't supposed to be. But I couldn't help it." She didn't sound sorry.

"You understand that Rizari destroyed one of Icarus's submarines today?" DeSante said. His tone when speaking to Iliana was a hundred times softer and warmer than it had been when speaking to her.

"We don't know the circumstances."

"I know the circumstances."

"Demetrius, please, don't do this."

"Iliana, you cannot play on my affection for you to manipulate me. I have a country to protect."

Iliana hung up the phone with a growl of outrage.

Serena didn't know how to play this. She was hopelessly lost. "President DeSante, before any further action is taken, we need to discuss this with Warrington."

"No, Your Highness. You do what you must, and I will do the same." DeSante disconnected the call.

Serena returned to her call with Warrington. He was no easier to talk with. She received the same hard-line response from him.

The best she could do was meet him to speak in person. Though she had previously declined the invitation, she agreed to meet Warrington in Rizari at the symphony hall, where he had scheduled a performance of the country's most popular orchestra, an annual event held the day after Katarina's birthday celebration. Warrington was unwilling to cancel the event, though there were clearly more pressing matters to attend to.

It was a strange place to meet, but if it brought King Warrington to the negotiation table, then she would go, talk, listen and try to defuse the situation. Serena didn't want war for Acacia and she had to stop this potential disaster before it spiraled out of control.

Casimir felt the shift in the atmosphere at the castle. Serena was doing her best to hold it together. As the

Mediterranean inched toward war, Casimir felt even more urgently that he needed to tell Serena who he was.

If he made his move and overthrew Warrington, he could prevent war. DeSante would back off if Samuel Warrington was no longer in power.

But overthrowing Warrington was not a simple task. Perhaps with Serena on his side, it would be easier. Would she support his play for power? Or would she be caught up in her anger at him for having lied to her and turn a blind eye to the benefits of helping him?

When King Warrington had requested that Serena meet him at the Grand Symphony Hall in Rizari, Casimir had followed her. He was not leaving Serena unprotected and he felt something was amiss. Though he had barely spoken three words to her, he'd stayed close. She'd been conferencing with one person after another—leaders of other countries in the region, the highest ranking members of the Assembly and her advisers. Her meeting with Warrington was next.

Of all the places King Warrington could meet Serena, why a musical performance? Samuel couldn't be trusted. Certainly, this event wasn't more important than the rapidly declining political situation between Rizari and Icarus. He was planning something and Casimir needed to get ahead of whatever it was.

Upon entering the theater, Casimir promptly spotted Serena. Seated in the king's balcony, she didn't know Casimir was watching her and he found her even more beguiling. She was quiet and unassuming, but her eyes were sharp. She had a guard on either side of her, the king's guards. Warrington had not yet arrived at the hall. Behind her was a heavy blue curtain, the same blue painted on the walls of the circular room. The gold trim was subtle, lining the balconies and stage without detracting from the aura of simplicity. Casimir's father had commissioned the symphony hall in honor of his brother, Samuel's father, and his love of music.

Out of the corner of his eye, Casimir caught a glimpse of Rolland, Demetrius DeSante's favorite and most trusted assassin. Rolland's most notable trait was that he was not notable at all. Average height and build, his dark hair was cut short, his eagle eyes sharp. Casimir tensed instinctively. His methods were unpredictable and he was loyal only to money. Raising the body count with innocents and bystanders wasn't a problem for him if it got the job done.

Rolland wasn't the type to patronize music and he did not exclusively work for DeSante. Which meant he was here on a job. Who was his target?

Casimir followed him in the crowd, while calling DeSante on the phone. But the president of Icarus wasn't answering. Casimir lost track of Rolland as people socialized and milled around.

He tried texting DeSante instead. Why is Rolland in Rizari?

The response came moments later. He's providing backup.

For? Who's his target?

Backup for you. You've lost focus and I need to get this done. No war. Target is Sam.

Casimir didn't need backup. Rolland would shoot first, ask questions later. He wouldn't care if he killed Serena and while assassinating Samuel held some appeal, a bloody coup made Casimir no better than Samuel. He wanted the throne in an honorable way. I have this.

Serena is meeting with our enemy to discuss an alliance. You had time. You failed. DeSante didn't mince words.

DeSante wouldn't stop Rolland. He had decided that Casimir wasn't moving fast enough. Rolland was exceptional at what he did. Accurate to a fault, he could slip away from any place unnoticed. He was untraceable and had so many contacts around the world, he could hide for months to let the fallout die down before reappearing somewhere else.

I am in control, Casimir texted, hating that he was being argumentative. His actions should speak for themselves.

Rolland stays on post.

DeSante was holding the line. Casimir knew his old friend too well. When DeSante set his mind to something, he rarely wavered. He had decided to kill Samuel and had sent in his best to do the job. If Casimir wanted Samuel alive so he could get the answers he needed, he would have to find Rolland and stop him.

When the members of the symphony began to tune their instruments, the lights in the hall blinked a few times. The crowd moved toward their seats. When the aisles were clear, the lights lowered and then the hall went dark. Casimir scanned for a red dot anywhere near Serena that would point to Rolland planning to take his shot at Samuel. He could have night vision goggles to assist him, but even a good marksman needed tools to hit his target in the dark.

The sounds of the orchestra rose up through the hall. Casimir moved from his position. He didn't want to be pinned down by trampling people if shooting started.

When the lights came on, Samuel Warrington was standing on the conductor's podium. Serena was in her seat. She appeared confused.

Noticing the king, the crowd erupted in applause. Samuel held out his hands to quiet them. "Welcome to you all, my dear friends, and please allow me to borrow the stage for one minute before the performance begins. This day holds a lot of meaning for me. As you know, this concert is a long-standing tradition held in the hall built for my father. He honored my mother with private performances here and I have continued that tradition in his absence. I have selected the score and heard some of the rehearsal. But before we enjoy the music, I have an important question for someone special."

Casimir felt panic for another reason, a reason besides an assassin roaming the crowd. The king was planning to propose to Serena. Though Casimir knew this was inevitable, he hated what was coming, hated that he would have to watch it. Most of all, Casimir hated the idea that Serena would belong to the king and the king to her.

Adding to his anxiety, given that the king had made himself an easy target, Rolland would take his shots.

"Serena Alagona, queen of Acacia, you have become the light in my world. If I have learned anything from the past several months, it's that life is too short. But it can also be sweet with the right woman at my side.

Together we can do great things. We can vanquish a common enemy. Will you be my bride?"

He had shoehorned in the problem with Icarus by reminding Serena and the crowd of their enemy, and forced the issue of the engagement.

Serena stood and appeared shell-shocked. She turned, presumably to exit the balcony to meet the king onstage. She would hate being proposed to in this public manner. Casimir hated it for a different reason. She would be close to Samuel, the target, while Rolland was somewhere in the building, probably gleeful about the spectacle he was about to make. Rolland liked his work to be appreciated and his efforts couldn't be fully valued when his directives included killing someone inconspicuously and hiding the body. The assassination of the King of Rizari would be in the open, in front of a live audience. It would be front page news for weeks.

Casimir rushed to intercept Serena. She was descending the stairs with the king's guards flanking her. "Serena!"

She whirled in Casimir's direction. "What's wrong?"

"No time to explain. There's an assassin here. You need to stay away from the king."

"Are you threatening the queen?" one of the guards asked. Casimir didn't recognize or know him. The man might think he was some nut stalking the queen.

"She is in danger. Not from me. Someone wants to kill the king."

"Every person here passed through security. The king and the queen are safe," the guard said haughtily.

Serena held out her hand to the guards. She addressed Casimir. "I need to talk to Samuel. He's waiting for my answer. Did you hear what he asked?"

He'd heard and though it wasn't the most pressing issue, he wanted to know her thoughts. "What will you say?"

Everything inside him needed her to say no. Despite what that could mean for their plans, no was the only acceptable answer. Her eyes were wells of sadness. "I will say yes. Our countries are on the verge of war. I can't rock the boat. I have to go, Casimir."

She wasn't thinking clearly because she was nervous and tense.

Three other guards swarmed closer and took him by the arms, dragging him away. Casimir had to find Rolland. The hall presented too many angles and too many places to hide. Struggling against their hold, he broke free of the king's guards and chased after Serena. The guards pursued, but they wouldn't shoot into the crowd, especially when the king was in range of flying bullets.

Serena wasn't wearing a vest. Casimir should have refused to allow her to pass him. He should have fought harder, but her answer had disarmed him for a moment too long. The king's guards, who were likely wearing vests, could take a bullet for her, but Casimir questioned their loyalty. The king's safety would be their chief concern.

Serena met the king on the stage. She was shaking and pale, but the nodding of her head was unmistakable. She was saying yes to his proposal. She would marry Warrington.

Casimir raced to the stage to warn them. The king's guards tried to stop him, but he was bigger, stronger and more determined. He stood in front of Serena and when the unmistakable sound of gunfire filled the hall, Casimir felt the impact when a slug landed in his chest.

Screaming. More gunfire. Casimir felt dizzy and had trouble pulling air into his lungs. He fought to take a deep breath. Serena was kneeling over him, cradling his head in her lap. He was in Rolland's eyeshot. She needed to go somewhere safe.

The king's guards were dragging the king to safety. The corners of his vision blurred and darkened. He tried to explain, tried to warn Serena to move to another location, to run to a safer place.

He couldn't make his mouth form the words. They came out as a gurgle.

Hers was the last face he saw before he lost consciousness.

Casimir felt as if he had been hit with a sledgehammer in the chest. Twice.

Serena was slapping his cheeks. "Casimir!"

Her hands moved down his body, poking and prodding. He moaned when she pressed his chest. He had taken a bullet in the vest. Rolland didn't fire tiny guns. He would have shot with serious power.

Serena was stroking his face. He preferred that to her prodding his body. "An ambulance is on the way. Just hold on."

Casimir opened one eye. They were behind the performance stage, as evidenced by a panel of lighting equipment on the wall and heavy blue curtains to his left. Serena was leaning over him, and he focused on her, her beautiful features filling his view.

"I'm fine. Vest." His bulletproof vest had taken most of the damage, but the impact would leave a deep bruise and maybe a few broken or cracked ribs.

Serena let out a cry of relief and threw herself on top

of him. He winced and she pulled back. "What were you trying to do?"

"Catch a bullet for you," he said, feeling out of breath.

Casimir closed his eyes, trying to think only of her face and not the throbbing in his chest.

When he woke, he knew immediately he was in her bed in her beach house in Acacia. The softness of her sheets and the scent of her surrounded him.

Serena was next to him on the bed, watching him. "How are you?"

Medical equipment was at the bedside, a blood pressure cuff was wrapped around his arm and a pad was taped to his chest.

"I feel like I've been shot," he said.

She touched his forehead. "You were shot. Twice. I have a nurse checking on you, but I thought you would be more comfortable recuperating here."

"I like it here. The smell and the sound of the waves. Where's Samuel?"

"I don't know. Not here. When the doctors confirmed you were stable, we took my plane back to here. I had X-rays taken of your chest. You've been in and out of consciousness. You hit your head when you fell."

He didn't remember much of anything. "Did I say anything stupid?"

She kissed his cheek. "No more than usual."

He smirked at her joke. "Can I see your hand?"

She held out her left hand. It was bare.

"No ring?" he asked. Had he misunderstood? Perhaps she and Samuel were not engaged. Had she refused him? Or had Rolland interrupted her answer?

She gestured to the white dresser across from the bed, against the wall. "It's there. On the dresser."

His chest ached all over again. "Why aren't you wearing it?"

"Are you trying to put yourself in more pain?" Serena asked.

He was fine. He'd had the wind knocked out of him by a couple powerful bullets. He wasn't down for the count. "You said yes." To King Warrington. To the man who had killed his father and destroyed his mother's life and who was seated on the throne that belonged to him.

"I had no choice. If I had said no to the king, it would have made the tensions between Acacia, Rizari and Icarus worse. I have to think of more than myself in these matters. If I get closer to Samuel, I can convince him that war is not the right response to the incident with Icarus."

Casimir would have preferred not knowing she belonged, at least in words, to King Warrington. "Run away with me."

"What?" she asked. "I had them look at your chest and your head. They said everything would be okay, but you sound crazy."

He felt crazy—and desperate. He had lost focus on his plan and his goals had changed. But the moment when he'd known Rolland was taking a shot at King Warrington, possibly gunning for Serena, too, nothing had been more important than her. "Run away with me. Let's leave this all behind."

"We can't do that," she said, but she sounded like she was considering it.

"You could have been killed today," he said.

"But I wasn't."

"Did they find the trigger man?"

She shook her head and laid her hand gently on his arm. "Everyone is looking for him. He won't get far. Someone snapped a picture of him."

"He's an assassin named Rolland. I know him."

Serena's brow creased. "What do you know about him?"

"That he's a sick, sadistic killer. He won't stop coming after King Warrington and I suspect he may come after me now," Casimir said.

"Why you?"

The ache in his chest was second to his worry. "You don't know Rolland. He's resourceful and slippery. I screwed up his assassination. He'll take that hard." Casimir didn't want to tell her that DeSante had sent Rolland. Keeping the peace between Acacia and Icarus was critical.

"You saved my life. Again. You have a funny habit of doing that. But my guards are here. They will keep us safe. It's my turn to protect you."

"I told you I would look out for you," Casimir said. She looked suspicious, as if she had more questions. If pressed, Casimir would answer them and then all the cards would be on the table. With the truth laid bare, Casimir would be taking a risk. He wanted to tell her. Wanted to give her a chance to be the woman he knew she could be, to see that he was a good man. "This isn't the life you deserve. Run away with me," he repeated, hating the begging in his voice.

Serena stood. "You don't mean any of this. You were hurt and you need to recover. Rest now. I'll wake you to eat in a little while."

Serena lifted his hand and kissed his knuckles. Casimir felt an ache in his chest, her rejection and the bruise of the bullets twisting in an unfamiliar combination of pain.

Casimir was talking crazy. It must be the medications he had been given for his injuries. Serena couldn't run away. It was her duty to serve as queen. She had taken an oath to serve Acacia. Walking away now was unacceptable.

She tried to reach Warrington again on his phone. He wasn't answering. Rizari and Icarus continued to circle each other and it was a matter of time before one took a swipe at the other and catapulted their countries into a full-on war. She had heard Warrington accusing Icarus of sending the assassin. If he confirmed it, war was inevitable.

Since she was engaged to Samuel, she would be dragging Acacia into Rizari's war with Icarus. Would he consider that before declaring war on Icarus? Would he consult her?

She had too much work to do and she needed to stay on top of the military and political situation between Rizari and Icarus, but she couldn't leave Casimir alone in the beach house. He was resting and injured. Could she bring him to the castle?

Serena looked around the kitchen. She needed to fix Casimir a meal. Her cooking skills were rough, but she had the ingredients to make soup. As she chopped vegetables, she thought again about what he had said to her.

Run away with me.

As if it was that easy. As if she could pack a bag and take off with him. Where would they go? What would they do for money? What about Acacia?

Yet he had seemed so earnest and so serious. He struck her as a man who thought through plans. Maybe his injury had affected him. Or maybe he had been telling her the truth. She couldn't wrap her head around it.

An hour later, she had a serviceable vegetable stew. She carried two bowls, two spoons and two cups of juice upstairs on a tray.

She watched Casimir sleep for a few moments and briefly considered letting him sleep as long as he needed to. He sensed her in the room—his protective instinct wasn't completely quiet—and he rolled over. He'd removed the blood-pressure cuff and pulse oximeter. He wasn't wearing a shirt and the location where the bullet had struck his vest was red and turning blue in places.

"I brought some soup," she said.

"Smells great."

He shifted and she caught his wince. She set the tray on her dresser and stacked the pillows behind him to make him more comfortable. She heard a creak on the stairs. Casimir said nothing, but tensed.

She brought the tray to Casimir. "Relax. My guards are watching the house. It's just the house settling."

A man with brown hair and weasel eyes appeared in the room brandishing a gun. "Your guards aren't watching anything. Your guards are dead, darling."

Serena turned and knocked the tray of soup off the bed. It splashed to the ground, burning her legs. "Get out of here!"

Casimir rolled to his feet. Gone was any sign he was in pain. "Rolland, you don't need to do this."

Rolland, the man who had tried to kill Samuel Warrington earlier that night had found her home. Were her guards dead or was he bluffing? If they were alive, where were they?

Rolland inclined his head. "DeSante didn't tell me you were sleeping with the queen. I thought she was engaged to the king of Rizari."

DeSante had hired Rolland. Serena touched her bare ring finger and put as much distance between herself and Rolland as possible. He had a wild look in his eyes. She didn't have any weapons in her bedroom. Throwing a lamp at him might distract him for a moment, but it wouldn't be effective against a gun.

Casimir didn't have a weapon to defend them either. Could he talk his way out of this without anyone else getting hurt?

"A marriage to the king of Rizari is a bad idea. I plan to put a stop to it," Rolland said. "Killing Casimir will be a bonus. He royally screwed up my plans. Excuse the pun."

"I'm not marrying the king of Rizari," Serena said calmly.

Rolland nodded toward the dresser where her engagement ring was sitting. "That ginormous rock says otherwise. And you forget. I saw you say yes to him." Rolland lifted his gun at her.

Casimir launched himself at Rolland. The assassin fought back, pinning Casimir to the floor and whipping him across the face with the gun.

Serena was about to throw herself at Rolland when Casimir roared up from the floor, slamming Rolland into the footboard of the bed. Relief washed over her. Casimir seemed to be in control.

Casimir grabbed Rolland's hand, pounding it against the floor. The gun popped free and Serena scrambled to grab it. It felt heavy and awkward in her hands, but she held it straight out, in Rolland's direction.

"Don't move," she said.

Casimir climbed to his feet and came to her side, taking the gun from her. He was breathing hard and covered in sweat.

"Serena, call for an ambulance. Rolland needs one."

Santino rushed to Serena and hugged her close. The police were on the scene and Casimir was speaking to them. Serena was worried about Casimir being up and around with his injuries, but he was handling the questions about Rolland. The bodies of her four guards were being loaded into ambulances. Rolland hadn't been lying about that. Tonight four men had died protecting her.

Their sacrifice wouldn't be forgotten. She would contact their families soon and offer her condolences and what she could to help them.

"I was so worried when I heard," Santino said.

"Worried because you feared I was with Casimir?" It was an unfair statement, but she wasn't ready to forgive her uncle for the mammoth pressure he had put on her to marry King Warrington and what he had said about her and Casimir.

In the end, Santino had what he wanted. She and King Warrington were engaged and she would sign the union agreement soon enough.

"I was worried about you being with Casimir, but not in the manner you mean."

Her uncle cleared his throat and extended to her a large envelope. "I've had Casimir followed. He may not be who he claims. I thought you should have eyes wide-open about that man."

Serena took the envelope, not sure of her uncle's intent with his accusations. "Who do you think he is?"

Her uncle didn't answer. He pointed to the envelope.

She sighed her displeasure and pulled a stack of photographs from the envelope. A few were impossible to place, close-ups of Casimir shopping, a couple from the wedding in Elion, a few with Fiona close to him. "What are you angling at?"

"Do you think it's strange that Casimir is always around when you need someone to rescue you? First, your father's birthday party. At the symphony hall during your engagement and then tonight."

Serena shook her head. If her uncle was implying Casimir was an assassin targeting her, he was wrong. "Someone is targeting me and Casimir is staying close. He cares about me and wants me to be safe."

Her uncle reached into the stack and drew out one of the pictures from the bottom. It was a picture of Casimir speaking to Demetrius DeSante.

"Casimir has been social with DeSante. I've been to those same functions and seen them speaking."

Her uncle rocked back on his feet. "Serena, you are painfully dense. They are more than casual acquaintances and you need to speak with him about that."

Serena would ask him about the extent of his relationship with DeSante, but Casimir had proven himself loyal. She felt bad about questioning him. Rolland had implied that DeSante had sent him. Casimir would not be part of a plot like that; his life had been in danger, too.

Her uncle held up a recording device. "If the pictures don't convince you, then you need to listen to this."

Serena's stomach tensed. "What's on the recording?"

"It would be better for you to listen to the recording. I don't want to give you the wrong impression or confuse you with my interpretation of what I heard."

Serena tried to process yet another bomb of information.

"Do you want me to alert King Warrington that we have a situation? How much have you told Casimir Cullen about your plans for Acacia?"

Too many questions. Serena looked at the recording device. Should she ask Casimir about it first and give him a chance to explain? Or listen to the conversation and draw her own conclusions? Serena couldn't remember every word she had spoken to Casimir about Acacia. He had never told her he was friends with Demetrius DeSante and they behaved like near strangers when they were in each other's company.

At best, Casimir had been hiding something from her. At worst, he was conspiring against her with DeSante as his partner. Was it the reason DeSante had positioned himself close to Iliana?

Serena held up her hand, silencing her uncle. "Enough. Give me time. I need to think about this."

Santino nodded once, bowed slightly and left her alone on the porch. Shoulders heavy, she entered her house and closed the doors behind her. She could see Casimir through her front windows, speaking with the police.

He looked handsome and strong but what she might hear next could devastate her. Her heart ached. Could

Casimir have been fooling her this entire time? Was he involved with her because of a hidden agenda?

She had given her heart to Casimir. She was thinking of ways to be with him, to escape her marriage arrangement with King Warrington. Was her uncle right that she was naive and overtrusting?

Feeling as if she was betraying Casimir, she pressed Play.

Some static and then Casimir's voice clear and strong. "I understand."

A long pause, then Casimir's voice again.

"She knows it's a mistake, but she's in a difficult position."

A pause.

"I haven't wavered from our plans."

What plans? If Casimir was indeed talking to De-Sante, it sounded as if they were working together. Working together against her? Why? What did they want?

More static on the line and then the recording ended.

The recording didn't prove much to her. How could she be sure that Casimir had even been speaking to DeSante? The recording was from her uncle, so considering the source, she gave it some validity. Was Casimir talking about her marriage to Warrington? He had expressed to her that he didn't want her to marry the king. That was nothing new. But what were the plans he'd mentioned?

She called to question the past several days. She and Casimir had made love. Was that only to keep her and King Warrington from growing closer? Was Casimir giving her advice based on his loyalties to President De-Sante and whatever they were conspiring to do?

Anger swamped her, mixing with sadness. She needed answers and only Casimir had them. She strode out of the house, directly to Casimir.

Maybe it was the look on her face or the fact that she was shaking with anger, but the entire yard fell silent.

"Leave us," she said. She was looking at Casimir.

The police and others fell back.

His scent, heartbreakingly delicious, lingered on her skin, tantalizing her. She grappled for her resolve. Casimir needed to explain to her what was going on between him and DeSante.

"What's wrong?" he asked and extended his hand to touch her.

She moved out of his grasp. "I need to know something from you. Whatever you tell me had better be the truth."

If he was a liar who was worried about being caught doing something wrong, he hid it well. His face was impassive.

She handed him the pictures. He glanced at them. "You had me followed?"

No accusation or hurt in his voice. Had he expected it because he was a liar who knew the truth would one day come to light?

"Do you want to explain what it is you're doing?"

He looked at the pictures again. "What do you want to know?"

He was pretending nothing was wrong and it infuriated her. She held up the recorder. "I have a recording of you talking to the president of Icarus. Care to explain that?" She felt shaken and broken, but her anger urged her forward.

"May I listen to the recording?"

She had hoped he would deny talking to DeSante. "Why do you need to listen to it?" So he could figure out what she knew and what lies he could tell to keep her in the dark?

"I think you may be misinterpreting things or taking words out of context."

Her anger was hot and she struggled not to escalate the conversation into shouting at him. "Explain how you know President DeSante."

"He and I are friends."

That would have been important information on day one. "Friends? You're friends with him? Are you also friends with King Warrington? Doesn't that make you a traitor? This recording makes it sound like you work for DeSante." And that he was working for him in a task that involved her. "Did you know the assassin's name because you were part of the plan to kill Warrington? Were you part of the plot to kill my father?"

Casimir lifted his chin and squared his shoulders. "I had nothing to do with your father's or your sister's deaths. I work for myself. I am friends with Demetrius DeSante."

When faced with the truth, why was he holding back? "What are you two planning?"

Casimir clasped his hands in front of him.

Silence? Didn't she deserve more? "If you do not answer me, I will have you arrested." Though the idea of Casimir in a jail cell almost gutted her, she couldn't allow someone—even the man she was falling in love with—to conspire against her and Acacia.

Casimir's eyes narrowed slightly. "Serena, there are matters you don't fully understand and can't possibly know. I need your trust. I need you to trust me."

He was withholding information and keeping secrets and he wanted her trust? "I cannot trust you if you will not tell me everything." The words burned in her throat.

Hurt flickered in his eyes. "I cannot tell you everything. I have too much on the line."

She had wanted him to bring her into his confidence. "Deceiving me sits well with you?"

"My plans have nothing to do with you."

He could not have spoken more hurtful words. She had believed that they had some future together, however difficult it might seem. But he was making his own plans; he was carrying out his own agenda. "What arrangement have you made with the president of Icarus?"

He hedged. "I cannot tell you that except to reiterate I had no hand in killing your father or your sister."

She fought against the negative thoughts that clouded her: Casimir was using her. He had been using her from day one. She had made a terrible mistake in judgment by trusting him. Her uncle and her detractors had been right about her.

Those soul-sinking ideas were too easy to hold on to. She went for broke. "Do you have feelings for me?"

"Yes," Casimir said. Except his face was once again impassive. If he cared for her, wouldn't he scramble to make this right?

"Why did you come to Acacia?" she asked.

"The answer is complicated."

"Lies usually are."

He met her eyes, but didn't respond.

She threw her hands in the air. Her emotions were a tangled mess. "Say something to convince me that you aren't a liar and a coward and a thief." A thief who had stolen her heart.

"I have not stolen from you."

She wouldn't admit she had lost her heart to him. "You have taken a great deal from me."

"The less you know the better."

Now he was insulting her. "Why do people say that to me? Because you think I'm an idiot who can't handle the truth?"

Casimir extended his hand to touch her and she jerked away before he could.

He didn't try again. That she wanted him to spoke of the depth of her feelings for him.

"There is a history you don't understand. There are situations that have unfolded and I don't want you caught in the cross fire. Look what happened tonight because you were in the middle of DeSante and Warrington!" Casimir said.

"How noble of you to want to protect me," she said, letting the sarcasm drip from her voice.

"I have honorable intentions for you. I don't want to hurt you."

Yet he had. Deeply. "You can tell me the truth or you can be escorted from here by the police."

Casimir stared at the sky. "You are asking me to either drag you into a war or keep you from it."

"But haven't you heard, Casimir? There will be a war. Countries are choosing sides and I will be dragged into the middle of this no matter what I do next. The only thing I know, here and now, is that you are guilty of crimes against Acacia."

She summoned her police and pointed to Casimir. "Arrest him for espionage and treason against Acacia."

Her heart broke at the words, but she made sure her

face betrayed no emotion. She had finally mastered the art of wearing her queen facade, but it wasn't a triumph. She felt as if she had lost everything that was important.

Chapter 11

Serena paced in her office. Iliana was sitting on the window seat watching her.

"You have something to say. Say it," Serena said. She was in a foul mood and hated to take it out on Iliana.

"You need to talk to him to find the truth," Iliana said.

"I asked him for the truth and he refused to give it to me."

"Give him another chance."

Give another chance to the man who had conspired against her with President DeSante?

"Are you hearing this from DeSante?" Serena asked.

Iliana shook her head. "No, Serena. My loyalty is to you. First to you. You know that. I haven't spoken to DeSante about this."

The hurt in Iliana's voice struck her. "I'm sorry, Iliana."

Her cousin waved her hand dismissively. "Don't be.

I feel like a moron. I blew things with DeSante out of proportion. He was using me and I think that's never been clearer before now. Please, don't mention DeSante. I'll just feel more stupid."

Serena understood. It was how she felt when sorting through what had happened with Casimir. "What was Casimir trying to accomplish?" Was his agenda to influence her to ally herself with Icarus? Was there more to his motives? Had she given away anything, said anything in front of him that gave Icarus leverage over her?

She had been foolish to fall for Casimir's charms. The setup and everything he had said and done had been too perfect. He could have studied her for months.

"The only person who can answer that question is Casimir," Iliana said.

"He's been lying to me. Why tell the truth now?"

Iliana stood. "You're right. He doesn't have to. But he cares for you. He saved your life." She pressed her lips tightly together and sighed. "The way he looks at you and speaks to you. He can't be pretending all of it. So give him a chance to come clean. Then decide."

Serena's heart ached to talk to Casimir. War was on her doorstep. DeSante and Warrington were ready to pounce on each other. Now was her chance to find the truth and ally herself with the right side.

Perhaps Casimir knew something about Icarus and DeSante or Rizari and Warrington that was critical. As a queen, Serena needed to know what that was. As a woman, she needed to know how he felt about her.

Casimir was inside a jail cell in the castle, with bars on the windows and the door locked. He wanted to speak to Serena, explain who he was and what he wanted. Outside at the beach house, he had been caught off guard. He had been scared for her after what had happened with Rolland and he had shut down his emotions and tried to think like a king and not like a man who wanted to protect the woman he loved.

He needed to speak with her now.

Yet asking one of the guards to see or talk to her would rush her. Serena had a methodical approach to everything. She would think and then would come see him. He would wait.

Casimir didn't have to wait long. The lock on the door creaked open and Serena entered the room. He noticed a change in her. Her timidity was gone. He read anger and hurt in her eyes. She moved like a predator and he liked seeing her strength.

He stood from the bare metal cot where he'd been sitting.

Serena remained near the door. "You will not be given another chance to talk. Tell me everything."

Casimir kept his hands at his sides. He wanted to reach for her and draw her into his arms, assure her that he had no intention of hurting her. He didn't want to manipulate her.

He started with the truth, the simplest fact. "My name is Constantine Casimir Warrington the fourth."

He gave her a moment to digest his last name. Her eyes flickered with recognition.

"My first cousin on my father's side is Samuel Warrington. He inherited the throne from my father, but I am the rightful heir. My mother was forced to leave Rizari while she was pregnant with me. My father never knew I existed. Samuel killed my father and his father in a hunting accident he arranged. His mother is partly responsible for my mother's exile from Rizari. I want revenge on both of them. I want what is rightfully mine," Casimir said.

"You believe the throne should be yours?" she asked.

"Yes." He was encouraged that she didn't immediately call him a liar and storm out of the room.

"How did you become involved with Demetrius DeSante?"

"My mother and I lived in Icarus after she was exiled from Rizari. When DeSante was a general in the Icarus military, I served under him for five years. I made a name for myself. I worked to become close to Demetrius, then I helped him topple the previous government and take over as president."

"He's a dictator," Serena said.

"Call him what you want. I told him the truth about who I am. He knows what I intended to do. He has been my ally in this matter because he knows that I will be a better king than Samuel. Better for Icarus and Acacia and Rizari."

She inclined her head. "What about me? What did you intend to do with me?"

"I didn't intend to hurt you. I came to your father's birthday party planning to kill Samuel Warrington. When my plans were interrupted by the assassination of your father, I realized I had an opportunity to find out what happened to my mother and my father and expose the truth."

"You planned to use me to do that?"

"Yes. But what's happened between us has been genuine. I didn't sleep with you to acquire information. I did it because I wanted you. Want you still."

He could read nothing on her face, but her knuckles were white from clasping her hands so hard.

He was getting to her and while he didn't want to use their chemistry to manipulate her, he ached for her. He ached to take her to bed. To make love to her and talk until they had cleared the air and she again looked at him with affection and respect. Would she ever look at him that way again?

He knelt at her feet. "I know you're hurt. I should have confided in you sooner."

She shook her head. "I can't trust you."

Her nipples were puckered under her blouse. It was strange to notice it now, but he was tuned in to her. "You can."

She shook her head. He would remember the look on her face for the rest of his life. Sadness, hurt and longing, all mixed into one.

"I need you to forgive me," he said.

"No." Her mouth said one thing, her body another. She reached for his shoulders and drew him closer.

"I want you, Serena. I'll always want you."

"What you want isn't relevant."

"Then tell me what you want and I will make it happen."

Serena narrowed her gaze on him. "You plan to take the throne from Warrington?"

"Yes. I will take the throne and expose him as a liar and a murderer."

"And then what? DeSante is spoiling for war."

"He is not spoiling for war. You have it mixed up. It's Warrington who wants war."

"If you become king of Rizari, you will make amends

to DeSante. Then you will release me from any obligation to Rizari. I will rule Acacia."

He nodded. "I can promise you peace and I have no quarrel with you ruling Acacia. I have told you before that you are the right woman for the job. I am glad that you've accepted it."

"Are you behind the assassination of my father and the attempts on my life?"

He had denied it before, but maybe she needed the words again. "No." The denial was immediate and adamant because it was the truth. The idea of hurting her was revolting to him. "I will never hurt you. If you trust me to do as I say I will, I will make it my goal to never, ever cause you pain again."

Serena closed her eyes for a long moment. "That is a promise you will keep, but only as the leader of Rizari. I will never again be yours in any way other than as the queen of Acacia."

The words burned through him, but Casimir wouldn't push now. He couldn't lose her, but it would take time. She was angry and lashing out. "I will need your help."

She tensed. "Now you want my forgiveness *and* my help?"

"To grow closer to King Warrington and expose his lies. To take my place as the rightful king."

He waited for her answer, knowing his plans hinged on her saying yes.

Serena understood anger. She understood wanting revenge for pain and loss. Her need to settle the score with whoever had killed her father and sister was dimmed by the overwhelming sense of grief that seemed to take up every spare inch of her emotional capacity.

She had to do what was right for herself and right for Acacia. Regardless of what Casimir had wanted, her country came first.

Serena entered her solarium, her head held high. Samuel and his mother were waiting for her. "Thank you for meeting me this morning."

Katarina took a sip of her tea and smiled thinly. "We are very busy and surprised by your invitation. After the assassination attempt on Samuel, we've been trying to stay out of the spotlight. Please explain what was so important that you must speak to us today."

Serena took her seat kitty-corner from Samuel and his mother and tried not to let Katarina's words annoy her. "I've read the merger agreement."

"I think you've found it's more than fair, given your position?" Samuel asked.

Serena laughed and shook her head. Samuel and Katarina exchanged looks. It was Serena's intention to set them off-kilter. "Not equitable at all. You have too many demands for me. You think I'm in the weaker position, but I have something that you need. I think this will make you feel more open to negotiations. Guards!"

Her guards escorted a handcuffed Casimir into the room. They stood on either side of him.

"What is this supposed to be? You're arresting your lover?" Samuel asked.

Serena clucked her tongue. "You misunderstand our relationship. I wanted to expose this man for the fraud he is. You know this man as Casimir Cullen. I've learned his identity is Constantine Casimir Warrington the fourth, rightful heir to the throne of Rizari." She took a moment to let Samuel and his mother chew on that before continuing. "If you want this information to remain between us, you will offer me better terms." She picked up her merger paperwork from the coffee table and handed it to Samuel. "You can read this over, but it's not negotiable. If you want Casimir in your custody, you will agree to do what I have spelled out in that document."

Katarina rose to her feet. "This man has no claim to the throne."

"The law of Rizari says otherwise."

"I'd heard rumors…but I thought they were just that," Katarina mumbled. She straightened. "That is ludicrous. You can't make demands. I will not let you destroy what we have worked for."

Serena inclined her head. "What is it that you've worked for exactly?"

Katarina narrowed her eyes on Serena. "You think you're so smart and you have it all figured out. I could kill you right now and no one would stop me."

Since both Casimir and her guards were in the room, she doubted that. "You would threaten me in my castle?"

"You seem fit to threaten the king of Rizari," Samuel said.

Katarina grabbed the gun from the guard to her left. She leveled it at Serena. "You've overplayed your hand. I have had more time to build allies. One very important ally who will swear that whatever I speak is truth. I won't cow to your threats. We will take this man, this fraud, as our prisoner and I will kill you to keep the truth silenced."

Confused by Katarina's declaration, Serena rose to her feet.

Santino entered the solarium. "Looks like I've arrived in time. Ladies, please. Let's not let this fly out of hand. Katarina, don't let your temper spoil our plans. We've worked far too long and hard to clear the way to allow a misstep to ruin us."

The familiarity between Uncle Santino and Katarina disturbed her. How did they know each other?

Katarina lowered the gun. "You have two minutes to convince me why I shouldn't kill your niece."

Santino glanced at Serena, his eyes flat and cold. "Because we can use her. Because if you kill her, the next heir is that twit Iliana. She is far less pliable and already close with Demetrius DeSante."

"Mother, what is this about? Someone had better tell me what's going on!" Samuel said.

Katarina held up her hand to her son. "Samuel, just shut up and let me handle this."

"Let you handle it like you handled killing King Alagona and Uncle Constantine? Like you killed my father? Like you killed Danae?" His rage was white-hot and Serena sensed he had known the truth, and it had been killing him.

"You monster!" Serena leapt onto Katarina, landing a punch across her face. The gun popped free and skidded across the floor. Casimir dove for it, his handcuffs swinging from his arm.

Casimir was now armed, as were her guards.

Before relief could settle on her, her guards turned their guns on Casimir. "Do not shoot him. He is not our enemy. Katarina is."

Santino came at Serena, grabbing her by the arm. "You little idiot! What game are you playing?"

"Let her go, Santino, or I will shoot you."

Santino threw her to the floor and whirled on Casimir. "You've made a grave miscalculation. The guards in this castle work for me. They always have. At my command, they will kill you before you have a chance to get a shot off. They've been following you at my direction. I knew you were more than a wealthy playboy. I was right. I should have had you killed weeks ago."

Katarina rose to her feet and appeared smug. "Everything I've done has been for my son and the good of Rizari. If that means I have to kill the queen of Acacia and her lover to clear the way, I have no problem with that."

"Enough! All of you!" Samuel said. "Danae was murdered because of you." He choked back a sob. "I won't allow this to go any further. I should have stopped you after she died. When she died, a piece of me did, too." Grief underscored every word.

Samuel had loved Danae. Seeing his behavior in that light shed nuances on his behavior and explained much of his distance and his treatment of her. Somehow, knowing he had loved Danae was a salve on that hurt.

"Don't be weak," Katarina said. "I've done this for you, Samuel, so you could be king."

"So you could have control of Rizari and use me to do it!" Samuel screamed. He picked up a crystal vase from the table next to him and swung it at Katarina. She screamed in pain as it shattered across her face.

Casimir aimed his gun at Santino. "As the rightful heir to the throne in Rizari, in union with the queen of Acacia, I command you to drop your weapons. You will be rewarded for your loyalty. Disobedience will be punished."

"Shoot him! Shoot him!" Santino screamed.

The guards exchanged confused looks. They didn't know whose direction to follow.

Casimir shot Santino in the knee and he dropped to the ground, screaming.

"Last warning!" Casimir said.

The guards laid their guns on the ground, raised their hands, and backed away.

Serena picked up the guns, never letting her eyes leave her uncle. Samuel sat on the couch and wept.

Santino was being loaded into an ambulance. He was handcuffed to his gurney. Katarina was being treated by another paramedic on the scene.

In exchange for a lesser sentence, Samuel was spilling everything he knew about his mother and Santino's plot to make him king.

Years earlier, his mother had driven a wedge between Casimir's parents, forcing Anna out of the country by accusing her of having an affair with the king's brother, Katarina's husband. Katarina had arranged for the murder of King Constantine and her husband while they were on a hunting trip.

Katarina had then planned the murder of King Alagona, hoping to put Samuel in a position of leadership and power when he married Danae, the heir apparent to the throne in Acacia. Danae's death had been an accident. The threats against Serena had been tools to scare her into agreeing to marry King Warrington and merge with Rizari.

Casimir had a legitimate claim to the throne and an investigation was under way to prove it. Demetrius De-Sante and Casimir had already been working on building the case. The matter should be simple to verify.

When Casimir assumed power, Acacia, Rizari and Icarus would have true and stable peace in their region for the first time in a century. His mother would have peace in her heart.

Casimir strode toward Serena, his shoulders back, his head high. He looked regal and unburdened. "I want you to know that I will do everything I promised. I will support Acacia as an ally and you as the queen. I will make peace with Icarus."

Serena folded her hands in front of her to keep from reaching for him. "Thank you, Casimir. You have everything you want now." He would be king of his nation. Why didn't he seem happier? Was he masking his emotions to appear in control?

"Not everything I want." He knelt in front of her, taking her hands gently in his. "I was bent on seeking revenge. But I've discovered that, more than revenge, I want you. I want you in my life. I will do anything you ask if you will give me another chance. I will walk away from all of this. I'll live with you in Acacia and be your faithful servant."

He was offering to abandon everything he had worked for. "What about Rizari? What about the throne?"

"I will pass the crown to someone else." The ease with which he could give up his kingdom told her that she was far more important to him than she had believed.

She ran her fingertips down the side of his face. "Casimir, you can't do that. You can't walk away from Rizari. Your country needs you."

His eyes shone with longing. "What about you? Do you need me?"

She felt tears welling in her eyes. What was being offered to her was rare and precious. All she had to do was reach out and accept it. "I do need you. I want you at my side whether that's on the throne, on the beach or in bed."

"Come here," Casimir said, dragging her into his arms.

"Don't you have work to do?" she asked.

He pressed a kiss to her lips. "Never too much work for this. Never too much to take time to tell you that I love you."

"I love you, too, Casimir."

"Then will you do me the honor of marrying me and being my wife?"

Joy erupted in her heart. She didn't think she could have been happier until that moment. "Yes, I will marry you, Constantine."

He groaned. "No one calls me that."

"But you're the fourth in a line of kings. What would you think about starting a family and giving you a fifth?"

Casimir kissed her long and hard. "I've always loved how your mind works."

* * * * *

"There's only...you."

All of the moisture seemed to dry up in her mouth. Her gaze slowly slid over him. The last time she'd seen him had been months ago. She'd wanted to talk with him then, but her brothers had been determined to keep her away from him.

Her brothers were keeping secrets from her.

Only fair, really, because she'd been keeping plenty of secrets from them, too.

Mark was a handsome man. Powerful and commanding. He had high, slanting cheeks, a long, hard blade of a nose and lips that were... sexy. Sensual. She'd spent far too much time thinking about Mark's lips over the years.

"What the hell are you doing here, Ava? I thought you were staying away."

Not from him, but from Austin. From the McGuire ranch, because that place held too many painful memories for her.

But when no place seemed safe, where were you supposed to go?

SUSPICIONS

BY
CYNTHIA EDEN

MILLS & BOON

Published in Great Britain 2015
by Mills & Boon, an imprint of Harlequin (UK) Limited,
Eton House, 18-24 Paradise Road, Richmond, Surrey, TW9 1SR

© 2015 Cindy Roussos

ISBN: 978-0-263-25316-0

46-0915

Harlequin (UK) Limited's policy is to use papers that are natural, renewable and recyclable products and made from wood grown in sustainable forests. The logging and manufacturing processes conform to the legal environmental regulations of the country of origin.

Printed and bound in Spain
by CPI, Barcelona

Cynthia Eden, a *New York Times* bestselling author, writes tales of romantic suspense and paranormal romance. Her books have received starred reviews from *Publishers Weekly*, and she has received a RITA® Award nomination for best romantic suspense novel. Cynthia lives in the Deep South, loves horror movies and has an addiction to chocolate. More information about Cynthia may be found at cynthiaeden.com, or you can follow her on Twitter, @cynthiaeden.

This book is for all of the wonderful
Harlequin Intrigue fans out there—
thank you so much for your support!

Prologue

"Help me!"

Her cry broke through the night, a long, loud, desperate scream.

Mark Montgomery had been standing on his front porch, staring up at the starry sky, but at that terrified call, he whirled around. At first he didn't see her. The darkness was too thick.

Thud. Thud. Thud. Thud.

He heard the unmistakable sound of a horse's hooves pounding across the ground. Someone was riding fast and hard, coming straight toward him.

He leapt off the porch.

"Help me!"

Her cry was even louder this time—and it was definitely a woman's voice. But there weren't any women at his ranch tonight. His mother had passed years ago, and there weren't any female ranch hands scheduled for a shift.

Then he saw the horse. It burst into the clearing near his house. The horse was a beautiful big black mare that he recognized—that was Lady. And Lady...Lady belonged to the McGuires, his neighbors who lived about ten miles away.

What the—?

A small figure was curled low on Lady's back, hugging the horse tightly. The horse's sides were shaking, its body wet with sweat after what must have been a brutal ride.

A ride in the middle of the night?

"M-Mark?"

And he knew that voice. Not screaming now, but soft, almost broken. He wanted to run toward that horse and rider, but he was afraid of spooking Lady, so he approached slowly, carefully. When the horse neighed, he reached out and softly touched Lady's mane. "It's okay." Then he reached up for the rider—Ava.

He could see her now. There was no mistaking Ava McGuire, not with that long, wild tumble of her hair. The moonlight and starlight spilled down onto her face, and the fear there made him lose his breath.

Some of his ranch hands had come into the yard, but they stayed a few feet back. "Get the horse!" Mark ordered as he pulled Ava off Lady.

She was like ice in his hands, and hard, heavy trembles kept raking her delicate frame. Ava had five brothers, all big, hulking military types, and Ava—the baby of the family—she was different. Delicate… Fragile… She was—

Crying. Because he'd just touched her cheeks and he could feel the wetness there. He wrapped his arms around her and held her tight. "What is it? What's happened?"

"Sh-shot…"

He could barely make out what she was saying.

"They…they were waiting…in the h-house…"

He caught her arms and eased back so that his gaze

could sweep over her. "Ava, did someone hurt you?" Rage pumped through him. Ava was only sixteen. If some jerks had hurt her, he would make them pay.

Her teeth were chattering. "Dead." She seemed to push out the word. "I'm scared. They're—dead."

Mark's whole body stiffened. "Who, Ava? Who are you talking about?"

She threw her body against his and started sobbing. "M-my parents! I saw them…the men…had guns! I heard the gunshots. I *ran*." Her sobs grew even harder. "I left them there…"

He held her as tightly as he could. There had to be a mistake. Her parents—they were fine, weren't they?

"Please," Ava begged him. "Help my parents. *Help them!*"

But there was nothing he could do. When Mark and his men went to the McGuire ranch, they didn't see the attackers. They just saw the blood.

Mark and his men made it to the ranch before the cops did. He was the first one in that place—and he would never forget the terrible sight that greeted him.

"Who would do something like this?" Ty Watts, Mark's ranch foreman, demanded as he stared at the brutal scene. "And *why*?"

There was no sign of the attackers. They were long gone. Mark stood there, the scent of blood heavy in the air around him, and he knew that he would be the one telling Ava that her parents hadn't survived.

He would be the one to give her the devastating news.

Mark bent down next to Ava's father. "I'm sorry," he whispered.

AVA STAYED AT his ranch for two days. During that time, she barely spoke. Her skin was too pale, her eyes far too wounded. She jumped at the slightest sound and during the night, she woke screaming. Again and again.

Mark didn't think he'd ever forget the sound of Ava's screams. He hated her pain and her grief, and he wished that he could do something to comfort her.

"I should have helped them." Ava's low voice had his head whipping toward her. They were on his porch, waiting, because Mark had gotten word that Ava's oldest brother had finally made it back to town. He'd learned of the slaughter at his family's ranch, and Grant McGuire had rushed home, flying back from some covert mission that had taken him to the other side of the world.

"Ava…" Mark sighed her name, and deliberately keeping his voice gentle, he told her, "The attackers had guns. What could you have done? You went for help!"

She shook her head, sending the dark locks sliding over her shoulder. "I left them to die."

She was breaking his heart. Ripping it right out with her quiet words.

"If you'd stayed," Mark forced himself to say, "then you'd be dead, too."

At first, Ava didn't speak. She stared down at her hands. Her fingers fisted. "I feel dead."

He strode toward her to pull her close. When she wouldn't look at him, he tipped back her chin. "Ava."

She flinched.

"You aren't dead." The thought of her dead—the thought of finding Ava… Ava with her slow smile and her warm green eyes…*dead*…that notion chilled him. "I won't let anyone hurt you."

He heard the sound of a car approaching. He didn't

let Ava go, but he glanced over his shoulder. Grant Mc-Guire had arrived. He'd come to take Ava away.

I don't want to let her go.

Because when Ava stayed with him at the ranch, he knew she was safe. He had his men on alert. They were patrolling constantly. But when Ava left…how was he supposed to watch out for her?

A car door slammed. Footsteps approached. But Ava was still staring up at Mark. He found that he couldn't look away from her.

"I'm scared," she whispered.

So am I. And very little scared him in this world.

"Ava!" That was Grant's voice. And suddenly Grant was charging up the steps. He pulled Ava into his arms and held her tight.

The guy's arms seemed to swallow Ava as she stood there, and Mark knew that Grant would be taking her away. The guy had flown halfway across the country in order to come home to Ava.

Grant turned toward him. "Thanks for watching my sister."

He forced his gaze to meet Grant's green stare. Green, like Ava's, but different. Colder. Harder. Fierce.

"I won't forget what you did." Grant shook Mark's hand. Then he looked back at Ava. "It's time to leave."

A tear slid down Ava's cheek, but she didn't make a sound. Mark's chest ached. He wanted to reach out to Ava and comfort her.

But Grant was the one to do that. Grant wiped away her tears before he pulled her close once again. "We're going to find the men who did this," he promised her. "They won't ever hurt anyone again."

And in that moment, Mark made a vow of his own.
No one would ever hurt Ava again.
Because her tears tore him apart.

Chapter One

Ava McGuire didn't have a lot of safe havens. And, outside of her family, there weren't exactly a lot of people she trusted.

In fact, only one person came to mind…

Mark Montgomery.

Ava slammed her car door and turned to the house. It was the middle of the night. *Not* the right time to be paying a visit to Mark's ranch, but she wasn't exactly overwhelmed with options.

I need to see him.

She straightened her shoulders and she marched toward his front door. She didn't let the memories swamp her as she climbed up the steps of the big wraparound porch. If she thought too much about the past, it would hurt. Those memories always did.

So she shoved the thoughts into the recesses of her mind, and she climbed those front steps. She reached for the doorbell but then the door opened.

Mark was there.

Tall, handsome, strong—*Mark*. His blond hair was tousled, and the light shone behind him, glinting off his shoulders. Very broad and bare shoulders because he wasn't wearing a shirt. Just a pair of low-slung jeans.

"Ava?" He reached out to her. As always, he seemed warm. His touch chased away the chill she'd felt since she'd first climbed into her car and begun the drive that would take her from her place in Houston to Mark's ranch in Austin. "What are you doing here?"

I needed to see you. I had to talk with someone...with someone who wouldn't think I was crazy.

Those words wanted to tumble out of her mouth, but she was trying to play things cool and not come across as the insane one. At least, not right away. She knew there were plenty of folks who already thought she was nuts or, much worse, a cold-blooded killer.

The rumors about her had persisted for years.

But...Mark had never seemed to believe those stories. He'd always stood by Ava and her family.

"I need your help," she told him quietly. She looked over his shoulder, hoping that no one else was there. The ranch house was huge, sprawling, but normally his staff stayed in separate quarters. She really didn't want anyone to overhear the confession she was about to make.

He pulled her into the house and shut the door behind her. "Ava, I'll give you anything you need."

Right. Because that was true-blue Mark. The guy who was always there to save the day. Or at least, that was the way she thought of him. Lately, though, her brothers had been acting differently when they spoke of Mark.

Her brothers had been friends with Mark for her whole life. And she, well, she'd been the tagalong. The little girl who bounced after the boys. *And who had always been in love with Mark Montgomery.*

Not that she'd ever told him that. Not him, not anyone. He kept his hand on her shoulder as they headed into his den. All of the lights were on in the place, and she saw a glass of wine sitting on the table.

Wine. No shirt...

Heat flooded her cheeks. "Do you have a…" *Not a lover, please, not a lover!* "Is someone here with you?"

One brow shot up. "Jealous?"

Wait, what? She shook her head. "I am so sorry. This—this was a mistake." What *had* she been think-ing? She'd just been scared and she'd run. But she hadn't run back to her brothers because she couldn't handle going to the McGuire ranch or…having them stare at her with pity in their eyes as they wondered if she'd finally cracked under the pressure of their parents' murder.

Poor, fragile Ava...she just couldn't handle it anymore.

She pulled away from him, spun on her heel and marched for the door.

Mark stepped into her path. His arms crossed on that massive bare chest as he gazed at her. "I'm not letting you go now." The words seemed to hold the edge of a threat. Or a promise?

"Mark?"

"I waited too long," he murmured.

She backed up a step.

"No one else is here." His voice was flat. "There is no girl waiting in my bedroom—if that's what you're thinking. There's only…you."

All of the moisture seemed to dry up in her mouth. Her gaze slowly slid over him. The last time she'd seen him had been months ago. They'd been at the funeral of Austin police detective Shayne Townsend. She'd wanted to talk with Mark then, but her brothers had been de-termined to keep her away from him.

Her brothers were keeping secrets from her.

Only fair, really, because she'd been keeping plenty of secrets from them, too.

Mark was a handsome man, powerful and commanding. He had high, slanting cheeks, a long, hard blade of a nose and lips that were…sexy. Sensual. She'd spent far too much time thinking about Mark's lips over the years.

He was big, easily a few inches over six foot, with those strong, broad shoulders that he'd used back in his high school football days. His skin was a sun-kissed gold, his eyes a dark blue. When he looked at her with those eyes, Ava sometimes felt as if he could see *through* her.

But right then, Mark's eyes held confusion and worry.

"What are you doing here, Ava? I thought you were staying away."

Not from him, but from Austin and from the Mc-Guire ranch because that place held too many painful memories for her. But when no place seemed safe, where were you supposed to go?

He's my haven.

"Ava?"

"I'm not crazy."

"I never said you were." His hands dropped and he took a step toward her. "Never thought it, either."

Others had. How many times had she heard the whispers over the years?

Is that her? Did she do it?

They should have locked her up…

She's either crazy…or she's a killer.

Ava swallowed and lifted her chin. "Someone has

been in my house." The little one-bedroom cottage in Houston that she called home.

"What?" Now a lethal fury had entered his voice.

"He didn't take anything. Nothing was broken, so I couldn't really report it to the police. I just… I know someone has been inside." It was the small things that had tipped her off to the intruder's presence. Things that most people probably wouldn't have noticed.

A confused furrow appeared between Mark's brows. *He doesn't believe me.*

"Pictures have been moved." Now she spoke quickly, the words tumbling out as she tried to convince Mark that she was telling the truth. "Like someone picked them up, but put them back down in the wrong place."

His square jaw locked. He had a faint cleft in his chin. Something else that was sexy about him.

"That's not all," she hurried to say because she knew the picture thing sounded flimsy. "My clothes were re-arranged." She felt the heat stain her cheeks. "He went through my dresser and…touched things. Moved them." Her underwear. Her bras. He'd been in her closet, too. The clothes had been moved—pushed to either side just a few extra inches.

At first she'd thought she was imagining all of these small things. But…then they kept adding up. And she hadn't been able to shake the feeling that someone was watching her.

No, worse.

Stalking her.

Now Mark was just staring at her.

"I'm not imagining this," she whispered as she gazed up at him. "It's happening. When I got home this evening, it had happened again. My back door…

it was unlocked. He just left it unlocked when he left."
Mark was still staring. He had to believe her! "I *triple-*checked that door before I went out. I know it was locked, I *know*—"

His hands wrapped around her shoulders. "Why didn't you call the police?"

"I did…the first time. They came out, looked around and said there was no sign of any intruder." The police had basically told her to stop wasting their time…only in a nicer way.

"Your brothers," he snapped out the words. "They own a PI business, for goodness' sake! They'd be on this thing in an instant. They'd—"

"Lock me up and throw away the key." Her words were brittle. "You know my brothers and exactly what they're like." Military through and through, and when it came to her…about a million times too protective. "I don't want to go back to the McGuire ranch. You know that. I *never* want to stay there again." Because every time she went there, Ava hurt. "This is just a jerk playing some kind of sick game with me. I want the game to stop. I want—"

Mark was shaking his head and his hold on her tightened. "Breaking into your house isn't a game. It sounds like someone is fixated on you! Stalking you!"

That was what she feared.

"What if he escalates? What if he decides to break into the house while you're there?"

Just why did Mark think she'd driven all the way to Austin? That unlocked door had sent her into a tailspin, and she'd been horrified at the thought of staying in that place for even one more night. She'd already put plans in motion to leave Houston, but tonight's little fright fest had moved up her departure by a few days. "That's where you come in," she told him.

His face was just inches from hers.

"I need a place to stay." He hadn't seen her car yet. So he didn't know… "I was already planning to move to Austin… I was offered a job at the art museum. I was scheduled to start in two weeks, but I already turned in my notice at my old job, and…" And she was talking way too fast. "Whoever was messing with me in Houston, he won't follow me to Austin. It's a new city." That's what she'd been telling herself. "I'll get an apartment here and vanish."

"Ava…"

"Until I find that apartment, I need a place to stay." She licked her lips. His gaze immediately fell to her mouth. Was it her imagination or did his blue stare heat up? "Please, Mark, can you let me stay here just for a few days? Until I find a more permanent place?"

Because she'd always felt safe with him.

But his jaw seemed to lock down even harder. His breath heaved out and he—he backed away from her. "If someone is stalking you…" He took another step back. "You need to call your brothers. They're the experts at this kind of thing. They'll find the guy—"

"If they even believe someone was in my place." She wasn't so sure they'd buy her story. They treated her with kid gloves as it was, always trying to hide the truth about their investigation into their parents' death. They didn't get that she wasn't some scared teen any longer.

He frowned at that. "Of course they'll believe you."

He sounded so confident. The cops hadn't believed her. Her neighbors hadn't believed her. "Do you believe me?"

"Yes." He gave a grim nod. "And you should have come to me *immediately.* I mean, how long has the joker been doing this to you?"

"A month." He believed her. Relief swept through Ava, almost making her feel a little dizzy.

Fury darkened his face. "You wait this long to tell me? You only come to me when you're terrified. You don't—"

"I changed the locks. My brothers had installed a security system—a top of the line system. I tried to stay safe." *On my own.*

"You have to tell them."

"My brothers haven't exactly been living the easy life lately," she muttered. Grant had nearly died a while back when he was working a case. He'd wound up in the hospital. And as for Brodie—he and his girlfriend had both just battled a monster from their past. They'd barely made it out of that nightmare alive. "They've had enough to deal with, okay?"

"You're their sister. They'd drop everything for you."

She glanced away from him. "I just need a place to stay tonight, okay?" Did he want her to beg? Because she was close to it. She couldn't stay in a motel. The walls in places like that were thin. "It's too late to call them now." If he'd just let her stay the night, she could figure out another plan for tomorrow.

"Bull. You came to *me* this late. Their ranch is just down the road."

Her gaze fell to the floor. "I wanted to be with you." But now that seemed foolish. He sure hadn't greeted her with open arms. "I shouldn't have come." She turned away and started heading back toward the door.

"No, you can't leave."

And he was touching her again, spinning her around to face him. Staring at her with fury and—and some other dark, turbulent emotion shining in his eyes. "You come to me," Mark continued, "telling me that some bozo is stalking you…and you expect me to just watch as you walk away in the night?"

She swallowed. "No, I expect you to give me a room…for old time's sake." Tomorrow, when she wasn't dead tired from fear and exhaustion, she'd work on another plan. One that didn't involve her brothers totally flipping out.

He gave a curt nod. "You can stay as long as you want."

Yes! That relief was so strong that she was *definitely* feeling a little light-headed. Or maybe that was just because she hadn't eaten since breakfast. "Thank you." Impulsively she stood on her toes and wrapped her arms around him. His rich masculine scent filled her nose. "You've always been a good friend to me."

Mark's body was rock hard against hers—hard and hot and so incredibly strong. His hands settled along the curve of her hips. "Is that what I am?" His voice was deeper, almost a growl.

She lifted her head and stared into his eyes. "Yes." Her own voice came out too husky, so she cleared her throat and tried again. "Yes, but you're also…more."

"Am I?" His gaze had locked on her mouth.

Her heart thundered in her chest. "You're almost family."

"No." An instant denial. His hold urged her even closer to his body. "I'm not family. Don't ever think that I am." His eyes were still on her mouth. And his head was lowering toward hers, closing that last little bit of space. "I'm not your brother, and I'm not some safe friend."

She trembled against him. "Mark?"

His gaze slowly lifted and met hers. "You should be careful with me."

Her drumming heartbeat seemed to shake her chest. She'd never worried about being careful with Mark. Mark was good, solid and dependable. The light in the dark. He was—

"Because I'm not sure how much longer I can be careful with you."

He was going to kiss her. Ava was sure of it. Mark was so close to her, the tension in the air had turned blazing, and she wanted him to press his mouth to hers. She'd wondered if he would ever actually—

He backed away. Again.

She suddenly felt very cold.

"You know the guest room is down the hallway." He pointed to the left.

Yes, she knew where the guest room was.

Just as she knew that Mark's room was on the other side of the sprawling ranch house. Far enough away… *that he won't hear me scream.*

She thought about going out to the car for her bags, but figured she'd just save that for another time. Her car was parked near the entrance to Mark's house, and the bags would be safe there for the time being.

For now, she'd crash…because she needed to slip away from Mark and his too-watchful gaze.

She turned on her heel and headed for the hallway.

"Tomorrow," he called after her, "we call your brothers."

She reached out and touched the door frame. "They

don't want me near you." Not now. She didn't know what had happened, but she'd been given that warning by more than one McGuire. Ava looked back at Mark.

He hadn't moved.

Had he even heard her? Sighing, she took a step forward.

"What do you want, Ava?" His low, rumbling words stopped her.

And an instinctive response…*you*…rose to her lips. But she managed to choke that word back.

"Ava?"

"I don't want to be scared anymore," she said, and those words were the truth.

Or at least, as much of the truth as she was willing to share right then.

Ava kept walking, and Mark didn't say anything else.

AVA WAS BACK.

Mark glanced down at his hands. There was a faint tremble in his fingers. He almost hadn't been able to let Ava go. Not when her sweet lips were so close to his.

Once it had been easy to stay away from Ava. But… Ava wasn't some scared sixteen-year-old girl any longer. She'd grown up and transformed into the most beautiful woman he'd ever seen.

When Ava was near, he ached. Because he wanted… what he shouldn't have.

He sucked in a breath and could have sworn that he tasted her. The scent of strawberries seemed to cling to Ava. A light, sweet scent. She'd been in his arms, her body pressed tightly to his, and he'd wanted to devour her.

He'd also wanted to destroy whoever was out there

terrorizing her. Because Ava had been afraid. Her body
had trembled, her breath had caught in her throat and
her green eyes had been bright with fear. Some jerk had
been stalking her for a month, and she was just *now*
telling him about it?

He spun away. Grabbed up his glass of wine and
downed the contents in one fast gulp.

First thing tomorrow he'd be calling her brothers.
Once upon a time he and Davis McGuire had been best
friends. There was no way he'd let Ava keep this dangerous secret from her family.

First thing tomorrow...

But for that night, Ava would rest. She'd be safe.

He started to pace. He'd keep watch over her now,
same as he'd done years ago.

The night she'd first run to him was burned in his
memory. How could a man forget a night of death? It
was impossible, as impossible as forgetting a woman
like Ava.

She'd grown up before his eyes. That terrible night
had destroyed the last of her childhood. At first she'd
been so brittle, so very breakable. He'd wanted to pum-
mel anyone who looked at her too hard, and there had
been plenty of accusatory stares. Sure, he'd heard the
rumors.

Some folks thought it was suspicious that Ava had
escaped from the killers without even a scratch while
her parents had died.

He paced toward the window on the right. *Suspicious?* No, there was nothing suspicious about her survival. She'd been lucky. He had no doubt that if the
killers had seen her, Ava would have died, too.

Years had passed since that night. Bubbly, happy

Ava had vanished. She'd become controlled, withdrawn and beautiful as she finished her college years. She'd gone to grad school, and she'd kept away from Austin.

But she's back now.

Back with him. In his home, but not in his bed. Though for the past two years, he'd sure imagined her there plenty. Ever since the night he'd tasted Ava for the first time. It had been a kiss that shouldn't have happened. A kiss that had changed everything for him.

His eyes squeezed closed. It was really going to be a long night.

AVA WAS IN the stables, stroking Lady's mane. She was humming a bit as she groomed her horse. Working kept her mind off the fact that she and her boyfriend Alan had broken up just hours before the homecoming dance. *Because he was a serious jerk with delusions.* And now she was there, alone with her horse, while all of her friends were out at the party.

Ava stopped humming. There would be other dances. And plenty of other guys—guys who weren't creeps and who—

Thunder cracked through the night. At the sound, Ava's whole body jerked. There wasn't supposed to be a storm that night. As the sharp crack died away, goose bumps rose on Ava's arms.

Was that thunder?

She whirled from the horse, ran from the stable. That loud blast still seemed to echo in her ears. As she ran, she looked up at the star-filled sky. There was no sign of clouds or lightning. Nothing at all.

Fear thickened in her veins. *Something is wrong. I don't think that was thunder.* She rushed toward the ranch house. All of the lights were blazing inside. She could see her dad standing a few feet in front of the picture window.

Only he wasn't alone.

Ava staggered to a stop. The lights were so bright in that house, and she could easily see the men with her father. Two men wearing black ski masks were pointing guns at her father.

Where's Mom? Where's Mom?

She inched closer, and when she saw her mother lying on the floor, a pool of blood gathering near her body, a sob tore from Ava. In that instant, her father whirled toward the window. His gaze locked with hers.

Dad!

"Run." He mouthed that one word at her.

Ava shook her head, too terrified to move.

But then her father whirled around to face the men in masks. He shouted something at them, words that drifted through the open window.

"I'll never tell you. No matter what you do. I'll never tell."

Boom! That time, she knew the sound wasn't thunder. She saw her father's body jerk. Ava watched in horror as he fell, and she was screaming, screaming—

"Wake up, Ava." Warm, strong hands wrapped around her shoulders and shook her once, gently. "It's okay. You're safe. I've got you."

Her eyes flew open. She saw that the lights were all on—and so bright—in that guest room. Mark was on the bed with her, his body curled protectively over hers.

"It's just a dream," he told her, his deep voice rumbling. "Dreams can't hurt you."

No, it was the men in black ski masks who did

that. Those were the men who appeared and wrecked your world.

Ever since that stalker had started playing games with her life a month ago, she'd been having the dreams—every single night. Before that, she'd been doing so much better. She'd even been able to go a few months without the nightmares.

But since the first time she'd noticed her pictures rearranged…it was as if the past had come rushing back to her.

His thumbs traced little soothing circles on her arms. "I didn't know you still—"

"Still woke up screaming." Her voice sounded raspy. How long had she been screaming before he'd rushed in? "That's why I could never have a roommate in college." Why she'd gotten the little rental house close to the campus. Her brothers had put in a security system there to keep her safe…and she'd really thought everything would be fine.

But someone still got in.

"The stalker, he brought it all back." She sat up in bed, but Mark didn't let her go. "I was getting better."

He didn't speak. His hands were so warm around her.

He'd come to her before, comforting her in the middle of the night. But she'd been a scared sixteen-year-old then.

She was still scared, but she wasn't sixteen.

And Mark…he wasn't leaving. Instead, he was watching her with an intense, turbulent gaze. She wished she could read his mind right then.

Wished—

His gaze fell to her body. She was wearing her bra and panties—she'd ditched everything else before she climbed into bed. Since his room was on the other side of the house, she'd hoped that he wouldn't hear her cries when the nightmare came.

He had.

His hands tightened on her. She could feel the calluses along the edge of his fingertips. Mark wasn't just some figurehead at the Montgomery ranch. He worked day in and day out. She knew he was the lifeblood of that place.

She also knew that she should feel embarrassed to be with him this way. She should probably reach out and pull up the covers. She didn't.

"Do you remember," Ava asked him, "when we kissed?"

Maybe he didn't remember. He'd been drinking that night. She had, too, or else she probably would never have gotten up the courage to kiss him. She'd just finished her undergraduate degree, and she'd been celebrating the holidays with her brothers—and with Mark. She and Mark had been alone for just a moment. The mistletoe had been right above them. She'd stood up on her toes and pressed a quick kiss to his lips.

Then something had happened. He'd taken over that kiss. It hadn't been quick. It had been deep and hot.

"I wish I could forget."

His words hurt, and she sucked in a sharp breath. "I—"

"Because if I could forget, then I wouldn't spend so much time wanting to taste you again." His right hand rose and sank into her hair, tipping back her head. "Like this…"

His lips pressed to hers softly at first, carefully.

But she didn't want careful. Not from him. Everyone else in her life treated her as if she'd break apart at any moment. *Not Mark, too.*

Her hands curled around his shoulders. Her mouth opened beneath his, and her tongue slid out to caress his lower lip.

His body stiffened, and she heard him groan. She loved that sound. Loved it even more when he stopped being so careful. She could feel his passion taking control. One minute he was holding her as if she were fine china, and the next he'd crushed her back into the bedding. He was on top of her, kissing her deep and hard, and she loved it.

For just a moment, the ghosts and fears from her past were gone. All she knew was the need she felt for Mark. The desire that was burning hot inside her, singeing her to her core. Her nails bit into his shoulders. Her breasts tightened, ached, and her nipples thrust against his bare chest.

Her hips were arching up. The covers were tangled around her legs, though, keeping her from feeling all of his body. She wanted those covers gone. She didn't want anything between them.

Her hands slid over his back. There were some scars there, faint ridges that rose beneath her fingers. She wondered how he'd gotten those marks, but then her hands kept moving because she wanted to explore every inch of him.

Ava knew plenty about nightmares. But because of Mark, she also knew a bit about dreams. And since he'd kissed her two years ago, she'd dreamed of being like this with him.

Only him.

His mouth pulled from hers and, for a moment,

she thought he was going to back away. He didn't. He started kissing a scorching path down her neck. She arched up against him as she moaned. She *loved* it when he kissed her at the base of her throat, and when he lightly sucked the skin, then scored it with his teeth…

"Mark!"

"Want to taste all of you…everything…"

She wanted to taste all of him.

He was still moving down her body, only now he'd just jerked the covers out of the way. She thought she might have heard the sheet rip, but Ava couldn't be certain of that. Her mind was focused on other things.

On him.

On the way he made her feel.

On the desire that was making her body ache.

His fingers slid under the edge of her bra. "Stop me," he said.

Was he crazy? Stopping him was the last thing she wanted. "Touch me," Ava said instead.

Because she was looking at his eyes, she saw his control break away. Saw his pupils swell as the darkness swallowed the blue of his gaze. Then he was shoving her bra out of the way. His fingers curled over her breasts, stroked her nipples and a ragged gasp tore from her. Yes, yes, this was what she wanted.

No fear. No pity. Nothing but pleasure.

Mark.

Then his mouth was over her breast. "So pretty," he whispered before his lips closed over her nipple. He sucked her, laving her with his tongue, and Ava nearly went crazy. Her hips bucked because the feelings coursing through her body were too strong. She needed him, wanted him. This moment had finally come, *finally*.

She felt as if he'd been staying away from her since that kiss, and Ava had feared that she'd imagined his desire for her.

But I didn't. He wants me just as badly as I want him.

There was no stopping. His hands were sliding down her stomach now, heading for her panties. There was—

An alarm shrieked, blaring through the house. Mark's head whipped up. He stared at her for a moment and shook his head as if he were coming out of a fog. Then he bolted from the bed.

"Mark!"

"Stay here!" he said as he rushed for the door. "Something set off the alarm near the stables—I know that alarm!"

He was leaving her.

Her breath heaved out. White-hot passion one moment…fear the next. That would *not* be the story of her life. Ava jumped out of the bed. Her knees did tremble but she stiffened them up, and she grabbed for her clothes. One minute later, she was running out of that bedroom door and racing to keep up with Mark.

Because if she'd brought danger to Mark's ranch, there was no way she was letting him face it alone.

Chapter Two

Mark rushed out of his house, his bare feet flying over the wooden porch. The alarm was still blaring up ahead, a security measure he'd put in after a psychotic SOB had torched his stables a few months back. The jerk had been trying to get at Brodie McGuire and Brodie's girl, Jennifer, and the fire had been set to lure them both into a trap.

No one will use me again.

He could see some of his ranch hands already running toward the stables. There was no sign of a fire, but something had sure set off the alarm.

The whole ranch was wired with state-of-the-art security, courtesy, of course, of the McGuires. He'd been watching the security feed when he'd first seen Ava pull into his drive earlier that night. Ava already knew the code to get past his gate, and he'd watched her, stunned to see her back at *his* place. Especially since her brothers had told him to stay away from her.

"Ty!" He yelled for his foreman because he had just come from the back of the stables. "Are the animals all right?"

Ty Watts hurried toward him. "Looks clear, Boss." Ty was close to Mark's age, with dark hair and dark brown eyes. "I didn't see anyone out back, and the men are in there with the horses now."

But something had set off the alarm—something or someone.

"What the hell do you think…?" Ty began. Then he let out a low whistle. "Sorry. Didn't realize company was here." His gaze was directed over Mark's shoulder.

Mark glanced back and saw Ava. Her hair tumbled around her shoulders. Under the lights that had flashed on with the security system, she appeared even more beautiful as the harsh glare lit up her body.

She was running toward Mark, clearly coming from the house.

In the middle of the night.

"Like that, is it?" Ty murmured.

Mark cut him a killing glare. "Yes," he told him flatly. "It is."

"What's happening?" Ava asked, her voice husky as her breath heaved out. The woman even sounded like sin right then. He'd had her beneath him moments before. His hot dreams had been about to become reality, and then—

The alarm had been a cold shower. A hard wake-up that had stopped him from making a terrible mistake.

Would it have been a mistake? Or would it have been the start of an addiction I couldn't end?

"Something set off the sensors at the rear of the stables, ma'am," Ty told her, his Texas accent rolling beneath the words. "After the recent fire, Mark here didn't want to take any chances with the horses' safety. Those sensors go off if anyone gets too close during the night."

A few more ranch hands came out. "Clear!" one of them shouted.

"Could have just been some animal checking out the place. Maybe a raccoon," Ty said. "It could even have been a coyote."

Ava was staring straight at Mark. "Do you have cameras set up back there?"

"No, not there," he said. "Not yet, anyway. The cameras are all connected to the main house and to the main road that led to the ranch."

"What if I led someone here?" Ava asked as she stepped closer to Mark. "What if I did this?"

"Nothing happened," he told her flatly. "You didn't do anything." He nodded toward Ty. "Have the men search the grounds just in case. We don't want to leave anything to chance."

Ty nodded and turned away. A few seconds later, Mark heard Ty barking orders to his men. Mark wanted to go and join the search, too, but he needed to make sure Ava was safe. "I thought I told you stay inside," he said as he leaned in toward her.

"I don't always stay where I'm put." Her voice held a distinct edge. "If there was a threat out here, I didn't want you facing it alone."

Ava…riding to his rescue. And some folks thought she was weak? Those folks didn't know her at all. "I just wanted you safe."

She stared up at him. "Are any of us ever really safe?"

With her past, yes, she'd wonder that.

"I want to help, and I don't intend to help by hiding inside your house." She straightened her shoulders. "If you're searching, then I'm going with you."

"Ava…"

"I...can't wait in there alone." Her voice was stark. "Don't ask me to."

He understood. He offered his hand to her. "Stay with me every step?"

Her smile flashed. "Of course. That's how I keep you safe, right?"

She had a gorgeous smile. One that winked dimples on each side of her mouth. He hadn't seen that smile of hers in a long time. He'd missed it.

The same way he'd missed her.

Ava put her hand in his.

FROM HIS HIDING PLACE, he watched Ava McGuire and Mark Montgomery cross the paddock. Ava was making a huge mistake. She couldn't trust Mark, not for an instant. She needed to realize how dangerous he was to her.

Mark had been keeping secrets from Ava for years. He'd been lying to her. And now she was going to turn to the man for help? *Wrong move, Ava. Wrong.*

In fact, that move could prove deadly for her.

Ranch hands were scrambling around, checking on the horses, trying to make sure they were all safe. Mark stayed beside Ava every moment, but he didn't think it was because he wanted to protect her.

You just want her.

In many ways, Mark Montgomery was just like his old man. When he saw something that he wanted, he took it, not caring at all for the consequences. Or for the shattered lives that he left in his wake.

Mark wanted Ava, so he thought he'd take her.

That won't happen.

Ava wasn't going to be destroyed. The Montgomerys had already wrecked enough lives. Maybe it was time for Ava to learn the truth about her so-called hero.

He slipped back into the shadows.

Maybe it was time for everyone to learn the truth.

THEY SEARCHED THE PROPERTY but found no sign of an intruder. Mark headed back to the house with Ava by his side. She seemed tense next to him, and he knew she had to be exhausted. They'd spent at least an hour out there because—

Because I wanted to make sure the jerk who has been harassing Ava didn't follow her to my home.

He shut the door behind them and set the alarm. "You should try to get some sleep." He wasn't touching her right then. Probably a good thing because the more he touched, the more he wanted.

I had her in the bed beneath me. Her breast in my hand. In my mouth. She was moaning for me. Ava wanted me.

And he'd been about thirty seconds away from taking the woman he wanted most.

He turned away from her.

"You're not going to talk about it, are you?" Ava asked him.

He locked his jaw. "The alarm went off. Maybe it malfunctioned. Maybe someone was here. I don't—"

She grabbed his arm and pulled him around to face her. "I'm not talking about the alarm. I'm talking about us!"

He tried to unclench his back teeth. "There isn't an us." Even though he spent too much time thinking about her. Even though he wanted to strip her right then and get her back on a bed once more. Even though—

"Why not?" Ava asked. Her eyes were big. Her gaze so deep. "Don't you want me?"

Wanting her sure wasn't the problem. He cleared his throat. "The age…difference between us is—"

"Bull."

He blinked.

"So you're a bit older than me. I'm not some kid. I'm in my twenties. I've got a graduate degree. I support myself." She waved the age difference away. "My brothers have dated plenty of women who are older and younger than they are, so don't give me that baloney. We're both legal."

"Your brothers…they are my friends."

She exhaled. "Are you sure about that? Because Davis told me just a few months ago… He said you weren't the man I thought you were."

And Davis had been acting odd around him ever since Detective Shayne Townsend had died. Mark didn't know what was happening, but the McGuires had definitely put the freeze on him.

"But I don't really care what Davis thinks about you. *I* want you."

Then she leaned forward, trying to wrap her arms around him.

He stepped back.

Hurt flashed across her face.

"Ava…"

"You were kissing me like a desperate man earlier. Like you didn't need anything more than me in the whole world." She shook her head. "Now you back away from me? *Why?*"

"Because I don't want to hurt you."

A faint line appeared between her brows. "You

wouldn't! You never have. You're the one who has always been there for me. Never judging, just accepting. You know all of my secrets."

"But you don't know mine, Ava." And that was the problem. He'd shielded her from that part of his life. Did the very best that he could not to taint her image of him.

But Ava didn't know the things he'd done. Ava didn't know about the dark core inside of him and, for her sake, he hoped that she never did.

Ava had always looked at him as if he were some kind of hero. He wasn't. He was about as far from hero material as a man could get. If she knew the things he'd done, Ava would never let him so much as touch her again. *And that's why she won't ever know.*

"Go to sleep," he told her because he had to put some distance between them. He couldn't be that close to Ava and not feel her sensual pull. "It's been a long day." He walked away from her.

Ava STARED AFTER MARK, narrowing her eyes. He was seriously just walking away? She wanted to scream at the man. Finally, *finally*, they'd been close. The desire had been burning between them. There had been no barriers. Nothing at all holding them back, and now—

Now he was pulling away.

It won't be that easy, Mark.

She headed back toward the guest room. Sleep wasn't going to come for her, not then. Adrenaline spiked her blood, and if she slept—well, she wasn't in the mood to deal with a second nightmare. No way.

Ava pushed open the door to her room. It was dark inside. Pitch black.

Ava hesitated. She'd been sure that she left the lights on when she ran out earlier. The lights had been blazing. She'd dressed as fast as she could and then rushed out after Mark.

And I didn't turn the lights off.

She glanced back over her shoulder. "Mark?"

It was just like before. Small things. Things that most people would overlook. But after a while, those little things had started to add up.

Ava pulled in a deep breath. Then her hand slid out, moving along the wall near the door. Her fingers touched the light switch. She flipped it on, fast, and illumination flooded the room.

The bed sheets were still tangled. Her purse was on the chair in the right corner—just where she'd left it.

The windows appeared to be closed and still locked.

She crept forward. Her body was tight with tension and fear. They'd searched the perimeter for the prowler, but maybe they hadn't found the intruder because he hadn't been outside. He'd been *inside.* The ranch house had been empty. It would have been the perfect time for the guy to sneak in.

No, I must be wrong. I left the lights off.

She bent and searched under the bed. Nothing was there. The closet was empty. She turned toward the bathroom. The door leading to the bathroom was shut, too. Ava tried to remember…

Did I leave it open or closed? She inched forward.

Open?

Another step.

Or closed?

Do not go back to her. Do not. The chant echoed in Mark's head, but his body wanted to turn around and go after Ava. She'd just looked so hurt.

And he'd never wanted to hurt Ava. He wanted to protect her. To keep her safe, always.

Why did he screw up so much when she was around?

Snarling, he turned and marched toward his bathroom. The door was partially shut, and he shoved it open. He flipped on the light—

The glass mirror was shattered. And letters were carved into the wall next to the broken mirror—rough letters that looked as if they'd been made with a shard of that broken glass.

Stay away from her.

"Ava!" He roared her name even as he whirled around and ran from the bathroom. The creep hadn't been outside. He'd been in the house. He'd drawn them out, maybe even set off the alarm deliberately so that he could get access to the home. *"Ava!"* Mark was in the den now and running fast. His heart thundered in his chest. He had to get to Ava, to see her. Had to—

She ran out of her room. "Mark?" Fear flashed on her face.

"He was here," he snarled as he grabbed her shoulders. "Someone was in my home."

She shivered before him. "I…I know." She pointed toward her door. "My light was off. I think he was in my room."

The sick joker might still be in there. Mark pushed her behind his back and ran to her room. The covers were tousled, and he had a flash of Ava in that bed, with him.

So close…

Until that jerk had come and sounded the alarm.

Her bathroom door was shut. Was the guy in there? Waiting for her?

"Be careful," Ava whispered. "I was just about to go in there…"

Forget careful. If someone was waiting in her bathroom, Mark would tear the guy apart. Mark kicked open the door. It slammed back into the nearby wall.

He saw the broken shards of the mirror on the floor. Just like in his bathroom. Words had been left behind for Ava, too. Only these words…

Don't trust him.

"We need to search the whole house," he said, voice flat and hard. "The video cameras were running, so we must have caught the bastard." He turned to find Ava behind him. Her gaze wasn't on Mark, though. It was on the message the intruder had been left behind.

The guy was trying to play games with them, but he was about to realize… Mark was an enemy he didn't want.

No one threatens Ava on my watch.

No one.

THE HOUSE WAS searched from top to bottom. Every closet. Every corner. There was no other sign of the intruder.

Ava's hands were shaking as she watched Mark pull up the video feed from his surveillance cameras. This was the first time the stalker had actually left any kind of message for her.

Don't trust him.

Did the stalker really think she was going to listen to him? She trusted Mark completely. He'd protected her on the worst night of her life. She'd never turn away from him.

"There he is," Mark muttered.

She leaned over his shoulder and…sure enough, she saw a man slipping out of the house.

The guy on the video feed was wearing a black ski mask. And as soon as she saw that ski mask, Ava lost her breath. For a moment in time, she wasn't standing there with Mark, looking at a computer screen. She was back at her old home, hearing the thunder of a gunshot and rushing toward her house. Her father was standing in front of the window.

Run.

And a man wearing a black ski mask was lifting a gun.

"Ava! Ava!"

She blinked. Mark was in front of her, breath heaving. His arms were around her and he was holding her tightly. *Get your control. Don't break in front of him.* Not in front of Mark. He was one of the few who didn't think she was already broken beyond repair. "He… followed me from Houston." She thought of that drive. The darkness. The stretching interstate.

All that time, she thought she'd been leaving him behind, but he'd been with her every step of the way. Had he watched while she'd packed up? Had he been there? Every moment?

Now she'd brought him to Mark's door. No, into Mark's house. "I'm sorry," she whispered, and she pulled away from him. Ava started walking toward the front of the house. Her steps were slow but certain.

"Ava!"

She didn't look back. She'd never wanted to bring danger to Mark, but now she'd put him right in the center of this thing—whatever it was.

But that black ski mask…that wasn't just a coincidence, was it? Was the guy trying to tell her something? *Was he one of the men who killed my parents?* Because those two men had been wearing black ski masks that night.

She reached for the front door. Mark caught her hand and pulled her back against him. Ava tried to break free of him, but he just held her tighter.

"What are you doing?" Mark demanded as she turned in his arms.

"Leaving you."

He flinched.

"I thought that was obvious."

"Why?" He seemed to grit out that one word.

"I'm not going to have you threatened because of me! I won't do that to you!" She owed him more than she could ever repay. Danger wasn't what he deserved.

"He left me a message, too."

Her breath caught.

"The fool told me to stay away from you."

He'd been intimately close to her before the stalker had come calling on them.

Mark's blue eyes glittered down at her. "That's not going to happen. The last thing I'm planning to do is leave you on your own. He wants you to run away. He's trying to put a wedge between us so that you'll be out there, vulnerable, and he can close in on you."

Ava winced. "But what about you?" She hadn't considered the risk to him when she'd driven to his ranch, seeking shelter for the night.

"I can handle anything this guy wants to throw at me." He said the words with such grim certainty. She wanted to believe him.

But, once upon a time, she'd thought another man

could handle any threat that came his way. Then her father had died. He'd died protecting her, and in that moment, she'd vowed—*no one else will ever suffer for me.*

"I want to leave," she told Mark softly.

He shook his head. "No way, baby."

It was the first time he'd ever used any kind of endearment with her. He probably didn't even realize he'd done it. The word didn't mean anything to him, but it had her body warming.

"Yes," she said as she gave a faint nod. "I'm not going to let him hurt you. I'll call the cops. I'll get my brothers involved." Because this situation couldn't be hidden from them, not any longer. They would go into their extreme mode—she had no doubt of that—but she needed to tell them. A strange man had followed her, broken into Mark's place—*he's just getting worse.* More dangerous.

A faint beeping sounded then, coming from Mark's study. His computer. He didn't let Ava go. His fingers curled around her wrist, and he pretty much pulled her back to the study. She stared at the screen there and saw the black SUV that was pulling up to the ranch's gate.

"You don't have to tell them," he said as her brother Davis's tense features came into view. "I think they already know."

"WHAT IS MY SISTER doing at your house—" Davis stalked into the den and headed straight for Mark "—in the middle of the night?"

Mark stood his ground. Ava thought about running for the door—leaving them both.

Instead, she cleared her throat. "It's actually getting

pretty close to dawn now." Davis's green gaze cut to her. She shrugged. "So that's more like morning, not the middle of the night."

He growled. Davis did that. He growled a lot. Once he'd had a much better sense of humor. Then he'd gone off and become a SEAL. Their parents had died—and Davis had locked down his emotions. Hard. Now there was pretty much just one setting for her brother…*ice*.

"How did you know I was here?" she asked him.

"I didn't, not until I saw your car outside." He huffed out a breath. "I was coming by because we're helping to monitor Mark's security system, and when I saw there was some trouble out here earlier, I figured I'd better check it out."

His words just weren't ringing true to her, and Davis hadn't looked her in the eyes while he'd been talking. When Davis lied to her, he never looked her in the eyes.

You're fine, Ava. No one thinks you were involved in what happened to our parents.

He'd been looking right over her shoulder the first time he'd fed her that line of bull. She'd wondered then…had her own brother thought she was involved? Or had he just already heard the rumors that folks were spreading around town?

"Are you sleeping with my sister?"

Now *that* had her eyes flying toward Davis. Her brother was big—as big as Mark. They both had the same broad shoulders and golden skin. But Davis's hair was dark, longer, and his features were rougher than Mark's.

Instead of answering Davis, Mark glared at him. His hands were fisted.

Ava leapt between the two men because it sure

looked as if they were about to come to blows. "Stop it!" Ava ordered. She turned her own glare on Davis. "Mark is my friend, okay? One of the few who stood by me over the years." There had been plenty who turned their backs on her. Folks who actually bought into the story that she'd either planned—or helped to commit— the murder of her parents. "So back off!"

Davis narrowed his eyes, eyes that were a darker green than her own. "What happened here tonight?"

She hesitated.

"Tell him, Ava," Mark urged her gruffly. "Your brothers will track down that maniac."

Exhaling heavily, she nodded. "Someone…someone has been stalking me."

Shock shot across Davis's face. *"What?"*

And she told him everything. From the pictures that had been moved to the cops who hadn't believed her. She told him about how she'd packed up her bags and driven fast to Mark's house…because—

"Why him?" Davis demanded. "Why did you tell him and not us?" He sounded hurt, and that was certainly the last thing she'd wanted.

"I had no actual proof that anyone was doing these things, not until tonight." She pushed back her hair, suddenly feeling very, very weary. The adrenaline high was sure starting to wane. "Then he left those messages here for us."

"What messages?"

"In my bathroom," Ava confessed.

"And mine," Mark added.

Davis's gaze assessed her. "You were sleeping in the guest room."

She nodded. Davis took off, heading down the hallway. In minutes he was back. His eyes immediately locked on Mark. "Did you get the same message?" he asked. "One telling you not to trust my sister?"

Ava glanced over at him. Mark shook his head. "No. Mine was different."

Davis vanished. She figured he'd gone to read the message for himself.

"What did it say?" Her voice was quiet.

His expression unreadable, Mark murmured, "He told me to stay away from you." His eyes glittered down at her. "That isn't happening."

Footsteps pounded—Davis was coming back. Fury was etched onto his face. "Based on what you've said, the stalker's events are seriously escalating! I've seen twisted stuff like this before. Too many times, and it doesn't end well. A man gets fixated on a woman…" His gaze snapped to Mark. "And he can't let her go."

Beside her, Mark tensed.

Then Davis was glancing back at Ava. "You're lucky that you weren't in that room when the guy broke in. Maybe he wouldn't have used that glass just to carve a message on a wall. He might have tried carving into you."

She held her ground. "You think I don't know that?"

Mark swore. "Stop it, Davis. You don't need to scare her."

Right. She was already scared plenty, with Davis adding to her terror.

But Davis fired back, "Maybe she needs to be scared. These incidents have been going on for weeks, and she didn't tell us. She's lucky she isn't already dead."

Ava flinched.

Mark surged toward her brother. "Don't." His voice was low and lethal. "Don't you tell her—"

"Ava is my sister. What is she to you?"

Mark's turbulent stare jumped to her. She thought of the kiss they'd shared in the guest room. Of how very close they'd come to sharing something else, too.

"Ava is—" Mark began.

"He's my friend," Ava said, her words clear and strong. She didn't know what else he might prove to be to her, but on that point, Ava was certain.

Davis opened his mouth to say something else, probably to launch some kind of attack at Mark, but she wasn't in the mood for that. "He was wearing a ski mask."

Davis's brow furrowed.

"A black one." She inclined her head toward the study area. "One of the video cameras caught sight of the guy leaving, so now we know—"

"He's big, probably about six foot one, maybe six foot two," Mark said. "Fit. And far too familiar with my home."

Because he'd just walked right in the door.

"We should get the cops out here," Davis immediately said. "Get them to run a fingerprint check and use their crime-scene team."

Mark's shoulders tensed. "He was wearing gloves in the video, so I don't think the guy left any prints behind. And after our last experience with the cops, I wasn't exactly chomping at the bit to get them here again."

Our last experience. She knew just what he was talking about. For years, the McGuires had been friends with Austin police detective Shayne Townsend. Most of the cops had seemed to give up hope of ever finding the men who'd killed their parents, but Shayne had kept working the case.

Or so they'd all believed.

But when Brodie and his girlfriend had come under attack, they'd all learned the truth about Shayne. The police detective had accidentally killed an unarmed teen years ago, and he'd been covering up the crime ever since. He'd been blackmailed into breaking the law.

And maybe even blackmailed into covering up the identity of the men who'd killed her parents?

That was sure what some of her brothers suspected.

"You never know who you can trust," Davis murmured, his head cocked as he studied Mark. "And who you can't."

There was something in his voice that put Ava on edge.

"We're calling the cops," Davis said. "And I'll want to talk with your men."

Ava shivered a moment, thinking about how close that unknown man had been to her.

Mark pulled out his phone. Spoke quietly.

Davis closed in on her. "Don't trust him."

"Right, I saw the message on the wall. I got it—"

"This message is coming from *me*." His gaze slanted quickly toward Mark, then back to her. "I don't know what you think is happening between you two, but there are things going on you don't know about."

Her back teeth clenched at that. She didn't know about those things only because her brothers liked their secrets. "He's your friend, too."

"I don't know what he is, not right now."

The whole situation was insane. "He saved me that

night." She'd never forget her first sight of him. Terror had filled her, and then—Mark had been there.

Davis exhaled on a rough sigh. "Right before Shayne Townsend died I asked him who killed our parents."

Her heart stopped before pounding again in a double-time rhythm. "What did he say?"

Mark was off the phone. And he'd—he'd closed in on them. "Yeah," Mark said, voice roughening, "what did he say, and why didn't you tell us before now?"

A muscle flexed along the line of Davis's jaw. "I didn't tell you because I know how Ava feels about her *friend* Mark."

She hated the stress he'd just put on that word. "You're friends, too—"

"Montgomery."

"What?" Ava exclaimed. "I don't understand—"

"The last word he said was…Montgomery." Davis turned his attention on a still-as-stone Mark. "So I have to wonder…why did Shayne use his last breath to name *your* family? Unless…the Montgomerys are responsible for the murder of our parents."

She hadn't thought the situation around her could get any worse. But it just had—so very much worse. Because as she stared at Mark, Ava could have sworn that she saw guilt creep across his face.

Chapter Three

"Ava, let me explain," Mark said as he followed her out to her car.

The cops had come out to the ranch. Uniforms who'd questioned them all and who'd collected pretty much zero evidence. Mark wasn't exactly holding his breath when it came to those guys breaking the case wide open. They were still nosing around the place, but Ava was fleeing.

At his words, Ava didn't slow down. Instead, she seemed to speed up as she hurried toward her vehicle. He reached out to stop her.

Davis caught his arm. "I don't think that's a good idea."

Most folks in Austin were afraid of the McGuire brothers. Their reputation preceded them just about everywhere they went. Grant, the eldest brother, was a former army ranger. Davis and his twin, Brodie, were both former SEALs. Mackenzie "Mac" McGuire had been part of Delta Force, and Sullivan, the youngest of the brothers, was an ex-marine. Yeah, most folks hesitated before trying to tangle with those guys.

Mark wasn't most folks. And he'd never taken any crap from the McGuires. "The game has changed," he said, his low voice carrying only to Davis's ears. "I'm not just going to sit back anymore. I thought she was safe. Happy. But she's not. She still wakes up screaming at night. And now some new jerk is out there terrorizing her." He shook his head. "That's not going to happen. She's not going to spend her days and nights afraid. I won't *let* that happen to her." He'd do everything within his power to protect her.

He heard Ava's car door opening. He forced his back teeth to unclench as he said, "Why didn't you come to me about this Shayne Townsend mess weeks ago? I wasn't involved in the murder of your parents! I had plenty of people here at the ranch who saw me right before Ava came galloping up!" The idea that he was involved was ridiculous. He was—

"I know you have an alibi. I already checked that."

Davis had been investigating him?

"It was your father who didn't have an alibi. No one could account for him an hour before the crime or an hour after."

Mark felt shock rip through him. "He was my… *stepfather.*" Like that distinction mattered. Technically, Gregory Montgomery had adopted him. Of course, most folks didn't know that Mark had hated the bastard with every bit of his soul.

"He committed suicide two months after my parents died," Davis said.

Mark glanced over at Ava. She was in her car, appearing for all intents and purposes as if she was about to drive away and leave him.

"Sometimes guilt can drive a man to take his own life."

Davis seriously thinks that Gregory murdered the McGuires!

And…and Mark couldn't say that he hadn't. Because he knew just how twisted Gregory could be.

Ava cranked up her car.

Mark jerked away from Davis. "Ava, wait!" He lunged toward the car. Her window was rolled down, and his fingers pushed through the opening and locked onto the steering wheel. "Wait," he said again, his voice softer.

She didn't look at him.

"I didn't hurt them, Ava."

She nodded. Blinked several times. Oh, no, was she *crying*? He couldn't stand it when Ava cried.

"I would *never* do anything to hurt you."

Again, she gave the faintest of nods.

Davis was a few feet away, watching them far too closely.

"Where are you going?" Mark asked her. "You said you were starting a new job in Austin soon. You can't just stay in some motel." Not with that creep out there watching her. "Stay here. You'll be safe."

Her head turned then, and she finally stared into his eyes. He didn't see any rage there. No accusation. Just the same trust that he always saw when she looked at him. "I don't want to bring any danger to you. He was in your house. Whoever this guy is…I don't want him hurting you."

And I'd be destroyed if he hurt you, Ava. Can't you see that?

"I'm going back to the ranch with Davis."

"You hate staying there." He knew Ava hadn't stepped foot inside the main house, not since that night.

She shrugged. "There's a guest cottage I can use."

"You can stay here." She'd been asking to stay hours before, and now she was running away.

But then Davis stepped forward. "We have better security at our place. He already got in here once. He won't reach her there."

Because the McGuire ranch had basically been transformed into a fortress after those murders. The brothers had wanted to make sure their home was always protected.

Even if that protection had come too late.

"I'm sorry I involved you," Ava said. Her hands were curled around the steering wheel.

He leaned forward a bit more and caught her chin between his thumb and forefinger. "This isn't over, Ava."

"Mark, I—"

He kissed her. A fast, hard kiss, right on her lips. And yes, he knew Davis was watching. So what? It was time all the McGuires realized that Mark would be taking what he wanted.

And what he wanted most was Ava.

He pulled back and held her surprised stare. "I'll be seeing you very soon." She wasn't getting away from him. Not this time.

THE COPS WERE USELESS.

He watched as they scurried around the Montgomery ranch. Were they seriously looking for clues? There weren't any to find. He was too good. He hadn't left any evidence behind, nothing that could be traced to him.

This isn't my first ball game.

And Davis McGuire was there, too. Stalking around, questioning everyone.

Some of the idiots there actually stuttered when they talked to Davis. Like he was some kind of big deal. He wasn't. None of the McGuire brothers were.

The only McGuire who mattered...that was Ava.

She'd left Mark. Good. She'd taken his warning. He'd already known that she was planning to move to Austin. He'd learned that during one of his trips to her place. He liked to keep tabs on Ava. To find out just what was happening in her life.

He was glad that she'd come back home. *Back to me.* He'd grown tired of waiting for her, so he'd started trying to...scare her a bit. Nothing too bad, of course. Just little nudges to make sure Ava realized Houston wasn't the place for her.

She was back now. She'd left Mark.

So it was finally time for him to move in...

I've been waiting, Ava. So patiently. Now you will be mine.

AVA HATED HER family home. It was beautiful, a sprawling ranch with a bluff and a lake, surrounded by old-growth trees. Her father had once said it was a slice of heaven. He'd told her that when her great-grandfather had emigrated from Ireland nearly one hundred years before, he'd taken one look at the land and fallen in love with the place.

Ava didn't think the ranch was heaven. To her, it was much closer to hell.

She parked her car near the small guest house and very much *not* near the main home. When she got out of the vehicle, she wasn't surprised to see Brodie already heading toward her. Brodie and Davis—identical twins who were both way too keen on the overprotective vibe. One look at Brodie's tense face and she knew that Davis had already spilled about the events of the previous night.

She thought he'd lecture her. Instead he pulled her into his arms, nearly crushing her in a giant bear hug. "It's about time you came home."

The words hurt. She knew he didn't mean to hurt her. Brodie loved her. She knew that. But when Brodie looked at the ranch, she knew he saw hope for the future. He and Jennifer were getting married and planning a family. Ava had no doubt the two of them would be deliriously happy there.

When she looked at the ranch, she saw her father telling her to run. She saw blood and death.

"It's…temporary," she told Brodie as she pulled back. "I'll start looking for a new place in the city as soon as—"

"He was wearing a black ski mask."

Right. He'd definitely already gotten the update from Davis. She bet that every one of her brothers had— and, knowing them, they'd be checking in with calls or visits ASAP.

"Give us a few days to figure out what is going on, okay? Then we can get you settled in any place you want to go."

Any place…

For some reason, she thought of Mark.

He'd kissed her before she left. Had Davis told Brodie that bit, too? Wasn't a woman supposed to have some secrets?

Brodie eased back and headed toward her trunk. "Let's get you settled."

Her gaze slid toward the stables. Lady was in there. She used to love riding Lady. Riding fast and hard and feeling the wind whip through her hair.

"Ava?"

"You all should have told me about what Shayne said." She glanced over at him. "I could have told you it was bull. Mark wasn't involved."

Brodie's gaze became guarded. "Can you say the same thing about his old man?"

Honestly, she barely remembered him. The man hadn't come over to their place very much, and he certainly hadn't socialized often in the community. Gregory Montgomery had kept to himself, and there had been some rumors that he drank…heavily.

But since Ava had been the topic of plenty of rumors that called her a murderer, she hadn't exactly believed those tales about Gregory.

"They were engaged once," Brodie said. "Mom and Gregory Montgomery."

"What?" She sure hadn't seen that little tidbit coming.

"But then she met dad, and everything changed for her. She broke off the engagement to Gregory, she eloped with Dad…and, well, you know how the rest of that story went."

The rest of the story ended with their parents *dying*.

"That's why Mr. Montgomery didn't come over much. Word is that he and our dad used to be good friends, but there are some things that can change a man."

She looked at the lake. The water glistened. She should stare at it and think it was beautiful. Instead, a shiver slid over her as she gazed at the water.

"We'll find the man doing this to you," Brodie promised her. "No one messes with my family."

No, those who'd tried—well, they'd found a lethal response waiting from Brodie in the past. "Is Jennifer

doing better?" Ava asked. Because his girlfriend—
fiancée, now—Jennifer had been attacked, and her
attacker had died. *Lethal response.*

He smiled. His dimples flashed. "She's great. She'll
be back in town tonight, and she can't wait to see you."

Jennifer was an interesting woman. On the surface,
Ava had thought the woman was a sophisticated, high-
society type. Then she'd learned the truth—Jennifer
was a tough ex-spy who'd worked to bring down some
of the most vicious criminals in the world.

"What you see..." Ava murmured...*is so far from
what you actually get.*

She headed around the car and grabbed one of her bags.

AVA HEADED INTO the city during the middle of the day.
She stopped by the art museum and checked in. She
spent a little time talking with her new supervisor, Kristin Lang. Ava wasn't scheduled to start for a few days,
but she still wanted to get the lay of the land. After her
chat with Kristin, she spent some time just walking
around the place and admiring the art.

When she'd first started college, art had been her
passion. On too many occasions it was the only way
that she could get through so many of those long nights.
She hadn't wanted to talk to a therapist or one of the
counselors at the college. After a couple of group sessions, she'd withdrawn from the group. Baring her soul
to them had just made her feel even more broken. Instead she'd painted.

Ava had painted canvases full of darkness and
rage. So much red—for the blood and the rage. Rage
that would course through her so strongly. She'd been
furious at the men who killed her parents and furious

with herself because she should have been able to help them, but she hadn't. She'd done nothing but run.

Some of her art teachers had seen her working at the studio. They'd wanted her to show her work.

But she couldn't. It was too raw. Too personal. Too… much of her soul.

So when she'd gone to graduate school, she'd focused on art history. She'd lucked out by getting this job. She'd thought about applying for a position far away, maybe taking a job up north or in the east—

"Ava?"

She turned at the call and found herself staring into a pair of warm golden eyes.

Her gaze swept over him. "Alan?"

"I thought that was you!" He smiled at her, flashing perfectly even white teeth. Then he opened his arms and pulled her into a big hug. "It's been so long!"

Years.

She pulled back. He'd changed from the boy she'd known so long ago. His features were sharper. His blond hair was stylishly pushed back from his forehead. His clothes—perfectly cut. Alan Channing had always been gifted with plenty of money and pull.

And once, he'd almost had her. At sixteen, she'd thought she loved him. She'd learned—just in time— that Alan wasn't the boy she'd thought.

The night my parents died, I was supposed to be with him.

"I heard that you were going to be working here." His grin grew even broader. "I was just appointed to the art museum's board, so we'll probably be seeing a lot of each other."

Her gut clenched at that news, but Ava forced a polite

smile. "Oh, really? That's just—" She broke off, unable to think of a polite lie because *That's just terrible* wanted to spill from her lips.

"I'm not the same, Ava." Alan's voice deepened as his smile slipped. "I'm not the same jerk I was back then."

She lifted her brows. "I don't remember calling you a jerk." Hmm…or had she?

Alan laughed. "Not now, but back then you did. Jerk and plenty of other things—and you were right. I didn't realize what a total screw-up I was." His face sobered. "Then…then your parents died. I saw how wrecked you were. Things changed for a lot of people back then."

How wrecked she'd been? And she remembered that Alan had tried to talk to her—at the funeral, at school in the weeks that followed. But she hadn't been able to talk with anyone back then. She'd been walking around in a fog, barely able to get through the days.

By the time she'd come out of her grief, the whispers had started.

Did she kill them? Was she in on it?

And she'd just wanted to run.

Maybe…maybe it was time she stopped running.

Isn't that why I took this job in Austin? Instead of heading up north? Because, deep down, she'd known that she couldn't run forever.

Her spine straightened as she stared at him. "I guess we both changed."

"We have." Alan's head inclined toward her. "Hey, how about we go out and grab some lunch? We can catch up, and perhaps I can start making up for being such a fool all those years ago."

Ava shook her head. "Sorry, but I have to go back and meet my brothers."

He took a step back. "Right. The brothers." Alan gave a little shudder. "You know, they used to terrify me. I was almost too afraid to ask you out."

She laughed at that. "Oh, Alan…they still terrify people." Then she eased past him.

"I'll be seeing you, Ava," he murmured, and his hand lightly caressed her arm.

For an instant, she stilled as a shiver slid over her. It wasn't the same kind of sensual shiver she got when Mark touched her. This was something else. Something…that was almost like a warning.

Her steps quickened as she hurried away from Alan.

Ava headed for the front of the museum. Her heels clicked over the marble floor and—

Mark was there. Striding through the entrance and heading right for her.

She stopped. Just froze for a second. His gaze swept around the museum, and then his eyes locked on her. It was rather like watching a hunter lock in on his prey. His saw her, his face tightened and then he began to stride right toward her.

Her breath quickened as she shook out of her stupor and hurried toward him, too. When they drew closer, she asked, "What are you doing here?"

His lips tightened.

"Did you follow me?" Her voice rose on that one. No, surely he hadn't—

"Some nut broke into my house and threatened you last night." He yanked a hand through his hair. "So, yes, that made me worry about you a bit. When I found out you were in town—"

"*How* did you find that out?"

"Brodie told me."

Well, wonderful, they were all tracking her now. That was what she'd feared. *Hello, hyperprotective mode.*

"Since he told me where you were, I guess that means he doesn't think I'm involved in what happened to your parents."

"None of them think *you* were involved." She didn't want to talk about his father, not then. "And I don't need you following me."

His gaze tracked over her shoulder. "Is that the little jerk you used to date? The one who stood you up for homecoming?" Anger roughened his voice.

She nearly rolled her eyes. She did quicken her step and head right for the gleaming glass doors that would take her out of the museum. "Yes, that's Alan Channing. And no, he didn't stand me up. I broke up with him right before homecoming." They were outside now, and the heat of the city blasted her. Memories were stirring in her mind, and she found herself blurting, "I heard him bragging about having sex with me to some of his football buddies. He was saying that he'd spend five minutes at the dance with me, then have me naked in the motel room ten minutes later." At the time, those words had shattered her.

Then she'd learned there were much, much worse things in life than just the words of some ex-boyfriend.

"He said *what*?" Mark demanded. Fury was stamped on his face. Then he spun on his heel and started charging right back up to the museum.

"Whoa! Wait!" She grabbed him as understanding hit her. He'd been going back in there to find Alan. And do what? "That was a long time ago."

"There's no expiration date on a whooping."

Her jaw dropped. "You are not serious!"

"If he said that about you—" his eyes were a blue fire "—then yes, I'm dead serious."

And she'd thought her brothers were bad. "He was a teenager. He said something stupid and I dumped him. End of story." She'd handled it on her own. "I don't need you fighting this battle for me." There was no battle there *to* fight.

"But he…hurt you."

For some reason, those words made her heart ache. "Do you know who I haven't thought about? Not once in all of these years?"

The door to the museum opened. Alan appeared.

Really bad timing, Alan.

"Him," she told Mark as she slid closer to him. Both of her hands were on Mark's shoulders now because she was more than a little worried he might break away and drive his fist into Alan's perfect smile. "Because he didn't matter after that night."

She could feel the tension in Mark's body.

"So let it go," she told him. "I sure have."

His gaze dropped to her lips. Then he leaned forward. Kissed her—not hard and deep. But softly. Carefully. "I just don't want," he whispered against her mouth, "anyone hurting you."

Warmth spread through her. Mark had to feel some of the same emotions that she did. And he was kissing her—again! Making her feel like she mattered to him. More than anything.

"Well…" That was Alan's slightly nasal voice. "I thought you were meeting your brothers, Ava."

"You should really let me throw at least one punch at him," Mark murmured.

"No," she snapped back at him. Then she looked at Alan. "You know Mark Montgomery, don't you?"

Alan nodded once, stiffly. "I believe you're on the board here, too, aren't you, Montgomery? When I signed on, they were telling me the names of a few others that I'd be working with."

"Yeah, I'm on the board." Mark's voice was flat.

Wait, both of them? And suddenly she was wondering just *why* she'd been offered the plum job at the art museum.

"I didn't realize the two of you were…involved," Alan said. He smiled at her, but it certainly wasn't the big grin he'd worn before. Far more forced and coldly polite.

"It's new," Mark said blandly. "She came back to town and—boom. I wasn't about to let her go again."

Alan's gaze slid to Ava. Softened. "I understand." He nodded to them. "If you'll excuse me, I have a meeting that's waiting."

A meeting that hadn't been waiting before when he'd asked her out to lunch?

He hurried down the stairs. She kept a close eye on Mark, making sure he wasn't going to go all macho on her and try to take a swing at the guy. "I think he's a bit afraid of you." Alan had sure fled fast enough. "Why would he be afraid?" she asked. Her brothers, she got. But Mark?

He shrugged. His fingers caught hers. He lifted her hand to his mouth and pressed a quick kiss to the back of her knuckles. "Don't know. Don't care."

"I…I have to go meet my brothers." They'd planned

a family dinner for her. And she wanted to check in and see if they'd discovered anything else about her stalker.

I didn't see anyone suspicious today or have the weird feeling that I was being watched. She'd felt that way a few times, back in Houston. Today had been different.

"Are you staying at the guest house?"

She nodded. "You know I can't stand the thought of sleeping in the main house." Honestly, being in that guest cottage was too close for her comfort.

"Then I guess I'll be seeing you soon." His fingers slowly released hers. But he didn't back away.

Neither did she, because she had to know. "Why?"

His brows lifted.

"You've been keeping me at a distance for so long." She wasn't going to waste time trying to hint around at this thing between them. "And now you're kissing me in public? Touching me?" *Almost having sex with me in your guest room.* "Why now?"

But he didn't speak. He just stood there.

Ava shook her head. "What is it that you want from me?"

"Everything."

MARK MONTGOMERY WAS a problem. The fool wasn't backing away from Ava. He was following her, trying to get closer to her, to kiss her.

And Ava—he'd warned her about Mark. Why couldn't she see him for the jerk that he was? Mark wasn't some hero to save the day.

He was a killer. Cold-blooded. Evil to the core. He didn't deserve Ava.

He didn't deserve any happiness.

It was time to make Mark pay for the things he'd done. And when Mark fell, when Mark lost all that he had, then Ava would see the man for the liar and betrayer that he really was.

He's not the one for you, Ava. I am.

When would she ever learn the truth? Just how much more would he have to do before she appreciated him?

Cars whizzed past him on the street. Ava pulled away from Mark. She hurried down the steps. Mark watched her, his gaze far too intent on her fleeing figure.

She's not for you.

Mark would learn that lesson soon enough.

Chapter Four

They had dinner at the guest cottage. It was sweet, re-ally, the way Davis prepared all of the food up at the ranch and then brought it over to her. Davis was actu-ally an amazing chef, and whenever she ate one of his meals, Ava knew she was tasting a bit of paradise.

Grant came with his wife, Scarlett. As soon as she'd entered the cottage, Scarlett had pulled Ava close and whispered, "Are you okay?"

Scarlett had her own violent and far-too-scary past, so if any woman could understand Ava's pain, it was her. Ava had nodded even as she blinked away the ri-diculous tears that had wanted to sting her eyes.

Brodie and Jennifer had come over for dinner, too. They'd talked, laughed and tried to keep Ava distracted. Oh, she'd recognized the technique for exactly what it was.

But when the meal came to an end, she got down to business. "Did you find out anything about the man who broke into Mark's house?"

Davis slanted a quick glance toward Grant, then shook his head. "No, the guy's pretty good. Made it on to the property without leaving any signs of a break-in.

He slipped inside during the confusion caused by that alarm sounding at the stables—"

"Betting he set that off deliberately," Brodie interrupted with a quick nod.

"Why?" Jennifer asked. "He made it that far without sounding the alarm, so why do it then."

"So that there *would* be plenty of confusion," Brodie said flatly as his gaze slid to Jennifer.

Brodie and Davis looked so much alike. The only difference? Brodie's face softened when he glanced at Jennifer.

And he glanced at her plenty. Jennifer's dark hair had been pulled back into a loose knot at the base of her head. Her dark eyes gleamed when she looked at Brodie. They…warmed.

It was obvious those two loved each other deeply. Just as much as Grant and Scarlett loved each other. Ava couldn't help but wonder…what would it be like to have a man love her that way? So completely?

"I think he did it to draw Mark away, too," Davis added. "No one was in the house but the two of them. With Mark gone, the guy had free access to Ava."

That sounded bad. Very bad. "He hasn't tried to hurt me before."

"He's escalating," Grant said flatly. "That's why you should have told us about this joker before. I mean, we're family and—"

"You had enough to deal with." That was a serious understatement. "And at first, I started to wonder if the cops were right. Maybe I was imagining things." Hadn't she worried in those first desperate days that she might be going crazy with the grief and the guilt that wouldn't end?

"Ava…" Sympathy flashed in Davis's eyes—sympathy and pity.

They weren't the same thing. Not at all. And she hated the pity.

Then Davis's phone rang. No, it didn't ring so much as it gave off a chiming alarm. He pulled out the phone and frowned at the screen. "I've got the gate's security system linked in here," he said as he lifted the phone. "It looks like we've got company out there." He tapped the display. "It's Mark."

Her body tensed. She looked up quickly—and found Scarlett's gaze on her. There was no pity in Scarlett's face, just plenty of speculation.

"What is he doing here now?" Brodie muttered.

"Can't a friend pay a visit?" Ava shot back as she jumped to her feet. If Davis wasn't going to key in the pass code to let Mark inside the ranch, then she'd go bring him in herself. "Let him in, Davis."

Davis tapped in a code on his phone.

Ava exhaled and hurried for the door. "Maybe he's found out something about the break-in."

"Yeah," Brodie drawled from behind her, "and he just had to come over and tell us in person instead of, you know, picking up the phone."

She stepped outside. She could see the lights from Mark's car coming up the curving drive. Mark wasn't heading for the main ranch house. He was coming to the little guest house—to her. Her family had filed out behind her.

"Do you know what you're doing with him?" Davis asked her softly. "Ava…there's more to him than you know."

She turned to stare at him. They were on the narrow

porch, and the front door light felt as though it was spearing down on her, bright, stark. "There's more to me than he knows, too." *More than you all know.*

She wasn't going to hide from the past any longer. It was time to face the nightmares. "I want in on the hunt."

"Ava, you don't need that pain," Grant said instantly.

"I've already got plenty of pain. Staying in the dark doesn't stop it."

Davis shook his head.

Brodie swore.

"You've tried to shut me out for years." Did they have any idea how much that had hurt? "You hunted for the killers, and you kept me in the dark."

"We were protecting you," Brodie grated out.

"I'm not a child anymore. I don't need you to shield me from the world. I can help. I *will* help."

Mark parked his SUV. He jumped out, then slammed the door behind him.

Ava could feel his stare on her as he approached. There was just something there—a connection that seemed to make her hypersensitive to him.

"I was coming back to Austin," Ava said, her voice low but firm, "even before this creep started messing with me. It's not about me running from him. It's about me…facing my life." A life that was there, in Austin.

"Thanks for letting me in," Mark said as he closed in on them. "I came to see Ava."

"Right," Brodie said, voice tight. "I heard all about how you *saw* her this morning and last night."

Jennifer slapped his shoulder. "Oh, Brodie, stop acting crazy. Ava's an adult, Mark's an adult and you need to chill out."

Mark braced his legs apart as he faced them. "If any

of you think I had something to do with the death of your parents, say it now."

Her brothers didn't say a word.

"The McGuires have been my friends for as long as I can remember. Yeah, Gregory used to get mad because he didn't want me around you all, but…he wasn't me. *And I'm not like him.* If he did anything, *anything at all*, to your parents, if he was involved in any way, I swear to you, I will find out the truth." His breath heaved out. "I protected that SOB while he was alive. I did it for my mother's sake."

A mother who'd passed away when Mark was a teen, right before his eighteenth birthday. Mark had vanished for a time after that and had only come back…right before Ava's parents had been murdered.

She wasn't sure what he'd done in those years, but judging from the way Davis kept talking about Mark, she strongly suspected her brother was aware of his secrets.

"He liked to hurt people." Mark's shoulders rolled back. "Me in particular. And yeah, you probably already know that he hated your father. He blamed the man for taking the one woman who Gregory said was perfect."

Ava couldn't move.

"He loved your mother, or at least, as much as he could love anyone. When my mom came around, he thought she was beautiful. I heard him say once that he had to claim the most beautiful woman around. That it would show the McGuires. I don't even know if he ever loved my mother. He sure didn't love me."

Ava broke from her stupor and hurried toward Mark. He was baring his soul in front of them.

"I stayed until she was gone, and I came back—

because I knew he was bad. I was taking steps to get him in rehab, but he didn't want help. He just wanted to die."

And he had. Ava stopped at Mark's side. But then she realized that wasn't good enough. She wrapped her arms around him and held him close. "I'm sorry," she whispered.

She and her brothers had been caught up in their own pain for so long. What about Mark? What about his pain and his life?

Even heroes needed help.

He was tense against her. "If he was involved, I'll find out."

She pulled back just enough to look up at his face.

Their gazes locked. Tension thickened in the air.

"Um…right…" Jennifer cleared her voice. "I think we should probably pack it in for the night. Brodie, Davis, how about we head up to the main house? Let's give them a chance to…to talk."

"Yes," Scarlett agreed instantly. "Grant, we should leave and head home, too. You're supposed to call your other brothers, remember?"

Because Sullivan and Mac were out working cases, they hadn't been able to join the dinner-slash-grilling-Ava-with-questions event.

Footsteps shuffled forward. Ava glanced over and saw Davis hesitate. He inclined his head toward Mark. "I know what he did to you. I hated it. I saw the scars, man. Not until too late, but I saw them. By then, he was already in the ground."

And Ava remembered touching Mark's back, feeling the raised flesh beneath her fingertips. Scars?

A dark picture formed in her mind, and nausea rolled

in her stomach. If her suspicions were right, then Mark had suffered far more than she'd realized.

"I thought about putting him in the ground myself," Mark admitted starkly. "That's why I left."

Davis glanced at Ava once more. They'd moved away from the light, so it was hard for her to see his expression.

"Ava has nightmares," Mark murmured. "I just… I want to make sure she's okay before I leave."

Jennifer was pulling Brodie toward the main house while Scarlett dragged Grant to their car.

Davis exhaled. "I guess Ava's always safe…when she's with you."

"I'd protect her with my life."

No, that *wasn't* something she wanted to happen. She never wanted him to be put at risk for her. She didn't want *any* of them put at risk for her. She had enough guilt on her soul to last several lifetimes already.

"So would I," Davis said softly. Then he turned and walked away.

That was the problem—they were all willing to risk too much for her. Didn't they get it? She was determined to protect them, too, at all costs. They all mattered to her. Her family. Mark. She'd protect them with her life. Because she would never run while someone she loved died. Never again.

She and Mark stood in silence for a few moments. Ava was waiting for the others to clear out before she spoke. There were some things she just didn't want her brothers to hear.

Like…

"How many secrets do you have?" Ava asked Mark, her voice quiet. The others were far enough away now that she didn't think they would overhear her. "I used to think that, with you, what I saw—"

"Surfaces lie. People lie." His words sounded gruff. "You should be careful who you trust in this world."

"I trust you." *With no hesitation.*

His hand lifted. His knuckles slid over her cheek. "I know."

"Are you trying to tell me that this is wrong? That I shouldn't?" Ava shook her head. "Because if that's the case, you should save your breath."

Then she turned and headed back to the guest house. He didn't follow her. Sighing, she stopped near the door. "Are you coming inside, Mark? Or did you drive all the way over here just so you could hang out in the dark?"

He gave a short bark of laughter, one that surprised her. She didn't think that she'd heard Mark laugh much over the years. And actually, Ava wasn't even sure she could remember the last time she'd laughed herself.

But I want to laugh again. I want to laugh and be happy and fall in love. I want to be just like everyone else. She was tired of feeling like a ghost, just drifting through the days. She wanted more from life.

I want to live and not just go through the motions.

"As tempting as the dark is—" his footsteps padded closer "—I came to see you."

Now that was what she'd hoped to hear. Ava opened the door and slipped through. Mark followed her. And as soon as he stepped inside, the guest house seemed even smaller.

No, she was just far more aware of him. Because they were alone now. No prying eyes. No overprotective brothers.

Time to find out just how much Mark would truly reveal to her.

Ava shut the door behind him. Then she braced her back against the wood and stared up at him. "I don't know how to play games."

He raised a brow as he gazed at her.

"My last boyfriend…that was Alan Channing. You know how that ended."

"Your last—" he began, voice incredulous.

"I've tried dating a few times," she said, cutting through his words. "But nothing clicked for me." Because by then…she'd already been comparing every man she met to Mark. "So I'm not used to all the sweet little lies that lovers are supposed to tell one another. And…I don't want to lie to you, Mark."

His expression hardened.

"So I'm just going to say this…I want you." She could feel her cheeks heat with her confession. "I know things are crazy now." When had they not been for her? "But when I kiss you, I'm not playing some kind of game. I'm kissing you because I need to do it. I ache when you're near."

His eyes squeezed closed. "Ava…"

"Why do you kiss me, Mark? Do you want me, too?"

His eyes opened. Desire was there, burning bright and igniting the blue of his stare. "More than you can even imagine."

Ava wasn't so sure about that. She could imagine a whole lot.

He moved toward her. The hardwood creaked beneath his feet. She tensed as he approached. It was a helpless, instinctive reaction. His hands came up and flattened behind her, effectively caging her between his body and the door.

"I kiss you," he told her, voice rough and rumbling—and making her toes curl a bit, "because I love the way you taste. I love it when you moan for me. When your breath goes ragged…"

Her breath was pretty ragged right then.

"I love the feeling of your mouth against mine. I've been thinking about that mouth of yours…" And his stare was on her lips. Lips that had parted as if she were waiting for his kiss. "Ever since that night two years ago."

"Christmas." Her whisper was husky.

"You were under the mistletoe. You weren't smiling and laughing like everyone else." His head lowered, came closer to hers. "You should have been. Beautiful Ava, you should have been the life of the party."

She hadn't even wanted to be at that party. She'd gone to the Christmas party at McGuire Securities for her brothers. She'd been wishing she could run away from that crowd. But then…

"I touched your hand. You looked up at me, and you smiled. Your first smile that whole night."

Had he been watching her that entire time?

"I kissed you. Even as I did it, I knew it was wrong. That you weren't meant for me."

She didn't want anyone else.

"Then I tasted you." His mouth was so close to hers. She wanted to taste him right then. "And I was lost. I knew I'd never get enough of you."

Her heart was a mad drumbeat in her chest. "But you…you stayed away." For so long. He hadn't tried to touch her again. Hadn't kissed her—

Until I was back at his ranch. In that bedroom.

"I'm not the man you need."

So wrong. "You're the man I want."

Then she stopped waiting for him to kiss her. Ava wrapped her arms around him and pulled Mark close. She kissed him, pressing her lips to his because she loved his taste, too. She loved the way kissing him made her feel. Already her blood was heating. Arousal deepened within her. She'd been waiting a long time for this man…and she was done waiting.

The wood was hard against her back, and he was so strong before her. In his arms, she wasn't afraid. She wasn't thinking about the past. It was just…him. That moment.

"I want to be with you," she whispered against his lips.

He kissed her harder. Deeper. His tongue slid into her mouth and she moaned. Her breasts were aching. She wanted him—wanted him in her.

This wasn't some frantic one-night stand. This was Mark. This was…everything.

His hands moved away from the wood. They locked around her hips, then slid down, curving around her and pulling Ava flush against him. There was no missing the force of desire.

He wants me, too.

"I can't even think clearly when you're close." His words were ragged. So deep. "I want you naked. I want to kiss every inch of your body."

Um, yes, that sounded more than good to her. It was a fabulous, fabulous plan. She'd love to explore his body. Kiss the scars she'd felt on his back. See if she could make him growl with desire. See if she could drive him as wild as he drove her.

"But I want to do things right with you." He pressed a kiss to her throat. Right there, at the base of her neck. The spot that made her quiver. The spot he'd found. "And I'm not going to rush you."

He pulled back.

No!

"You're not rushing me." How was he missing this? She felt like jumping him!

"Your brothers are watching, waiting for me to leave." He shook his head. "When I take you, I'm going to want the whole night. Because when I get you in my bed, I'm not planning to let you leave anytime soon."

She didn't want him leaving then.

"Mark…"

He kissed her again. "I needed you to know," he murmured against her lips, "that you can count on me."

She already had known that.

"My secrets, my past—I won't let them hurt you."

Ava shook her head.

"Lock the door behind me," he said.

He was leaving? "Stay," she said.

She could see the struggle on his face.

"Mark…"

But he reached for the doorknob. "You need your rest, and you also need to think about what's going to happen when we cross this line between us."

The line between friends and lovers. She was ready to race across that line. Full speed ahead!

"There won't be any going back." His words were a warning, and his expression had darkened. "I don't think I can have you once, then watch you walk away."

She wasn't going anyplace.

"I've seen a man's obsession for a woman wreck his world."

He had to be talking about Gregory Montgomery.

"I already think I'm half-obsessed with you. You should…be very careful with me." He opened the door.

She caught his hand. "You're nothing like him."

"I don't have his blood, but I lived in his house for years. There were things that happened there, things I don't talk about much."

"He hurt you." And that knowledge enraged her.

Mark stared down at her.

"I touched the scars on your back."

His shoulders lifted in a small shrug. "When he didn't like the way I worked the ranch, he'd use his belt."

Ava flinched.

"I was thirteen the first time he came after me. And I didn't know what I was supposed to be doing at the ranch. I learned, fast, not ever to make the same mistake twice."

"Mark…" She started to wrap her arms around him, but he stiffened.

"I don't want your pity, Ava."

And wasn't that why she responded so deeply to him? Because he didn't look at her with pity in his beautiful gaze? "I don't pity you," she said clearly. "I just want to hurt Gregory." In that instance, she figured it was a shame the dead couldn't be hurt.

"He never touched my mother. Never let the ranch hands see what he did. I was dependent on him. He'd adopted me, taken us both in. I knew that if we left him, my mother and I would have nothing. Everything, *everything* was his."

Her hands fisted. "You should have told us. My brothers—"

"Like Davis said, he figured out what was happening. It was right before my mom died. When she passed, I didn't care anymore. I left. Rode out fast and hot, and I *wanted* that bastard to die, too."

But Gregory hadn't died, not then. He'd lived for years—and then Mark had come home.

And my parents died just a few days later.

"You are not like him," she said, the words tight. *He was a monster.* Mark wasn't. He was good and strong and—

"Everyone has darkness inside. We can all be pushed too far." His breath heaved out slowly. "Remember that, when you're making your choice. Because I've got more darkness in me than you probably can even guess."

Davis...he'd said something before about Mark and—

"I want you too much. Maybe you should play it safe and tell me to stay away."

She shook her head. Why couldn't he see she wanted him the same way? "I'm not afraid of you." Not of any part of him. Good, bad, darkness, light—whatever, it didn't matter.

"Maybe you should be." He inclined his head. "Lock the door, Ava."

Then he was striding away and heading back to his SUV.

She shut the door.

Locked it.

A few moments later, she heard his vehicle crank. Mark drove away.

Maybe you should be.

THE GATES OF the McGuire ranch shut behind him. Mark paused a moment, his vehicle idling. He was trying to do the right thing with Ava, but every time he got close to her, he just—wanted.

Wanted her naked.

Wanted to see her flush with pleasure.

And—

Her voice, soft and husky, echoed through his mind. *My last boyfriend...that was Alan Channing.*

And that guy was a serious grade-A jerk.

His fingers tightened around the steering wheel.

Keep moving. Drive away. Now.

He shifted gears and drove down that dark road. He hadn't been kidding when he'd told Ava that he worried he was already half-obsessed with her. He thought about her too much. Wanted to protect her at all times. Wanted to destroy anyone who threatened her—

I should let her go. She deserves more.

Because he'd lied to Ava before. Lied to the McGuires. Lied to the police. There were things he'd done that would always darken his soul. Things he never wanted Ava to know about.

Some secrets were better left buried with the dead. They couldn't hurt anyone then. They couldn't destroy a life.

He headed east, traveling back to his ranch. He thought of Ava as she'd last been, standing there with her eyes so big and deep, with her cheeks lightly flushed and her lips slightly swollen from his kiss.

Walking away from her then had been one of the hardest things he'd ever done. He wasn't sure he'd be able to pull away from her next time. He'd warned Ava. Now the choice was hers.

There were no other vehicles on the old dark road. His headlights cut through the night as his SUV ate up the distance to his ranch. He paused at his gate, slowing while he waited to head inside and—

The gunshot blasted. It hit his windshield, the boom like that of a firecracker exploding.

Even as Mark slammed down the gas pedal and the SUV shot forward, more shots were firing, striking the windows and the hood of his SUV in fast succession. Glass rained down on him and a bullet blazed right across his arm.

He needed to make it inside his property. He could get help if he could make it inside—

A bullet hit his front tire. One bullet, then another in fast succession. The SUV swerved as he tried to steady the wheel, but it was too late. The SUV broke through the fence, then barreled into a tree.

AVA PACED AROUND the guest cottage. Tension was knotting her gut. She kept thinking about Mark. About the choices people made in life.

About the choices she'd made.

No more running.

She stared out the window. It was so dark out there. She couldn't even see the stars right then because storm clouds had rolled in. She'd heard the forecast for that night. She knew a powerful storm was supposed to sweep into the area before dawn.

As she gazed at the dark sky, lightning flashed for a moment, a bright streak that stretched like spindly fingers in the night.

Then she heard the crack of thunder. Only...

Her phone beeped. Ava turned around. She took a

few steps and found her phone on the table near the door. When she picked it up, Ava saw that she'd just gotten a text from Mark.

Ava, I need you. Come meet me at my ranch.

Her breath caught and her fingers tightened around the phone. No, there would be no more running away for her. This time, she'd be running *to* someone.

She'd waited long enough. Time to start living.

She hurried from the guest house. Lightning flashed once more.

MARK'S EYES CRACKED OPEN. The pain hit him first, exploding in his head and he realized that he'd slammed into the steering wheel. His air bag hadn't deployed—and the dash was smashed, pretty much caging him in the SUV. Broken glass littered the area around him. He could feel cuts on his arms, and the skin near his right shoulder burned—

Because some SOB took shots at me!

His memory returned in a flash. He'd wrecked and hit his head so hard that he must have lost consciousness for a few moments. He pushed against the mangled steering wheel and dash, trying to twist out, but there was no give there. He was pinned too tightly.

Fumbling, he tried to grab for his phone, but—

It wasn't there. It should have been in the dock near the radio. Who knew where the thing had flown in the crash? The *dock* was gone. The driver's side door was open, swaying drunkenly, freedom so close.

But he couldn't reach it. He was trapped.

And that psycho with the gun could still be out there.

Fumbling, he tried to reach for the glove compartment. He kept a screw driver in that glove box. Not much of a weapon, but far better than nothing. And maybe he could use the screw driver to help pry himself out of that tangled mess. He stretched and his fingers slid over the edge. Almost…almost…

He couldn't reach it.

Blood dripped into his eyes and lightning flashed.

He was a sitting duck. The shooter could come in for him at any moment, and Mark wouldn't even be able to move.

DROPS OF RAIN pelted down on Ava as she hurried to her car. She glanced up at the ranch house. Lights still glowed up there. If she just vanished in the middle of the night, her brothers would worry.

Her phone chimed again.

Ava, don't make me wait long.

Her breath rushed out.

Come alone, sweetheart. I want to make love to you again.

Her drumming heartbeat grew even faster right then, because—she and Mark had never made love. And he'd never called her sweetheart.

Baby. He slipped up and called me baby *once. But not sweetheart.*

She ran toward the ranch house. For an instant, the past and present blurred. It was another night. She'd heard thunder—

I heard thunder a few moments ago.

She was running to the house, looking toward that big picture window...

Ava skidded to a stop. The big picture window was gone. Her brothers had remodeled the ranch house. The window she remembered from her nightmares had been torn down long ago.

The house looked so different now. A new place. There were flowers running around the house, and—

Lightning flashed.

Ava ran toward the door. She pounded her fist against it. *Hurry, hurry.* They weren't answering fast enough. She grabbed the doorknob and twisted, but it was locked. So she pounded again and again and—

"Ava?" Davis had yanked open the door. "What's going on?" He grabbed her wrist and tried to pull her into the house. "Is someone here? Did something happen?"

She jerked away from him. "Mark's in trouble!" She was certain of it. "We have to go help him, *now*!"

Chapter Five

Low, rough laughter reached Mark's ears.

He stopped struggling when he heard that sound.

"She's coming…" the voice rasped. It came from too close by.

His headlights must have been busted out because they weren't throwing off any illumination. The interior of the SUV was a dark hole.

"She thinks that she's coming to you. Ava is racing to see her lover again, but she won't find you." The voice was still low. The jerk was trying to disguise himself.

Mark rammed against that steering wheel once more. Had it shifted just a little bit?

"She won't find you, though. I'll be waiting for Ava."

No, no, that couldn't happen. "You stay away from her!" Mark yelled as he heaved with all of his strength.

"You're the one who should have stayed away." It sounded like the guy was moving. Circling around the SUV? Yes, Mark could just see the guy's outline. He was near the smashed front of the vehicle, raising his arm as lightning flashed. In that instant, Mark saw the gun gripped in the other man's hand. "I warned you, but you just didn't listen, did you?"

Mark surged against that wheel. Yes, *yes*, it had

shifted, just an inch, but an inch was all he needed. He could slide out now. But first he had to get a weapon. He also had to distract the assailant who had Mark locked in his sights.

"Ava isn't yours. She was never meant for you."

Mark forced himself to laugh. "Let me guess. You think Ava belongs to you?" His fingers slid over the passenger seat. He found a chunk of glass that had once been part of the passenger-side window. That chunk would have to do. Not a knife, but he could still do some serious injury with that thing.

Another part of my life that Ava doesn't know about. I learned to kill, maybe too well.

He had more in common with her brothers than Ava realized.

"Ava is mine!" The voice was even lower. Mark had to strain to hear it. His eyes were trying to adjust to the darkness, and he thought the guy was wearing a hood…no, a mask.

Lightning flashed again.

A dark ski mask.

"I've had plans for Ava ever since she was sixteen."

Mark's blood turned to ice in his veins. "You killed her parents."

Laughter. Laughter that he hated. "I'll kill anyone who gets between Ava and me. She came back for me, and now I get to keep her." He was raising that weapon. Mark saw the guy's hand lift—

Mark jumped out the driver's side door. The bullet erupted less than a second later, slamming into the driver's seat. Mark hit the ground hard, and he rolled, twisting and coming up as fast as he could. There were trees all around there, plenty of space for cover, and he leapt for them, his heart racing fast and his legs pumping furiously.

Another shot sounded, and a chunk of bark flew off the tree near his head. *Missed me! Guess you can't aim so well in the dark.*

No wonder it had taken the guy so many hits to crash the SUV.

But the man hadn't given up. He'd kept shooting and—

"You should never have touched Ava!" The other words had been a rasp, but those were a scream. "She was mine. She was waiting for me! And you ruined everything!" A high, sharp scream.

Mark ducked behind a tree. He swiped his hand over his eyes to get rid of the blood that slid down from his forehead. He had his makeshift weapon. Now he just needed to find the right moment to attack.

Then he heard the growl of an engine. One that wasn't coming from his ranch but instead seemed to be coming from the main road—the road from the Mc-Guire ranch.

Ava's coming. She thinks she's coming to find you…

His phone had been missing from the SUV. The driver's side door had been open… That guy must have used it to contact Ava! He'd lured her in with Mark as the bait.

Now he was waiting out there, armed with a gun, and Ava would have no clue what kind of hell she was walking into tonight.

I can't let him hurt her!

He heard the thud of footsteps. His attacker was moving, probably rushing to better ground so that he could attack Ava when she approached. He'd fired at Mark's vehicle, sending him crashing. The guy was planning the same kind of attack on Ava.

No! Mark left his cover and ran after the attacker. Mark could see his shadowy form moving fast. The guy was rushing toward the road and the approaching vehicle.

"She isn't yours!" Mark yelled out.

The other man froze. Then he started to swing around to face Mark.

Mark tackled him. They hit the ground, and the attacker's gun flew from his fingers. Mark brought his weapon up and put it against the man's neck. He definitely had on a ski mask, one that completely shielded his face, but his neck was open, and the glass pressed to his skin. "Make another move," Mark snarled at him, "and you're a dead man."

The growl of the engine was coming closer and closer.

But the guy just laughed. "Left…a little surprise for sweet Ava." His voice was a rasp. "Won't ever see it coming."

Mark's head whipped up. It was so dark. He could only see the flash of Ava's headlights as she drove—too fast—toward his ranch. "What did you do?"

And then he saw the headlights swirl. They spun around as the car seemed to lose control.

"I left some spikes in the road for Ava."

He heard a crash, and terror clawed inside Mark's chest.

"I didn't want her getting to you too fast," that rasping voice told him.

Mark slammed the guy's head into the ground, and the masked man's body seemed to go limp. Mark jumped to his feet and roared, "Ava!" as he started running toward the crash. Pain and fear twisted through him. He had to get to her, to find her. He pushed himself to run faster. Pushed so he could *get to Ava*. She'd been coming to help him, and if she was hurt, he didn't know what in the hell he would do.

His feet thudded over the earth. His breath heaved out. Ava. He had to reach Ava.

"Freeze!"

And suddenly a bright light was shining on him.

"Mark?" That was Ava's voice, coming from behind the light. "He's bleeding!"

Yeah, he was probably bleeding from about a dozen different spots. So what? Ava was there—she was alive. She was also running to him. He could see her clearly now. She threw herself against him and embraced him. "I was so worried," she whispered.

The bright light was still on him, and Mark squinted, trying to see past it, even as he held Ava as tightly as he could.

"What is happening?" a sharp voice demanded—Davis's voice. He was the one with the light, and as he approached, Mark realized Davis was also holding a gun.

Brodie was at his twin's side. "Someone put spikes in the road," Brodie muttered.

"He's back there," Mark said, pointing behind him. "I left him on the ground." Each word seemed to take way too much effort, and the blood was dripping in his eyes again.

But Ava is safe. She's in my arms. I won't let anything happen to her.

"He…shot at me when I drove through the gate. Crashed, and he was waiting…"

"Where is he?" Davis demanded.

"About fifteen feet in front…of the line of trees… west side…"

Davis took off running with his gun drawn. Brodie was a step behind him.

Mark didn't join the hunt. He wasn't about to leave Ava. His hand curled around her chin. "I heard the crash," he whispered. "Baby, are you okay?"

"I'm not the one bleeding all over the place," she said. "We have to get you to a hospital."

Yeah, he could probably use some stitches—or maybe a few dozen. But… "I was scared," he told her, the words little more than a growl. "Knew he was… going after you. Can't let him…can't let him hurt you."

"And I didn't want him hurting you!" Her voice was sharp. She pulled out her phone and called 9-1-1. As she talked, Ava kept one hand on him, almost as if she was afraid of letting him go.

He knew he couldn't let her go. Ava mattered too much.

DAVIS'S LIGHT SWEPT over the battered remains of Mark's SUV. The windshield was gone, and bullet holes littered the vehicle.

Behind him, Brodie gave a low whistle. "Someone was playing hard."

"He wasn't playing." His backed away from the vehicle. It was so dark out there, and the light he was shining made him a target. He'd searched where Mark indicated, but there had been so sign of the man who'd tried to kill Mark. He and Brodie had branched out and scanned the area, but the guy had seemingly vanished.

"He didn't realize just how hard Mark would be to take down." Davis killed his light. He wanted to get back to Ava and Mark just in case the man they were searching for had decided to circle around for another attack. "His mistake."

Because Davis knew just how Mark had spent his years away from Austin. He'd kept secrets for Mark over the years, just as Mark had kept quiet about Davis's past. There were some things that shouldn't be shared.

The world already had enough nightmares.

He and Brodie hurried back to Ava. There were too many trees around them. Too many places to vanish. He hadn't heard the sound of a car, so the guy they were hunting must still be on foot.

If he was lying in wait out here, then he must know the area. To vanish so quickly in the dark, he has to be familiar with this land.

There were some old trails leading away from Mark's ranch. The guy could've escaped on one of those and had a ride waiting in the distance.

Or the man could still be out there, hiding and waiting for a chance to take another shot at his prey.

You won't get a shot at my sister. No one messed with his family. No one.

When he got back to Mark and Ava, he wasn't surprised to see that Mark had moved them closer to Brodie's smashed car. They'd hit the side of a tree after going over those spikes, but the body of the vehicle was still rock solid. Mark and Ava had taken shelter back there.

"I called the ranch," Mark muttered to him. "Help's on the way. Until the cops get here, my men can hold that jerk who—"

"We didn't see him." But they had found a gun the guy had left behind. He'd tucked it into his waistband so he could give it to the cops.

"He's still out there?" Mark demanded, and Davis saw Mark instantly pull Ava closer to him.

He'd known how Mark felt about Ava. When the guy looked at her, his eyes always got that too-intense expression in them. But Mark had been keeping his hands off Ava for years. He'd stayed away.

Looks like he's not holding back any longer.

Instead, he was holding her tight.

Davis knew that any man who tried to take Ava from Mark Montgomery would have a fight on his hands.

"I'm not like Gregory." No, Mark wasn't, but he was still one very dangerous man. How would Ava respond when she learned about Mark's past?

He heard the approach of vehicles then—several, by the sound of things. The cars weren't coming from the main road. Instead, they were coming from the Montgomery ranch. Had to be Mark's staff, rushing to help. Good. He could use them. They could fan out and search the area. Because if that guy was still close— *and he has to be*—then they still had a chance of stopping him.

The vehicles braked. Car doors slammed. The men hurried forward.

"Mark, buddy, are you okay?" Davis recognized the voice of Ty Watts, Mark's foreman and friend.

"He's not okay," Ava said, her voice shaking. "He's bleeding too much, and the ambulance needs to hurry."

Davis tensed. He hadn't examined Mark's wounds because the guy had looked strong when he ran toward them. But Mark was an ex-soldier. If he was at death's door, he'd still probably race straight ahead, showing no weakness.

"We need your men to search," Davis said, his words sharp. "We have a man out there, possibly armed." He didn't know how many guns the guy might have brought to the ambush. "He was here a few minutes ago, and we have to find him."

Before he decided to attack again.

Brodie led the men on the search.

Davis slapped his hand on Mark's shoulder. "How bad?" he asked softly.

"I've had much worse."

Davis noticed that Mark's hand was still wrapped around Ava's as if he couldn't bear to let her go.

"We'll get him," Davis assured him before he started to turn away.

But Mark's words stopped him.

"I should have killed him," Mark muttered, "when I had the chance."

"No!" came Ava's instant denial. "Mark, you're not a killer. That's not who you—"

Mark's laughter was bitter as he finally eased his hold on Ava. "Oh, baby, there is so much you don't know about me."

"Mark?" Now her voice was hesitant.

"Next time," Mark promised, the words heavy with lethal certainty, "he won't walk away. He's not going to have you, no matter what that sick freak thinks."

Davis tensed.

"He said you're his, Ava." Mark seemed to be gritting out the words. "He thinks he's going to have you."

An obsession. One that had sure escalated tonight.

"I don't—" Ava began.

"He told me…that he had plans for you. That he'd had plans since…" Mark's voice roughened, and he stopped.

Mark was holding back. They couldn't afford that.

"What did the guy say?" Davis prompted Mark.

Mark's hand lifted as if he'd touch Ava again, but then his hand fell back to his side and his fingers clenched into a fist. "I'm sorry, Ava."

This wasn't good.

"Mark?" Fear threaded through his name as Ava reached out—and she didn't hesitate. She touched Mark. She curled her fingers around his hand and held tight.

"He said…" In the distance, Davis could finally hear the faint sound of an ambulance approaching. "He said he'd had plans for you…ever since you were sixteen…"

MARK MONTGOMERY WASN'T DEAD.

He was still very much *alive* and the man was currently with Ava. *With my Ava!*

And Ava…she'd been bad. He'd told her to come to him. She should have come alone, but instead, she'd brought her brothers with her. Those two McGuire men had leapt out of the vehicle with their guns in their hands. They'd been searching so desperately near the crash scene. They'd almost—*almost!*—seen him. They'd found one of his guns. Luckily he'd been wearing gloves so there wouldn't be any fingerprints on the weapon. They *shouldn't* be able to trace it back to him, but…

He eased deeper into the shadows. Men were searching all around the area. But there were so many dark spots hidden beneath the trees. He'd prepared well for this night. He'd learned the area far better than anyone else. He knew how to disappear.

And I know how to bide my time.

Because he would have to wait for Mark to lower his guard once more. Then he'd attack. Mark Montgomery wasn't going to get away from him.

As he watched, Ava reached out. Her fingers curled around Mark's as if…as if she just had to touch him.

No, Ava, he's not for you!

Ava had to understand. She would never be with Mark. Mark was a dead man walking. The guy just didn't know it yet.

But you will, Mark.

Mark had never belonged there. He and that sick bastard Gregory Montgomery had no right to that land. They weren't worthy.

He'd taken everything away from Gregory. At the end, the old fool had begged. He'd promised the world to him.

But it hadn't mattered. He'd killed Gregory, and no one had even known. Gregory hadn't been his first kill and wouldn't be his last. Any people who got in his way—they would all be eliminated.

I will take what I want.

And the thing he wanted most…was Ava. Sweet, beautiful Ava. He'd already done so much for her. Did she even realize it? Did she even know?

I killed for you, Ava. And I'll do it again and again.

THE EMTs WERE dragging Mark into the back of an ambulance. He was trying to stay, despite the fact that he was bleeding all over the place.

"Ava!" Mark tried to push toward her.

"Go with him," Davis told her as he gave her shoulder a quick squeeze. "I'll keep searching here."

She moved forward, her body feeling numb. Mark's words kept replaying in her head. *He said he'd had plans for you...ever since you were sixteen...*

Nausea was rolling inside her as she climbed into the back of that ambulance. Mark finally settled down then, and he let the EMTs start checking out his body.

There was so much blood on him. Dripping from a gash on his forehead, coming from scrapes and cuts on his arm—

"Looks like a bullet grazed you here," one of the EMTs murmured as he studied Mark's right shoulder.

"I just need a few stitches," Mark told him. "I'll be fine. Check Ava—her car crashed, too! You need to make sure she's okay."

"I'm fine," Ava said. "And it wasn't my car—it was Brodie's." She was fine, physically. But her mind was a wreck right then. This man after her—if he'd been making plans since she was sixteen, had he been one of the men who killed her parents? Had they truly died because of her?

Her fingers were shaking. She looked out the back of the ambulance and saw Davis staring at her. His expression was hard, angry. Did he blame her, too?

Davis slammed those back doors shut. The ambulance's siren screamed as the vehicle lurched forward.

"Sir, how many fingers am I holding up?" Ava heard the EMT ask Mark.

"Two, and get 'em out of my way." His response was a snarl. "Ava? Ava, you're trembling!"

And she was. She'd slid back into a corner of the ambulance, hoping to make room for the EMTs to work, but heavy tremors were running through her body. "He tried to kill you," she whispered.

One of the EMTs turned toward her. "Ma'am? Ma'am, where do you hurt?"

In her heart...

"He was attacking you because of me." She knew it.

Mark gave her a grim smile. "Baby, I'm a hard man to kill."

That didn't make her feel any better. In fact, his low words, spoken in a hard voice that she'd never heard from him before, just made her feel even worse. Because she realized right then—*I don't know Mark nearly as well as I thought.*

His blue eyes had turned cold and icy, and for a moment, she almost felt as if she were staring into the gaze of a stranger.

Chapter Six

They hadn't found the man who'd attacked him. Mark had talked to the cops. He'd repeated his story at least four times to them.

But he hadn't seen the man's face. He hadn't recognized that low, rasping voice. He knew the guy had been close to his own height and that he had been well muscled. He suspected the man was familiar with the area because he had known just where to wait for his ambush—and he'd been able to disappear so quickly. But other than that, he hadn't been able to give the cops much information at all.

He's a psycho and he'd obsessed with Ava. Those had been Mark's words to the cops. Ava had stood there, far too pale and far too tense, during the interview with the police. *He said I wouldn't have her. That she was his.*

Ava had actually flinched when he said those words.

She'd spoken very little. And when they'd left the hospital, she'd seemed to withdraw completely from him. Now he was in the vehicle with her and Davis, heading back to his ranch, and he was—what? Just supposed to leave Ava?

There were at least a few more hours before dawn.

With that maniac still on the loose out there, he didn't want to let Ava out of his sight.

She was in the front seat with Davis. She hadn't looked back at Mark, not even once. *What is happening?*

He leaned forward. "Don't bother going to my ranch tonight. I already talked to Ty. He'll have extra security out there."

Now Ava did slant him a quick glance. Finally.

"Take me to Ava's place," he said flatly. And Davis had better not even try arguing with him. After everything that had happened, he wouldn't be separated from her.

"You think you're spending the night with my sister?" Davis asked him. Apparently, he *was* going to try arguing.

"I think I'm going to be your sister's guard until dawn." Because Ava would be scared and because—fine, *he* was the one who was scared. Scared that the man out there might attack Ava again when Mark wasn't close. What would he do then?

"Brodie and I can watch Ava." Davis's voice was flat. "You need to rest."

Right. Like he'd be able to rest with the adrenaline rush still coursing through his veins. "I let him get away," he said. "I should have—"

"Don't." Ava's voice was brittle. "Don't even say it, do you understand?" And she turned to glare at him. "Don't say that you should have killed him. That's not you. That's not what you do! You don't kill people! You help—you save people, just like you saved me!"

Not always, Ava.

"You know I can keep her safe," Mark said. Davis

was one of the few people who knew all about his past. "Don't you want as much protection for her as possible?"

He saw Davis give a grim nod. Good, because if Davis had taken Mark back to the Montgomery ranch, he just would have forced his way back inside the McGuire place.

The rest of the ride passed in silence. The road was pitch black. Mark kept glancing around, hyperaware now that threats could come at any time. Until that guy was caught, he knew he'd be looking over his shoulder.

And trying to keep Ava as close as possible.

Davis took them through the big gates at the McGuire ranch. The vehicle eased up the drive until they got to the guest cottage. Ava hurriedly jumped out of the car, and Davis followed her.

Mark exited, but he stood back a minute, waiting to see what went down between Ava and her brother.

"You should stay up at the main house," Davis told Ava. "Jennifer got a room ready for you—you know you'll be safe there."

"I'm starting to think no one is safe…anywhere."

Mark had to strain in order to hear her words.

"Come to the main house," Davis said again.

But Ava shook her head. "I'm staying here with Mark."

Yes.

Davis turned toward him. "You see anything suspicious, you call me, got it? You sound an alarm, and you get me here."

If he saw an attack coming, Mark would be striking back with all the power that he had.

Davis paced toward him. He leaned in close. His

voice no more than a breath of sound, he warned Mark, "And you keep your hands off my sister, got it?"

No, he didn't. Mark grabbed Davis's arm, stopping him before he could leave. Keeping his voice just as low as Davis's had been, Mark said, "Ava's an adult. What happens between us…it's just between *us*." If Ava wanted him, the last thing he'd do would be to turn away from her.

Davis could get angry. The guy could try to take a swing at Mark, but there was no way Mark was staying away from Ava. Not now.

Davis's expression was unreadable in the darkness. But when he said, "You hurt her, and I'll break you," Mark understood his threat.

Then Davis was heading back to the car.

Ava had opened the door to her cottage. Mark rushed forward, not wanting her to go in alone. He caught her hand. "Let me check it out."

"The…the alarm's still on. The place should be safe."

It should be, but he still wanted to check in there. Mark hurried inside and did a sweep of the guest house. The den was clear. So was the kitchen, the bathroom, the bedroom and—

He opened another door. The room there was mostly empty except for about a dozen canvases that had been stacked near the walls.

"No one here but us," Ava said, her voice still sounding brittle. Sharp. Not at all like Ava. "I told you the place was safe."

He turned to look at her, but Ava's eyes were on the canvases. "I store them here because I don't want anyone else to see them." She seemed to hesitate. Then she said, "Maybe I should just throw them out."

He'd never seen Ava's paintings before. He didn't think anyone had. He took a step toward those canvases.

This time, she was the one to reach out to him.

"We all have…secrets, don't we?"

Yes.

Her gaze rose to hold his. "Who are you?"

Mark shook his head, not understanding.

"Are you the man who kept me sane all those years ago? The white knight, riding to my rescue?" She swallowed. The faint click of sound was almost painful to hear. "Or are you the guy who talks about killing a man in a way…in a way that makes me think you'd really do it? That you wouldn't hesitate at all?"

Her fingers were so soft against his skin. Like silk. "If your life was on the line, I wouldn't hesitate." He would do anything for her.

Who are you?

"I'm both men." Good and bad tangled together.

Ava was so close to him. Her gaze searched his. "Should I be afraid of you?"

He shook his head. "I won't hurt you." It was a vow he'd made to himself long ago.

"Can I trust you?"

There were things she didn't know, but when it came to her safety… "Yes."

Ava glanced back toward the canvases. He couldn't see what she'd painted on them, and he wanted to stride forward.

But he also wanted her to keep touching him.

"You told the police that the man who attacked you said I was his."

His back teeth clenched. "Yes."

"What do you think he'll do…to me?"

If he had the chance… The image flashed in Mark's mind, and rage burned inside him.

"That's what I think, too," Ava said, seeming to read Mark's thoughts. "Why? Why does he want to hurt me? I don't even know him."

He wrapped his arms around her shoulders and pulled her against him. "Because he's sick, Ava. You didn't do anything. It's this guy. He's just—"

"If he started making plans when I was sixteen, then do you think… Was he one of the men who killed my parents?"

Mark was afraid that he just might be.

"Why?" Her head titled back as she stared up at him. "Why is he doing this? Why is he focusing on me?"

"I don't know." He wished he had words to comfort her.

Her gaze slid over his face, then up to his forehead. The docs had put in a few stitches there, and they'd stitched up his shoulder. The wounds didn't hurt him. He'd had much worse before, courtesy of Gregory and the life he'd led after leaving the ranch.

"I'm sorry he hurt you." She stood on her tiptoes and pressed a light kiss to his cheek. "The people I care about always seem to get hurt because of me."

Her scent teased him. Strawberries. Ava.

He closed his eyes as he just drank her in for a moment.

"I'll…get some covers for you. You can sleep on the couch. Or, I mean, if you want, you can take the bed."

He opened his eyes.

"You're the one who was hurt," she whispered. "I can easily bunk on the couch while you take the bed."

He'd rather be in that bed with her.

"I heard the doctors…" She exhaled softly. "They said you might have a concussion. Is it even safe for you to sleep—"

"I'm not planning to sleep." Too much adrenaline pumped through him. He wouldn't be sleeping anytime soon. "And you…you take the bed, Ava. I'll be fine on the couch."

She nodded and slipped from the room. Her soft footsteps padded away.

He stared at the stack of canvases. Ava had made those, and because they were hers…part of Ava…he found himself striding across that room. He wondered what she would paint. When she'd been in her early teens, she'd always taken a sketchbook around the ranch with her. He'd found the sketchbook once. It had been filled with drawings of her horse, her brothers. Even… *Me*.

He'd been blown away by her work. It was so beautiful and detailed for someone so young. What would her work be like now?

He picked up the first canvas.

Mark sucked in a sharp breath.

Her work…it was still beautiful. But it was dark. She wasn't sketching anything anymore. Not painting horses or people. The art was abstract. Angry reds and turbulent grays. He picked up more canvases, going through them, seeing the same emotions jumping out at him again and again.

Rage.

Pain.

They were twisted together in her paintings, so strong he could feel the emotions battering at him as he gazed at her work. So strong that—

The last canvas was a painting of a man. Ava's father. He was staring back from that canvas, his eyes filled with fear even as his face was twisted with rage.

The floor creaked. Mark's head snapped up. Ava stood in the doorway. She had a pillow and a blanket in her arms. She gazed at him, her eyes wide. Hurt.

"Ava—"

"Not so beautiful anymore, are they?"

He didn't speak. The paintings *were* beautiful. In a dark and almost unearthly way.

"You told me once that my sketches were beautiful."

He put down the last canvas and took a step toward her.

"When I pick up a brush now, it's all so…rough." She gave a hard shake of her head. "It was supposed to be therapeutic, doing that. At least, that's what I read in one of those crazy self-help books. 'Paint your emotions.' But I guess I didn't realize my emotions were so violent."

Because there was violence in her work.

"I…want them to pay."

He took another step toward her.

"I want the men who killed my parents to suffer. I want them to hurt, just like I hurt." Her voice dropped. "My brothers want to shut me out and hunt these men on their own, but…it's about me. Don't they get that? I was there. My father's last moments—he was staring right at me."

With fear in his eyes and rage on his face.

"I won't be shut out." Her laughter held a desperate edge. "Especially since I know they died because of me." She pushed the pillow and the blanket into his arms. Then she spun on her heel.

"It wasn't because of you." He wanted to be clear on that.

She looked back over her shoulder. "But that man tonight—"

"If he was involved, that has nothing to do with you. You didn't ask him to kill your parents."

Ava flinched. That *had* been one of the vicious rumors circulated about her. That she'd hired men to kill her parents. That they hadn't approved of her secret lover and she'd had them killed. How else had she escaped that night? Ava must have been involved. At least, that was what the gossip said.

He'd hated those stories. Every time he'd heard those tales, he'd jumped to Ava's defense. And when a few fools in a bar had been dumb enough to mouth off about Ava and her parents, Mark had started a bar fight that wound up costing him over five thousand dollars in repair fees. He'd torn that place down because those drunks had been raging about her.

They didn't even know her. Ava would never do something like that.

Because Ava… She was one of the few good things left in the world. In *his* world, he sometimes thought she might be the only good thing left.

"You didn't do this," he said again, because he wanted Ava to believe that.

"I want to give them justice. Sometimes I think if I can just get them justice—" her smile was bittersweet "—maybe I'll be able to sleep without them haunting me."

Then Ava slipped away.

AVA LAY IN BED and stared up at the ceiling. Mark was just outside the bedroom. She'd heard him getting settled for the night. Moving quietly, but the creaking floor had given him away.

Now there was only silence from the den.

She'd been so afraid earlier. So terrified that she wouldn't get to him in time.

Her fingers curled around the sheets. Mark could have died that night. And what would her life have been like then?

You have to keep going. Davis had told her that after they'd buried their parents. *We can't crawl into the ground with them. You think they'd want that? No, they'd want you to live and to be happy.*

She pushed aside the covers. She'd changed into a pair of loose shorts and a T-shirt before she'd climbed into bed.

If Mark had been killed, everyone would have expected her to soldier on.

They wouldn't have realized that her heart had been cut out of her chest.

What am I waiting for?

Ava crept toward her bedroom door. The sound of her breathing seemed far too loud to her. Her fingers touched the doorknob. She turned it and the door opened with a little squeak.

The den was dark, but her eyes quickly adjusted. She could see Mark on the sofa. Not lying down but sitting up. She inched forward.

"Did you have a bad dream, Ava?"

In a sense, yes.

"It's all right," he told her softly. "You know nightmares can't hurt you."

She stood in her doorway and tried to keep her backbone straight. "There's…there's plenty of room in the bed." She sucked in a quick breath. "There's enough space for us both. You don't have to stay on that couch."

Silence.

Her cheeks burned. As far as seduction routines went, hers was extremely lame. It was just that this moment mattered so much to her. No, *he* mattered.

"Ava…" he said her name like a caress, and she shivered in the dark. "Are you inviting me into your bed?"

"Yes." That was exactly what she was doing.

She saw his shadowy form rise. He walked toward her, big and menacing in the darkness. She didn't back away when he approached. This time, there was no hesitation. Life was too short to waste on doubts.

"Let's be very clear." His voice held an edge she couldn't quite interpret. Desire was there. Demand, really, but…more. "Are you offering me a place to sleep…"

She waited.

"Or are you offering me more?"

Ava reached out, took his hand and laced her fingers with his. "I'm offering you everything."

His fingers tightened around hers. "There won't be any going back once we cross this line."

"There's no other place that I want to go."

She turned and led him back into the bedroom. Her heart was racing in her chest, and she wondered if he could feel the nervous tremor in her fingers. She wanted to appear sophisticated and in control, but the truth was that her knees felt like jelly. This moment with him—it mattered so much to her.

"I was waiting for you," he said.

She stopped at the bed and turned back toward him. "Waited so long…for you…to come to me." His left hand rose and sank into her hair. He tipped her head back, and his head lowered toward hers. "I thought I'd go insane from waiting."

And she hadn't even thought he really wanted her, not until that kiss at his ranch.

"Is it safe?" Ava asked, a fast worry pushing through her. "With your stitches?"

"What stitches?" Then he was kissing her. Softly at first, then harder, deeper. "I don't feel a thing but you," he said against her mouth.

And *he* was all *she* could feel as he surrounded her with his strength. His chest was bare, and when he pulled her closer, his muscles flexed against her.

Her mouth opened more for him. His tongue slipped past her lips, and her hands rose to grip his shoulders.

"No interruptions this time," he said. "Just you and just me."

She moved a bit to the side, and her knees hit the mattress.

"Just you," she repeated. "Just me."

His hands curled around her hips, and he lifted her onto the bed.

Ava caught the hem of her shirt, hesitated only about half a second—because this was Mark!—and pulled the shirt over her head.

She thought that Mark was going to come closer to her then. That she'd feel his touch. Instead, the bedside lamp flashed on. She blinked against the light and saw Mark standing there, his hand still near the lamp but his eyes on her.

"You really thought…I'd take you in the dark?" He shook his head. "No, baby, I want to see everything, because I'm never forgetting you."

His gaze slid over her body, down to her breasts. Her nipples were tight and aching for him. She wanted him to touch them. She wanted him to lick them.

Mark drew in a deep breath. "Take off the shorts."

She eased back onto the bed until she was lying down. With her eyes still on him, Ava arched her hips and pushed the shorts over her hips and down her legs. When the shorts were near her knees, Mark caught them, easing the material the rest of the way off.

He dropped the shorts onto the floor. His gaze was on her underwear, a pair of black cotton panties. She wore nothing else.

"You are the sexiest thing I've ever seen."

He said the words as if he meant them. She knew Mark had probably been with plenty of lovers—he had money and power, and the guy was pure walking sex appeal—but when he stared at her, there was such stark desire in his eyes.

Like I'm the only woman for him.

That was perfect, since he was the only man for her.

His hand lifted, and he touched her shoulder. Lightly. Carefully.

That wouldn't do.

Ava shook her head. "I want everything from you that you have to give." Passion and need and a desire that burned right through any thought of control.

Their gazes held.

"Take off your jeans," Ava ordered him.

Staring at her, he did.

Her breath came faster. If possible, the need within her built even more. Desire was raging within her blood, a heat that flooded her veins.

He slid into the bed with her and kissed her, not carefully, not softly—wildly. Hard and fierce and deep, and it was exactly what she wanted from him.

Mark pushed her legs apart and slid his hips between her thighs, positioning himself at their juncture. He braced his arms, and then his mouth was moving down her neck. Licking and sucking and letting her feel the edge of his teeth in a sensual bite.

Down, down he went, and when his mouth closed over her nipple, Ava hissed out a breath because it felt so good. She arched toward him, demanding more. Now that this moment was here, she wanted to take all he had to give. She intended to savor every single moment of pleasure.

He kissed his way to her other breast. Light stubble coated his jaw, and it rasped lightly over her skin, heightening her sensitivity to him even more. He licked her nipple and sucked it deep into his mouth. Her hips jerked against him, a helpless reaction, and his long, thick arousal pressed to her core.

Her panties were the only thing between them. She wanted those panties gone. She'd longed to feel him inside her for too long already, and she didn't want to wait any longer. "Mark, *now*."

But he was kissing her stomach. Working his way down her body and caressing her with constant touches that were driving her to the very edge of reason.

He moved his body, taking away that wonderful aroused flesh, and she cried out in frustration.

"Don't worry, baby. I'll take care of you."

Then he was touching her through the thin fabric of her panties. Stroking her, but it wasn't enough. Not even close. She needed him too much right then, and she heard herself demand, "More!"

He bent and put his mouth on the panties.

She nearly came off the bed. "Mark!"

He jerked the panties down, and she heard the faint rip of the fabric. Then he was sliding his fingers against her sex and into her. She bit her lip because the feelings were so strong. But she didn't want just to be touched by his hand. She wanted him—all of him.

"So beautiful," Mark whispered. "So perfect for me..."

She was going crazy. "Don't make me wait," she told him. She'd waited long enough. "Now, Mark, now!"

He pulled away from her, and she cried out in frustration, but he was just reaching for his jeans to grab his wallet. She realized he'd brought protection with him.

Talk about being prepared. Another thing she adored about him.

In seconds he was back. She parted her legs eagerly. He positioned his shaft at the entrance to her body, and his fingers threaded with hers. She stared into his eyes as he thrust deep.

The pain was fast. A quick burn that was lost in the tide of pleasure, but Mark's eyes went wide. "Ava?" Shock was there, and he tried to pull back.

She wasn't about to let him go. Ava locked her legs around his hips and arched toward him. He was filling her completely. She was on the edge of her release, and she just needed—

He kissed her. Hot, deep, just the way she liked.

Then he withdrew and thrust back into her. The bed seemed to shake beneath her. Again and again he thrust. Her head tipped back as the pleasure lashed through her. Ava's release was so close. So—

His hand pulled from hers. His fingers slid between

their bodies and then he was stroking her, pushing right against the center of her need. He thrust and caressed and her climax rolled over her. Ava's body shuddered as the waves seemed to consume her with so much pleasure that she lost her breath. She could only hang on to Mark and enjoy that wild, sweet ride. Her heartbeat was drumming in her ears, a thunderous rhythm, and her body was slick and sated beneath him.

He was still moving within her, thrusting deeper, harder, and making aftershocks of pleasure course through Ava. Another thrust—

His eyes seemed to go blind as he stared down at her. The darkness of his pupils spread, covering the blue of his gaze. He jerked within her, growled out her name as an expression of pure pleasure swept over his face.

Her body shivered beneath his. He was all around her. Strong and warm. And when he slowly pulled out of her body, Ava whispered a protest because she didn't want the pleasure to end.

"I'll be right back. Promise."

The mattress shifted when he rose and padded to the bathroom. Ava stretched, her muscles aching and her body feeling so incredibly good. Her eyes started to drift closed, and then she felt the soft, wet warmth of a cloth between her legs.

"Was there something you wanted to tell me?" He moved the cloth, then eased back into bed with her.

Exhaustion was pulling at Ava. She smiled and told him, "I want to make love with you again. Soon." Because he'd sure been worth waiting for.

"Ava." He said her name with a tenderness she hadn't heard before. "Did I hurt you?"

With her eyes closed, she shook her head.

"You…you should've told me that you hadn't… not before…"

He sounded so flustered that she forced her eyes to lift. "What did it matter?"

"Ava…"

She smiled at him. "I wanted you, Mark. I didn't ask who you'd been with before, and you didn't ask me, either."

"You *hadn't* been with anyone."

"Because I haven't trusted anyone else, not the way I trust you." That was the simple truth. She didn't trust him just with her body. She trusted him with her heart. Did he even realize that?

"You should have told me. *I* should have asked! I should have—"

He looked so cute and confused. She kissed him. "It was wonderful."

His hand sank into her hair. "You were wonderful."

She pulled him down beside her. "Stay with me." It just seemed natural to say those words to him. After the day they'd had—the night—she wanted to sleep with him.

His arms curled around her. She could hear the drumming of his heart beneath her ear. That strong drumming was the last sound she heard before she slipped into her dreams.

MARK MONTGOMERY WAS spending the night with Ava.

He hadn't stayed at the hospital. He hadn't returned to his ranch. He was with *her*.

Fury surged within him. He'd told Mark that Ava was his. The fool should have listened.

Mark had put up much more of a fight than he'd

anticipated. He'd thought the guy would be so easy to take out, just like Gregory had been. Gregory had been so easy. The fool had been drunk, no match for him at all. Gregory had tried to fight—too late—but there had been no point.

One blast of his gun, and he'd been done. Then all he'd needed to do was set the scene to make it look like a suicide. The cops hadn't questioned Gregory's death. Mark hadn't questioned it.

He figured everyone had just been glad the old man was dead.

He stared out into the night, so quiet and still. Ava was behind the heavy gates and security at the McGuire ranch, but she couldn't stay there forever. And Mark— he wouldn't be at Ava's side every moment. He would have to leave her sometime.

There would be a moment when Ava wasn't guarded. A moment when he could move in…

Then she truly would be his.

Mark won't take you from me. No one will. Ava had finally come back home. He wasn't going to lose her now.

Chapter Seven

When Ava opened her eyes, Mark was gone. She sat up quickly, her gaze flying around the room. She'd crashed, hard, and for the first time in longer than she could remember, she didn't know if nightmares had haunted her.

She couldn't remember anything about her dreams.

As she gazed around that room, the only thing she knew for certain was that… *I'm alone.*

Swallowing, she rose from the bed and made her way toward the bathroom. She hurried into the shower, and a quick jerk of her wrist sent the hot water powering down on her. Ava put her head under the stream, letting the water soak her hair.

Mark is gone.

What had she expected? Honestly, Ava didn't know. She hadn't thought much past the passion of the moment with him. She'd just wanted to grab on to him, wanted to hold tight and see if reality would be any match for her fantasies.

Reality had rocked. But she hadn't thought about the morning after.

A burst of cold air hit her, and Ava whirled around. The shower door had been opened and Mark—Mark was standing there, staring at her. He was dressed in jeans and a T-shirt. His hair was tousled, and his eyes seemed to be eating her alive.

The water kept pounding down on her. He kept staring at her. Yes, he definitely had the look of a starving man.

Ava's fingers flew out and turned off the rush of the water. The *drip-drip-drip* seemed incredibly loud in that moment. "I thought you'd gone."

A faint line appeared between his brows.

She was so not sounding sophisticated and cool. But sophisticated and cool were incredibly hard to do when a woman was standing naked in the shower, dripping wet, and her lover was fully clothed in front of her.

"I made you breakfast," he said, his voice gruff.

Her lips parted in surprise. He'd cooked for her? That was…nice.

"But the food's going to have to wait," he muttered and he stepped into the shower. She automatically glanced down and saw that he wasn't fully dressed, after all. His feet were bare—

He kissed her. Mark pushed her back against the tiled wall, and his mouth took hers. This wasn't a getting-to-know-you sort of kiss. They were far, *far* past that stage. When his lips touched hers, she felt as if he were claiming her. Only fair—she definitely wanted to claim him. Her wet hands grabbed for his shirt, and she shoved it up and out of her way. She wanted to touch him, skin to skin. The press of his lips against hers had ignited a firestorm of desire within her.

His hands were sliding over her body, caressing her breasts and stroking her aching nipples. Then down, down his hand went. She was slick from the shower, and he pushed his hand between the folds of her sex.

Ava rose onto her tiptoes, gasping because his touch felt so good.

Everything about Mark felt right.

"Am I…hurting you?" He seemed to force out the words.

She pressed a kiss to his neck. Bit him, then licked the skin. "Only if you stop…" Because the pleasure had risen so quickly.

Her left hand jerked open the snap of his jeans.

"I've got…protection."

Good. because she wanted him, right then.

A few moments later, he was lifting her up against that wall, holding her easily as he drove inside her. The wall was cold and hard behind her, and he was hot and strong before her. *In* her.

He was lifting her up against him, then bringing her down, and every stroke, every move had her desire swelling even more. Her breath panted out, her heartbeat drummed like mad in her ears and her nails dug into his back.

"I love the way you feel," Mark whispered right before he kissed her again. "So perfect…like you were made for me."

The release hit her. Even harder than before. Deeper, longer, and Ava tried to muffle the sound of her scream.

Mark was with her. She felt his aroused flesh jerk within her, and the contractions of her inner muscles seemed to push him over the edge. But he didn't muffle his cry. He roared her name, and then he held her so tight.

So tight she wondered if he'd ever let her go.

BREAKFAST WAS A cold, soggy mess. Not that it had been much better *before* he'd seen Ava in the shower and pretty much lost his mind. The eggs were runny, and the toast—well, maybe the toast was still edible. Maybe. And—

"You didn't have to cook for me."

Ava's voice had him turning around. She stood just a few feet away. Fully dressed now—unfortunately—in a pair of jeans and a white T-shirt. She'd pulled her hair back into a ponytail, and her skin gleamed. She gave him a smile, one that showed her gorgeous dimples. "But thank you."

He smiled back at her. Ava just made him feel… good. "I don't think you should thank me, not until you actually taste the food."

She laughed. He loved that light and sweet sound. Her laughter was far too rare, and just to hear it right then, he felt as if he'd won the lottery.

Ava headed over to the little table. She sat down and actually reached for those runny eggs. He caught her wrist. "Don't." He sighed. "Baby, this stuff has to taste like garbage."

She laughed. "Yes, I'm pretty sure it does."

He stared into her eyes. The green was gleaming. Her cheeks were flushed a light pink and her full lips curved. She didn't look like a woman who'd been beaten by life. She looked—*perfect*.

"Ava—" he began.

But there was a knock at the front door.

"That's probably Davis," she said.

Or Brodie. Either man equaled trouble. Because Ava's neck was a little red from where his stubble had chaffed her. Her lips were swollen from his kiss, and it was going to be obvious to her brothers that Mark had not kept his hands off her.

He wondered who would throw the first punch. He knew from past experience that Davis had a killer right hook.

Ava rose and headed for the door. Mark followed her, and when the door opened, he braced himself. Sure enough, Davis was waiting on the threshold.

Big surprise.

Davis's gaze—a harder green than Ava's—raked over her. That glittering stare immediately turned on Mark, then narrowed.

"Don't," Ava bit out when Davis opened his mouth to speak. "I've seen you with far too many lovers in your life, Davis. And I haven't ever said a word about them. So don't even think of launching into Mark right now."

Davis blinked.

"I'm the one who seduced him," Ava continued, her voice tight with anger. She even moved, placing her body right beside Mark's. "So back off."

Mark had to fight to keep the smile off face.

A muscle jerked in Davis's jaw. "There have not been that many lovers," he muttered. Then he rubbed the back of his neck. "And you're my kid sister!"

"I'm a woman. And what happens between Mark and me…that's our business."

"You're the one shouting about seducing him!" Davis pointed out.

Ava blushed, but she stood her ground. "And you're the one acting like I'm still sixteen. I'm not."

Davis backed up. "I just wanted to make sure you were both okay this morning."

Mark was feeling pretty good. He'd woken up with Ava—that was a whole lot better than his usual routine…when he woke up, wishing she was close.

"No alarms were triggered last night," Davis continued. "So I don't know if the guy just decided to lie low or if he's biding his time for a reason. Now that the sun's out, I want to head back to where you crashed and see if I can find any trace evidence the guy might have left behind. Maybe something we missed in the dark."

That sounded like a good idea to Mark.

"Can you come and walk me through things?" Davis asked him. "Show me exactly where you were when he attacked?"

Mark nodded. He wanted to walk through that area, too. He glanced over at Ava.

"You can bet I'm coming," she said quickly. "Let me just grab my bag and I'll be ready." Ava hurriedly backed away.

Mark didn't move from the doorway.

Davis held his gaze. "Remember what I said before," Davis murmured. "You hurt her…"

"I won't." Hurting Ava wasn't even a possibility for him. He'd kept his emotions locked down for so long. No one realized how he felt about Ava. He was just starting to understand the full depth of his emotions. Ava mattered—plain and simple—more than anything.

"I'm ready," Ava's voice was a little breathless. Her cheeks were flushed, and he had a quick flash of seeing her in that shower. The steam had been rising around her. Her delicate skin had been tinted pink. She'd been naked, her body wet, and she'd nearly brought him to his knees.

Did she have any clue just how much power she wielded over him?

Ava's stare met his. "Are you ready?"

To head back to the scene where someone had tried

to kill him? Mark gave her a grim smile. "Always." Because it was time to turn the tables on that guy. The stalker wasn't going to keep hunting them. It was time for him to become prey.

MARK'S WRECKED SUV had been towed away. Ava stared at the broken glass that still littered the scene and at the smashed gate. A shiver slid over her. Mark had been so lucky to walk away.

"He came to the vehicle while I was trapped inside," Mark said as he stepped over shards of glass. "He was about to shoot me, but I managed to get out before he fired off another shot."

Ava's eyes closed.

"I ran to the woods, over there, because I was trying to get to shelter."

Ava opened her eyes, exhaled and followed the men to the trees.

"I could hear another car coming—I thought it was Ava's car," Mark said, his voice deepening, "and I knew I had to act. He still had a gun, and I was afraid he'd shoot at her."

Mark had saved her again. She'd thought that she was racing to his rescue, but he'd been looking after her. Ava edged away from the men. They were searching the ground, scanning the area so carefully.

"I knocked him down here," Mark said. Ava was about ten feet away from him. "The gun flew out of his hand."

"Yeah, that's where I found the weapon." Davis hesitated. "Did you see where the guy ran off to?"

"No, I was too busy trying to get to Ava. I'd heard the crash, and I didn't know how badly she was hurt."

He turned toward her. "I just needed to get to her," he said softly.

Ava backed away, sliding closer to the line of trees and then—then she turned because she could hear the sound of a horse's hooves pounding on the earth. Mark and Davis hurried toward her just as a stallion burst out of the trees. It was Mark's horse, Legacy. And he was running fast—wild—heading straight toward her at a furious gallop.

No, no, Legacy shouldn't be there. He should be back in his stables.

"Ava!" Mark shouted.

But she'd already leapt to the side. She hit the ground, hard, but she escaped the dangerous crash of the horse's hooves as Legacy raced by her.

Mark gave a loud whistle, trying to signal the horse, but Legacy just reared back. The horse cried out—a sound like a high, sharp scream—and he raced toward Davis with a shaking head and rolling eyes.

Something is wrong with him!

"Legacy, no!" Mark yelled, his voice sharp with command.

Davis swore and dodged for cover. Like Ava, he wound up in the dirt. But the horse kept coming for him, stomping, thrashing.

There was no saddle on the animal. No reins. How had he gotten out there? Legacy was Mark's prized stallion. He should have been safe in the stables.

The horse whirled around and ran toward Ava again.

"No!" Mark was there in front of her. "Legacy." His voice held only powerful command, no anger, just deadly control. "Legacy, stop."

The horse wasn't stopping. He was—

Legacy collapsed. Just fell right there in the dirt.

Ava rushed toward him even as Mark and Davis closed in on the animal. He was sprawled in the dirt, his eyes still wild, his breathing hitching.

Mark put his hand on Legacy's chest. "His heartbeat is out of control." He gave a hard shake of his head as he stroked the animal. "Something has happened to him! This isn't—this isn't Legacy!"

White foam was forming near the animal's mouth.

Davis yanked out his phone. She heard him calling, asking to speak to Dr. Myers—she knew Jamie Myers was the veterinarian in the area who took care of the horses at both the McGuire and Montgomery ranches.

"He should be in the stables," Mark muttered. "Legacy should be secured in the stables!"

But he wasn't. He was on the ground before them, his whole body convulsing.

Ava fell to her knees beside Mark.

And Legacy's eyes closed.

"POISONED?" MARK DEMANDED as fury burned in him. "You're telling me that my horse was poisoned?"

Jamie Myers exhaled slowly. They'd managed to transport Legacy back to the Montgomery stables, but it sure hadn't been an easy task. The animal had had repeated spells of rearing and thrashing during the journey back, and Mark had barely managed to keep him controlled.

"I'll have to do more blood work to know for sure, but yes, he's exhibiting all of the signs," Jamie said with certainty. She pushed back a wisp of blond hair that had escaped from the bun at her nape. "His heartbeat is too accelerated, his breathing isn't stable and these spells he keeps having—"

Spells where the horse tried to break free.

She ran her hand over Legacy's back. "I'm going to stay with him and figure this thing out."

Jamie had been taking care of Mark's horses and the horses at the McGuire ranch for the past year, ever since she'd come into the area, seeming a bit out of place in her fancy clothes but more than ready to get her hands dirty as she worked on the animals.

Jamie had come from the Northeast. She never talked about her family, and from what Mark had been able to tell, she didn't get too close with many people.

He respected that about her. She was a woman with secrets.

Secrets she didn't want shared.

"He'll be okay, Mark," she promised him. "He's already getting more stabilized. It's a good thing you found him when you did. If he'd run into the road when cars were coming out this way…"

Legacy could have died. The stallion had almost run *them* down.

When it came to the ranch, Mark wasn't too sentimental about many things, but Legacy mattered. Mark and his mother had bought Legacy. Legacy was *theirs*.

The horse was the only thing of his mother's that he had left.

"I'll check all the horses," Jamie said. The faintest hint of a New England accent whispered in and out of her voice. "If any of the others are affected, I'll let you know."

He nodded. He stared across the stall at Legacy.

There was no food in the stall. The place didn't appear to have been disturbed at all.

The security feed.

If someone had come into the barn to poison Legacy, the feed would have caught it. "I'll be in the house," Mark said abruptly, "if you need me."

Jamie nodded, but her attention was on Legacy, not Mark.

He hurried out of the stall and—

"Is he okay?"

Ava was there. She'd been standing with her back propped against the side of his stables. He looked around, but he didn't see any sign of Davis.

"Mark?" Ava marched closer to him. "How's your horse?"

"Poisoned." He raked a hand through his hair. "At least, that's what the doc thinks." And he was about to figure out just who had been given access to his horse. He caught Ava's hand and hurried toward the main house.

When he stepped onto the porch, Ty rounded the corner of the house. "Boss!" Ty called out. "Boss, I got something you're gonna need to see!"

Mark glanced over at him.

Ty held up a syringe. "I just found this out back." His face darkened. "With Legacy acting so wild, I'm betting this is the cause."

Mark's jaw was clenched so tightly it hurt as he stared at that syringe. There was a thin, white label wrapped around. The name of whatever drug had been inside it? Hell, that was exactly what they needed! "Take it to Dr. Myers. She's with Legacy."

Ty nodded curtly and headed for the stables.

"Wait! Did you hear anyone last night?" Mark demanded.

Ty looked back. "I patrolled out here, but I didn't see a thing. Whoever this guy is…" Ty shook his head. His eyes hardened. "He's good. And he knows your ranch. He knows how to slip in and out without being seen by anyone."

But had he managed to avoid the video cameras?

Mark and Ava headed into the ranch house. Ava was quiet beside him as he keyed up the video feed. He fast-forwarded through the footage, watching, looking for any sign of the masked man who'd been on his property before.

You're just making yourself at home here, aren't you?

But…there was no one on the tape. No one but Ty, going in for what Mark thought must have been a quick check on the horses.

"No one's there." Ava leaned over his chair, and her hair slid over his arm. "He was too smart this time. He must've figured out where the cameras were positioned."

Maybe.

The scent of strawberries hung in the air around him.

"I know how important Legacy is to you," Ava told him as she rubbed his left shoulder. "I'm sorry this happened."

Everyone in the area knew how much he valued Legacy. "He tried to hurt me by taking him out." He looked up at her. "He could have drugged him last night after the accident."

Ava sucked in a sharp breath. "When you called your men to the scene—"

"It was the same technique he used before. Distract

and attack." The guy must have seized the opportunity. Since he hadn't been able to take out Mark, rage would have been riding the guy hard. And he'd let that rage out on Legacy.

Ava backed up when Mark stood. "He's going to be okay," she said. "Brodie has talked about Dr. Myers plenty of times. He said she knew her animals better than anyone he'd ever seen."

Yes, she did. They returned to the stables, but before they could enter, the doors swung open and Dr. Myers hurried toward them. Ty was right behind her. She smiled when she saw Mark. "He's going to be okay!" She had the syringe in a plastic bag. "I know what to give him to counteract the effects. Legacy will be fine."

Some of the heavy tension left Mark's shoulders.

"If Ty hadn't found this syringe..." She glanced over at the foreman. "Well, let's just say I'm very grateful. Now, if you'll excuse me, I need to call my office so I can get the right medicine for him." She took off jogging to her car.

Mark clapped his hand on Ty's shoulder. "I owe you."

But Ty shook his head. "No way, man. I'm the one who owes you. And we both know it's more than I can ever repay."

Mark's jaw tightened. He and Ty had become friends in school. Ty's mother had never seemed to care about her son at all. She'd seemed more interested in drinking her way to the bottom of a bottle and, most nights, Ty and Mark had hung out together. When Mark had come back to town, he'd sought out Ty. The guy had been one step away from living on the streets. He'd given Ty a place to stay and offered him a job.

Ty was one of his oldest friends—and, no, the man didn't owe him a thing.

"I'm guessing you didn't see anything on the video," Ty said, his lips twisting.

Ava stepped forward. "No one was there."

"I'll step up the guards tonight," Ty promised. "You'll be safe here."

"I'll be staying with Ava tonight," Mark said. That night, and every night until they caught the bastard.

Ty glanced over at Ava. "I sure am glad you're all right."

She gave him a weak smile. "Mark was the one who got hurt."

He'd forgotten about his stitches. They didn't matter.

Dr. Myers had returned from her car, and she was heading for the stables once more.

"Go on," Ava told Mark, pushing him forward. "Check on Legacy. I'm going to meet up with Davis."

Right. Because Davis was still searching the area near the crash.

Mark pulled her close to kiss her hard. "If you need me…"

"You'll know," she finished as she gave his arm a quick squeeze. "I'll call. But don't worry, I'll be with Davis." Then she waved a quick farewell to him and Ty.

As she walked away, Ty gave a soft whistle. "You must be feeling pretty brave to go up against all the McGuires, buddy."

Ava was worth tangling with her brothers.

"She knows," Ty began carefully, "about your past?"

His past. Those lost years when he'd slipped from Texas. "No."

"Aw, man." Ty gave him a pitying look. "What do you think will happen when she learns the truth?"

He didn't intend to find out. Maybe there were some things that Ava would be better off not knowing.

AVA HAD ALMOST reached Davis when her phone rang. Frowning, she lifted it up, but she didn't recognize the number that appeared on her screen. "Hello?"

"He's dangerous." The words were so low she could barely understand them.

"Who is this?" Ava demanded, but…she knew.

It was him. The stalker.

"I'm just trying to protect you from him. Can't you see? I want to take care of you."

Her fingers tightened around the phone. "You almost killed Mark last night."

She heard laughter—low and bitter. "And you think Mark hasn't killed? You don't know him. Not really. He's been lying to you for so long."

"No." Ava could see Davis striding toward her. She waved to him, hoping he'd hurry forward.

"Have you asked him about the night your parents died?"

Her heart slammed against her chest. "Were you there when they died? Did you kill them?"

"Ava, I only want to take care—"

"Did you kill them?" Ava screamed.

Davis ran toward her.

"Mark is lying." His voice was still so low. "He's going to hurt you. Don't trust him."

Davis was just steps away from her.

"Ask Mark. Get him to tell you…what your father said before he died."

What?

"My father was dead when Mark got to him." She knew because Mark had told her… *I'm so sorry, Ava. There was nothing I could do. He was gone.*

"Liar, liar," that voice mocked. "You'll see soon enough. You put your trust in the wrong man."

The line went dead.

Ava stared at Davis, stricken. No, no, that creep on the phone was the one lying to her. Not Mark.

"Ava?" Davis touched her arm. "What did he say?"

"Dad was dead."

His brow furrowed.

"By the time Mark got to him, Dad was dead, wasn't he?"

Mark had said—and Davis—

Davis looked away from her.

She grabbed his shirtfront. "Dad was dead!"

"He only lived a few moments, Ava." The words were soft, sad. "He didn't have a chance of surviving."

And it felt as if she'd just been shot in the chest. "No. Mark said…you—you *both* said that he was dead. That nothing could be done!"

His fingers curled around hers. "I read the medical reports. There *was* nothing that Mark could do. Dad had lost too much blood. His wounds were too bad. But, yes…" Now his voice turned hoarse. "He was alive, just for a few minutes. Mark told me—"

"But no one told *me*!" No one but that freak on the phone. The man who was tormenting her.

"We didn't want to hurt you, Ava! That's why we held back. We didn't want you to know…" His voice trailed away into silence.

Too late. She knew exactly what he'd been about to say. "You didn't want me to know that when I left him, Dad was still alive."

Run.

Her whole body felt numb right then. "What did he say to Mark?"

Davis frowned at her.

"Before he died, what did Dad say to Mark?"

But Davis shook his head. "Nothing, Ava. Mark never told me about anything our father said to him."

Was it another lie? Or the truth? She'd trusted her brothers—and Mark—blindly for all of these years. But they'd been holding back on her.

She turned away from Davis, but he caught her shoulder. "Ava, you were so close to breaking back then…"

Everyone always thought she was so fragile.

"We were just trying to protect you."

Ava glanced at him. "I've never lied to you."

Pain flashed on his face.

"How many lies have you told me?"

He didn't answer, and that very silence terrified her.

"What else are you keeping from me? What else is Mark holding back?" Mark, the man she'd thought of as her white knight. Now he, too, seemed surrounded by secrets.

"Mark's past is his own to share." Davis swallowed. She saw the quick dip of his Adam's apple. "And anything I've done, it's all been for you."

Was that supposed to make it right?

"Let me go, Davis."

His hand lifted.

"I need some space."

"Ava…" A warning edge entered his voice.

She stiffened her spine. "Despite what you think, I'm not close to breaking apart. And I don't have a death wish. I just want to be by myself for a few hours. Is that so wrong?" She needed to get away, to stop feeling watched. "I'm going to the museum." Because she actually did have a job waiting for her. Ava's boss had called earlier and told her that they were setting up a new exhibit. More hands were needed. Kristin had said that if Ava was available to come in early, her help would be appreciated.

A couple of hours at the museum—yes, that would be just what she needed. Work, to take her mind off the insanity around her.

"If anything happens…if you need me…"

Ava looked back at him. "I need you to figure out who just called me." She tossed her phone to him. He caught it easily. "And I want to find out how he knew our father lived until Mark arrived. He said…he said that Dad spoke to Mark."

Davis stared down at her phone. "Mark never mentioned anything—"

"Yes, well, as you said, people lie." Her breath heaved out. "And I think it's long past time that we started sharing the truth."

He pulled out his phone. "Take mine. Just in case—"

"In case a crazy stalker tries to ruin my life again?" She took the phone from him. "Got it."

Then she turned and walked away. Davis didn't seem to get just how much his words had hurt her. She was tired of being in the dark. Tired of her brothers thinking she couldn't handle the danger that had haunted her family for years.

She wasn't going to break. She wasn't going to shatter into a million pieces.

No matter what happened, she'd survive.

One way or another...

Chapter Eight

"That looks amazing!" Kristin Lang said as she headed into the museum's main gallery. Her red hair was in a long braid down her back, and the large hoop earrings she wore swayed with her movements. "You've grouped them perfectly! Those colors—the lighting—fantastic!"

Ava dusted off her hands on her jeans as she glanced over at the museum's director. Kristin was only a few years older than Ava, and she seemed to be bursting with energy. A wide smile lit Kristin's face as her gaze traveled around the display.

Ava had been working with the docents there for the past three hours. They'd arranged, then rearranged the artwork until everything was perfect.

"Hiring you was the smartest move I've made in months," Kristin said, with a decisive nod.

"Uh, yes, about that…" Ava cleared her throat as she closed in on the other woman. "Why did you hire me?"

Kristin's smile slipped a notch.

And Ava's stomach knotted.

"Well, because of your credentials, of course!" Kristin told her, that smile appearing again, only it wasn't quite so full this time. "You graduated at the top of your class. You have a keen eye—" she waved her hand around the gallery "—obviously! You know your work and—"

"How much influence did the museum board have on your decision?" Because as she'd worked, she'd had time—too much time—to think about things. About the perfect job that had opened up and brought her right back home. A job that had been arranged for her... courtesy of Mark?

"The board?" Guilt sparked in Kristin's eyes. "They can make recommendations, certainly, but the final call is mine."

And Ava knew her suspicions were dead-on. "A board member told you to hire me."

"I simply went over the list of applicants, and you were personally recommended—"

"Who recommended me?" She kept her tone polite, curious, when she wanted to demand. But she couldn't demand. This was her boss, after all, and she needed the job. With everything else in her life going to hell, this position was important.

Kristin appeared hesitant.

"I have to thank him...or her," Ava said, forcing a smile of her own. One that felt incredibly stiff on her lips. "I'd hoped to get a job at a museum like this one, and that recommendation...it made my dream come true." And that was the truth.

Kristin's shoulders relaxed. "I knew you'd love this place! After our interview, I thought for certain you'd fit perfectly here! And they were both so adamant that you were the right choice—"

"Both?" Ava asked her carefully.

"Why, yes, two board members were very supportive of you. Alan Channing and Mark Montgomery. They both vouched for you, and with references like those, I wasn't about to turn you away."

Right. Ava's gaze fell to the canvas near her.

"Is everything okay?" Kristin asked as she edged closer. "You *are* enjoying the job here, aren't you?"

Ava nodded and smiled again. She hoped the smile didn't look as fake as it felt. "Of course." But…she wished Mark had told her that he'd pushed to get her the position. There were a lot of things that she wished Mark had told her.

"Wonderful." Kristin clapped excitedly. The woman really had a lot of excess energy. "And I think we're done for the day. I owe you a million thanks for coming in and helping today. You are a phenomenal addition to the museum, and I know we're going to be doing great things together."

Then Kristin was hurrying away, her high heels echoing in the museum. Ava glanced down at her watch. It was nearly five o'clock. Another night was closing in, and she still didn't have any clue who that jerk out there was.

Grant had called her twice—checking in with his usual big brother style. She'd assured him that she was fine.

I can't be afraid every moment.

Ava hurried back to her office and reached for her bag. As she'd told Grant, she couldn't let this guy control her life. She couldn't stay with a guard every moment—that was no way to live. *I won't let him win.*

Winning and losing—as if this were all some sort of sick game. Unfortunately, Ava had started to think of this whole mess as a cat-and-mouse game. She was the mouse, and the guy was just playing with her.

A few of the other workers called out to Ava as they left. She waved to them and quickly finished organizing her office. When she was satisfied, she reached for her keys. The parking garage was on the level right below the lobby, so she headed for the elevator.

"Wait for me!" Kristin called.

Ava held the elevator door for her. Kristin hurried in, carrying a big briefcase. "Late-night work," Kristin told her with a light laugh. "I've really got to learn how to leave this stuff here. Working all night doesn't give me much of a social life."

The elevator dinged when it reached the parking garage.

"Got big plans for the night?" Kristin asked her. "I know you've got family here—"

The elevator opened.

"—so I'm sure they're glad to have you back—*aah!*" Kristin's words ended in a scream because she'd just stepped out of the elevator and run right into a man wearing a black ski mask. A man armed with a knife.

He struck out with the knife, but Kristin lifted her briefcase. The blade sank into the case, and Ava grabbed Kristin, hauling her back while the man in the mask tried to yank his knife out of the leather. When Kristin was safely out of the way, Ava leapt forward. She shoved into the case, into the attacker, and he fell to the floor.

"Ava!"

At Kristin's cry, Ava jumped back into the elevator. Her hand slammed into the elevator's control panel. "Shut, shut, shut," she screamed. The doors started to slide closed.

The attacker was on his feet again. He had the knife in his hand.

He could have lunged forward—could have gotten in there with them.

He didn't move.

The elevator doors slid closed, and the elevator rose up to the next floor.

Kristin had a death grip on Ava's arm. "We have to call the cops!"

They had to get someplace safe first. The elevator doors were already opening. "We have to get out of this building." Ava shot out of the elevator. "Because he could be coming up the stairs." And the stairwell was just a few feet away. Was it her imagination? Or did she hear him in that stairwell right then?

They ran. They raced through the museum. Everyone else seemed to have gone, but Ava knew the security guard would still be at the front desk. They just had to get to Frank Minnow. He'd help them. He'd—

The lights flashed off.

And Ava knew that her stalker was hunting them.

"SO...YOU'VE BEEN honest with me, haven't you, Mark?"

At Davis's slow words, Mark glanced up at the guy. They were in Mark's barn, and Dr. Myers had finally gotten Legacy stable. She'd had to give the horse several injections, but he seemed calm now.

When he glanced over at Davis, Mark saw that the other man's eyes were on the pretty doctor.

"I don't like it when people lie to me," Davis continued softly.

Right. So while the guy might appear to be staring at the doc, Mark knew Davis's attention was wholly on him. "If you're going to accuse me of something, then do it." He wasn't in the mood to play games.

"You told me that my dad was still alive when you got to the ranch that night."

Mark locked his jaw. "He was." But he hadn't lived long. When he'd first seen him, Mark had thought he was already dead. There had been so much blood.

Then he'd caught the faintest sound—a whisper. He'd rushed forward and tried to stop that massive blood flow, but it had done no good.

"What did he say to you?"

Surprise pushed through Mark.

Davis turned away from the stall and focused his assessing stare fully on Mark. "Before he died, what did my father tell you?"

Mark shook his head.

"He *did* say something to you, didn't he?"

"How do you know this?" Because he hadn't thought anyone knew. Those last few moments had been so chaotic. He'd barely heard the man's rasping words.

"That psycho who is stalking Ava called her today. He told her that Dad was still alive when you got to the ranch."

Mark squeezed his eyes closed. Now he'd have to explain to Ava why he hadn't revealed that to her before. *Because I didn't want to hurt her. I didn't want Ava to know her dad was in agony until the very end. Choking on his own blood and struggling for every single breath.*

"I tried to trace the number, but it didn't work. The jerk probably was using a burner phone that he ditched right after he made the call to her."

Mark's hands were clenched into fists.

"He knew my dad was alive, and he knew that my father spoke to you before he died." Davis took a step toward Mark. His voice dropped even more as he said,

"You never told me that, man. We've spent years trying to find out who killed him, and you've been holding out on me, haven't you? You have! I can see it in your eyes."

Mark didn't speak.

Davis lunged forward. He grabbed Mark by the shirt-front. "What were you keeping from us?" Now his voice was a snarl.

Mark didn't speak.

"Stop it!" Jamie Myers yelled as she hurried toward them. "What are you two doing?" She pushed between them. Put a hand on each of their chests. "What is happening here?"

So much that the lady didn't understand.

"It didn't matter," Mark finally gritted out to Davis.

"It matters to me." Davis's breath heaved out. "What did he say to you?"

Mark looked away.

Jamie just stood there. "Please tell me that you two aren't about to start fighting. Because if that happens, someone is going to the hospital. I patch up animals, not people."

He wasn't going to fight Davis. He wouldn't do anything to hurt the guy, because then Ava would just get hurt. Wasn't that why he'd kept silent for so long? Because he didn't want to hurt her? *Everything* he did... it was all for Ava.

"Tell me," Davis demanded.

Mark raked a hand over his face. "He said...'I'm sorry.' That's all he was saying, all right? Over and over, he was trying to say he was sorry. Like it was his fault that he and his wife had been murdered."

Davis blanched.

Mark lunged forward, pushing past Jamie. He

grabbed his friend's arm. "He didn't know what was even happening then. He was out of his head. Your father wasn't to blame. No matter what—"

"He said something else." Davis's face was stark. *"Tell me."*

Jaw locking, Mark told him, "He…he said, 'My fault.' That was the last thing, okay? He was saying, 'My fault that she—'" Mark stopped because Ava's father had stopped. "He never finished that sentence."

Because he hadn't taken another breath.

Davis turned away from him.

"You were all hurt enough!" Mark yelled. "That wasn't going to help you!"

Davis kept walking.

THE MUSEUM'S ALARM was sounding. A long, desperate shriek. Kristin and Ava were running for the front doors. They rounded a corner.

"Freeze!" It was Frank, holding up his gun and flashlight.

They froze.

"Ms. McGuire? Ms. Lang?" He started to lower his weapon. "I thought everyone had already left!"

Ava shook her head. That alarm was still shrieking. "There's a man in the parking garage. He's got a knife."

Frank surged forward.

"He tried to stab me," Kristin said, her words and her body shaking. "He nearly killed me!"

Frank's light shone behind them. No one was there. But that guy in the ski mask could be *anywhere* right then.

"The police are already on the way. They were con-

tacted the minute the alarm sounded," Frank said.
"Let's get you two someplace safe."

But at this point, Ava was starting to wonder if any
safe place existed.

*He's always playing his games. And tonight, Kristin
was almost caught in the crossfire.*

They hurried down the hall. Frank stayed close, and
he kept his weapon at the ready.

When they made it to the front of the museum, Ava
saw the blue swirl of police lights. Frank opened the
door for her and Kristin. As they rushed out, the cops
rushed in. Ava glanced back—and saw all of the lights
in the museum flash back on.

Cat and mouse. How long would it be until the cat
decided to eat that mouse and end the game?

Kristin was talking quickly beside her. The other
woman's words were tumbling out as she spoke with the
uniformed cops. Ava stood there, and she just felt…cold.

I want this to end.

A car braked nearby, the squeal of its tires jarring
Ava enough that she glanced to the right. She saw Alan
jump out of a Jaguar. He hurried toward her. "Ava! Kristin! What's happening?" Worry darkened his face. "Was
there a break-in at the museum?"

Ava shook her head. The attacker hadn't been trying to steal anything. He'd just been after her. *And he
was willing to hurt Kristin because she was in his way.*

"A man tried to attack me!" Kristin said. "He was
waiting in the parking garage with a knife. He—"

"It's my fault." Ava knew her voice was too low.
She cleared her throat and tried again. "I'm…I'm sorry,
Kristin."

Kristin's lips parted in surprise.

A young uniformed cop stepped closer. "Ma'am? You want to explain that a little bit more to me?"

She shivered. Alan took off his jacket and wrapped it around her shoulders.

"I…a man has been stalking me." Her temples were pounding. *Kristin could have died. Just like Mark could have died when the stalker went after him!* "I've already spoken with some detectives at the station. They know…he's been following me. A man in a black ski mask. A guy about six-foot-two, maybe one hundred eighty pounds."

"Ski mask," Kristin repeated, and she wrapped her arms around her stomach.

"He shot at a…friend of mine last night." Her gaze fell to the ground. "He's not stopping," she said, voice breaking a bit. "I don't think he's ever going to stop until he gets what he wants."

"And he wants…?" The cop stared at her, his eyes suspicious.

"Me."

MARK CAUGHT DAVIS right before the guy climbed into his vehicle. "Wait, man, *wait*!"

Davis looked back at him.

"Your father was a good man. We both know that. He was out of his head at the end. He was just talking crazy. I wasn't going to repeat what he said because I knew the gossips would run wild with all kinds of stories." Just like they'd done with Ava. "I didn't want your family hearing or seeing stories about your father being in on the attack…or him doing something to get your mother killed."

Davis's eyes were angry slits of green fire.

"You saw what they did to Ava!" Mark shook his head. "I was trying to protect you all. I didn't want you to hurt anymore." And they'd all been suffering through hell.

"What else aren't you telling me?"

Mark stilled.

"Because you see, Mark, I'm wondering…maybe I shouldn't be trusting you quite so much." He stepped closer. "I know what you're capable of doing. I saw you in the field. No hesitations. Anything necessary to get the job done."

Mark's back teeth had clenched. "You were the same way."

"I know." Davis eased out a breath. "That's what scares me."

Before he could speak, Mark's phone rang. He pulled it out of his pocket, then frowned at the number there. According to the name on the screen, Davis was calling him.

Only Davis was standing there, glaring at him.

Mark took the call, turning it on speaker. "Hello."

"Mark." Ava said his name in a quick rush. He could hear her fear, and every single muscle in his body locked down. "He was here, at the museum."

"Are you all right?" he immediately demanded. "Ava—"

"The alarm went off, and the police are here now. They're looking for him." Her breath whispered over the line on a soft sigh. "He had a knife."

Bastard.

"My boss, Kristin, was with me. He tried to stab her." Davis swore.

"We're both okay," Ava told them. There was no

emotion in her voice, and that scared Mark. Everything about this messed up situation scared him. "The security guard was still here. The guy after us—he turned off all the lights in the museum. He was hunting us."

But they'd gotten out. This time.

He looked up and saw the same fear and fury he felt reflected in Davis's eyes. "Stay with the cops," Mark said. "We're on our way."

HE DROVE SCARY fast to get to Ava. Mark hadn't been able to find Ty before he'd left the ranch, but Jamie had been there, still keeping watch on Legacy. He'd given orders to a few of his other ranch hands to help her— and to keep an eye on the place.

Davis was in the car with him. With every second that passed, Mark's fury grew. Why couldn't they seem to catch this guy? Why was he always a step ahead—a step that put him far too close to Ava?

When he got to the museum, he counted five police cars at the scene. The area looked like chaos, with the uniformed cops all running around. He knew the system must have automatically sent an alert to the authorities when the museum's alarm had triggered.

I hope you left a trail behind this time.

He jumped from his vehicle and hurried toward the building. Then he saw Ava. She was standing to the side, talking with two cops. Alan Channing was with her. As Mark watched, Alan wrapped his arm around Ava and gave her a hug.

Mark hurried toward them.

"I'll take Ava home," Alan was saying. "Until this bastard is caught, I feel like she needs someone to stay close to her."

Ava rubbed her left temple. "I don't want anyone else getting pulled into this mess. I'm fine on my own."

But Alan shook his head. "You need—"

"Ava." Mark slid past the police officers.

Alan stiffened. His arm dropped from Ava's shoulders.

Mark reached out to her. His hand skimmed down her cheek even as his eyes searched every inch of her for any sign of injury. "Did he hurt you?"

"No. He—he almost stabbed Kristin." She pointed to the right. The redhead was talking animatedly with more cops. "The knife went into her briefcase instead of slicing into her, and I shoved him back."

Davis pushed Mark to the side. Mark glared at the guy.

"The elevator closed, and we got away from him." Her gaze drifted to the museum. "Then the lights went out."

"Where were you when the guy attacked?" Davis asked.

"The parking garage. We were leaving. The doors opened, and he was just there."

Because he'd been waiting on her.

"The others had just left a few moments before. There's so much security at the museum, I-I thought I was safe."

He'd thought she was safe there, too. So when Davis had told him earlier that Ava had gone in to work a few hours at the museum, he'd figured she was getting some much needed downtime.

"When he cut the lights, he might have thought that also disconnected the security system," Davis muttered.

"It didn't. The alarm was shrieking so loudly, I thought my eardrums were about to burst."

Maybe that alarm had scared the guy away.

Davis hugged her. Ava seemed stiff in his arms. And actually, Mark realized that when he'd touched her cheek earlier, Ava hadn't moved at all.

"I was about to take Ava home," Alan said. "That is…if you're done talking with her?" he asked the cops.

They nodded.

"I can take my sister home," Davis said, voice tight. "But thanks, Channing."

"Actually, I can take myself home," Ava said with a tired smile. "But thank you, Alan. I mean it. I appreciate the offer."

Alan hesitated. His gaze seemed to soften as it slid over Ava's face. "I wouldn't ever want anything to happen to you."

Ava shrugged out of the coat she'd been wearing and gave it back to Alan. "Thank you."

And the guy still lingered.

Ava hadn't looked at Mark, not directly in the eyes, since he'd arrived. He'd been expecting something else. What, exactly, he didn't know. But Ava just seemed cold, and that wasn't her. Ava was passion and heat and emotion—not this.

"Kristin is shaken," Ava said, her gaze troubled. "We need to make sure that she gets home all right."

"We can take her," Davis immediately began.

But Alan told them, "I've got her. Don't worry. I'll see to it that Kristin gets home safely." He inclined his head toward them, letting his stare stay on Ava a bit too long. Then he turned and made his way toward Kristin.

Davis pressed even closer to Ava. "Were you able to tell anything else about the guy this time?"

"He was still wearing a ski mask."

Mark wanted to pull her into his arms and hold her tight. But she was actually inching away from him.

"The garage was well lit, right?" Davis pressed her. "Did you see his eyes?"

Ava pushed back her hair. "It all happened so fast. The doors opened, and he was just there with that knife. Kristin lifted her briefcase, and the knife came down." She licked her lips. "I pulled her back and shoved him down. I don't think…" Her head tilted as she seemed to remember the scene. "I don't think I ever saw his eyes. I don't remember them, anyway. So fast…" Her words trailed away.

"I want to talk with Kristin," Davis said. "See if she can remember anything else about the guy." He hurried toward the redhead.

Mark stayed right there. Ava still wasn't looking at him. Was it because of what that jerk had told her on the phone call?

"I've had enough," Ava said.

His heart stopped right then.

"I'm not going to let him hurt anyone else just because he's after me." She whirled away from Mark and stared out in the darkness. "He's out there right now, watching me."

"Ava…"

"First you, then Kristin. Who will be next? Who is he going to hurt because he wants to get to me?" Her voice was getting louder, sharper. A few of the cops glanced their way. "No one else," she said. Her words seemed to ring in the night. "You want me? Then just come for me. *Leave everyone else alone!*"

Silence.

Ava's breath heaved out.

Mark wrapped his arms around her. He hated her pain. If he could, he'd take it all way.

"Leave everyone else alone."

He almost smiled when Ava shouted those words. Finally she understood. This was just about the two of them. The way it should always have been.

As he watched, she jerked away from Mark. She was realizing that Mark and his lies were no good for her.

Ava didn't have blinders on any longer. She wasn't hiding. She was ready to face all of the dark truths out there.

She was asking for him. Calling out to him because…

Ava is ready for me now.

He was certainly ready for her.

Chapter Nine

"Ava." Mark held her tight, his mouth close to her ear as he said, "Baby, you're tearing me apart."

As always, his touch seemed to warm her, but her pain was strong right then. She was tired of others being at risk for her. The next time that stalker attacked, he could wind up killing someone.

She pulled away from Mark. A fast glance to the right showed her that Davis was with Kristin. No doubt grilling her. So much for the fresh start at a new job. When you nearly got your boss killed, that made one heck of an impression.

"Let's go back to the cottage," Mark told her.

Back to hide again.

She looked around once more. He was out there. She knew it. Would he follow her back to the ranch? *I want this to end.*

"Ava!" Davis called her name, and she looked up to see him jogging toward her.

"I'm going home," she said. Because she needed to think. Just standing out there with those swirling blue lights was giving her a headache.

Davis looked at Mark. She sighed. "I have my own car. I can get home just fine—"

"I'm sure that's what Mark thought last night," Davis drawled, "until the guy opened fire on him."

Ava flinched.

"For me, please let Mark take you home."

Her lips thinned.

"I want to stay and talk to the cops, and I kind of need your car so that I can get back home." He rolled his shoulders back. "When Mark and I realized what was happening, we both just jumped into one of the cars he keeps at his ranch."

She fished for her keys and held them out to Davis. "Be careful."

His fingers closed around the keys. "Always."

Ava headed toward Mark's car. A quick glance over her shoulder showed Ava that Davis was already closing in on Kristin Lang and the cops near her.

"Maybe the guy who did this left evidence behind this time," Mark said.

Or maybe he'd gotten away clean again.

Ava slid into the car. Mark didn't shut her door. He knelt down so that they were eye to eye. The open car door was behind him, partially shielding his body. "I know that he called you."

More pain. She was so tired of the pain. "You lied to me."

"I was—"

"Please, don't say you were protecting me," Ava told him as she rubbed her throbbing right temple. "Right now that's the last thing I want to hear."

His gaze held hers. He gave a grim nod and rose.

She caught his hand. "What did my father say to you?"

He looked away. *Another secret.* They sure were

piling up. "What did my father say?" Ava asked again. "And how did *he* know?"

"Your father said that he was sorry."

His words squeezed her heart.

"And that it was his fault."

Ava started to shake her head.

"That's what your father said. It was his fault. Those were his last words to me, Ava, I swear it." The faint lines near his mouth deepened. "There was no point in telling you what he'd said back then. The last thing I wanted to do was hurt you any more. You were in enough pain. As it was, Davis and I were already afraid—" He broke off and looked away. As if he couldn't quite bear to look her in the eye.

But Ava knew what he'd been going to say. "You thought I was going to hurt myself, didn't you?"

He nodded.

"I didn't want to die back then, Mark. Not then, not now." She pulled her seat belt into place. He slammed the car door and hurried around to the driver's side.

Mark started to crank up the car, but she stopped him. Her fingers curled around his wrist. "You still didn't tell me... How does my stalker know what my dad said?"

"I don't know. I didn't think *anyone* had heard him speaking to me. I was there with Ty and a few other ranch hands, but they weren't close, not during those final moments."

Ty? "Where is he now?" Ava asked softly. "Where's Ty?"

Mark turned to stare at her. "He wasn't at the ranch when I left. So I don't—*you think it's Ty?*"

"I think the man who called me on the phone...he

was disguising his voice. Probably because he was afraid I'd recognize it—him—if he didn't. I think he's around Ty's height and build, and I think Ty is one of the few people who knew that my father spoke to you before he died." She pulled in a deep breath. "And right now, the thing I want most…is to find Ty."

He cranked the car. "Then let's hunt him down."

"I DIDN'T SEE his eyes. I'm sorry," Kristin Lang said as she swiped her hand over her cheek. "I just saw the knife coming right at me."

Davis had sure hoped that Kristin would remember more about the attacker.

"He was waiting down there." Her voice was hollow. "Other people had gone into the parking garage before us, but he must have been hiding. *Waiting*," she said once more.

For Ava.

"Is he going to come after me again?" Kristin asked him, her eyes wide with fear and her lips trembling. "Ava said that he's been stalking her. Do you think he'll come back to the museum?"

Davis thought the man had to be stopped—yesterday.

"Let me take you home, Kristin," Alan said. He put his hand on her shoulder.

She turned toward him, nodding. "Th-thank you."

Davis watched them leave. Something was nagging at him. "Kristin!"

She looked back at him.

"He struck out with his knife once, right?"

Biting her lip, she nodded.

"He didn't try to attack again?"

"Ava pushed him down. He had to yank the knife out

of the briefcase. By the time he got back up, the elevator doors were starting to close." She shuddered. "I've never been so afraid in my entire life."

Alan led her away. His Jaguar waited near the corner.

Davis turned and strode into the museum. Most of the cops there knew him, so they let him into what normally would've been a closed crime scene. In moments, he was down in the parking garage, searching the scene. There were no video cameras down there. No wonder the guy had been lying in wait in that particular spot. Instead of going into the museum, it would have been much easier just to sit back and have his prey come to him.

Davis paced a few feet away from the elevator. A large column stretched to the ceiling. It would have been easy enough to hide near the column and still have a perfect view of that elevator.

You thought Ava would come down alone, didn't you? But she wasn't alone, so you had to try and get Kristin out of your way.

He edged around the column. The stairs were to the right. It would have been easy enough for the man to rush up there…

Davis pushed open the door. It groaned. The stairwell was dark. He took his time going up those stairs, searching carefully. Then he was at the first floor. He eased into the hallway. And saw the first sensor near an exhibit on his left.

You set off the sensor. You never intended to come this far, but you couldn't let Ava get away, could you?

And when the alarms had started shrieking, the man would have gone for the fastest exit—and that would have been the stairwell again. He would have gone out that way.

Davis headed back downstairs. Only a few cars were left in the garage.

Did you just drive away while the alarms were shrieking?

He walked out of the garage, heading for the main street. He took the same path that a vehicle would have needed to take. And it was there, about ten feet from the garage's exit, that he found the discarded ski mask. It had been tossed into a garbage can, one the city had placed right at the edge of the road.

Davis stared at that mask. "Got you." Because he was sure the man he was after had left trace evidence in that mask. Maybe something as small as a hair, but it would be *something*.

He looked up and realized that…Alan Channing had been parked right at that same spot. His Jaguar had been there moments before.

And now he was gone…with Kristin Lang.

WHEN MARK PULLED up at his ranch, the place looked quiet. Too quiet. The doors to the stables were shut. No one was out patrolling. The lights in the main house were all turned off.

"Where is everyone?" Ava asked.

He killed the engine and climbed from the car. "Let's find out."

Ava hurriedly exited the vehicle and followed him. He went to the stables first and pushed open the doors. He braced himself before he entered, more than half-afraid that he'd discover his horses had been attacked again.

But when he entered the stables, Jamie was still

there. She turned and saw him and Ava, and the doc smiled. "He's doing great." She stood next to Legacy and patted the horse. "Give him a day and he should be as good as new."

His breath expelled in a rush. "Thank you."

She inclined her head toward him. "I'm just glad I could help." She made her way out of the stall. "But you should know…it was close, Mark. Someone didn't just want to hurt that animal. Someone deliberately poisoned him with a very high dose of drugs. That person wanted Legacy to die."

Because that SOB was trying to hurt me.

She made her way past Mark and Ava. "Hopefully you won't need me again." She reached for the door. "But if you do, you know where I am." The door squeaked when she left.

Mark stared at Legacy. The horse walked toward him, and Mark reached out to stroke Legacy between his eyes.

"I'm sorry," Ava said as she edged closer to him. "This should never have happened."

No, it shouldn't have happened.

Jaw locking, Mark turned around. He had quarters for his ranch hands out back. And if the men weren't patrolling, then he should be able to find them there. His steps were fast, angry, as he went straight to that area. Ava rushed to keep up with him.

The main ranch house had been dark, but the quarters for the men—they were lit up. He could hear the sound of voices and laughter drifting in the air. When he got to the door, he pounded his fist against the surface.

The door was opened quickly, and one of the youngest hands on the ranch, Pape Forrest, stood there. The guy, barely nineteen, swiped his hair back and straightened when he saw that Mark was the person who'd been pounding on his door. "Boss? Did you come to join the game?"

Mark looked over Pape's shoulder. The workers were gathered around a table—poker night. Right. He'd forgotten all about that. Sometimes he joined in the games. They were a great way to let off steam after a hellish week.

But he wasn't there to play. "I need to speak with Ty."

Ty stood. A line of chips was spread out in front of him. "What's up?"

Ava was silent behind Mark. "Let's go outside," he told his friend. Outside and away from the eyes and ears of the other men there.

Ty took his time heading toward Mark. He pulled the door shut behind him. The sun was setting, the sky darkening, and shadows were snaking across the ranch.

Ty looked at first Mark, then Ava. He exhaled heavily. "Why do I feel like I won't enjoy this little talk?"

He is my friend. He'd been close to Ty for years. The man knew all his secrets. "Where were you earlier?"

Ty frowned at the question. "I went to visit my girl, Mary, at her apartment. She'd made a late lunch for me."

Mary. Right. That would be Mary Angel. A sweet blonde who Ty had dated on and off for a few years. Mark had thought that Ty and Mary were currently off, but maybe they were an item again.

"What's going on?"

Ava stepped forward. "You were there the night my father died."

"Yes." Sadness whispered in his voice. "And that's a sight I won't ever be forgetting."

"You knew my father was alive when Mark got to him."

Ty's stare jerked to Mark. "You told her?"

"No, the man who has been stalking her did that." He kept his voice emotionless. "He called Ava and told her about her father's last minutes and about her dad's final words."

Ty took a step back. "He *spoke* to you, Mark? I-I didn't know. He was breathing, but it was a bare thing. I can't believe—*he spoke to you*?"

His shock seemed real.

"I didn't know." Ty shook his head. "I mean, I knew he was hanging on, barely, but the guy was bleeding all over the place. I almost fell in the blood that covered the floor—"

Ava gave a choked cry.

"I'm sorry!" Ty said at once. He yanked a hand through his hair. "You didn't need to hear that. You didn't need…" His words trailed away. His head cocked as he studied Mark. "Why are you asking me these questions? About where I was? About what I *might* have heard all those years ago?"

Mark braced his legs apart. "Ava's stalker made an appearance earlier. He came to the art museum, armed with a knife…and isn't Mary's place just a few blocks from that art museum?"

Ty's mouth dropped open as he seemed to understand Mark's questions—and his suspicions. *"You think I went after your girl?"*

At this point, Mark didn't know what to think.

"No, *no*." The denial was sharp. "Call Mary. She'll

back me up. I didn't do that. Come on, you *know* me, man. I would never do anything to hurt a woman. Not after the hell I saw my own mother endure."

Because she'd been a victim, too. Ty had never mentioned specifics to Mark, but he'd let just enough slip over the years that Mark had realized Ty's mother had been abused by a lover. To escape from that pain, she'd turned to booze. *It numbs everything for her.* Ty had told him that long ago.

"I've always had your back," Ty told him, voice roughening. "Even when old man Montgomery passed—right after you—" He stopped, his chin jutting up in the air. "I never said a thing to the cops, did I?"

Mark's drumming heartbeat filled his ears. He was aware of Ava stiffening. "There was nothing to tell the cops," Mark said flatly.

"You threatened to kill him, man. Said he should pay for all the pain he'd caused. I heard you tell him that you knew what he'd done to the McGuires…" Ty cast an apologetic look at Ava. "And the next day, he was dead."

"Mark?" Ava's voice was stunned.

"I didn't say anything to the cops," Ty continued quickly. "Because I have your back. Always. So if you think I would ever do anything to hurt your girl, you are dead wrong."

ALAN CHANNING LIVED in a high-rise condo in downtown Austin. Davis rode the elevator up to the guy's floor, his body tight with tension. He'd turned over that ski mask to the cops, but even before the crime scene techs had collected the important evidence, he'd seen the hairs stuck in the material.

Blond hairs.

The elevator opened, and Davis stalked down the hallway. The thick carpet muffled the sound of his footsteps. In moments he was in front of Alan's door. Jaw locking, Davis lifted his hand and knocked.

Silence.

He waited, his impatience growing by the moment. He'd called Grant on the way over, and his brother was already digging into Alan Channing's past. The guy had been at the scene tonight—too conveniently so—and if those blond hairs were linked to him...

You will go down for hurting my sister.

The door creaked open. Alan's eyes flared in surprise when he saw Davis.

"Wh-what are you doing here?" Alan asked him. "Is Ava all right?"

Ava. "Mind if I come in?" Davis asked.

Alan blinked. "Uh, of course, come on in." He stepped back. "I just got in myself. I had to stay with Kristin for a little while. She was quite flustered after the attack tonight."

Davis thought "flustered" was quite an understatement. His gaze darted around the condo. The guy had obviously used an interior designer on the place. It looked like something out of a magazine—something perfect but untouched. There were no personal pictures in the place. No mementos. Just cold class.

"Ava is okay, isn't she?"

Wanting to gauge his reaction, Davis turned his full attention back on the other man. "She left with Mark. I'm sure he's keeping a very close eye on her."

Alan's lips tightened. "I thought you were taking her home."

"Ava wanted Mark."

Ah, there it was. A flash of anger on the guy's face. "Ava could do far better than Mark Montgomery."

He eased closer to the man. "Why were you at the museum tonight?"

Alan stepped back. "I'm on the board. I often go the museum—"

"But it wasn't open to the public today." He knew. He'd done plenty of checking. "They were working on a new exhibit. It was staff only."

"I'm on the board!" Alan said again. "I was appointed recently, and I like to check up on things—"

"You've been making a lot of trips over to Houston in the last few months." That was a total shot in the dark. Yes, Grant was checking for trips like that right then—but they didn't know anything about the guy so far. All Davis had was his growing suspicion.

But at his words, Alan's lips parted in surprise, and his head jerked. "That's business! Just business!"

Well, well...

"My business takes me all over Texas. And yes, I have to visit Houston frequently. What does that matter?"

It mattered a great deal because... "Ava was living in Houston."

Alan nodded. "Right, but Ava hadn't seen me in ages. We ran into one another recently at the museum, we talked about grabbing a bite to eat together—and that is all." The guy was sweating.

"Interesting phrasing you have there... Ava hadn't seen *you*. But had you seen Ava?"

Alan's chin hitched up. "I worried about her. She had a hard time after her parents died."

Davis's body tensed. "You don't have to tell me that. She's my sister. I know all about her."

"No," Alan said softly. "I don't think you do. You still see her as that lost sixteen-year-old, but she isn't that girl any longer." Like he needed this guy telling him anything about Ava.

"Ava is so much more than you realize," Alan continued, voice almost passionate. "I've always known that about her."

The guy was talking about Ava as if he were still in love with her. And when Davis had seen them at the museum, Alan's face had flashed with jealousy when Mark got near her.

Alan straightened his shoulders. "I don't understand why you're here."

"I'm here because some psycho has been terrorizing my sister, and I don't like for Ava to be afraid."

"I don't, either," Alan said at once.

Davis smiled at him. He knew it wasn't a pretty sight. "You don't want me for an enemy."

Alan's cheeks flushed red as he sucked in a sharp breath. "Are you threatening me?"

"No, I'm stating a fact. You don't want me for an enemy, and you don't want Mark Montgomery for an enemy."

"I'm not afraid of Montgomery!"

You should be.

"Why was Ava at the museum tonight?"

Alan's hands flew up in the air. "This is ridiculous! Obviously the woman was working. Kristin had a big project, and she needed all hands on deck."

"And you knew all about that project?"

"I told you—"

"Right, you're on the board." This guy was pushing all of Davis's buttons. "But Ava wasn't scheduled to start at the museum for a few more days. Why would Kristin call her in early?"

Alan glanced away.

"I think I'll call Kristin and find out," Davis murmured.

Alan ran a shaking hand through his hair. "I told Kristin to call Ava in."

I thought as much. You wanted Ava out in the open, didn't you? Where you could get to her?

"I knew how qualified Ava was. This—this would have been a great opportunity for her—"

"Or for you."

Alan inched back another step. "I don't know what you mean."

"It was a chance for you to get to Ava." His hands clenched into fists. "I found the ski mask you left behind."

"What ski mask?"

"The one you were wearing when you tried to stab Kristin. Only she wasn't the target, right? It was Ava. You were waiting in that parking garage for her, but when the elevator opened, Ava wasn't alone. Kristin was with her. You had to get rid of Kristin, so you attacked."

"No!" Alan shook his head. "I wasn't in any parking garage! I was outside. I was coming by to see— to see if Ava wanted to have dinner with me. I didn't attack anyone."

"I found the ski mask," Davis said again. "Your hair is in it."

"My...my hair?"

"You left evidence behind. Very sloppy. But I guess

you just couldn't stand it anymore, could you? Seeing how close Ava was getting to Mark. She was supposed to come back for you, right? Not him?"

"Get out," Alan spat.

"Just how long have you been obsessed with my sister?" Davis demanded as the rage heated in his gut. "Because now I'm wondering…did it start all of those years ago? She broke up with you, right? On the same night that our parents were killed."

Alan marched to the door. He yanked it open. "Anything else you have to say to me…you can say through my attorney."

"Don't worry," Davis took his time strolling toward the door. "I'm sure the cops will have plenty to say to you *and* your attorney real soon."

Alan's body seemed to be practically vibrating with rage.

Davis stopped right next to the man. "Stay away from my sister."

Alan's eyes burned with fury. "I'm not scared of Mark Montgomery, and I'm not scared of you, either. You think because you were some hotshot SEAL that I'm supposed to tremble when you're near?"

The guy *was* trembling.

"I would never hurt Ava. Everything I've done has been to help her." He gave a rough laugh. "So do your worst. Rip into my life. Go digging for all my secrets. You'll see I'm not the one you're after."

"You'd better not be," Davis told him. "Because if you are, I will make your life a living hell."

Then he strolled out of the condo.

Alan slammed the door shut behind him.

Davis took out his phone and called Grant. "Hey,

man, you need to get that info on Alan Channing yesterday." He glanced back at the door. He knew that Brodie and Jennifer were at McGuire Securities with Grant—they were all working to dig up information on Alan Channing right then. "Because I think we may just have found Ava's stalker."

Chapter Ten

They were back at the guest cottage on the McGuire ranch. Mark turned off the car's engine, but he didn't make a move to leave the vehicle. Ava was beside him. She'd been pretty silent ever since Ty had dropped his bombshells.

He looked over at Ava. She sat there, as still as a stone. He told her, "I didn't kill him."

Ava flinched. She fumbled, opened her door and hurried from the vehicle. He followed right behind her and caught her before she could go inside the cottage. "Ava, please, wait!" He turned her around in his arms. "Listen to me, okay?"

She stared up at him. The porch light shone down on her.

"There were plenty of times when I wanted Gregory dead," Mark confessed. *More times than I can count.* "When he hurt me, when he raged and drank… I wanted him to die." The words were brutal and true. "I stayed here for my mother." She'd been sick those last few years, battling heart disease, and she'd had no idea what Gregory had done to Mark. "When she passed, I didn't plan to come back, ever."

He'd tried to hide this part of his life from Ava

because he'd been afraid she would turn away. Now he was desperate to do anything, to say anything, if he could just convince her to stay with him.

"Where did you go?" Ava asked him.

He half smiled. "Maybe I was more like your brothers than I realized back then. I joined the army. Served a tour and then I...went independent."

Most folks didn't call the contractors "mercenaries" any longer. He'd worked on jobs in so many different parts of the world. He'd seen things that he'd never be able to forget. And he'd realized...a man can only run so far from the ghosts that chased him.

"I got word that Gregory was bad. Drinking, going days without eating. He'd gotten a diagnosis of cancer, and it had driven him over the edge."

She inhaled sharply. "I didn't know—"

"No one did but me. His lawyers called me. Told me what was happening. He couldn't take care of the ranch any longer, and if I didn't come back, he was afraid he'd lose the business." Only when he'd come back, he'd learned that Gregory was still interested destroying everyone around him. "I wanted him to get clean and look for treatment options. But he told me to screw off. Said he didn't need me and never would."

"What had he done to my family?"

His hand dropped back to his side. "Your father had been plagued by poor supply shipments and overzealous creditors for years. Did you know that?"

She shook her head.

"Yeah, I didn't, either. Not until I came back. By then, Gregory wasn't able to hide his secrets from me. I found records of all the times he'd tried to cause havoc in your father's life."

Ava's eyes were so wide and deep.

"He thought he loved her," Mark said. "In his twisted way. Though I doubt he could actually love anyone. And he wanted to punish your father for taking her away."

"My mother?"

Mark nodded.

"That night—the last night he was alive—I'd found all the paperwork that showed what he'd done over the years. And even with your parents gone…" This was so hard to say to her. Especially when she was staring up at him with trust in her eyes. "I learned he was still trying to cause trouble. He should have been fighting the cancer! But he was scheming like mad and trying to get a team to come in and buy the ranch out from under your brothers."

She stepped back.

"I told him it wasn't happening. And, yeah, I said I should kill him myself. But that was just anger talking. Rage." Fury at a man who'd abused him for years— and who'd enjoyed hurting so many people. "I told him that he was a disgrace and that maybe he was better off dead. Then I left him." Guilt rose then, knifing through him. There'd been no love lost between him and Gregory but… *I would wish that death he'd suffered on no one.*

"Mark?"

"When I came back the next morning, he'd shot himself in the head."

"I'm sorry."

Her kind reaction shocked him. He had to touch her then. Had to wrap his arms around her shoulders and step even closer to her. "I told you what he did to your family."

"He was the only father you knew."

"He was a sick bastard who left me with more scars that I can count, and he harassed your family for years. No one should mourn him. No one should—"

"I'm sorry," she said again. Her voice and her touch were so very gentle. "Because I know it hurt you. No matter what he'd done, I know it hurt."

And it had. He put his forehead against hers.

Ava's hand rose and caressed his jaw. "I know you," she continued. "Even if you think you're keeping your secrets from me, I know who you are inside."

"I didn't kill him." Those words came out so gruff.

"I know."

He'd seen suspicion on so many faces—even Ty's. *Ty thinks I did it. So do others at the ranch.* But he hadn't pulled that trigger. He hadn't fired since his days in the Middle East.

Yet...

I would kill in an instant if it meant protecting her. That understanding went straight to his soul. He would truly do anything for Ava.

He pressed his lips to hers. When Ava was close, Mark felt better. Stronger. She made him want to be better. A man who was worthy of her.

The kiss deepened as he pushed her against the door.

Her taste made him heady. Desire surged through him. He couldn't be near Ava and not want her. She'd gotten beneath his skin, and he knew that he'd never be able to escape the pull she had on him.

"Come inside with me," Ava told him.

Like he needed to be asked twice.

Ava opened the door. Mark followed her inside. The

cottage was dark as he reset the locks. Ava didn't linger in the little den. She walked straight for the bedroom.

He hesitated.

"Don't be shy now," she told him, her voice light, soft, and banishing the grief and rage that had clung to him for a moment. "I'm waiting on you."

"I don't have a shy bone in my body."

She slipped into the bedroom. He followed right behind her. The room smelled of Ava. Sweet strawberries. He turned on the light because he wanted to see every inch of her body.

She stood next to the bed and stripped. There was no shyness from her, either. Her clothing hit the floor with a soft rustle and she stood before him, her body bare and perfect. Her breasts thrust toward him. The pink tips were tight, and he wanted to taste them. Her waist curved into the flare of her hips. Just staring at her pretty much made him ache.

He stepped forward.

"You still have your clothes on," Ava pointed out.

Mostly because he couldn't wait to touch her. His hand curled around her breast, then stroked that tight nipple. Ava gave the little moan that he loved—Mark was sure he'd already grown addicted to that sound.

He lifted her up against him, holding her easily, and he took her nipple into his mouth. Her fingers sank into his hair as she arched toward him. He kissed that sweet flesh. Licked. Sucked. His mouth pressed to her as he carried her to the bed.

He put her down on the mattress, and for a moment he just stared at her. Lost. "You're supposed to be afraid of me."

She reached up and slid her hand under his shirt. "I'm shaking with fear."

No, she wasn't. "When I was in the army, and after... it wasn't an easy time, baby. I did things—"

"Your mission."

Yes, but some of those missions had been horrible. Blood and death and sand and battles without end.

"I don't think I've ever been afraid of you." Now her hand was at the snap of his jeans. "And I don't think I ever could be." She unzipped his fly.

His erection sprang into her hands, and when she stroked him from root to tip, his eyes nearly rolled back in his head. Earlier he'd remembered to put another condom in his wallet—very lucky because he wasn't sure anything could have stopped him from being with her tonight.

She kept stroking him, and a growl slipped from his throat. He leaned over the bed, over her, and he braced his hands on the mattress. Mark kissed her, a caress of his lips against hers as he explored her mouth and put a stranglehold on his desire.

But Ava pulled back. "You don't have to go slow with me. I want you. I want you to make me forget everything else."

He ditched his clothes, put on the condom and went straight to her. But...

"Why do you want to be with me?" The question was pulled from him even as he caressed the slick folds of her sex. He wanted Ava so badly he hurt, but did she just want the oblivion that pleasure could give to her? Would anyone work for her right then? Would—

"Don't you know?" Her eyes held his. "Because I love you."

Time seemed to stop. He stared at her a moment, and he even shook his head, certain that he must have misheard.

But Ava smiled up at him. Her dimples flashed. "I've loved you for a long time."

She broke him.

He drove into her, thrusting deep and hard. His control had shattered as his need for her erupted. There was no holding back. No taking things slow or careful. There was only need. Only desire. Only him trying to take everything that he could—even as he gave Ava all that he had.

The bed was squeaking and slamming into the wall. Ava was gasping. Her nails dug into his back. He kissed her neck. Let her feel the score of his teeth. He wanted to mark her right then, to show others that Ava was his—because he was hers.

He didn't have the words to give her. He wasn't even sure what he should say, and all he could do right then was feel. Feel the hot heaven of her body and her silken skin.

Taste...

Taste Ava. Her lips. Lush and full, red and wet.

Take.

Take her until she screamed for him. He could feel the way her sex was squeezing around him. Ava was close to her release. So close.

"Mark!" She slammed her hips up against him, and her inner muscles clenched tightly around him.

He came, following her on that hot and heavy tide of release. He emptied into her until he was sure he had nothing left. His heart thudded. Sweat slicked his skin. And he didn't let her go.

I love you.

He knew that he'd *never* let her go again. Ava belonged with him, and now both of their fates were sealed.

DAVIS'S FOOTSTEPS WERE slow as he walked through the ranch house. The place was so quiet. Brodie and Jennifer had opted to stay in the city—they were planning to head out at first light so that they could go to Houston and learn more about Alan Channing's visits to that city.

And to see if he was watching Ava during those trips.

Exhaustion clawed at him. He'd gone back to the police station. Told the cops all he knew about Alan. The cops had promised to keep uniforms near Alan's place just as a precaution.

So you'll see what if feels like to be watched.

Mark was with Ava. They were settled in at the guest house. He'd called earlier and woken Ava from her sleep. Her voice had been husky when she told him that she was safe. That Mark was close.

He knew that Mark would die before he'd let anything happen to Ava.

I've known how the guy felt about her for years. But he'd still tried to keep Mark away from Ava. Why?

He walked through the quiet halls of the house.

Because I didn't want to lose Ava.

He climbed into bed and stared up at the ceiling. Family was the thing that mattered most to him. He knew many people thought he was a cold-blooded bastard, but his family…his family was his life.

He'd already lost so much in the past.

Too much.

The house here—this sweet spot in Texas—it was his haven. It was—

Davis smelled smoke. He could hear…the faint hiss and crackle of flames.

Fire! He lurched up and leapt for the door.

SHE'D DONE IT. Ava turned in the bed, and her gaze slid over Mark's features. She'd actually told him that she loved him.

And Mark hadn't said anything back to her.

Talk about awkward—and painful.

The sex had been incredible. They had combustible chemistry. There was no denying that. But for her, it was more than just physical, and it was far more than just sex.

I've loved him for years.

She still had no clue how Mark felt about her.

She'd slept for just a little bit and had woken to find him still in the bed next to her. His arm was curled around her stomach. He looked so…relaxed right then. Peaceful, even. She hadn't seen him look peaceful very many times in his life.

Moving so very carefully, Ava eased from beneath his arm. She grabbed a T-shirt—his—and slid it over her head. Then she tiptoed out of the room. Ava didn't take a full breath until the bedroom door shut behind her.

The little cottage was so quiet. Ava glanced around as her eyes adjusted to the darkness in the den. The porch light was spilling through the front window. She stared out that window for a moment.

When will it end?

She turned away and headed toward the back room

in the cottage. The room that housed her paintings. She opened the door. She'd poured her rage and pain into those canvases. Then she'd tried to hide them—the same way she'd tried to hide her feelings ever since she was sixteen.

But Ava was done hiding.

She flipped on the light. Then her breath choked out in a sharp cry of shock and dismay.

The canvases—they'd been slashed.

At first Ava could only shake her head. No, no, that wasn't possible. Her brothers had installed the *best* security at the ranch. No one could get inside…

But someone had. The canvases littered the floor. It looked as if someone had taken a knife to them, and she remembered the knife that had swung out at Kristin in that elevator.

Ava backed away, moving slowly out of that room, but then she bumped into something—someone—and she whirled around, screaming.

Chapter Eleven

"Ava!" Mark caught her hands when they swung out to attack him. "Baby, what's wrong—" But then he broke off because he'd just caught sight of those canvases.

"He's here." In contrast to her scream, now Ava's voice was a low whisper. "He got past the security, and he's here on the ranch."

Mark swore and pulled her from the room. No one should have been able to get on the ranch. The McGuires were fanatical about the security out there. "We need to get dressed," he told her, "and get out of here." He wanted her safe, and then he wanted to hurt this guy. Because if he was still close by...

Then I will find you.

They hurried back to Ava's bedroom and dressed as fast as they could, and then—

The lights went off.

He heard Ava suck in a sharp breath. "That's the same way it was at the museum. He killed the lights there—*he's playing with me.*"

Mark reached for his phone and called Davis. The line rang and rang—no answer.

"Mark?" Ava's fingers curled around his wrist. "Are my brothers okay?"

He put the phone in his pocket. In the dark, she couldn't see his expression, so she wouldn't know the worry that pierced through him. "Of course," he told her, forcing his voice to sound calm. "You know them—no one can take down the McGuire boys."

Get her out of here. Get her to safety.

He didn't have a weapon in the cottage, but he had one waiting in the car outside. They headed for the door, moving slowly, carefully. Mark opened the door.

And found himself staring down the barrel of a gun.

The moon was overhead, its light spilling down, so it was easy for Mark to see the weapon pointed right at him. And the man there—

"Ava," the guy demanded, his voice gruff. "What is happening?"

The man holding the gun wasn't an enemy. Mark recognized his voice even if most of the guy's body was in shadows.

Ava pushed past Mark and ran to the guy, giving him a tight hug. "Mac," she whispered.

No one can take down the McGuire boys.

And another McGuire was standing right there, holding Ava with one arm while his other hand still gripped that gun. Mac McGuire was probably the wildest—and, if the stories were true, deadliest—of the bunch. Former Delta Force, Mac seemed to enjoy looking for danger. An adrenaline junkie, some had said. Mark had always thought Mac rushed after the danger because he was running from his own demons.

"I didn't think you were in town," Ava said. "Davis told me that you were working a case in Atlanta."

"Sully and I just finished up there," Mac said, his voice gruff.

Sully—yeah, that would be the youngest McGuire. Sullivan. Ex-marine. Icy green eyes, dangerous temper.

"We came down here as soon as we could," Mac replied. He was still holding tight to the gun—and Ava. "When the lights went off, he went to the main house to check in, and I came here." He hesitated. "Ava, what is happening?"

"We all need to get up to the main house," Mark said. "The jerk who has been stalking Ava has been here."

"Then why are we just standing out in the open?" Mac demanded.

Good freaking question.

They hurried out to the cars. Mark's gaze narrowed when he looked at his tires. "Someone slashed them." *He was here...while I was in that cottage with Ava.* And Mark had been so lost in her that he hadn't even been aware of the danger.

"Is the cottage clear?" Mac's gaze had turned back to the house.

"I don't know." Mark slid closer to Ava. "I just wanted to get her out of there and..." His breath came out in a rush. "Davis wasn't answering his phone. I wanted to make sure he was safe up at the main house." That they'd all been safe.

Once again Mark pulled out his phone. This time, instead of calling Davis, he tried for Brodie. The guy answered on the second ring. "Brodie! Man, I was getting worried." Because this was not a good scene. "We think the stalker is on the ranch. He's been in the cottage, and he's—"

"What?" Brodie's voice was a roar. "Is Ava okay?"

"Yes." His gaze slanted toward her. "We wanted to make sure you, Jennifer and Davis were safe."

"I'm not at the ranch."

Mark heard Jennifer's voice in the background.

"We're in town, but we'll be there as fast as possible," Brodie continued.

Mac was heading toward the cottage's door.

"Is Davis with you?" Mark asked. His guts were knotting. This setup wasn't good. Every instinct he possessed was screaming *danger.*

"He's at the ranch."

Then why isn't he answering his phone?

"Protect my sister, Mark," Brodie said, his words rushing out. "Keep my family safe."

"Mac is here. We'll find out what's happening." He shoved the phone back into his pocket.

Mac was about to head into the cottage. "If he's here, he's not getting away—"

"I smell smoke," Ava said, her voice sharp and breaking with fear. "Don't you smell it?"

Mark's stables had been set on fire a few months ago, and he remembered the rush of fear he'd felt when he scented that smoke. Only the smoke had come with an explosion—one that had blasted right through the stables.

"Something is burning." Ava hurried away from the men. "It's coming from—*it's coming from the main house!*"

The main house… Was Davis there?

Mac ran and jumped into his truck. Ava and Mark pushed in with him. It wasn't far to the main house, and even as they drove up the lane, Mark was frantically trying to reach Davis on his phone again.

Then the truck came to a screeching halt. The ranch house was just feet away, and it was on fire.

The flames were flickering inside the house, rising in orange and red waves. Mark could see someone at the door, a man who appeared to be trying to break down the main entrance.

They all leapt from the truck and raced toward the house.

"Help me!" the man yelled. It was Sully. He was driving his shoulder into the door again and again. "It's stuck and I think Davis is inside!" But, then, before they could run to him, he turned and hurried toward the window in the front of the house. He lifted his hand and drove his fist straight into the glass.

Smoke billowed out as the glass shattered. Mark knocked as much glass out of the way as he could. Sully crawled through the window even as the crackle of the fire grew louder.

Mac headed in after him.

And Mark remembered another fire. The fire at his stables had been a trap. The man who'd set the blaze had been trying to get Jennifer. He'd set the fire to lure her out so he could grab her.

Mark swung around. Ava was right beside him. She pushed against him. "I need to get in there!"

But he caught her arms and held her back. "Mac and Sully will get Davis out."

Brodie's words rang in his mind. *Protect my sister.* That was exactly what he intended to do.

She struggled in his hold. "Mark, let me go!"

The flames were growing bigger. The scent of the fire was so much stronger. Mark needed to call 9-1-1. He had to—

A gunshot rang out. The blast was so close. Mark

could feel the heat of the bullet whipping by him before it plunged into the side of the house.

He yanked Ava forward, and they hit the ground.

SOMETHING WAS WRONG.

Davis tried to open his eyes, but that one small feat seemed to take way too much effort. His head was hurting, throbbing with a constant agony that had nausea rolling through him.

What happened?

He was on the floor, and he coughed because there was…smoke around him. His eyes cracked open, and he could see the tendrils of gray rising. His hands flattened on the wooden floor. Fire. That was right. He'd smelled smoke. He'd run out of his room and…

Did someone hit me? Because things were dark after that moment. He couldn't remember what had happened after he'd left his room.

He crawled forward, coughing more. He could hear the flames crackling and what sounded almost like laughter around him. Fire was racing up the walls, and he wanted to roar his fury. This was his home. He'd rebuilt it—he and Brodie had worked so hard to save this place.

Ava hated the ranch. She saw only pain there.

But it's my home. My life is here.

The flames grew bigger. Hotter.

"Davis!"

His head jerked when he heard the cry of his name. Through the smoke, he saw two dark figures surging toward him.

"Davis, are you all right?"

He would know that fierce, growling voice anyplace—

it was Sully's voice. And Sully was grabbing him, trying to help Davis get to the door.

"No, he's not all right," another sharp voice said. *Mac*. He slid his shoulder under Davis's right arm. "Come on, let's go!"

They half pulled, half carried him out of the hallway. The flames were racing across the den, moving so fast, and the sight of them made Davis's heart hurt. Not this place. It couldn't be destroyed. They needed it too much.

I need it.

They were close to the front door.

"That's why it wouldn't open," Sully said.

A table had been shoved against the door.

"Someone didn't want you getting out," Mac said.

Davis tried to speak but could only cough.

"Move that thing, Sully!" Mac ordered him. "Hurry!"

AVA STARED UP at Mark. He'd slammed into her and taken them both down to the ground. She knew he was trying to protect her from whoever was shooting at them.

The same man who set the house on fire.

"We have to help my brothers!" She pushed against Mark's shoulders.

But he didn't move. He wasn't moving!

"No, Ava, stop!" He caught her arms and pinned them in the dirt. "If we move, he'll have a perfect shot at us. That's what he planned, don't you see? This is a trap to lure us—*you*—out here. He's waiting for his moment to attack. The first shot missed, but the second? I don't think it will."

They were on the side of the house, low, hidden for the moment. But her brothers were in the fire. "Let me go," she told Mark, her voice sharp. She wasn't going to hide while her brothers died. *"Let me go!"* She bucked against him, heaving with all of her strength.

"Ava—"

Another shot rang out. Only this one…it hadn't been aimed at them. Mark's hold eased on her, and Ava twisted, rolling away from him. She stayed down, out of sight, but she saw that the bullet—and another one that had just blasted—had hit the front door of the ranch. A door that had opened just a few inches.

My brothers are trying to get out of the flames.

But whoever was out there—he was shooting at them. If her brothers ran out, he'd kill them. Ava knew this with utter certainty.

"No," she whispered as her heart splintered.

Mark's hands closed over her shoulders. "Stay here, baby, please," he told her, his voice so soft she barely heard his words. "I'll get them out. Just—*stay safe.*"

Then, before she could respond, Mark was up and running away. He was heading right for the front door, and he didn't have any weapon with him. "He's got a gun!" Mark bellowed. "Go out the back! Go!"

And gunfire erupted again.

"No!" Ava screamed. And she didn't stay there. She didn't hide.

She leaped to her feet.

"Somebody is shooting at us!" Sully yelled as he held tighter to Davis.

They were at the front door. Mac had yanked open that door moments before, and air—clear, sweet air— had whispered inside. Davis choked and coughed because that clear air was gone, and the smoke was rising too fast.

The fire was burning all around them.

"He's got a gun! Go out the back! Go!"

Davis heard that frantic shout, and he looked over his shoulder. Flames were behind him. Where had all those flames come from? How had anyone gotten onto his ranch? *How?* The place should have been secure.

"We can't go back." Mac's voice was low and grim.

No, they couldn't.

"Let's head for a window. We'll break the glass, just like we did before," Sully said. And then Sully started pulling Davis toward the right.

In the next instant, Mac heard the thunder of gunfire. More bullets. Then—

"Stop!" Ava's scream, clear even above the flames. *"Leave them alone! If you want me, I'm here!"*

"No," Mac whispered.

Then the gunfire…it came again.

AVA LEAPT IN FRONT of Mark even as the gunfire exploded. She thought the bullets were going to slam into her. Mark was yelling and trying to push her behind him—

The bullets didn't hit her.

They slammed into the house.

Mark froze.

"He's not going to kill me," Ava said, her voice breaking. "He wants me alive, don't you see?" So he wouldn't shoot her. But if he had a shot at Mark, she didn't doubt for an instant that he'd take it. "If I'm here, he won't shoot."

And her brothers would have a chance. Because they *had* to get out of that fire. If they could just get out of the house and to the safety of Mac's truck or Sully's SUV, they'd make it.

"Hurry, Sully!" Ava called to her brother. The smoke was getting so thick out there. If it was bad on the narrow porch, what was it like in the house?

She risked a glance over her shoulder. Mark had finally let her go, and he'd shoved open the door to the house. He rushed inside—

And Ava stood there, her arms spread over her head, her feet braced apart. She was a target. She knew it. But more, she was a shield for her brothers and for Mark. For the men she loved so much.

Hurry.

"Come to me, Ava!" A hard, angry voice cried out from the darkness. "Come to me!"

She didn't move. Ava feared his words were just a trick. If she moved, then he would shoot.

"I'll kill them if you don't!" His voice was such a terrible roar.

"You'll kill them if I do." She wasn't budging and… yes, she could hear Mark behind her again. Mark and her brothers. They were coming out of the house. She moved then, but only so she could better shield them with her body.

He won't fire at me. He hasn't hurt me. He wants me alive. She just had to remember that.

"Ava!" Her name was a cry of absolute rage.

"Get to the vehicles," she told her brothers. They were low, crouching behind her. "Run!"

Run. Her father had said the same thing to her.

Despite the heat of the fire, Ava felt goose bumps rise on her arms.

"Move away from them!" the man in the darkness screamed.

But Ava wasn't about to abandon her brothers or Mark. So when they ran forward, she ran forward. She tried to stretch her arms and her body as much as possible to cover them.

"Ava!"

She flinched at that bellow of fury. And an instant later, gunfire erupted. But the bullet hit over her head, plunging into the wood of the porch.

Then another bullet hit about a foot away from her shoe.

Ava's breath sawed out and—*they were at the SUV.* They crouched behind it, and Ava reached for Davis. He was so still. When her fingers touched him, Davis flinched.

"Looks like the joker out there knocked Davis out," Sully said, "and then just left him to die in the fire."

A scream built in Ava's throat, but she choked it back.

"I'm calling 9-1-1," Sully declared.

Ava's fingers slid over Davis's jaw. "Are you okay?"

His hand lifted to curl tightly around hers. "Takes more than this...to stop me."

More than a fire? One that was destroying the home he'd worked so desperately to save? That house had been everything to Davis. She'd refused to set foot in the place, seeing only the pain there. But to him and Brodie, it had been so much more.

It had been...hope?

Now it was burning.

"I've got my weapon, and I'm going after him," Sully said. "Police and fire trucks are on the way."

But they'd get there too late for the house.

Mark had his phone out, too. "Bring every man and woman over here," Mark snapped into that phone. "We've got a fire at the McGuire ranch."

He put down the phone, then stared at Davis. "You and your family have always been there for me. Time for me to repay my debt."

Sully was already slipping away into the darkness. Ava wanted to grab him and hold on tight. The shooter out there wouldn't hesitate to fire at him.

But Sully—Sully was too fast. One instant he was there. The next he was gone.

Davis groaned. Mac leaned toward him. "You're bleeding so bad, man. What did he hit you with?"

And she could feel the blood streaming down his head. Davis. Her strong and tough brother. Another one who'd been hurt because he was trying to protect her.

"He'll get away," Ava said. Because if the guy had been good enough to sneak past their security, then he'd know a way off the property. Before help arrived, he'd be gone. "I have to stop him." This wasn't something she'd just leave to the others. Ava eased away from Davis. "Take care of him," she told Mac.

Mac was shaking his head. "Ava, whatever you're thinking—"

"I'm thinking that he won't shoot me, but he'll happily kill you all." This man was sick. And he was out there right then. "I'm going to draw him out."

"What?" Mark grabbed her arm. "No, baby, no!"

"Be ready," she told him as she straightened her spine. "I'll pull him out, and you get the bastard. Don't let him hurt anyone else." Then she leaned forward and kissed Mark. Fast, desperately. "Don't let him hurt you."

"Ava…"

She jerked away from him and ran. Not away from the ranch house, not this time. She wasn't going to leave those she loved behind, no matter the cost. Instead, she stood in front of the flames. Ava raised her hands high above her head. "I'm here!" she shouted. "If you want me… *I'm right here!* So come out and face me!"

AVA WAS CALLING to him, standing in front of those flames as they destroyed the house she hated. Did she realize he'd set the fire for her? To rid her of that terrible pain that she carried?

Her arms were open. She was yelling for him, and he wanted to turn and go to her so badly.

Ava. Sweet Ava. It had all been to prove his love to her. She didn't need Mark. She didn't need her brothers. She needed only him.

He heard the snap of a twig behind him.

He realized too late that he'd been hunted. His eyes had been on Ava, and he hadn't seen the threat closing in.

"Drop the weapon, you bastard," a low, guttural voice told him. "Or I will shoot you where you stand."

Slowly, never taking his eyes off Ava's form, he dropped the gun. It was one of the brothers who'd snuck up on him. The brothers had always been such an annoyance in his way, trying to block him from getting time with Ava.

Her parents had been in his way, but they'd been eliminated.

Now for her brothers…

"Take off the ski mask and turn to face me."

Taking his time, he lifted off the mask. He tossed it to the ground.

"Why the ski mask?" the brother demanded before he could turn to confront the fellow.

"Because I wanted to remind Ava." It was the truth. "I wanted her to remember that night whenever she looked at me."

"Did you kill our parents?" Ah, so much hate was in those words. He understood hate. Fury.

Fury could make a man careless.

Smiling, his hand slipped down to his waist. He had another weapon there, tucked in his waistband. His fingers curled around the gun. "I wish I had." He lifted it up and whirled in one movement. "Like I'm killing you!" He fired.

But—but the man had lurched to the side. Instead of hitting him in the chest, the bullet slammed into his prey's shoulder. And the man fired at him—a fast, rapid succession of shots.

One sank into his shoulder.

Another into his side.

No!

Pain tore through him, and he fired even as he staggered away. This wasn't supposed to happen. This wasn't the way things were supposed to end.

Not for him. Not for Ava.

Her brother stopped firing.

He ran for the sheltering darkness, even as the blood poured from his wounds.

Chapter Twelve

At the sound of the gunfire, Ava's breath caught in her throat. But those shots weren't aimed at her or the house or even at the SUV. They were coming from the west, from the line of trees just past the bluff.

"Sully," she whispered. Because he'd been out there, looking for the man who'd set that fire. If he'd found him— *"Sully!"*

And then she heard the growl of vehicles approaching. Lots of vehicles, from the sound of things. They were roaring up the drive, and all she could see was the bright flash of lights.

Then Mark was there, running to meet them. Shouting orders. She realized that help had come in the form of his workers and friends.

"We busted through the gate," she heard one man tell Mac. "Sorry about that, but the boss said we needed to get over here fast."

And they had. They were shining lights around the scene. Men were grabbing hoses and buckets of water and trying to put out the fire, trying to save the house.

A house she'd scorned for too long.

In the distance, Ava could hear a siren. An ambulance, coming to take care of Davis.

"Where's Sully?" Ava asked. Sullivan still hadn't appeared.

The men and women who'd arrived were fighting the flames, but no one was searching for Sully.

Ava started running toward the bluff.

Then she was grabbed from behind. Hard hands swung Ava around. "You're not going anyplace without me," Mark said.

She stared up at him, but a cloud had slid over the moon, and she couldn't see his face clearly. The scent of the fire was all around her, and so many memories were in the air. The past—the present—everything was tangling together.

Mark laced his fingers with hers. "Not without me," he said again.

He had a gun. She could see it in his other hand. Ava didn't even know where he'd gotten that weapon. From one of his men? From Mac?

But there was no time for questions. They ran toward the bluff. Mark's steps were sure, and she moved too fast to stumble. "Sully!" She cried out his name, but there was still no answer. She tried to keep her body in front of Mark's just in case the stalker was out there waiting for another shot, but Mark kept moving, trying to protect her.

When I want to keep him safe instead...

"Ava..." Her name was low, rough. And very close. She whirled to the left because she knew the sound of her brother's voice.

She and Mark leapt through the brush.

The clouds slid past the moon—

Sullivan was on the ground. He had a gun in his hand, and he was struggling to sit up. She ran to him and sank to her knees. "Sully!" When she touched him, she felt the sticky wetness of blood on him. So much blood.

"Shooting arm…went numb," he muttered. "Bullet's still in me…"

More than one bullet, judging by the amount of blood she felt. "Help!" Ava screamed, because the others back at the house had to be close enough to hear her. "Help—"

"No," Sully growled. "He's still here, Ava. He's close."

Mark swore. "Where?"

"Slid away to the…right…moving slow 'cause my bullets hit him, too…"

And Mark rushed to the right. Ava jumped up, wanting to follow him, but Sully had too tight a grip on her wrist. "Stay," he said. It wasn't an order but a plea. She didn't think tough Sully had ever pleaded for anything in his life.

Sully had been injured just a few months back. He'd gotten out of the hospital, supposedly with a clean bill of health, but…but he'd been taking fewer missions since then. And the way he was holding her hand so tightly…

She swallowed to clear the lump in her throat. "It's not just a bullet in your arm, is it? Were you shot somewhere else, too?"

"I…love you, Ava…"

Tears stung her eyes. No, no, this *wasn't* happening. Sully had survived so much. He was supposed to be invincible. He'd been her confidant for most of her life. The youngest brother, he'd been the closest to her age. The one who'd always taken the blame when she did ridiculous things because he'd said it was his job to keep her safe.

No matter what.

"Sully, *no*." Her voice thickened. "Don't you do this to me. *Don't!*"

"Always hated…that I wasn't here when you needed me."

No, no, he was talking as if he were about to leave her. The final words of a dying man, and that couldn't happen. She *wouldn't* let it happen. "I'm going to get help. I'll be right back."

But he wasn't letting her go. His grip was so strong.

And tears were sliding down her cheeks.

"I'm sorry…" Sully told her. "I wanted…you safe…"

That too-tight grip went slack, and terror drove straight through her. "No!" Ava yelled. "No, no, Sully!" Her hands flew over his chest. And she'd been right. There were more wounds. His shirt was soaked with his blood. "Sully!" She wasn't even sure that he was breathing. She put her hands over those wounds, trying to apply as much pressure to them as she could. "Help me!" Ava screamed. But…but the fire was still raging. Would anyone hear her? Help was so close. She just had to run and get it.

"I'll be right back," Ava told him. She pressed a quick kiss to Sully's cheek. It was…chilled. No, *not Sully*. She staggered to her feet and turned to run back for help. Her shoes thudded over the earth as she hurried back toward the house and flames. As she ran faster, she could hear the horses screaming in the stable. The men were shouting and—

"Ava!"

She nearly ran into the shadowy form right before

her, but his hands flew out, and he grabbed her shoulders to steady her.

"Ava, what's happening? Are you hurt?" Ty demanded.

Ty. Right. He must have come with the group from Mark's ranch. "It's my brother," she said. "He needs help! Sully's been shot!"

The ambulance she'd heard was finally coming up the drive. She could see its shining lights.

"Take me to him," Ty ordered her. "Right now, Ava! Hurry!"

But Sully would need more than just Ty's help. They needed to get those EMTs to him. She tried to pull free. "I have to get to the ambulance—"

And something shoved into her side. Something cold, hard.

"You won't get to that ambulance," Ty told her, his words low and cutting. "And if you make one move to scream or try to fight me, I will shoot you where you stand."

That was a *gun* digging into her side.

Ty! Ty! Mark had been suspicious of him, but Ty had seemed to be so innocent. Oh, but he'd played that role far too well.

"You won't shoot me," Ava told him. Then she opened her mouth to scream.

His left hand slapped over her lips. "I will shoot you, and I will shoot every person who comes to your aid. I won't stop until there are no more bullets in this gun."

Over his shoulder, she could see the flames. The fire. Brodie had just arrived at the scene. Jennifer was with him.

"Do you want to see how many of them I can kill?"

Ava shook her head.

"Then you come with me, and you don't make a sound."

Brodie was looking at the house. He didn't see her. Ava swallowed, and then she nodded.

HE COULDN'T FIND the guy. Mark ran back through the brush, his gun clutched tightly in his hand. He hadn't wanted to get too far away from Ava. *But I wanted to find that bastard!*

He rushed back to her, but…

Ava wasn't there.

Sullivan was sprawled on the ground. Fear spiked in Mark's veins. "Sully!" He raced toward the man, but when he touched Sully, he knew the guy was in much worse shape than he'd originally realized. Sully's breath was barely whispering past his lips, and his skin was far too cold to the touch. "Sully, man, open your eyes. *Look at me!*" But Sully wasn't moving at all.

Mark glanced around, frantic. Where was Ava? She'd been there just a moment before.

I left her. I thought she was safe. I left her!

"Ava!" That wasn't his desperate call for her. Someone else was yelling out for her. Footsteps thudded toward him, and a flashlight shone in Mark's eyes. "What the… Mark?" The light dropped to the ground. *"Sully?"*

And then Brodie was running forward. Brodie's voice was a little harder and sharper than his twin's— that tone was a dead giveaway for his identity. Brodie yanked out his phone. Then he was saying, "I found Sully! West of the bluff, about fifty yards. Get the EMTs out here, now! He's hurt." His voice dropped and he added, "He's hurt bad."

Brodie tossed the phone aside. "Where's Ava?" he demanded.

"I don't know," Mark said, and the words actually hurt.

Brodie's head snapped up. "Where is my sister?"

Mark was already on his feet. *"Ava!"* He roared her name.

More footsteps thundered toward them. Help, coming for Sully.

But where was Ava?

Mark shouted her name again as he spun around. And fear—a dark terror unlike anything he'd ever known—tightened like a fist around his heart.

MARK WAS CALLING her name. Ava blinked, trying to stop her tears. He was so close—they were all so close. If she just called out to them—

"Mark will be the first to die," Ty promised her. "He can't hide behind you now."

"He was never hiding behind me."

"He wasn't worth your time. He was no good, a useless bastard who should never have touched you." He jerked her back against him, forcing her body even closer to his. "Knew you were meant for me…that very first night… I knew."

And he was dragging her back. Away from the lights. Away from her family. Away from Mark. Ava knew that if she didn't get away from him soon, there would be no escape.

"Thought they'd keep me from…you…" His breath rasped out. He was bleeding. She'd felt the blood as he held her so tightly to him. "No one can. Figured out how to slip in…and out of this ranch…"

He lived so close to the ranch. He'd had plenty of time to study the security system and find a flaw there. Her brothers had probably even talked with him about the system. After all, they'd thought Ty was a friend, just like Mark had.

They hadn't realized the secret side he'd been hiding.

I've known him for years.

He stumbled a bit, and Ava used that moment to let her knees buckle. She slid down, acting as if she couldn't stop herself, and they both fell. The gun slid away from her body. The weapon slammed into the ground and discharged.

The bullet blasted, and Ava screamed. She screamed desperately—because she hoped that her brothers or Mark would hear her, and because that flying bullet had just sunk into her side. The pain was white-hot and burning. Like someone had shoved a fiery poker into her skin. Ty was on top of her, struggling to subdue her, but she was fighting him with all of her strength. Fighting and screaming and hoping—

Hear me over the fire. Hear the sound of that shot. Get to me!

Ty yanked Ava to her feet. He'd grabbed the gun again. "You shouldn't have done that… You'll *pay* for that, Ava."

And she knew…yes, she would pay.

Because he wasn't letting her go.

MARK'S HEAD WHIPPED to the right. A gunshot. He took off running even as Brodie shouted behind him. He shoved his way past the EMTs, and he kept bellowing Ava's name.

But he couldn't see her.

And the echo of that gunshot had already faded away. No, no, he couldn't let her go.

I love you. Her words whispered through his mind. He'd been stunned when she spoke those sweet words to him. Ava…actually loving him? That was the only dream he'd had. A dream so far-fetched that he'd never dared voice it. When she'd said those words to him, he'd been stunned.

And I didn't tell her how I felt. He'd been struck dumb. So freaking happy, he'd been at a loss for the first time in his life. He should have held her tight. Kissed her deep and hard and told her that he loved her more than anything. That she was the one thing that mattered most in the world to him.

Ava. Always…Ava.

"Ava!" Mark yelled. *"Where are you?"*

And if he lost her, Mark knew nothing else would ever matter to him again.

THE EMTS WERE forcing Davis into the back of an ambulance. He didn't want to go. Ava was missing! He needed to search for her. He needed—

"Get in," Jennifer told him flatly. "Before you pass out."

And then he saw Sully being loaded into the same ambulance. Only Sully looked bad. Scary bad. His skin was ashen, and the bright lights in the ambulance showed the blood that was pouring from his wounds.

"No," Davis gritted out. This couldn't be happening again. He tried to go to Sully, but the EMTs shoved him back.

"Mark hasn't found her."

His head snapped up at Brodie's words. His twin

stood at the back of the ambulance, fear stamped on his face. Jennifer reached for him, curling her hand around his arm.

"He's searching—running around like mad, but she's vanished." Fear cracked in those words. "I called Grant. He's coming...*but she's gone.*"

Rage was giving Davis the strength to stay upright. His head still pounded as if a sledgehammer was shoving against his skull, but he had to say this... "Alan... Channing..." The stalker had to be that jerk. "He...took... her..." If they could get an APB out on the guy, then they could track him. They could find Ava. They could—

"No..." That weak rasp came from Sully.

Davis looked over at him. Sully's hand had risen and locked around the wrist of the EMT. The guy held a syringe in his fingers, but Sully was stopping the him. He was saying— "I...saw him... Not Ch-Channing... Tell Mark...it was...Ty..."

Ty?

Davis shook his head.

When he looked back out of the ambulance, he saw that Brodie had already whirled away. The guy was running for the cops.

Another EMT started to slam those doors shut. Davis lurched forward and out of the ambulance before they could close him inside. He nearly fell on his face, but Jennifer helped to catch him. Davis looked back at the stunned EMTs. "Take...care of my brother..." Davis said.

Because he was going to help his sister.

MARK RAN INTO the stables at the McGuire ranch. The horses were crying out, no doubt scared by the flames and the smoke. He rushed through the stalls, stopping only when he neared Lady.

Ava's horse. A beauty who wasn't shaking like the others. She came toward him, lowering her head. He reached out to her. "Help me find her." Because he could cover so much more ground on that horse's back.

In moments, he had her saddled up and ready to go. He urged the mount forward, and Lady galloped out of the stables. He could barely breathe because fear was clawing into his chest. Ava's image flashed in his mind. She'd been so determined to protect him and her brothers and so sure that the stalker wouldn't shoot her...

I hope she's right. Please, God, let her be right. Maybe the stalker wasn't hurting her. If Mark could just get to her in time...

"Mark!" Brodie ran toward him. "It's Ty! He's the one who took Ava! Sully told us...it was him!"

The fury within Mark coalesced, seeming to freeze his heart with an icy fire. He went numb then, operating on pure, cold instinct.

Brodie's breath heaved out. "Where would he take her?"

Someplace close. Someplace where he could hide her. Maybe he thought Sully was dead. Maybe Ty thought no one knew that *he* was the one who'd attacked that night.

"The security system is back up and running," Brodie said. "It looks like he slipped in via the south gate."

The south gate. The gate that was closest to Mark's property.

"Then that's how he's going to try to get out." Mark urged the horse onward. "I'll get her back," he shouted to Brodie. Brodie was running into the stables, too, and so was…Davis? Staggering, yes, but still trying to follow his twin.

Mark leaned low over the horse's mane. He urged Lady to go faster. To run harder.

Years ago, Ava had made that same desperate night journey with Lady. She'd gotten to him safely, and now Mark was frantic to get to her.

I'm coming, Ava. I'm coming.

TY WAS DRAGGING AVA, pulling her and trying to force her to run, but every step was agony for her. She was sure the bullet was still inside her. She hadn't felt it come out, and the pain wrenched through her.

"We'll get clear of the McGuire ranch, and then I'll take you away," he said. He'd been talking to her, muttering constantly, as he hauled her through the darkness. "It'll be just you and me, Ava. The way it should have been. Then I'll get rid of Mark, and everything—*everything will all be mine.*"

He was insane. Straight-up certifiable.

Ava slipped and fell, but this time, the stumble wasn't a fake-out designed to gain her freedom. Her legs just wouldn't go anymore, and she hit the ground.

"Get up!" Ty screamed at her.

Ava tried, but she couldn't.

"Get up!" He grabbed her hair, jerked her head back and put the gun in her face. "Or I will shoot you!"

She stared up at him. "You…already did."

"Wh-what?" And there was fear in that one word. He'd hurt so many people—and yet he sounded terrified in that moment. "When?" His hand flew over her, and when he touched her wound, Ava hissed out a breath. *"No!"* Ty bellowed.

No? He was the one screaming as if he were in agony, but she had the bullet in her side.

He hauled her to her feet. "You'll be okay." Was he saying that to convince her or himself? "Bullets grazed me, too. I'm still going…" The words came faster. *Faster.* "You'll be okay…"

"Didn't…graze me." She swallowed, trying to clear the thick lump in her throat. "It's…in me." She sagged to her knees before him.

He froze. "I didn't mean to hurt you." The words were low and hoarse and so absolutely insane that she had to bite back the hysterical laughter that rose to her lips. "You shouldn't have fought me. You should have just come with me."

And he shouldn't have tried to kill her brother. Or set fire to her family home. Or terrorized her for so long.

Ava stared up at him. The moon was behind Ty. Big and full and bright. "Why?" She just didn't understand. "Why…me?"

His hand stroked over her cheek. "Because you're just like her."

She shook her head, not understanding.

"He was obsessed with her, and I'm… I'm consumed by you."

Her body shuddered.

"He couldn't have her, and it drove the old man crazy. I'll prove that I'm better than he ever was. I'll have you."

The old man… Understanding clicked for her. "Gregory? Gregory Montgomery?" He'd been—wait, he'd dated her mother but—

"He wanted her, always her. My mother wasn't good enough. He treated her like garbage." His fingers slid down her jaw. Tightened. Bruised. "He hurt her. Again and again...because she wasn't the woman he wanted."

Gregory had been involved with Ty's mother?

"I'll have you...you're the one I want. Mark thinks you're his, but he's wrong. He got everything else. Even though he wasn't the bastard's real son. *Everything else*, but he won't get you."

She heard the thunder of approaching horse hooves pounding across the earth.

"That's him," Ty said. He uttered those words with such certainty, and when his head moved just a little bit, she realized he was smiling. "He thinks he's coming to the rescue. He doesn't know that I've planned for him to die all along."

Ava shook her head. "Please don't."

"Don't beg for him!" His fingers were so tight she feared he'd break her jaw. "He's nothing! He got *my* life, and he should have been tossed into the streets years ago!" His voice was cracking. "Then he locked his sights on you. He wanted you... I knew it... Mark wanted you more than anything. More than *my* ranch. More than the life that was *mine*. And I wasn't going to let him have you. I was going to show him—the thing he wanted most was *mine*!"

The horse and its rider were getting closer. And Ty was still right in front of her with his gun. Ava gathered her strength. She wasn't going to let Mark die. Any pain, any sacrifice, would be worth his life.

"You can watch him die," Ty told her. He said the words as if he were offering her some kind of gift. Maybe in his messed-up mind, he was. "Then you'll know...it will just be you and me. Forever."

No, it wouldn't be.

"Ava!" That was Mark's voice. So strong. So fierce. He'd spotted them. Did he see Ty's gun? *"Get away from her!"*

But Ty just slid closer to her. "Watch closely," he told Ava. "Sully didn't see my weapon, either, not until it was too late."

Sully. She pressed her lips together to stop their trembling. She wasn't going to watch anything—especially not Mark's death. "You said…you didn't mean to shoot me."

"I don't want to hurt you," he whispered.

She tipped her head back even more. Could he see her smile as clearly as she'd seen his? "Guess what? I *do* want to hurt you." Then Ava surged up. She ignored the pain of her wound. She pushed her fear away. And she hit him. Ava slammed into him with all of her might. Her head hit his nose, and Ava was sure she heard the crack of his nose breaking. He howled and tried to strike out at her.

The gun was coming close to her, but he was falling back. Falling—and crashing into the ground. Ava leapt away from him and started running toward Mark. "Go back!" Ava screamed. "He's got a gun! Go back!"

Mark was racing forward on the horse.

Her legs were shaking and—

"Down, Ava! Down!" Mark's wrenching cry.

Ava fell.

And Mark—Mark fired the gun he held. *Boom. Boom.* Her hands pushed against the earth, and she glanced over her shoulder. Ty was on his feet, the gun in his hand. Had he been about to shoot her? Or Mark?

As she stared at him, Ty staggered. The gun fell

from his fingers, and his knees hit the ground. "You… were…mine…"

Ava shook her head. "No, you bastard. I wasn't." She rose, slowly, her hand pressed to her side. She could feel the blood spilling through her fingers. Lady neighed behind her, but Ava didn't look back. She was afraid to take her eyes off Ty. Afraid that he'd be like one of those horrible movie monsters that just rose again and again and kept attacking until everyone else was dead.

"Ava!" Mark was there, wrapping his arms around her and holding her tight. She still didn't look away from Ty. He was sprawled on the ground now, his body heaving. He'd hurt so many people.

"I was afraid I wouldn't get to you in time," Mark rasped. He pressed a kiss to her cheek. "I think I lost about fifty years of my life when I was racing on Lady."

She wanted to look at him. She needed to hold him.

But her body had frozen. "He's not dead," she told Mark. Her voice sounded too husky. As if she'd been screaming for hours, but she hadn't. Her knees had locked so that she wouldn't fall. She didn't feel cold any longer, and her wound didn't ache. She didn't feel the wound at all.

More hoofbeats thundered toward them.

Mark pulled Ava back. His touch was so careful and gentle. He didn't know just how much Ty hated him. Not yet. Ava found herself easing over, trying to stand in front of Mark.

"No." Now his voice was hard. "Don't ever risk your life for me again."

"I love you." Again, her words were too soft. "It's what I do." You protected those you loved. It was a McGuire rule.

Brodie ran past Mark, heading toward the prone figure of Ty.

Mark stepped in front of Ava, finally blocking her view of the fallen man. "Ava, please, look at me."

Her gaze rose to his face. The moon shone down on them.

"I love you," he said, his voice strong and clear. "And that's what I do."

A sob built in her throat, but she wouldn't let the sound escape.

"I would risk my life for you in an instant. I would kill for you. Baby, I would do anything for you." His lips came down and touched hers. "Because you are the one thing in this world that I cannot live without."

And she didn't want to live without him.

The kiss was bittersweet, and the ice around her began to melt as he held her close. Mark—he was safe. Brodie was safe. Ty—

"He's still alive," Brodie snarled.

Mark pulled her close. He turned his body as he glanced over at Brodie, and Ava saw her brother's hands fist in Ty's shirt as he yanked the other man up to a sitting position and cursed. Brodie's voice was a low, lethal drawl. "You are going to rot in prison for what you've done to my family!"

Ty laughed. "You…need me. I…know."

"What do you know?" Brodie shook him. "You're a psycho who doesn't even—"

"I know…who killed them."

Ava's heart slammed into her chest. Her fingers pressed harder to her wound. She still didn't feel the pain. What had happened to the pain?

"I was…watching Ava. Saw them."

She shook her head. No, no, he'd been at the Montgomery ranch when she rushed over there that night—right? But when she tried, Ava couldn't remember seeing him that long-ago night. She'd just seen Mark when she arrived at the ranch. He'd sent out his men. She'd assumed Ty had been sent then, too.

"You…need me." And Ty kept laughing.

Davis advanced from the darkness. His steps were slow, cautious. Davis wasn't the cautious type. She reached out to him.

"Ava…" He pulled her away from Mark and into his arms. He whispered a confession in her ear. "You scared me."

She squeezed her eyes shut. She could hear Brodie talking to someone—he was barking orders and demanding the cops rush over, so she figured he had to be on his phone. Mark was close, right at her back. And Davis was holding her so tightly that she could barely pull in a breath.

Davis and Mark had been afraid they'd lose her. She'd been afraid they'd be hurt. But they'd all made it out of that mess alive.

Mark loves me. He'd said she mattered more than anything to him. There was too much fear still swirling in her heart for his words to sink in, but they would—she knew they would. Then she'd be happy. This nightmare would finally be over.

"Sully?" She had to force out his name. For some reason, it was getting harder to talk.

"On the way to the hospital," Davis quickly told her. "He's alive, Ava. And he's a fighter. All the McGuires are. You know that."

Yes, they were fighters.

Davis let her go, and Ava started to fall. She just didn't have the strength to stand any longer. She expected to hit the ground and she couldn't even brace for the impact, but Mark caught her. His arms wrapped around her as he cradled her so carefully. As if she were precious to him.

I love him. Probably more than he'd ever realize. Enough to trade her life for his without any hesitation.

"Baby?" His hold tightened on her. "Ava? Ava, what's wrong?"

She heard Ty's laughter again. Wild. Cruel.

"You won't have…her!" Ty promised. "She's gone… you lost her…you lost!"

Mark's hand pressed over her wound. Ava's breath hissed out, and he looked down at her side.

"No," he said, voice gone hoarse with horror. "Ava, *no*!"

She licked her lips. They were so dry. And the pain had come back.

Mark was on his feet and running with her cradled in his arms. "I'll get the EMTs! You'll be fine, you'll be—"

"I love you," she told him, needing to say those words once again. Her eyelids were sagging closed. "And…don't worry…"

"Ava!"

"You heard…Davis… McGuires are…fighters…" She would fight for him—for their chance at a life together—with every bit of strength she had.

He loved her. She loved him. And Ty *didn't* get to win.

AVA DIDN'T OPEN her eyes. Not yet. She knew she was in a hospital. She remembered the frantic ambulance ride there. The way Mark had clung so tightly to her hand. The way he'd said—

I love you.

Over and over again.

The bullet had been taken out. She'd been stitched up. Things were really foggy after that point.

She expected pain. But…there wasn't any. Just a heavy lethargy that seemed to weigh down her body.

"Mark." She whispered his name because he was the first person she thought about. The one she needed most.

Warm fingers curled around her hand. "I'm right here."

She opened her eyes. He was beside her. Stubble lined his jaw, and dark shadows swept under his eyes.

"Right here," he said, "with you. The one place I always want to be."

Happiness spread within her. They'd made it. They'd— "Sully?"

"Right here, sis," said a low voice. She turned her head to the left. There was another bed in that hospital room. Sully was there, looking tired but still managing to smile. "You know I'm hard to kill."

Her breath heaved out in a sound that was a cross between a sob and a laugh. Yes, he was hard to kill. He was a fighter.

A McGuire.

And they'd won.

Mark's fingers swept back her hair. His touch seemed to sink right through her. "I want to date you, Ava."

His words—after everything that had occurred— had her shaking her head. "What?"

"I want to date you, properly. The flowers and the

dinners and anything and everything you want." He swallowed, cleared his throat. "And when you're ready, I want to marry you. If you'll have me."

If?

"Because I do love you, and I'd like to spend the rest of my life making you happy."

Her lips parted.

"Aw, man, Ava, I should've gotten my own room!" Sully groaned.

She ignored him and focused on Mark. "You don't need to date me."

Worry flashed in his eyes.

"But you do need to marry me." They'd been through hell together, and they'd come out stronger for it. "Because I don't want to spend any more days or nights without you."

A wide smile spread across his face.

"Definitely my own room," Sully muttered.

Mark leaned forward. "I love you."

And Ava knew that the nightmare was over. Finally, everything was going to be all right.

Epilogue

Mark walked into the small interrogation room at the Austin Police Department. Davis was right at his heels. He didn't know what kind of strings Davis had pulled in order to get this little one-on-one chat, but Mark figured he'd owe his brother-in-law-to-be for this one.

Ty glared at him. His ex-foreman and friend was handcuffed to the little table. He wore a garish orange prison uniform, and hate burned in his eyes.

Mark stared at him a moment as the past swam in front of him. Those brown eyes…filled with burning hate…he'd seen them before.

Eyes in another man's face. The same hate reflected in a gaze just as dark.

"You're his son," Mark said. Because he'd put all the puzzle pieces together after he talked with Ava and Davis. "Gregory Montgomery's son."

"His *real* son!" Ty shouted. He tried to surge forward, but the handcuffs yanked him right back down. "You were nothing to the old man, but he still left you everything! He gave you everything!"

And he had. Gregory Montgomery's will had stipulated that all of his holdings were to pass directly to Mark. There'd even been some legal mumbo jumbo

about no additional heirs—even biological offspring—
ever being able to claim his assets. At the time, Mark
hadn't paid any attention to that clause, but now...*it
makes sense.* "He knew about you."

"He never thought I was good enough!" That hate
just burned hotter in his stare. "Never thought my mom
was good enough. But I showed him!"

Davis propped his shoulders against the wall on the
right. "Just so you know," Davis murmured, "you're
being watched and recorded."

Ty's gaze slanted toward the one-way mirror. "You
think I care?"

He should. He was about to talk away any chance he
had at ever seeing the outside of a prison.

"I've been robbed my whole life, and I'm *glad* to tell
the world now." His chin jutted up. "That old bastard?
The one you let punch you around? I'm the one who
was strong enough to stand up to him. *I* killed him."

Mark had already suspected as much.

"Then I found out about that bull he'd put in his will.
He'd told me—weeks before!—that I was gonna get
what I had coming to me. He *lied*!"

"No." Mark shook his head. "He gave you exactly
what he wanted you to have."

Nothing.

Gregory had always been a twisted bastard.

Davis pushed away from the wall and headed toward the table.

"I was gonna show him," Ty said, his words coming out so fast and hard. "I was gonna take Ava...he
couldn't get her mother, but I would get her. Ava was
even prettier. She was perfect. She was—"

Davis slammed his hands down on the table in front of Ty. Ty flinched.

"If you say that my sister was going to be yours," Davis told him, "then I will slam my fist into your face and break your nose again."

Because Ava had broken his nose the night of the fire, and Mark's bullets had kept the man in the hospital for over a week.

"Do you think I had it easy?" Mark asked him, curious now. "You know what he did to me."

Ty's lips twisted. "I guess you've never seen my back. He did the same thing to *me.*

"You won't let me go to prison." Ty leaned forward. He seemed cocky now. So confident. "You'll make a deal for me." He inclined his head toward Davis. "Because if you do, then I'll tell you what I saw that night. I'll tell you who killed your parents."

Silence.

Then...

"You attacked my sister," Davis said. His voice was low and cutting. "I don't care what you know. You're going to rot in jail." He looked back at Mark. "I think we've got everything we need. The cops heard him confess to killing Gregory. They already had him dead to rights on the other attacks. He's done."

Then he turned his back and walked away.

"No," Ty whispered. "No!" He tried to shoot to his feet, but once more, the handcuffs just pulled him back.

Mark stared at him. He wanted to hurt the man. To destroy him the same way Ty had tried to destroy everything Mark held dear, but...

Ava was waiting for him. *Life* was waiting.

"Goodbye, Ty." They'd gotten the confession that the cops needed.

Ty was screaming when they left him.

THE RANCH HOUSE had been saved. Mark figured that was pretty much a miracle. His men and the firefighters had been able to contain the blaze. The den, Davis's bedroom and the hallway were charred, but the structure of the place was fairly intact. The home could be repaired. Rebuilt.

"How much pain," Davis asked quietly as he gazed at the house, "do you think one place can stand? How much…before you just have to walk away?"

Mark put his hand on his friend's shoulder. "Ava is here."

Davis's head whipped toward him.

"She's on the bluff."

Davis shook his head. "Ava…doesn't like this place."

Mark just stood quietly with his friend.

A few moments later, Ava joined them. Davis stared at her as if she were a ghost.

"I have some ideas," Ava said as she cocked her head and studied the house. "About how we can repair this place."

"You…you want to rebuild?" Davis's voice was strangled.

Ava nodded. Her left hand reached for Mark's. Their fingers threaded together. "Yes. After all…it's home."

Davis was still as stone.

Ava's right hand reached out to him. Her fingers threaded with his, too. "Home is important," she told Davis. "So is family."

"Nothing's more important than family," Davis agreed, his words a rough rasp.

Ava smiled at him, she winked at Mark and then she looked at the house once more. "I have some ideas..." she said again.

A few minutes later, Ava climbed into the car. They were about to head back to Mark's ranch, and he couldn't wait to get her back there and into his bed. But first...

Mark looked over at Davis. "You know you aren't going to let things end this way."

Davis was staring at the house. "Ava wants to rebuild." He sounded dazed.

Mark shook his head. "That's not what I'm talking about."

Davis turned to face him.

"If Ty knows who killed your parents, we have to make him talk."

Davis smiled then, and the sight was chilling. "Oh, don't worry, he'll talk." His eyes glinted. "I've already put plans in motion."

A cold chill slid up Mark's spine.

"I *will* find out who killed my parents. Before I'm done, Ty Watts will be begging to tell me everything he knows."

Staring into Davis's cold gaze, Mark believed him. But then, he knew just how deadly Davis McGuire truly was. "If you need me," Mark told him, "you know where I'll be."

Davis nodded. "With my sister...protecting her with your life."

"Always," Mark promised him. Then he turned and headed toward the car—and Ava.

DAVIS WATCHED AVA and Mark pull away. Mark loved Ava. Of that, Davis had no doubt. Ava was happy, safe.

And now—now he could focus on the past once again. Every day he felt as if he learned a new piece of the puzzle that was his parents' murder. Every day he got closer to the truth.

Yes, Ty would talk…sooner or later.

The guilty would be found. Davis wasn't going to rest until he gave his parents the justice they deserved.

McGuires were fighters, and he still had plenty of fight left within him.

* * * * *

MILLS & BOON®

The Italians Collection!

2 BOOKS FREE!

Irresistibly Hot Italians

You'll soon be dreaming of Italy with this scorching six-book collection. Each book is filled with three seductive stories full of sexy Italian men! Plus, if you order the collection today, you'll receive two books free!

This offer is just too good to miss!

Order your complete collection today at
www.millsandboon.co.uk/italians

MILLS & BOON®
INTRIGUE
Romantic Suspense

A SEDUCTIVE COMBINATION OF DANGER AND DESIRE

A sneak peek at next month's titles...

In stores from 18th September 2015:

- **Reckonings** – Cynthia Eden *and*
  High Country Hideout – Elle James

- **Navy SEAL Spy** – Carol Ericson *and*
  The Rebel – Adrienne Giordano

- **The Agent's Redemption** – Lisa Childs *and*
  Texas Takedown – Barb Han

Romantic Suspense
- **Second Chance Colton** – Marie Ferrarella
- **The Professional** – Addison Fox
